MOR'ANH

Spear of the Sky . . .

Everything about Mor'anh set him apart from other
men. While still a boy, he had begun by
killing a leopard unaided. Still only nineteen, and
hence four years into manhood, he yet bore the
scars of successful kills of wolf, and of bear.
The tiger he had killed had not even marked him.
Best of wrestlers, greatest of hunters, he had
never yet failed at anything he had attempted.
And beauty lay on him like sunlight on the Plain.

More, he was beloved of his family and Tribe;
he was a priest, touched by the Gods,
Chosen of Kem'nanh, and able to commune
directly with his God. Mor'anh should
have been the happiest of the Sons of the Wind.

But Kem'nanh gives his blessing for a purpose.
Mor'anh was troubled and restless. There was
no maiden of the Tribe he could not have—
except the one he wanted, and much worse,
he hated with reasonless passion the Golden Ones
who were the delight and the terror of his people.
Where they were awestruck, he felt only savage anger.
He did not know where this alien, passionate
feeling would lead him, nor how desperate
a decision the God would thrust upon him.
But he was a Khentor, one of the Dark Ones—
and he had never run from anything . . .

THE GREY MANE OF MORNING

by

JOY CHANT

with an introduction by
BETTY BALLANTINE

and text illustrations by
MARTIN WHITE

BANTAM BOOKS
TORONTO   NEW YORK   LONDON

THE GREY MANE OF MORNING
A Bantam Book / September 1980

PRINTING HISTORY
Originally published in Great Britain by
George Allen & Unwin Ltd.

ISBN 0-553-01200-2

Published simultaneously in the United States and Canada

Bantam Books are published by Bantam Books, Inc.
Its trademark, consisting of the words "Bantam Books"
and the portrayal of a bantam, is Registered
in U.S. Patent and Trademark Office and in other
countries. Marca Registrada. Bantam Books, Inc.,
666 Fifth Avenue, New York, New York 10103.

PRINTED IN THE UNITED STATES OF AMERICA

0 9 8 7 6 5 4 3 2 1

INTRODUCTION

Joy Chant's world of Vandarei was first encountered in a magnificent fantasy entitled "Red Moon and Black Mountain." That was a story of a time very much later than the setting of the present book. In chronological order, THE GREY MANE OF MORNING is a prequel—a tale of one of the earliest heroes of an enchanted land, of a time before the world was even given the name of Vandarei.

Then, as in all ancient times, people lived as the land demanded they should. The Khentorei, Gentle People of the Plains, drifted in small tribal groups, pushed by the varying seasons over a vast domain—a not particularly kind or safe existence, but one that was rich with excitement, laughter, intense loyalties, and a glorious joy in the magnificent Horned Horses, the Davlenei, which they alone could ride and which the God had given them to guide their wanderings.

Each seven years, the God chose one particular Davlani who became Dha'lev, the God Horse, his spirit imbued with the wisdom of the God Kem'nanh, Ruler of the Wind, Lord of the Herds. The Sons of the Wind measured time by the passage of earth signs, celebrating many with Festivals—the Moon of New Grass, the Moon of Yellow Flowers, the Moon of Burning Trees . . . and at the proper times and seasons the Dha'lev would grow restless and lead the way to new pastures or to safe winter valleys.

The Khentorei had no enemies, nor did the Tribes war with one another. Free as the wind, they rode, they danced, they drummed, they hunted, they celebrated their life and worshipped their Gods, and no one kept any reckoning of their comings or goings. Except for the Golden Ones, those tall, handsome, blond people who lived in houses behind walled towns in the hills, worked metal, wore cleverly dyed clothes and, once a year, in their lordly way, took tribute from the awestruck Gentle People of the Plains.

Nothing had changed for centuries—not that anyone bothered to measure the centuries—things were simply the way they had always been. Especially was this true of the Alnei, a Tribe blessed with a wise and powerful Dha'lev and with, unusually, a brother and sister both also touched by the Gods. Between Mor'anh and Nai there had always been a closeness, something sacred, an unspoken communion. They were priest and priestess and the children of the leader of the Alnei. More, Nai was known to bring Luck to the Alnei: their herds had been strong and prolific, their pastures good, the living easy. Everyone recognized that they would therefore, in logic, pay greater tribute to the God-like Golden Ones. None questioned this—except Mor'anh. For in Mor'anh, named for the Lightning, the God had planted a seed that questioned the immutable laws of custom.

And when the Golden Ones ripped Nai away from her Tribe to be raped and thrown into servitude, Mor'anh's doubts flowered into savage rage. But there seemed little he could do—even his father, leader of the Tribe, reluctantly accepted Nai's fate.

Mor'anh had to acknowledge it was impossible to fight the Golden Ones, to throw the Tribe into bloodshed and horror just for the sake of one girl. But he was not idly named Spear of the Sky. When the time came, Mor'anh knew he must and would act. Whether his decision for vengeance would bring death to his Tribe, or freedom, he could not know. One thing was sure, the ancient pattern of life on the Plains and in the Hills would never be the same.

BETTY BALLANTINE

SOME OF
THE PEOPLE
AND PLACES
OF
VANDAREI

THE HORSE PEOPLE
The Khentorei

also known as:
Wandering People
People of the Plains
The Gentle People
The Dark Ones
Sons of the Wind
Men of the Wide Land

The Khentorei are divided into several tribes. This story is chiefly of the Tribe called Alnei, the Tribe of the Wolf. Only the Khentorei men can ride the magnificent horned horses (Davlenei), and among the Davlenei, the God selects one—the Dha'lev, the God Horse. The Dha'lev is holy and powerful and magic, God's Chosen to lead the Tribe.

KEM'NANH
the Khentorei deity who chooses the Dha'lev. Kem'nanh
is Ruler of the Wind, Lord of the Herds.

IR'NANH
a Khentorei deity, the God of the River,
the Trees, also known as the Dancer, the Lord of Destiny,
and the Lord of Life. A very powerful God.

NADIV
Khentorei Goddess, served by the women of the Tribe. Among
the Alnei, Nai is priestess to Nadiv, the Sacred Mother.

HAR'ENH
the title given to those through whom the God speaks, not
always, or necessarily, a priest or priestess. However, in the case of
the priest Mor'anh and of the priestess Nai, both are Har'enh.

HORN-BLOWER
the call to death. It is said of the Old One that Horn-blower
has forgotten his name.

TEMPLE OF HAR'ENH
Tent of Kem'nanh, the God's Tent, a sacred place.

SOME KHENTOREI FESTIVALS AND SEASONS

The Fire of Gathering—held in the evening, when the Tribe comes together for a particular event, or a celebration, or to discuss problems.

The Grass Dance
The Feast of the Mother
Moon of the New Grass
Moon of the Sheep Shearing
Moon of Long Days
Moon of the Dances
Moon of the Great Feasts
Moon of the Flocking Birds
Moon of the Storms
Moon of the Burning Trees

CHIEF CHARACTERS IN THE ALNEI TRIBE

LORD ILNA—*Grey Wolf*

Has been Lord of the Alnei for eighteen years.
His grey hair is worn in braids and he rides the davlani Hulakhen.
His wife Ranuvai has been dead for ten years.

MOR'ANH—*Young Wolf*

Son of Lord Ilna and a priest, Chosen of Kem'nanh. Mor'anh rides the davlani Racho. Mor'anh is nineteen, wears his black hair short. He is oddly named, for Mor'anh means Spear of Heaven, Lightning Bolt. He is a mighty warrior, excelling at the hunt and at drumming. He is also spear-brother to Hran, who is in love with his sister Nai.

NAI

Daughter of Lord Ilna and sister to Mor'anh. She alone among all the women can raise her voice at the Fire of Gathering, for Nai, a poetess and prophetess, is also Chosen of Nadiv, the sacred Mother. Her relationship with her brother Mor'anh is deep and close: they share a common dedication to the Gods and can sense one another's feelings.

HRAN—*the Eagle*

Son of Yorn. He rides the davlani Ranap and excels at hunting and dancing. Hran is in love with Nai, and spear-brother to Mor'anh.

RALKI

Hran's bold, gay sister, and his favorite dance partner.
At one time Mor'anh courted Ralki.

YALN

Ralki's husband.

MANUI

Manui is plump and pretty and rides her pony Otter
as well as any of the men ride their davlenei. She is in love
with Mor'anh, her friend and sometimes her lover.

RUNI—*the Leopardess*

She is well named Runi, meaning leopardess, for she is tall and
lithe and reckless. She wears her thick, dark hair loose, clinging to
girlhood, denying the responsibility of becoming a woman.
But Mor'anh loves her passionately, obsessed by her sensuality.

DERNA

Runi's brother.

DURAI

Hran's younger sister.

OLD ONE

So ancient none can remember the years of his life or even his
name. But his memories are important to the Tribe.

THE GOLDEN PEOPLE
The Kalnat

They are tall, strong, golden-haired and blue-eyed. They live in
the mountains, in stationary houses within walled towns. They are
skilled at the working of metal and their artifacts include swords,
spears and long knives. They wear brightly colored clothing and cultivate
fields. Their diet is largely vegetarian as they do not hunt. The Horse
People regard them as demi-gods to whom they give annual tribute.
The God of the Golden People is Akrol, the Soul of Light.

SOME CHARACTERS AMONG THE GOLDEN PEOPLE

MADOL
Nephew of the Master, i.e., son of the Leader's sister.

MARAT
Madol's sister. Her mother was a Horse Woman taken in tribute.

KARINIOL
A big man with thick yellow hair, sympathetic to the Horse People.

HANIOL
He negotiates for tribute with the Horse People and keeps a tally.

KUNIOL   )
KELDOL   ) young male friends to Madol
DARINOL   )

KERATOL
Master of the Golden People

THE PEOPLE OF THE CITIES

YU-THUREK
Lord of the City Jemaluth, the City of the Wise, in the country of Bariphen.

YA-BUREN
Translator—he spent some time with the Alnei
when Mor'anh was a small boy.

PRINCESS JATHEROL
Daughter to Lord Ya-Buren and heiress to the throne.
Inheritance is through the female line.

PRINCE YO-PHERIL
Son of Lord Yu-Thurek.

Redorh

MOUNTAINS

THE
NORTHERN
PLAINS

Danamol

Black Mt.

Rennath

Eron Nes

Nelimhon

The Downs

H'ara Tunij

KUNO

Kuniuk

Emneth

REALM
OF
KEDRINH

LUNETH

NETHARUN

Kedrinhel

REALM
OF THE
ISLANDS

Janorh

Merenkh

Equator

Nadirh

NEVIRH

Nevirh

THE CONTINENT OF
VANDAREI

MILES

0 100   500

Mountains

Forest

Scrub

Palm Trees

Marsh

Desert

- - - - Mor'anh's
Route

Rai

PART ONE
The
Son of Ilna

1

he moons had set long since. First the red disc of sullen Hega had slid below the horizon, then silver Vani's waning crescent. But the Plain was not dark. There was little cloud to hide the massed stars of northern Khendiol, and Vani at her brightest scarcely outshines their pulsing splendour. The grass shimmered, and the camps of the wandering tribes lay drenched in pale, shadowless light. Night drew near its end. Above the stillness, the tireless stars turned. A thousand years would pass before their secrets were shared, their true names known. There was none to read in them of the changing of an age, as they danced about the one that the tribesmen name the Picket Star.

Peace lay over the realm of the *Men of the Wide Land,* the *Khentors.* For generations they had lived on the Plain, hunting and herding, living the life ordained for them in the land the Gods had given them. They were not yet the wielders of a mighty power, and many lifetimes would pass before they were the companions of the Starborn. Yet though they did not understand the starry dance above them, still that dance went on. They looked for no new age. Time to them was the present, and the unreckoned centuries brought little change to the *Khentorei,* who live to this day much as their fathers did then. But the time when no tribe was greater than another tribe, nor man than another man, was passing; had passed nearly twenty years before, when at the Autumn Feast the young priestess *Ranuvai* had faced a man in the firelight and seen what she had never seen before, the face of a stranger.

In the camp of the tribe called the *Alnei* (there was no potency yet in that name) men slept, but their herds grew wakeful. The air was changing. *Racho* tossed up his head and snuffed the wind. His nostrils flickered; he smelt the coming dawn. The starlight glinted in his eyes, frosted the tip of his curling beard, gleamed on the pale twisting horn which parted his forelock. For Racho was a davlani, one of the great Horned Horses which lived on this plain and nowhere else in the two-mooned world. Save for his horn and beard, he looked like a beautiful, long-limbed horse, but he was not, and surpassed horses in all, in intelligence, in strength and speed, in stamina, in hardiness. None rode the Horned Horses but the Khentor men, and no one might call himself a man who did not ride a davlani.

Even the plainsmen called them 'horses' as often as davlenei, for they had known horses first, and from them had learned their mastery as riders. But when their wandering took them deeper into the Plain they met the davlenei; and thereafter the horses had only pulled the waggons. They were fine, strong animals, and the Khentors took great pride in them still; but they had always been their servants, never, as the davlenei were, their brothers. They still at that time called themselves the Horse People, using the name of the lesser breed; but upon the love between them and the davlenei their world was founded.

Racho stooped to nudge the young man sleeping at his feet, but the young plainsman only sighed and turned over, pulling closer the black bear-skin which covered him, and the horned head came up again. Racho was light-horned, his body dappled storm-grey, his mane and tail, beard and feathering white as sunlit cloud. He

4

was just entering the prime of his strength, and so splendid was he, so perfect at every point, that the tribesmen accorded him the highest praise in their power, and called him a 're-davel.'

Not all the Alnei slept. The herds were not left unguarded, and between the herds and the tents *Hran* was keeping the Dawn Watch. The drums were slung before him over Ranap's withers, their harness heavy across his own thighs, and the great horn was hanging at his side. The wind that Racho had felt blew cool upon him. He stirred and stretched, his gaze upon the eastern horizon. The grey mane of morning was in the sky, but it was not yet day. The eastern stars were dimmed by a pallid cheerless light. Ranap's neck and horned head were losing the beauty lent by starlight, growing firmer, though still without colour and warmth. Hran shivered, and felt for the drumsticks; for however unworthy he found it, this grey chill was the outrider of dawn. Lord Ja'nanh, Rider of Heaven, he thought, you should do better than this dull smirching of night. You are light and splendour and warmth and glory; come, Lord, and banish fear!

The drums thundered like the voice of his fear. Ranap's ears twitched and swivelled, and he scraped a hoof. Hran bent lower and pounded the drums urgently. For to the Horse People this half-light between night and the day was part of Hargad—the void, the un-world, the half-lit limbo of wraiths and evil dreams. It was not like the good dusk of evening, when fires grew bright and the Tribe drew together, when there was talk and rest, sleep for children and dancing to drums. When the old and sick died, they died in Hargad. It was the time when the tethers of all souls were loosened, and Creation's heart faltered.

He calmed his fierce tattoo. Already, down in the camp, fires were blossoming. He was no longer alone. In the grass near him, birds were chirping tentatively, and there was a new warmth in the sky. Keeping a steady beat on the drums, he felt for the Horn, his eyes on the east.

This was the good part of keeping the Dawn Watch; this drove Hargad from mind. O God of Day, loose your bright flock in the plain of heaven, O Lord of Glory, come. . . .

A rim of fire-gold crested the horizon; tongues of flame reached out north and south, consuming the darkness. Spears of light pierced the sky, the stars paled, the clouds were touched with delicate fire, and in the same moment Hran's horn groaned out in sonorous ecstatic welcome to Ja'nanh the Rider of Heaven, climbing the sky in his chariot of light. Around the god the sky was woken to blue, above the Plain the mighty music beat the air, light and sound swelled and mingled, and for a magic confused space it was hard to tell which had called, and which obeyed the summons.

A thin mist was sinking back into the river; the dark cattle around their wade stood breast-deep in it. *Mor'anh* rode past them through a world awash with light, with the low sun flooding the mist and burning vividly through each dew-drop into glowing colour. When he had passed the sheep and the goats, drinking upstream of the cattle, their fleeces had been sparkling with the fog-dew. Nothing could compare with the tingling, skin-tightening call of the Plain in spring; but this time of early autumn, when gold mingled with green in the grass, held its own enchantment.

The place where the men bathed was far enough below the cattle-wade for the water to have cleared. Mor'anh dismounted and looped the reins about Racho's neck, then stripped and plunged into the river. The chill struck through him, but he did not heed it, only diving and thrusting into the current just strongly enough to keep the pale blur of his body motionless. Then he broke the surface, his moustache and the black cap of his hair streaming water, rubbed himself vigorously, and tossed his head a few times before swimming to the bank. He waded out and snatched up a rough woollen cloth that lay by his leather clothes, and began drying himself.

He was the perfect figure of a Man of the Wide Land; the proud wary head with deepset slanting eyes and sombre mouth, broad shoulders tapering through strong waist and hips to long, taut-muscled legs. A compact leather-hard body, well-muscled, and not tall—though he was the tallest of the Alnei, save for Hran. His skin was the dark ivory of his race, and was marked with scars that made him the envy of every young man in the Tribe. On his left shoulder and upper arm, the marks of a wolf's mauling. On his left flank and dragging across his ribs, the traces where the bear's terrible claws had raked him. In his right thigh, the fading marks of a young leopard's fury. These were badges of honour which they all coveted. Few men had collected such an array and lived; none, when as young as Mor'anh. He was nineteen years old, though if asked his age he would only have answered that he had been a man four years: and as a hunter he was already a byword to his people. He alone of living Alnei had won all four of the skins of honour; and the tiger he had killed with his spear had not even marked him.

Down into the camp came Hran who had kept the Dawn Watch, eager to be gone to the river and his friends. But he rode first to the centre of the camp, for he had with him things too precious to be long in his care. Ilna, Lord of the Tribe, came out from his tent as Hran dismounted, and the young man bowed to him, right fist to left shoulder, then straightened smiling. Ilna inclined his wolf-grey head and smiled back, and took from Hran the drums and the great horn. They were ritual objects, of special meaning to the Tribe, as witnessed by the wolf-signs painted on them and the wolf-tails hanging from the drums. Ilna carried them into the Tent of the God, where the most precious and most holy things they had—their few metal tools, ritual head-dresses and ornaments for the sacred dances, the marvellous fire-stones, and the great stone cleaver—were kept under constant guard. On the left of the door, a tribesman with a spear; on the right a wolf-skin on a pole, the eye-slits of the mask black and watch-ful.

The God's Tent, the Tent of Kem'nanh, was made of leather dyed deep green, decorated with patterns painted in white and black, its roof-edge fringed with black and white horse-hair. It was bigger than any other tent, and the Alnei thought of it as very old, for although all parts of it were often renewed, it had never been remade. It was in fact one tent within another; only the Priest or the Har'enh of the God might enter the inner, secret place. Its outer circle was hung with wolf-masks and wolf-tails, some white like the Door-keeper, mostly grey. For this was the Tribe of the Wolf, and they prayed to the Horse-God who cared for them for the courage, cunning, and nobility of their namesake.

The Tent of the God stood at one horn of an arc, at the centre of which stood the Lord's tent. Between these two was the Priest's tent. About to mount Hran paused, then went to it and pulled back the flap. As he had expected, it was empty. His friend's spears stood in the rack around the king-pole, the grey-striped tiger-pelt over the bed gleamed silver in the dim light: but plainly Mor'anh had not slept there, and Hran ducked out.

But as he did so, there was the soft sound of a door-flap falling from the tent beyond Ilna's and Hran's heart leapt to his throat. Ilna's daughter stepped out, her bare feet soundless, her head bent. He drew a breath, but let it out, for she looked neither right nor left, unaware of the world. He stood motionless, watching her, and she went to the outermost tent of the crescent, that facing the Tent of Kem'nanh: and when she laid her hand on the door-curtain he hastily averted his eyes, lest as it opened he should see anything forbidden. For this was the Tent of the Goddess, and it too was guarded. Before the door smoke rose from a round pot of fire; before that, a circle was drawn. On the left of the door a woman sat, cross-legged under her skirt, hands in her sleeves.

The smoke ceased to waver from her passing, and the

door-curtain hung heavy and still. Hran waited a few moments before riding away, but she did not re-appear.

Ja'nanh's golden waggon rolled steadily up the sky. The gold of the day burned richer; the sky was deep, clear blue, with no drift of cloud. Nai stood gazing at it, but she did not see it, and her hands rubbed up and down her arms as if she were cold.

She began to walk slowly forward, still looking up. The women on the river bank dropped their voices as she drifted by, and when she was gone sought each other's eyes perturbed. The men stepped aside for her; the children who came running to catch her skirt stopped short, abashed. With a slow entranced tread she passed among the tents and out through the waggon-circle. Several times she turned from fires at the last moment, and once almost stumbled on a pegged-out hide; but she did not falter until brushing through the grass she startled a feeding bird. It rose from her feet with a great clatter and outcry, and she started back, looking about her bewildered as birds rose on all sides, calling and wheeling about her. In a short while they settled; Nai felt the sun warm on her throat, and looked into the sky with waking eyes.

She sank to her knees, and took a new-fallen flower in her hand. 'Great Mother: Holy Nadiv:' she whispered. 'I beg you, speak to me. What does this fear mean? Vani is dark thirteen times in a year, and I never felt my heart wane with her before. What is there to dread in the dark of the silver moon? Tell me, Good Goddess! Kem'nanh has sent my brother no warning. What is it? Is sickness coming to the Tribe? Have we angered you, Holy One? Tell me, that I may tell them. Dear Lady, speak clearly to me!' She turned the flower one way and another, touching it delicately. 'Or is it for myself? For me alone? Let it be so! Let the danger be only to me. O Mother, let the Tribe be safe!' So she prayed from her heart; but tears pricked at her eyes, and after a moment she whispered, 'Great Nadiv; have mercy on me.'

9

The stallion gave another scream of anger, tossing his head in a storm of white mane, then beating it against his forelegs, trying to free it. He reared, lashing the air, jumping sideways; but the strong tether and heavy picket stone pulled at his head, dragging him in a circle. He came down at last, hacking the ground in fury, and screamed again. Once more he ducked his head and kicked out high to the back, whipping the air with his white tail, tearing at the earth with his horn. Then he planted his hooves firmly and strained at the picket with his mighty neck arched, until the great stone actually dragged a little from its place. He bucked a few times, then snorted and stood still, trembling with anger and weariness.

His mares milled and fretted, their foals crowding against them. They were frightened by their lord's rage, half longing to run, daring neither to leave his protection nor to approach him too closely. The sacred herd was in a ferment; the half-grown horses careered around in coltish panic, always preparing flight, always turning back at the edge of the herd as their nerve failed and the cracking whips of the drovers warned them away. Even the young stallions with full-grown horns dared to leave their place at the outside and come, ears pricking and eyes bright and wary, to see what was wrong with their leader.

The plainsman set to watch him looked at his sweat-darkened sides, and guilt and awe were mingled with his compassion. Awe to see his unyielding spirit, and to guess how the God must ride him; guilt that they had dared again to bind him, the Dha'lev. The aura of power and holiness present in all horses was most potent in him, the God's chosen. The title they gave him was greater than Lord, higher than any they would ever give a man. The Dha'lev: the sanctified-to-rule: the King. He was Kem'nanh's regent in their midst, their sign, their oracle, their sacrifice. No man was held so high. The Lord of a Tribe, and the Priest, received the God's words, but heard them dark and twisted as men do; and not even the

God's Har'enh could guide them to grass and water. Their life depended on the Dha'lev, and so when the God's call came to him they must picket him, lest he lead his herd away before they could strike camp and follow. Tomorrow they would loose him and follow him to better pasturage; but until then he must feel the weight of his royalty, and endure the picket stone.

Manui sighed and turned over, burying her head under the covers and trying to muffle the noise; but sleep once lost, there was no regaining it when the King was making such an outcry. She sighed again, and, yawning, slid out from the enfolding skins.

It could not be long until dawn. She would begin to pack now. She groped for her underdress and put it on, then felt for a taper to light the lamp. She shivered when she opened her door; she had forgotten how cold it could be in the last watch of the night. There was no moon, and the thick stars blazed unchallenged. In its shelter by her door, her fire-pot glowed dimly. As she knelt to kindle her taper the Dha'lev screamed, and she shivered from another cause. It had happened that he had caught his leg in the picket rope and fallen; then someone must go in to free him, lest he hurt himself. She thought of the huge hooves, the snapping teeth and deadly horn, all that strength and royal rage to vent on whomever was nearest. She paused, sheltering the taper's flame, and tried to recall the names of those watching the God's Herd; but she did not find any name to frighten her, and went in.

The lamp lit, she finished dressing, and packed her few possessions—little more than her cooking utensils and the clothes she was not wearing. Then she shook out the sheepskins and coverings of her bed, arranging them on the big shiny bull-hide that had been spread under them, rolled the whole neatly and tied the roll. Next she took up the lower inner wall that kept draughts out of the tent. A small wind came slipping in to her. Soon the Drum would sound; and she thought, with sudden hope, that maybe he was keeping the Dawn Watch.

11

All else done, she began the dreariest task, taking up the matting of the floor. She was binding the first bundle when all at once her eyes stung fiercely. She gasped, straightening her back, and rubbed angrily at her tears.

She could not deceive herself. She had not heard his name. He was not on patrol, nor watching the horses, nor was he on the Dawn Watch. And still he had not come.

He came in the morning. He passed as she was lowering her tent, and stopped to help her. Manui stood by as he folded it, watching him with a smile, holding his cloak, the great bear-skin that he had tossed to her so carelessly, the proof of his prowess. She buried her fingers in its silky blackness, once or twice touching her cheek to the coolness of the fur. She had to keep gathering it up as it slipped, for it felt heavy in her arms, and she wondered how he could wear it so lightly, swinging it easily from his shoulders. She noticed anew the weight of it whenever it covered her; the weight, and the warmth. She laughed softly, then flinched from a sudden thought. He was very merry, and pleased with himself. Who had lain under the bear-skin this night past?

Yet even that thought could scarcely hurt her while he was there. While he stayed, neither past nor future could touch her: but he never stayed long enough. He had tied the folded tent, he had taken back his cloak, he was riding away to his father's side; he was gone, and with no more at parting than a wave of his hand.

2

t was three days later when the Lord Ilna planted the tribal banner, and they pitched camp. The Dha'lev had led them far to the south and west, until the mountains were a green barrier against the sunset which could not be ignored. The Plain itself was no longer flat, but tumbled into deep hollows and rises, rippling and flowing up to the west, swelling into the foothills not a morning's ride away. In the lee of one such slope they pitched their tents, loosed their herds beside the circling river, and turned their backs to the west. The long hummock felt good behind them, like a shoulder hunched against the wind; but they could not entirely blot out the sight and knowledge of the peaks beyond.

In the evening of the first day Mor'anh, the son of Ilna, and Hran, the son of Yorn, rode away from the tents, through the great circle of waggons, past the herds and out of the camp. Racho and Ranap whinnied as they passed the horses, and from here and there came soft answers. The Dha'lev swept up his snow-crested head, and the young men saluted him respectfully; he watched them calmly for a moment, then dipped his head again to graze.

The grass was shorter here, barely reaching their horses' bellies. Out in the deep Plain it often reached their waists even on horseback, but now their boots brushed against the feathery heads, loosing a cloud of pale powder. It was good to look out over the expanse of swaying green, to see the subtle, changing patterns of shadow, the nodding of the heavy seed-heads. The flowers were mostly past, but sometimes among the blades glowed richer colours of berries and ripe pods. The birds no longer sang the bold, shining songs of spring. They did not sing in autumn for love or combat, but for pleasure and content, sweet bubbling songs poured from the sky, or from the blue throats of the birds who clung to the dancing grass-stems. The great hunters preferred the deeper grass; over this smaller world hung an air of quiet fruitfulness, the hustle of spring and summer past.

'Euch,!' cried Mor'anh, 'Lai! Eu-*ha!*'

Racho neighed and sprang forward. Hran clenched his thighs as Ranap plunged after him, then collected himself and caught up with Mor'anh. 'Yellow dog! Could you not leave me dreaming?'

'Vech, you dream too much these days. Kem'nanh preserve me from seeing the sun rise anywhere but in the eastern sky.'

'Surely Ja'nanh must preserve you from that. And Young Wolf, you speak in envy.'

'Ja'nanh save me, then; and shall I be envious, and she my own sister? Y-*hai*, Racho!'

He urged his horse on, leaning into the wind, and Hran followed. On the move, this joy was denied them. Except when patrolling, they must move at the speed of the lumbering waggons. Even those who escorted the sacred herd found that the Dha'lev kept a pace within a foal's endurance. Now they were free to taste again the delight in the strength and speed of the horses that made them men, to exult in the grace and power they controlled. The thunder of the hooves, the hiss of the grass, the song of the wind, blended into a music as potent as the dark rhythms of the throbbing drums. They rose from their saddles and leaned forward, lips parted as if they drank life from the wind that streamed coolly through their hair and poured caressingly over their bare chests. When they rode into it, it pressed against them and tugged importunately at their open coats. When they turned and rode before it, it flurried around them, flapping their cloaks, tumbling their horses' manes, urging them forward; then swept on past them, singing its soul-stealing song away into the vastness of the open grass.

But they did not follow. Instead of yielding to the aching emptiness and dwarfing breadth of their world, they turned back to the tribe as to a picket-stone. They did not return to the camp, however; they raced each other past it, sweeping in great curves and circles, turning and weaving, sidling and halting, testing their own and their mounts' skills in a dozen ways. It was done in play, but it was serious play. The davlenei were life to them. Between horse and rider there must be perfect confidence, perfect understanding. Men had died because their horses did not trust them enough.

They were moving all the time westward, and suddenly Mor'anh turned Racho and sped straight towards the sinking sun. Following, Hran saw him halt at the top of a low hill, and become at once still, a motionless silhouette against the flaming sky. After a moment he turned and signed to Hran who, sensing some gravity, slowed Ranap and trotted to his friend's side.

The grass was barely knee-deep where they stood; beyond them it grew shorter yet. The rise sank away from their feet and ended in a trench not two hundred paces from where they stood: and beyond the trench they saw the sight which of all others the Horse People most revered and most feared, their dread and their desire. Three young men standing and two girls sitting on the grass, enjoying the last sunshine. The men leaned on long-bladed slim-shafted spears; a dog whose silky coat glowed the colour of the spear-blades lay nearby; one of the girls was combing her hair. The men saw the two riders first, then the girls. They turned to look, then turned unconcernedly away. One of the girls laughed;

15

the other tossed her head and flicked her wrist, and the hair she combed flashed bright gold.

The Golden People . . .

Hran's heart tightened. He drew a deep breath, for once heedless of his friend's reaction. Mor'anh's face was stormy, and fire was gathering in his black eyes. But Hran did not notice.

To the Horse People, the Golden Ones were both demigods and demons, their terror and their delight; but above all they were their masters. Years past reckoning had it been so, for generation upon generation beyond the reach of memory. While a tribe stayed in the depth of the Plain it was safe; but once near the mountains, their shadow fell on the tents. The Golden People claimed tribute of the tribes—tribute of cattle and furs, leather and musk and ivory; and sometimes women. For though they despised the lithe, hard-muscled men and saw no beauty in them, it was another matter with the women, whose fine bones and wide, dark eyes had cost many their happiness. If any ornament a man wore caught their eye, he had lost it; they had taken from Mor'anh in the last year of his boyhood, the first hunting trophy he had ever worn. Only horses were safe from them; they feared and disliked horses. Indeed, to the plainsmen it seemed that one law was the symbol of the Golden People's mastery; the long-remembered decree that no horse could cross the boundary of their land.

Such were the tokens of their bondage, and bitter they were; but they were less regarded than they might have been. The dark-haired horsemen had sucked in the bitterness with their mothers' milk, and habit robs hardship of the worst of its sting. And should they ever grow resentful, it needed only for them to meet the Golden Ones again, and they were humbled. Surely the Gods had made them rulers and ruled, for the Golden People lived in walled towns and the earth brought forth as they commanded; they wore garments of bright cloth, their eyes were blue as heaven, and they had shining yellow

16

hair; and the Horse People did not reach to their shoulders. So they paid their tribute, looked on their lords with awe, and did not pull against their tether. Or so did almost all.

Mor'anh urged Racho slowly down the hill. Hran looked at him, startled, wondering uneasily what his friend might do. The Young Wolf was no fool, but he had always been headstrong; he might dare anything.

But Mor'anh turned Racho's head and rode across before the group, along the edge of the boundary ditch, very slowly. His bearing was haughty and he stared at them with defiance, a look of stony hate so unmistakable that a man and a girl turned away their faces, ill at ease. Then he turned away, his face bleak with a helpless bitterness, a bitter helplessness. He would not make himself foolish with empty gestures; and what could he do?

Feeling silly with relief, Hran cantered after his friend. Such moments were part of the price of friendship with the Young Wolf, for Mor'anh's mind could go where Hran's could never follow; and at such times Hran would feel almost afraid, ashamed that he could not understand his spear-brother, and against his will even jealous.

There was nothing about Mor'anh which did not set him apart from other men. Had he not begun by killing a leopard unaided before he had even reached manhood? Did he not wear his hair cut short, as no other man had ever done? Best of wrestlers, greatest of hunters: he had never yet failed in anything he attempted. Even his appearance singled him out. Other men might be good to look on—Hran was one. But Mor'anh was to them as the sun to the stars, surpassing them in this as in all else. Beauty lay on him like sunlight on the Plain, beyond the reach of age or injury.

Right from the womb it seemed the Gods had marked him: for at his birth his mother, who had been a priestess with much deep knowledge, had given him a strange and ominous name. For whereas men usually bore names

17

Following, Hran saw him halt at the top of the low hill, and become at once more still, a motionless silhouette against the flaming sky.

taken from the animals—Ilna the Grey Wolf, Hran the eagle—Mor'anh was named for the lightning-bolt, which sweeps the Plain with fire.

Vani, the silver moon, was almost dark, and Hega, the red moon, two nights from the full. Nai watched them through the thin smoke from the Fire of Gathering, and thought, 'There can be no luck at such a time.' Perhaps this was the reason for the dread that grew in her nightly. She had prayed again and again for a clearer warning, but the Goddess was silent. The sacred cat was healthy and content, and She accepted all the offerings. Yet if it is not the Goddess who is angry, thought Nai, why is it I who am afraid?

Hran, idly spinning a dice with Mor'anh for the bright red seeds they used as stakes, was only half attending to his score. Vanh the Singer had finished his songs some time ago, and sat plucking a few low, quivering notes from his instrument. This was the time when Nai sometimes sang, and he wondered if she would begin. He glanced over his shoulder, but she was looking at the moons, and he turned back. Mor'anh looked at him with half a smile, as Hran absently pushed his stake across, regardless of having just won.

'If you looked at the dice half as often as you look at her, you might give more sport.'

Hran look startled, then grinned self-consciously. 'I am waiting for her to sing.' Mor'anh made a derisive noise. 'So are half the people here. She has a voice like gossamer.' Mor'anh rolled his eyes and Hran laughed. 'Just because you cannot sing—'

'Eu-ha! My win. I cannot sing like her, I cannot dance like you, but I have taken all your seeds. Now you can watch Nai all you like.' He rolled over to recline on his rug, and Hran leaned on his elbows, looking away from the fire. Nai's folding stool was set a little way from the smooth, old wooden chair of Ilna the Lord. She did not sit on the ground like others, for she was the luck of the Alnei, their poetess, priestess, and prophetess. She alone of the women might raise her voice at the Fire of Gathering.

Khentors were governed entirely by the men, and women's voices were little heeded. It could not be otherwise; they were nomads, hunters and herders, and danger and the honour went all to the men. Yet there had been a time, long ago, when women had held a much higher place among them, and in this one thing, in the reverence they gave their Priestess, it was remembered. Khentors gave to no other the adoration given to Kem'nanh the Mighty, Lord of Herds, Ruler of the Wind; but they held the Great Goddess in much awe. On Her their life depended, the Giver of All Good Gifts, She who made herds fruitful, the bestower of grass and the Mother of Mares. She gave or withheld children, and the best pleasure of life was Her gift. And the women had never yielded Her mysteries to the men. In those rituals alone could they feel themselves still powerful; and the worship of Nadiv the Mother had become a thing of darkness and secrets, jealously guarded from the men, who now held the Goddess in as much fear as honour. So they treated with deference the Priestess who placated and interceded with that sullen power, giving her equal honour with the Priest, calling her Lady, and Luck of the Tribe.

But the Alnei were blessed beyond belief in the children of Ilna. For Nai was more than Priestess, as her brother was more than Priest; she, too, was the Har'enh of the One she served, and the Goddess spoke through her. Maybe once in a generation one of the Horse people would be thus singled out; that two should come, in one tribe, in one generation, of one flesh, was most wonderful.

Yet Nai did not seem awe-inspiring as she sat there upright, small hands clasped in her lap, her face grave; and to Hran she was not Har'enh and Luck of the Alnei, but much less and much more. He gazed at her, and wondered again if all people thought her as beautiful as she seemed to him. Her braided black hair fell heavy and glossy beside her ivory cheeks; her eyebrows, so exactly like her brother's, were pure and perfect curves. But her greatest beauty lay in her eyes, which were large and brilliant, shadowed by thick lashes. He sighed. As she sat looking so remote and calm it was hard to think of her being otherwise; to believe this was the same woman with whom he talked, and argued, and made love.

He sat up, looking away from her. It was time they began the dancing. There were few things Hran loved more than to dance, and he was the best dancer in the Alnei. It sometimes gave him guilty pleasure to know that there was at least one thing he could do better than Mor'anh . . . but if the Young Wolf did not excel as a dancer, no one could make drum-music as he could. Mor'anh could beat the drums so that the music forced men to dance. It was best to dance, thought Hran, with Mor'anh on the drums, and with his sister Ralki for a partner. Ralki's dancing made other women seem spear-shafts. He caught her eye across the circle, and raised his hand to her. She was leaning on her man's shoulder, laughing, which was shockingly improper, but very like Ralki. She was tall and bold and gay, almost too mannish to be pretty, but it had been a surprise to many when she went to Yaln's tent. He was wiry and rather ugly, but Ralki had thought even Mor'anh no rival to him.

Hran glanced at Mor'anh, remembering with amusement his friend's youthful courtship of his sister; then he looked away annoyed. The Young Wolf was gazing with something not quite a smile on his proud mouth, at someone beyond the fire. Hran could guess who it would be. It was like Mor'anh to choose her; he loved to test his prowess against difficulty.

He let his eyes turn back to Nai; and found her watching him. She snatched her eyes quickly away when they met his, and stared into the fire. Hran looked at her insistently, willing her to look again, and she began to bite the corners of her mouth against a smile. But it grew for all that she could do and at last she turned her face to him, laughter breaking from her. She shook her head at

22

him, then turned to speak to her father. Hran smiled to himself, and lay back. He had no fear of her denials. Whatever she pretended now, later she would not turn from him. He knew he was as secure of her love as she was of his. He had lain with other women before her, and she with other men; but they were all forgotten. He wanted only Nai, and she would never again give herself willingly to any man but him.

inter was in the wind. The children who a day or so before had been running naked were clothed now, and Mor'anh wore his cloak clasped, not swinging loose behind him. Black anger was in his face. He knew the women watched him with surprise, that he was still in the camp. He would not speak even to the children, and when they saw his face they swerved hastily out of his way.

He had more than one cause for anger. The nearest, the plainest, and almost the worst, was that as they had gathered for the hunt, one of the youngest of the men had begun to show off his horse. They were close together, and when the horse had grown frightened at being made to turn and dance with so little space, he had bucked and kicked Racho on the leg. No great harm was done; Racho would not be lame more than two days. But for those two days the Young Wolf could not ride; and worse, he had been unable to go on the hunt.

He clenched his teeth. It was well for Hran, in the glow of his good humour, to try to calm him, saying the young man had not meant the harm he did, he had only been thoughtless. Only thoughtless!—as if a man could be anything worse! It was poor relief to have sent the young fool away white from the savagery of his tongue. Let Hran see Ranap hurt and limping from someone's carelessness, he thought, and then let me see him be patient!

They had been dismayed that he could not hunt. They would have no luck without him, they said: and in the soreness of his heart he had almost hoped they were right. But when he caught himself in that thought, he checked in shame. Even his present anger did not reach such a depth.

Mor'anh's rages were fortunately rare and short-lived, but while they lasted they were frightening. Only Nai dared face him in one of them. He would not have fallen into such a black passion even for Racho's sake, had not so many other things angered him that morning.

Coming towards him he saw a group of *banyei: girls who had loosed their hair from the plait of childhood, and not yet become women in the worship of the Goddess.* He turned aside. Runi was at their head, and he had had enough speech with her for one day—or even many days.

He was well beyond the waggon-circle when he paused, the heat of his fury cooled to a tired angry bitterness. He looked about him. On the sunward side of a slope not far away sat an old man, the grass before him scattered with children. Mor'anh laughed drily. Well, he thought, since I am left with the children, I will go to hear the Old One's stories.

They called him simply the Old One; they had no idea of his age, only that he was older than anyone else in the Alnei, older than they thought it possible to be. They did not reckon their age from their birth, but from their manhood; but the Old Man had lost count even of those years. He had outlived his horse, which was a thing unheard of; he had outlived all his children, and the oldest of his grandchildren were growing grey. Bowed, white, and incredible, he lived on. Horn-blower, like everyone else, had forgotten his name.

For the Horse People, there was no slow decline towards death; it came as an ambush, the sudden call of the Horn that could not be defied. The Gods, on giving them

25

their span of years, had been sternly practical; they lived long enough to rear their children. Maybe for a year it was said, 'He is old; is not his second son a father?' But unless they were close friends, it was likely they saw no change. Their vigour need fail very little; they lived hard, sometimes violent, lives. On the Plain, people did not grow old; only too old.

The children stared up at Mor'anh as he walked among them, then gazed at each other as he stretched out on the grass near them. To them the Young Lord was very little, if at all, lower than the Gods. The Old Man peered at him from the mass of wrinkles in which his eyes were almost hidden, but did not pause in the telling of the story. The children settled again, only glancing sometimes at Mor'anh to see if he was enjoying it. But he gave no sign. He leaned on one arm, shredding grassblades with strong, impatient fingers, a settled frown on his brow.

'Well, then, it is finished,' said the Old Man at last. The children did not stir. 'Are you going to your mothers?' They shook their heads slowly. 'Are you waiting for another story?' They nodded, more vigorously. Mor'anh, remembering the familiar ritual, smiled faintly.

'Well, well,' grumbled the Old One, shaking his white braids in pretended annoyance. 'If there is no other way to be rid of you. But you must choose the story for me. Which is it to be?'

They were silent, looking at Mor'anh. His presence tied their tongues. They would not make a choice that might be unpleasing to him. The silence was broken only by their little, smothered laughs, until Mor'anh looked up, surprised at their slowness. Then meeting the dozen pairs of eyes he understood, and smiled at them. His smiles were brilliant, and the children began to giggle.

'Are they waiting for me to choose for them, Uncle?'

'Do you ask me? Are you not closer to them than I am?'

'You know I am not. Well, I will choose.' He looked down at the grass, then frowned again suddenly. 'Have you told them of our coming to the Plain?'

The old man looked at him. 'Always the same story. Have they come, then?'

'Yes,' he said curtly. 'They came this morning. Did you not hear them? It was after the hunt had gone.'

The Old One nodded. 'So. Hear then, children. This is how the fathers of your fathers' fathers came to be the Horse People.

'Long ago before ever a man made a roof of hides, in days so far past they were before the time of my grandfather's grandfather, we, the children of The God, *Kem'nanh*, lived not on the Plain but far away in holes in the sides of mountains. In those lands there were no horses, or great herds, or deep grass. Ja'nanh was fiercer, and rivers smaller: so the story says. Our long-dead ones were a poor, unskilful people, who lived by hunting but did not know the true hunter's craft, and served the demons of Hargad in fear. They had no knowledge of any good thing. They could not work and sew leather as we can, and they wore the skins almost as they took them from the beasts. They had no crafts. All they had were their dances and their drums, and with them they made the magic to keep the demons out of their holes, and to make the animals plentiful. So they lived, in fear and little pleasure, in the stony mountains.

'Then came the Golden Ones, the Gods' beloved. They came down the mountains in their might and their beauty, and our fathers fled before them. They killed the men, and they thrust their red spears through the skins of the sacred drums so our fathers could not make holy music to drive them away, and they scattered the fires; and they drove our people down into the Plain.

'Our fathers were afraid, and wept; but this was good fortune for our people, and blessed the time that the Gods sent the Golden Ones to us. For in the deep Plain Kem'nanh was waiting for his children, and he put his arm about us. He was kind and loving, he showed us his face, he spoke to us. He showed us the ways of life. He taught us the right way to worship the Goddess, and

27

Ir'nanh, and Ja'nanh; and he taught us that we were his children. He showed us new dances, and the hunter's skills, and the laws of the Plain. And best, he gave us his other sons for our brothers; he taught us to know the davlenei, that we had never known before.

'Yes, yes, it was then that our fathers learned to ride on the backs of horses and to master them. Then they were afraid no more, for they were free of the Plain. They built waggons, and sewed tents, and listened to the wind. Then they knew that the Gods had been good, to send the Golden Ones. For had they not come, maybe our fathers would never have come to the Plain, and we would never have known that we are the Men of the Wide Lands, the children of Kem'nanh.'

The old voice died away, and the children stared in silence. This was not like the stories they had heard before. They looked uncertainly at each other. Then one boy rose to his feet, bowed once to the Old Man and once to Mor'anh, and went; and then they were all rising, bowing respectfully, then running to their games. Mor'anh did not move, and the old man went on nodding gently. There was a long silence after the last child had gone. Then the Old One said with a shadow of reproach in his quavering voice, 'You have frightened away my friends.'

Mor'anh looked up and shook his head. 'Not for long, Uncle. They will be back. We always come back to you; and I most often—Lai?'

'Yes, you oftenest. And always asking for the same story. I am ashamed to tell it before you now, you must know it so well.' He watched the tall young man rise up above him. He had seen three generations, but never one of the Tribe—not even his own sons—so dear to him. 'Mor'anh, you are troubled,' he said gently. 'And I think it is more than the sorrows of youth.'

'Lai, Uncle, it is more. I am troubled.'

'What is it? What are you thinking?'

'I am thinking—', he paused, 'I am thinking of the kindness of the Gods, in sending us the Golden Ones.'

At such times, he always sought the river. When the hunt returned Hran found him on the bank, leaning against Racho's side, watching the sliding water. He did not look up as his friend approached.

'How is his leg? Is it well?' said Hran.

'As well as may be. I have salved it and bound it. How went the hunt? You were long away.'

Hran grimaced. 'The hunt went ill. When you are not with us, Kem'nanh turns away his face. We had much labour for little good.' He glanced at Mor'anh's face. It was very bleak; but there had been Runi, too, that morning.

'You missed the Golden Ones,' said Mor'anh abruptly. 'They came this morning.'

Hran had no reply to make. After a long silence, Mor'anh looked round at him. 'You have little to say, for once. What has lamed your tongue?'

Hran felt suddenly resentful, and looked at him challengingly. 'Maybe it is not my tongue at fault, but your ear. Tell me, then, of what may I speak with safety? Racho? Runi? Nai? The hunt? Which will make you least angry?'

Mor'anh flinched slightly, and his mouth tightened. He turned with a brief flash in his eyes, then mastered himself. 'Euch, maybe you are right. Well, of those, Nai is the safest. Now let me hear you talk.' Hran looked startled, then could find nothing to say, and Mor'anh laughed.

'What, did you think I would find words to praise her? I am her brother, not her lover!' Then he sobered. 'No, let us not talk of Nai . . . maybe you were right, maybe I am a little jealous. You mean to claim her, then?'

Hran was utterly taken aback. Mor'anh's changes of mood could be sudden, but twice about in one speech!—and as for his abrupt question . . . He might be his spear-brother, he might be Nai's brother, but so flat, so direct a demand—almost brutal in its curtness—it was against all custom, all courtesy. Slanted teasing was one thing, friendly and correct; but until a man had actually

29

cast his spear, such an unveiled reference was so imper-
tinent as to be almost insulting, and the worst of bad luck
also. He saw that Mor'anh was himself aghast and wishing the words back, but that did not help now. He set his
teeth and hit back.

'Attend to your own courting, and leave mine to me.
Yes, and if your heart is set on the Leopardess, you will
find there is more to winning her than "meaning to claim
her"—you are like to need all your luck there, Young
Wolf, and more than all your skills too. I am going to
bathe. If you are coming to the Fire I will see you there.
And you will be better welcome if you bring your manners with you!'

He flung away. Mor'anh, almost starting after him,
checked and bit his lip. He would let Hran cool before he
begged his pardon. He did not wonder at his anger. He
had shocked himself. The wounding retort had been
milder than he deserved. A man needed to work hard at
it, to make Hran lose his temper.

He put his arm up under Racho's throat, leaning his
cheek against the davlani's smooth neck, and sighed. Of
late these moods had often taken hold of him: an impatience that galled and never left him, a tension bursting at
times into unreasonable fury. It was as if his people came
between him and something he needed to hear; as if
someone were talking on a hunt.

And Nai . . . She was his sister. Let others think what
they wished, he was still the closest to her. There was a
bond between them not always present between
brothers and sisters, a bond which they hardly understood themselves, which had little to do with the blood
they shared. They might grow to love others more, but
they would never find the same understanding. And
Mor'anh knew that Nai was afraid. She hid her fear from
their father—even, it seemed, from Hran. From Mor'anh
she could not have hidden it if she would, but still she
would not speak it aloud. Yet she gave no hint of ill
omens from her Goddess, and her love prospered; of
what could she be afraid?

He gave a quick shudder, and turned from the river. 'It does no good to think of it,' he told himself. 'If it is something, the God will show me in time. Maybe it is just my own anger. That is enough, today at least.' He bent and ran his hand down Racho's leg. The great horse shivered and snorted, moving his other feet nervously; but Mor'anh's hands were gentle. The young man straightened, and gazed again into the river. 'It was my anger only,' he thought; because of her, and Racho, and because they came. I will go to the Fire now, and ask Hran's pardon. He sighed, and stretched his arms; and all at once he thought of Manui. Manui was to him as the river was, a refuge; he would go to her, to be healed of his anger.

4

ran brought Ranap at a slow, springing trot along the lanes between the tents, sitting very erect, his lips dry with nervousness. He was looking his best, freshly shaved, his moustache trimmed; the glossy, black hair falling about his shoulders was newly washed, and from the thong that bound his top hair back from his face fluttered gay, scarlet feathers. His boots and clothes showed no speck of dust, and his necklaces and bracelets bounced as he rode. He sat without moving on Ranap's back as the davlani danced and sidled through the camp, tossing his glowing mane and sweeping his tail, displaying himself in obedience to his rider's unseen commands. He gleamed like the red metal the Golden Ones worked. Hran grasped a spear in his hand as he rode.

He met them near the centre of the camp: Ilna, Lord of the Alnei, with his son and daughter with him. Mor'anh, seeing Hran, grinned and held back, while Nai lowered her eyes. Hran turned Ranap to block their path, and the horse pricked from foot to foot, tossing his head; Hran drew rein and he half reared, sinking back on his haunches until his tail lay like a pool of fire on the ground. Hran said, 'Terani!'

'Hran, son of Yorn?'

Hran turned the spear in his hand and threw it; it thudded into the ground at Nai's feet. Hran looked at Ilna.

'Terani, I would be your son!'

The people nearby craned, interested. Hran watched, pale with dread. Suddenly it seemed possible that Ilna might give back his spear—or Nai!—no, never that. Nai looked at the throbbing spear. She could not say she was surprised, but she felt oddly shy and excited. She turned to meet her father's smiling eyes, and answered the question in them with a quick nod. Ilna pulled the spear from the ground and showed it to Hran.

'I have your spear, my son,' he said; then he raised his own spear and hurled it to strike the ground before Ranap. The horse shied back, but Hran urged him forward and jerked the spear free. He bowed to Ilna and to Nai, unsmiling; then swung round and cantered away.

Nai took a step or two forward, watching him out of sight; Ilna smiled and turned back, but Mor'anh waited. She gazed after Hran smiling, then said something and laughed joyously, clasping her hands behind her head. Mor'anh stepped up to her. 'What did you say?'

'I was wrong!' she said. He looked at her puzzled, half smiling, and she laughed again. 'I said I was wrong to think there could be no luck at such a time!'

Madol of the Golden People dug irritably at the grass with his spear-butt, and looked again over his shoulder. 'Where are they?' he demanded again. 'The third hour after noon, they were told, and it was almost that when we came out here. Where are they?'

He had had other plans for this afternoon, but his uncle had ordered him to oversee the rendering of the tribute. If the Dark Ones were much longer, there would be no time left to take his dogs out. He thrust moodily at the ground again, with the red bronze of his spear-blade this time. Kariniol watched him thoughtfully. He had never liked Madol, one of his childhood's chief tormentors, but when a man was the son of the Master's sister, it did not do to quarrel too often with him.

'They will be here soon enough. What tribute do they bring?'

The oldest man answered. 'Thirty-five ewes, twenty cows, eight deer carcases and hides (one with head and antlers complete—that for the Master). Fifteen other hides, six furs, and a bag of dumachat root.' He paused, then added reflectively, 'Keldol says we should have asked for some of that bark they gather too; but it's too late now.'

Several men looked round, and Kariniol whistled; 'How big is this tribe?'

'I don't know. Normal size, I suppose. Why?'

'Surely that is heavy tribute?'

Haniol shrugged. 'We should be lucky to see the Wanderers again before winter.' Kariniol frowned a little, but Madol laughed at him.

'Of course it is not heavy! You must learn to understand these things, Kariniol. And if they do not bring it swiftly, I will in the Master's name make it heavier by one cow!' He thought a moment, then laughed again. 'Now that is a good idea. How if I command them, because they were slow, to bring another cow tomorrow, and when they are late then, to bring another, and so forth?' Several of the young men laughed loudly. Haniol turned away from them, and Kariniol shook back his thick, yellow hair impatiently. 'Madol, do your dogs ever bite you?'

'My dogs?' Madol looked blank. 'No. Why?'

'I am surprised, then.'

Madol crimsoned with anger. He half raised his arm; but whatever Kariniol's rank, he was the biggest man in Maldé, and he lowered it again, scrubbing angrily at the beard that only nobles were allowed to wear. Kariniol turned from him contemptuously. Then Haniol said, 'There they are.'

About twenty of the Horse People came over a rise. Ilna rode at their head, Mor'anh was there, and Hran; and

Nai. Her presence was strange; but she had insisted. Why she was compelled to go, she did not know. She only knew that, again, she was afraid.

They could not take their horses with them; they dismounted, and Nai stayed with the horses, by a pony laden with hides. She watched as the tribute animals were driven across the narrow ditch which marked the border that no horse might cross. The fair-haired men came to meet the tribesmen; their hair, their tanned limbs, the colours of the woollen tunics, glowed in the rich sunlight. The metal blades of the long slender spears they bore gleamed and flashed; it was as if they wielded flames. When the men came together, she saw how only Hran reached even the Golden Men's shoulders; and not he to the shoulder of the tallest. The Horse People looked like boys among them, and she shivered, touched by dread. She leaned back against her own pony for comfort, rubbing his nose. Great Goddess, I do not understand, she thought. Why did you make me come? What do I fear?

Madol found the business going too slowly for him. Haniol, who had done this job for years, was unhurriedly discussing the animals with the Lord Ilna and the two herd-masters of the Alnei, but Madol had nothing to do, and was there merely to oversee. He felt the afternoon slipping away from him, and grew irritable again. 'Come on, come on,' he said, 'get some more of that stuff down here.' He hustled some of the younger plainsmen up the slope again, and saw Nai's figure by the horses. She was wearing trousers as the women always did to ride, and he took her for a boy. 'Hey, you!' he shouted 'Bring that pony down here!'

Startled, Nai shrank back and looked about her. The women never learned the tongue of the Golden People, and she did not know what he asked. But she saw plainly enough that he was angry, as he sprang over the ditch and came towards her, and she drew back among the horses, fearful. Madol came up shouting at her, and went to the pony with the hides. He untied the straps and pulled them off, still cursing in his own tongue, then, having lifted the hides to his shoulder, turned back to aim a blow at the disobedient boy. Nai gave a scared gasp and flinched; but his arm remained motionless.

She had never seen a Golden Man so near. She was overwhelmed by his height, his breadth, the red of his tunic. She saw the muscular weight of his arm, the brown skin gilded by hairs as yellow as the thick hair of his head and beard. And Madol realised his mistake. He saw the heavy braids of her hair, the wide, frightened eyes, the delicacy of the hand with which she had hoped to ward off his blow; and the hides slid from his shoulder. The impatience on his face died into appreciation. His eyes travelled over her slender body, lingered on her face. Nai, watching him in fascinated terror, tried to scramble backwards, but his arm shot out and a hand that could have broken her wrist with one twist closed around it. 'Well, what have we here?' he laughed; and she cried out in fear. Then he whooped, and dragged her running down the slope.

'Hey, look!' he shouted. 'Look what I found!'

Nai screamed, wildly; she resisted, digging in her heels, struggling to free her arm, but the big man did not even notice. He swung her across the boundary, and she screamed and beat his arm. 'Mor'anh!' she cried. 'Hran! Father!'

They had turned at her first cry, and were frozen, staring. For a moment, Hran did not realise what it meant. Then when she called him, Mor'anh gave a fierce shout and leapt forward, and in the same instant Hran understood, and sprang towards Madol. Two tribesmen seized him, and Kariniol flung his arms around Mor'anh, holding him back. 'Don't be a fool!' he said, 'There are some here would spear you without thinking, long before you reached him!' But Mor'anh only gave him a blank, wild stare and struggled harder. Nai was crying for help, pinned by one arm against her captor's side.

Madol pulled her over to Haniol, still laughing. 'For being late!' he said. 'Better than a cow, isn't she? I'm keeping this one.'

Ilna, his face grey, looked at Haniol. 'This is not the tribute asked,' he said, 'We have paid the tribute. Give back my daughter. This was not asked.'

Kariniol shouted to some Alnei, and gave the furious Mor'anh into their charge. 'Hold him, or they will kill him!' Hran was fighting frenziedly. Mor'anh cursed and twisted, demanding they release him.

'Nai!' called Hran. *'Nai!'*

'Hran!' Madol was holding her by her hair, but still she strained to reach Hran, and the young Golden Men shouted with amusement. Mor'anh trembled, and stiffened; he would not be a show for them. Planting his feet apart and throwing back his head, he watched Madol with a black blaze of hatred. Kariniol saw it, and shuddered suddenly.

'Let the girl go, Madol. It's true enough, they've paid the tribute. Let her go. Haniol!'

Ilna, pleading desperately with Haniol, looked to the tall man with a gleam of hope. Haniol might have told anyone else to release Nai—not from compassion so much as a liking for orderly procedures—but Madol was a noble, and he dared not. He shook his head, and Kariniol looked exasperated.

'In the name of light! What does Madol want with another girl?' A fresh burst of laughter answered him, and he grew angry. 'Madol, give her back, before there's trouble!'

'Trouble!' said Madol. 'What trouble? I've a right to take her if I want. And who do you think you are giving orders to? No-name.' His friends sniggered, and Kariniol set his teeth at the old insult. 'Ah, look at Red Feathers. He wants her back. I'm not surprised either.' He swung her round to show his friends. 'Look at her. How often do you see one as good as this? I'll bet she's not a virgin, though. Pity. Look, Kariniol; even you must see—'

Madol was holding her by her hair,
but still she strained to reach Hran.

'Lord, let us take her back. She is our Priestess—'

'You hear that, Madol? The girl's a witch. In Akrol's name, let her go before we all regret it.'

'Witch! Regret!' Madol's voice was derisive. 'You can save your breath. I shan't let her go. I want her.'

Haniol caught Kariniol's arm. 'Let it go, Kariniol,' he said softly. 'Arguing only makes him stubborn. I don't want to offend you; but you are the last person he would heed, and he could make trouble for you. What does it matter?'

Kariniol looked past him, at Ilna's face, at Hran's anguish, at Mor'anh—'What does it matter? Of course it matters!'

'Yes, but you are doing no good, Kariniol.'

Kariniol shook off his hand angrily. 'They paid the tribute in full. And they have not tried to give less than the best of anything. Why should he take their girl?'

'Still on about the tribute?' said Madol. 'Here, hold her.' He pushed Nai to one of his friends and walked over to the tribute. He drove out a cow, and threw a fur and a deer-carcase at Ilna's feet. The lord stared at them blankly. 'There. And that's generous. I'll remit that much tribute for her. My Uncle can claim it from me.' The cow lowed, puzzled; Madol reclaimed Nai. Haniol's face cleared.

'They can't quarrel with that, Kariniol. If we had asked for a woman they would have to give one, and nothing would have been remitted. I think he's being quite fair.'

'Do you?' said Kariniol quietly. 'But we did not ask.'

'Well, I think it's fair. And he won't give her back, anyway.'

Kariniol did not answer. He looked at Ilna. 'I am sorry,' he said, and turned away. Nai shook her head, tears filling her eyes. 'No! oh, no!'

Hran stared at the little heap at the Lord's feet, and the cow. Was that the worth of Nai? He gave a cry and began struggling again; the men hung grimly to his arms. Mor'anh stood unmoving, watching. Ilna looked dazedly at Haniol.

40

'Well?' said Haniol harshly. 'It is over. You may go now. Go. What do you stay for? Go!'

Ilna turned blindly away. Madol began walking towards their town, and Nai realised she was looking her last on Hran, and her father, and Mor'anh. She began to cry out again, straining against Madol's arm, kicking him and trying to bite. Mor'anh gave a bellow of fury, and thrashed against the men's restraint, making them stagger. Ilna came and gripped his shoulders. 'My son! My son! Stop!' Mor'anh paused, panting. 'It is no use. They will not give her back. They will kill you if you defy them. Am I to lose both my children?'

Mor'anh shuddered violently, and was still. He stared after the Golden Ones, watching Nai out of sight, his mouth twisting at her cries. Hran still fought. Kariniol, going last, looked back. He was ashamed, and sorry for them. Then his eyes shifted to Mor'anh; and he shivered, and hurried on.

They drove the cow back to the camp, and took the other restored tribute. Ilna wept, without attempting to conceal it. Hran rode with a stricken, and Mor'anh with a rigid, face. The whole party was silent and afraid. Nai was more than simply one of their women, for whom they need only grieve. She was the Har'enh of the Mother, the Luck of the Tribe. What might become of them, now their Luck was gone?

The tiding spread through the Alnei like the first breath of winter, a tremor of grief and dread. Hran went out of the tribe into the Plain, to grieve in secret. He could not forget that Mor'anh had spoken too early of his love for Nai; could not help but blame him for the disaster that followed. Ralki wept, for Nai and for Hran. Manui, Nai's closest friend, mourned her bitterly, and ached for Mor'anh's pain. Of them all, Mor'anh alone did not weep for her. In a silent passion of rage and grief, he closed himself in the Inner Tent of the God. There he beat at Kem'nanh's ear with his fury and his pain, storming at the great god until far into the night, crying out against

41

his loss, until the smothered hatred in his heart seared him with agony, and from his bitterness was pressed a cold desire for vengeance. Dry-eyed he remained; but with the dryness of burning ice, or a winter sky too cold for snow.

5

he sun grew dark in Hran's eyes, because of the loss of the daughter of Ilna. The Alnei turned south, and to break the camp where Nai had been claimed and lost tore his heart. It seemed that to do so was to finally abandon her, and he could hardly bear it. He suffered much; and the moons made his pain not less but more.

Yet even he did not understand Mor'anh. He could only think that grief for a sister was of a kind unlike a lover's grief, for Mor'anh seemed to feel anger rather than sorrow, and a stubborn disbelief. Hran thought, 'It must be because he cannot remember a time without Nai, that he will not believe that she is gone. My love for her is hotter, but his is older. She was a companion of his hearth when she was only a name to me. It must be that.'

Mor'anh did not understand himself. He could not resist Kem'nanh, when he drove the Dha'lev after the sun, but in his heart he raged at the God for taking him further from his sister. His strange, baffled anger shook his whole life. He could not give up hope of Nai, whatever he was told. Ilna, for all his grief, had accepted his loss, but his son could not. Worst, he could explain to no one. The thoughts that beat in his mind like birds in a dark tent could not be caught with words. His soul was shaken with storm; but the spirit which possessed him was dumb.

'It is fate,' they said. 'This is not an uncommon thing. We were lucky to have been free of it so long. It was her fate. What can we do? Can men master their fate?'

And Mor'anh was silent. But in his heart he thought, They can try.

The second new moon since Nai had been taken shone, and in the circle around the fire a girl looked up at the thin curve with wideset, green eyes tilted under winged brows. She was tall, for one of her people; lithe and agile, with thick, glossy hair still falling loose, the hair of a girl not come to womanhood. Her skin was almost as pale as Vani herself; her proud and lovely mouth was curved in a faint smile. From the darkness beyond the firelight the Young Wolf watched her, wishing her smiles were less rare, and sometimes for him.

He went to her. 'What is this, Runi?' he said, crouching at her feet. 'Do you not dance to Vani tonight?'

She looked at him coolly. 'We did so at moonrise; when else?'

'Ai, ai; I had a hope there that you had forsaken the banyei at last.' He shook his head regretfully, and she laughed at him.

'That I shall never do, Young Wolf.' She met his eyes with a challenging lift of her chin. 'And so I have told you.'

'Often. But I still hope.'

'Ah, be comforted. Why do I say it? I know you will be. You will never die of loneliness.' He laughed, and seeing heads turn to them she smiled a little. She looked back at Mor'anh, catching the hooded fire of his eyes and the oddly disquieting curve of his mouth, and raised her brows. 'What are you thinking?'

'Of how beautiful you are, leopardess.'

She coloured faintly, tossing her head. 'Always the same. Can you think of nothing else?'

'No,' he said.

44

Her colour deepened despite her. Her eyes grew resentful and defiant. 'I wish I had been given some other name,' she said; for the Horse People, the leopard was the lover's symbol. Mor'anh laughed softly. 'And I wish you would deserve the one you have.'

She met his eyes. 'All may wish, son of Ilna,' she said coldly. 'Few wishes are granted. Yours will not be one.' Then she turned haughtily away and would speak to him no more. Mor'anh closed his lips and stood up. He bowed to her, fist on shoulder, and walked away.

For a few strides he stared angrily before him, resolving that in future he would treat her as a woman in one thing at least, and not speak to her before others. Then reluctantly he turned to look at her. He gazed at her loose hair, her slender, untouched body, and ached with longing. It was foolish for one who should have gone to the Goddess in the same feast as Nai to be still a girl. Indeed, it was sacrilege. Yet, as he looked at her, it was not desire he felt most, but a tenderness that seemed to melt his bones. She turned all his strength to weakness, and his bold assurance to baffled supplication. He waited a few moments, but she did not turn her head.

Runi sat quite still for a while, showing how little she cared for the White Wolf, though he bowed to her before them all. Then from under lowered lashes she slid her eyes around the circle, and seeing the stares and whispers bit her mouth to hide a slow, triumphant smile.

Mor'anh found Racho grazing, and leaned against him, fondling him; then he leaned folded arms on the davlani's back and laid his head on them. There was comfort in his warmth and the rich smell of his body. He could feel the horse's slow strong heart-beat, and the easy surge of his muscles. Occasionally Racho swung his head and rubbed his great cheek against Mor'anh. It was soothing, consoling, to stand and be warmed by that deep, uncomplicated love.

After a while he roused himself and wandered to the river, Racho ambling beside him. In the dark night it shone faintly, its daylight sparkle changed to a mysterious glimmer, its low voice clear in the stillness. The banks receded into the dimness, and only the water's shine showed where the course ran. Mor'anh stood and gazed, feeling the cool stream flow through the turmoil in his mind.

He had never been able to explain the spell the river cast on him. In part, he thought, it was its certainty; it flowed without hurry or hesitation, never faltering or turning aside, sure of its way. Then there was the endless wonder of where it went, a question that had intrigued him since boyhood. Once, he had said that he wished to follow the river to its end, but Hran had laughed, not taking him seriously. Such a thing was impossible; to do it, a man would have to leave his Tribe. And where had the river begun? That must be a very holy place, where the Dancer's heel had struck. And again, what of its end? Or had it no end? Could it end? How could the water cease flowing?

Yet it was not questions alone that troubled him. If he gazed into the sliding water for long it swept his soul away like a leaf, and he sank into a stillness so deep he seemed near to hearing what that low voice said. There was a mystery in the river, something he needed to understand; but Ir'nanh did not speak to him as did Kem'nanh. But the river was very holy. The water alone was nothing, yet the river was alive; it was the power of Ir'nanh in it, the Lord of Life. Indeed, to Mor'anh, the river, dancing, inexhaustible, changing and changeless, seemed so full of the Dancing Boy, the Lord of Destiny, that at times his fascination was close to fear. Now, tonight, its depths were full of stars.

Much later, Hran came along the bank. Mor'anh did not notice his approach, and when greeted he did not speak; only raised his head and looked at Hran, rapt. For a moment he scarcely seemed to see him; then his eyes cleared a little, and he said, 'Hran: the river has spoken to me.'

Hran looked startled. Mor'anh said, 'Listen. It is hard to say what I mean. The river, and its banks; which is

46

lord? I mean, when there is a bend, has the river turned, or have the banks?'

'Mor'anh, what are you talking about? Both have, of course!'

'No! Which chooses? Which guides the other? Which is horse, which rider? Can you see? The river is Ir'nanh's, and he is Lord of Destiny—do you not see, it is important! Does the river flow in the bed laid down for it, or does it choose its own way?'

'Lai, I do not know! It is a foolish question; what does it matter?'

'Much, Hran; much. It does matter. For if the banks guide the river, then maybe all is fate as they say; but if the river makes its own bed—why—then—'

Downstream from the camp a group of women were working; their young children playing in their sight. They were weaving rushes, scraping hides; for once Runi was working among them, plastering the insides of small baskets with clay and setting them to dry in the sun. They would be long about it; the year was dying, and the sun had little heat. They were camped now among the hills where they would spend the winter.

Once Nai had made one of this group, and this was the first time since her loss that the lack of her had not cast a shadow. But they were laughing now, and Ralki was saying, 'I had been sick already, but vech! when Yaln brought me the mare's milk I was almost sick again. I did not believe it would be so strong.'

'You will learn to like it.'

'Since I must drink it for eight moons at least, I hope I will.'

'Maybe you will be like me,' said another woman with pride. A young child, thumb in mouth, gazed over her shoulder, and a baby lay kicking at her feet. 'I like it now. Since I began, I have always had one on my back, one at my breast, and one in my belly.' She laughed, and others with her, while one of the older women laid down her work and said, 'Sadi, have you quickened *again*?'

'When I am not with child,' said Sadi with dignity, 'be sure I shall tell you of it.'

Why could they not talk of something else, thought Runi as they laughed again. It was almost as if they enjoyed it.

'So, Ralki, you will not dance for us for a time?' said the older woman.

'Ve, there is no reason to stop yet.' She put her hands on her slender waist and swayed her skirt, adding thoughtfully, 'I shall not come down to dance at the Feast, of course.'

Mention of the Feast cast a cloud. This year there would be no Nai to make their prayers for them. They were silent, until one said, 'And you, Runi?'

'What of me?'

'Do you go to the Mother this year?'

'Not this year, or next, or any year.' She heard their murmur of disapproval, and tossed her head. Ralki said, 'You cannot stay a child forever, Runi.'

'I am not a child. I am of the banyei, as you all were once.'

'Yes; and that is to be neither child nor woman nor man. Some day you must change.'

'Why should I change? To bow my head to a man, as you all do? I have no love for men!'

'So you say; and yet you try to follow them. Do you think that Kem'nanh has a davlani for you? You will never be a man, Runi; you can never equal them at their own tasks. You cannot ride a great horse, nor draw a man's bow, nor throw a spear. Why will you not be what the Goddess made you?'

'No!' She was made angrier by hearing her voice shake. 'What, to work always, never to please myself, never to ride, or—or have any pleasure—'

'There are other pleasures,' interrupted Sadi with a chuckle.

'—to always bend my will to a man's, never to be thought of, and to bear children year after year until I am no longer light, and at the last to die as my mother died,

48

too worn to bear her last child. I saw her—so much blood—I will not! No!'

'That is not fair, Runi!' Kani the midwife spoke. 'It was not because your mother had borne so many other children; she was as healthy as any woman could wish to be. I have seen young women with their first child die of that flow of blood. It is as the Goddess wills.'

'Still, she died! I will not be used so by a man, no, not when they care as little as my father did—'

'Now, that is enough!' One of them stopped her angrily. 'Your father loved your mother. Why else are you called leopardess? But when a man is left alone with children so young, he must take another woman if he can. You were of the banyei then, a grown girl; but you would not care for them. What should he have done? He did not take a young woman out of desire, though still few would have refused him. He sought a widow with children of her own. What is wrong in that?'

'I do not care! Even if he did grieve, *he* was alive, and *she* was dead! I will not—no, I will not—' She stopped on a gasp, and stood up. 'Anyway, what is it to you? I will be a banya all my days, and go to the Goddess as I came from her! No man is worth so much!' She turned and ran from them, angry and ashamed. The women sat looking at each other.

'I am sorry I spoke of it,' said Ralki. 'I did not mean to distress her.'

'She is mad!'

Manui bent her head over the mat she was weaving, half ashamed to be thinking, 'Do not let her change her mind.' Aloud, she said in her low voice, 'She is afraid. That is not to be mad. I was afraid, at my first Feast.'

'Who was not? But we did not all hide.'

The oldest woman there snorted. 'Afraid, vech! No: "loose hair, no burdens". That is what it is. I remember my three summers too; saying what I pleased, speaking to whom I chose, doing as I wished—oh, yes, a good time. But I wearied of it, we all wearied of it; we wanted to be women, and take our own place in the Tribe. If we

49

all clung to girlhood as she does, what would become of the Alnei? I can remember others who never bound their hair, but they did not receive the Goddess's sign, or they only had the mind of a child. Runi has strength and sense. What does she think—that refusing womanhood will keep her young for ever? How will that loose hair look, when there is grey in it?'

'She cannot mock the Goddess,' agreed Kani. She sighed. 'It was a pity she was there when her mother died. But how could we have known? It was time she learned; and Leni had always given birth so easily. So she did then, but then came the blood. Poor Runi. But there: she cannot mock the Goddess.'

In the summer, these stony hills were burned bare of grass, and the streams shrank; then the herders shunned them. But in winter, when the Old Woman pitched her tent on the Plain and the sweet, tall grass was hidden by snow, then the tribes drew back among the wooded hills, for the nights of frost were fewer there and less cruel, and the grass did not all die.

Among those, boys no longer, who brought new-won davlenei back to the Alnei that autumn was Derna, brother of the leopardess. His sister's joy in greeting him was beyond measure, for him at least Runi loved better than herself, and she had feared for him. But Derna, finding her stubborn in her girlhood still, was not pleased. He was as much in awe of the Lord's son as others of his age, and his sister's conduct filled him with shame.

For the women, winter's work was much like summer's. The meat they dried, the hides they cured, were from the autumn sacrifices, and not hunts; they spun less and wove more; but their tasks changed little with the seasons. But for the men, winter was another life. The herds needed them no less, though milking dwindled; but for five moons they did not hunt. Their work hardly took them beyond the herds, no further than they need go to find the wood and the flints they needed, and that the deep-soiled Plain did not yield. They became craftsmen in winter, making and mending; and artists, carving in the firelit evenings. No man spent less than a fourth part of his waking hours giving his horse the care it needed to stay in good fettle. They still had the boys to teach, but now they joined their sons at their target practice, lest they lose their own keenness of eye. Even the games they played changed in winter, not only to better suit the uneven, rocky ground, but because they served a different end; not just for play, but to keep their bodies hard.

Winter was the only time Tribes were encamped close together, and there was much riding from valley to valley, making and renewing friendships, exchanging news, sitting as guests at other Fires of Gathering, receiving guests at their own. The days in winter were crowded; but the darkness was long, and made the season a slow, quiet time, full of old tales and songs. It was a season for dreaming, for thinking and talking, for brooding over memories, and making plans. And that year, most of all so for Mor'anh. As the new men laboured day by day at the teaching of their horses, so he daily struggled with his mind.

6

he Old Man's winter clothes, sheepskin with the fleece turned inward, made his outline strange and bulky. His white braids hung down beneath a sheepskin cap. He sat in the shelter of a large rock, out of reach of the wind's cold probing. But it blew on Mor'anh, stretched at his feet, stirring the long, black hairs of his cloak to show the grey down between them, and pale stripes of the skin beneath. Mor'anh held it close about him, his face pale with cold. The wind tumbled his black hair. He was silent, listening to the Old Man's quiet voice, hardly louder than the wind itself.

'Why do you ask me this? Is the son of Yorn no longer a friend to your mind?'

'Hran is the brother of my heart, but he had no answer for me.'

'And your father?'

Mor'anh's mouth tightened a little, and he lowered his eyes; but he said only, 'My father could not say, either.'

'And so you bring it to me. Am I wiser than Terani, then? Or do I know you better than your spear-brother? Do you look for an answer from me?' He peered down again, but the White Wolf neither spoke nor moved.

'Why do you think I will know? Because I am old? It is true that the world speaks louder to me now. I have time to watch and listen, time to smell every breath I breathe. Does this make me wise?'

He paused. The wind moaned a little, coming over the shoulder of the hill. Mor'anh shivered and huddled his cloak up to his ears, but did not speak.

'Age does not bring wisdom, Mor'anh. It may take it away. Age has given me patience, because it has taken away desire; there is nothing before me that I wish to hurry to meet. And long life has given me many memories. In that is all the wisdom I have. Memory puts it into my power to say I have seen this before, and this is what came after. Often this is good. But if I have not seen a thing before, what can I say? The old are not wise in new things. About new things, they may be less wise than the young.'

Mor'anh took his chin out of his cloak, his eyes kindling. 'Is the river new?'

The Old One smiled slowly. 'No, the river is old. But the thought you have, and would share with me—that is very new.'

The young man sat up, a quick blaze of delight in his face. 'Uncle I thank you! I knew you would not fail me!'

'I? Have I not?' He sounded surprised. 'I have given you no answer.'

'No, no.' Mor'anh stood up. 'No, you have not. But I do not think I came expecting an answer like that. I came in the hope of having my question understood. You hear what I am asking. Nai would hear. But they did not. Hran thinks it is foolishness, and my father too; he says it is a thing of no importance.'

'Of no importance.' The Old One repeated the words slowly, closing his eyes. 'A thing of no importance. Ah, no, Young Wolf. It is not that.'

Mor'anh waited to hear if he would speak again; but he did not open his eyes, and soon his head drooped in a doze. Still, as he walked away the Young Wolf felt his loneliness lessened. It never ceased to hurt and surprise him that Hran could not always keep pace with his mind or catch the thoughts he could not speak. It was at such times that he felt most his need of Nai, the pain of his severance from her total sympathy.

When he reached his tent, Ilna was just emerging from his own. Mor'anh stiffened, remembering how they had parted, but his father greeted him smiling, and nodded towards the porch of the God's Tent.

'One of the boys brought some firestones.'

Mor'anh scooped them up, exclaiming with pleasure, and struck them to see the sparks leap out. He did not mean to speak; but before he knew, he had said, 'Father, we were saying—'

'No!'

His own words had taken him by surprise, but not so much as the sudden violence of Ilna's reply. He stepped back and stared at the Lord, who looked at him exasperated.

'You have said enough, Mor'anh; and it is all folly. You do not know what you would say. What makes you speak so wildly? I know what it is. Something has hurt you, so the world must change. My son, the sky sends down hailstones. Will you punish the sky? When the winter blows, what then? Will you turn it back? Some things must be endured. Can you resist the Gods? Dare you try?'

Mor'anh closed his hands carefully around the firestones. He felt dizzy sickness surge through him, and with it dread of what he knew was coming. He felt the familiar tightening of his head, the stiffness of his neck; felt the storm swelling within him. The God was coming. He swallowed and clenched his teeth, breathing carefully. His hands shook, with impatience, or fear, or strain. Words would not come. Formless knowledge beat in him, and thoughts without a name. He tried to speak, but his tongue would not obey him.

'It is bad, my son, I know.' Ilna's voice was gentler. 'But it is as the Gods will.'

'No!' Mor'anh cried out as his spirit leapt with protest. He shook with tension; he felt as if he were bound with strong ropes. He looked at Ilna with desperate appeal. 'No! No longer!'

54

The Lord turned back. 'What do you mean?' He spoke sternly, but the anger in his voice could not quite hide the fear. 'What do you mean?'

He shook his head. 'I do not know!' He felt stifled. His arms ached as though they held an unbearable weight, but only the firestones were in his hands. He struck them convulsively together, and suddenly began, 'Nai—'

Ilna said harshly, 'Forget Nai!' He glanced at his son, then away. 'Let her go. It is useless. We shall never see Nai again. Kem'nanh has told me so.'

'Kem'nanh—' repeated Mor'anh stupidly, staring at his father. Confusion and doubt clapped about him. Why should Kem'nanh say one thing to him, another to his father? Could the God lie?

'I have prayed,' said Ilna, 'I have wept, and pleaded. But always I am answered "You shall not see her again." She is gone forever. Mor'anh! Mor'anh! Do you think I loved her less than you? But can I fight Kem'nanh?'

His whole body throbbed and hurt, and his head spun. One of us is wrong, he thought. Is it I? Am I mistaken? Is Kem'nanh deceiving me? But as he formed the thought, he knew it was impossible. He could not doubt Kem'nanh. What Ilna heard did not matter; on that he would not be shaken. 'I must listen to the God when he speaks to me,' he thought, 'and not when he speaks to other men.'

He heard his own voice from far away. 'They should not have touched Nai. She belongs to the Goddess.' And all the time through the spinning darkness in his head he knew it was not Nai, not only Nai; but that was all his father would understand. He was standing against a mighty wind which smote and buffeted him, and which if he yielded would tear him to pieces. It wailed within him. He could not endure much longer. His blood pounded, and ran burning through his limbs.

'Then she is the Goddess's to defend.' Ilna's distant voice came to him with words that quivered in him like arrows. 'Not for us. The Golden Ones are our lords; if they command what can we do but obey?'

The question went through him like a spear, and all the baffled rebellion in him leapt with pain.

'—Disobey!'

The cry was wrenched from him; it came like blood from a wound. The strong, cold wind howled exultantly through him and left his head clear; and he saw his father's face, grey and old with shock.

'What did you say?' he whispered.

'Disobey!' There was a wild, delicious terror in the word. 'If we can obey, then it is plain we can also disobey!'

'You are mad!' Ilna's voice shook. 'Mad! How could we? And have you thought what their revenge would be? For one woman? This is worse than wildness!' He struggled to calm himself. 'You must bend your neck, Mor'anh. "Only a King lives unbridled." I know your heart, I know your pride. But you must rein them both, or they will destroy you; and maybe more than you.' His eyes fixed for a moment, and he checked; then went on, 'This is bitter broth, I know; but we must all swallow it. Why must it choke you? Learn to live in the world as it is, my son, before you break your heart.'

Mor'anh thought wearily, 'He still does not understand,' and it hurt him a little. But he was weak and shaken, and needed quiet; he kept silence, and Ilna turned away.

Mor'anh stood still for some time. He heard again, 'They will destroy you and maybe more than you,' and saw the flicker in his father's face. Mor'anh: Lightning-bolt: Destroyer. He stared at the firestones in his hands, turning them over and over. But no matter which way he turned them, there was no where they did not strike fire from each other.

He knew when he woke that the day had gone. His cloak had not covered him as he lay, and he was cold. When he opened his eyes he wondered where he was; then he became aware of the God, and knew he was in the Secret

Place. And he smiled, remembering that a clear word had come to him at last.

He stood and stretched, feeling the surge of muscle in his arms and shoulders, the braced power of his body, and he laughed, exulting in his strength. He felt full of vigour and high spirit, like a stallion full of summer grass. Within him all was sun and white clouds. It was a surprise when he stepped out of the Tent to find rain, and a cold, gusting wind. The Fire was a dying glow, and few remained around it. He caught his cloak around him, and walked over to Hran.

'I did not think it was so late,' he said, crouching by his friend. Hran shook his head.

'It is not. No one wished to stay tonight. It is no night to lie under the stars; I will find myself sleeping by the door.' In the communal tents used by the young unmarried men and women, the first comers took the places by the king-pole; latecomers risked sleeping in a draught.

'Use my tent.'

'I hoped you would say that. May I have some of your covers also?'

'Be comfortable; take the whole bed.'

Hran turned his head, an amused glint in his green eyes. 'Do you not sleep tonight?'

'Yes,' replied Mor'anh absently, then caught Hran's eye and laughed. 'Vé, yes, but not yet. I have hardly woken.'

'Not yet, and not in your tent?'

'And not in my tent,' he agreed, standing up. 'Sleep well, my brother.'

The women had all gone. He would have to seek, and he hardly knew for whom. One face then another came to his mind as he walked. He thought of Durai, Hran's young sister who had gone to the Goddess at the last Feast. Her quick tongue made him laugh, and he enjoyed her half-resentful fierceness. But he did not want Durai. Then he thought of Manui, and desire quickened; he turned towards her tent.

57

It was not usual for a young woman to have her own tent. Young people might share a tent with younger brothers and sisters if they did not like the communal tents, or they would sleep in the open. Mor'anh and Nai had tents because they were Priest and Priestess, not because they were the Lord's children. But the Great Sickness which had wasted the Tribe ten years before, in which Mor'anh's mother had died, had killed all Manui's family save her, her youngest brother, and the oldest of her five sisters. This sister had gone in the same year to her man's tent, and had cared for the younger ones. The brother still shared her hearth, yet a child, but for several years Manui had lived alone in the tent which had been their father's.

Mor'anh often wondered whether her times of quietness were due to this disaster of her childhood; for even when she was merriest she had an air of holding her happiness delicately, as if it were brittle. Yet he could not remember that grief had seemed to weigh too long on her, as a child. Grave and shy she had always been; but whatever shadow lay on her heart, it had fallen since her womanhood.

He turned into the lane where her tent was pitched. Ahead of him, vague in the uncertain light, he saw a man and woman, and slowed to let them draw away. The tone of the man's voice, though not the words, reached him; a young voice, and he grinned to hear the persuasion descend to mere pleading. But it was not until the man reached out his arm and the woman, avoiding it, laughed, that he recognised Manui.

The shock robbed him of breath; then he could not think why it should, nor why he should feel such cold dismay. He had never thought he was the only man ever to share Manui's bed. Had he ever considered it, he would have assumed that she gave herself to others also. To sleep alone was no virtue. Manui was in the third year of her womanhood, and well he knew the heat of the fire beneath her gentleness. And yet, the thought of her with another man gave him pain.

The wind drove cold rain against his face. He stood still, feeling utterly foolish. How could he have come so confidently, so arrogantly? How could he have been so sure he would find her waiting? Were other men not to desire her, or was she to keep her welcome only for him? He felt angry with himself, and ashamed, and strangely hurt.

He stepped back quietly, and had turned to go when he caught Manui's voice again, but not laughing. He hesitated; but when she spoke again, her distress was plain. So he went towards them, taking care not to be heard; they saw him, and moved apart.

'I greet you,' he said formally. 'Manui, is anything wrong?'

She could have wept with humiliation, but she said steadily, 'Nothing, I thank you, Mor'anh. Linhai is just going.'

'I am not!' retorted the young man, flushing angrily. Mor'anh knew him now; he was entering his second year of manhood, and had probably meant no real harm. It was punishment enough to speak to a woman in front of him, as if his presence were of no importance.

'You are!' whispered Manui fiercely.

'Most certainly you are,' agreed Mor'anh, 'if Manui asks you to.' His voice was easy, but his relaxed stance was a quiet threat. Linhai's mouth tightened, then he shrugged and bowed sarcastically.

'Manui knows her wishes best,' he said. 'I yield to you, Young Wolf.'

Manui's face flamed, and she bent her head. She hardly knew which would be worse—that Mor'anh should think that she admitted other men to her bed, or that he should know that she did not. Mor'anh watched Linhai go, then looked at her and paused irresolute. He had been meaning to go at once, but looking at her he did not want to go. He wanted to stay; but for the first time, he was unsure of his welcome.

The silence was not long, but seemed very heavy; they were not usually ill at ease together. Then Mor'anh moved as if to depart. Although at first Manui had wished him to go, she felt suddenly desolate, and looked up to meet his eyes. He was smiling, but doubtfully, and with a look of appeal which overwhelmed her.

'Must I go?' he said.

She thought, 'If I had any pride I would send him away.' And she thought, 'Alas, I have no pride.'

'Why should you think you must?'

'You sent Linhai away.'

'Oh, Linhai; he is so young,' she replied; then added with a faint laugh, 'And he had only come for shelter from the rain.'

His eyebrows rose. 'You think so!' he said; then, 'It is still raining. Will you send me away for that?'

'Oh,' she said as if considering, 'you have a tent of your own, if all you want is a roof over you. Besides,' she smiled, 'you do sometimes come at other times.'

He followed her into the tent, but when he would have kissed her she slipped laughing out of reach, and left him to fasten the door-curtain. She untied the braids of her hair and shook it loose to comb it, while he sat down and looked about him. It was warm, for her fire burned at the back of the tent, the roof opened a little to draw the smoke out. It always seemed comfortable in here, he thought; better than his own tent, or his father's; or even than Nai's. There was a coloured blanket over the bed, not only skins—Manui was a better weaver than most Khentor women. And she burned something on her fire that covered the stinging smell of the smoke. He stretched and took off his cloak, casting it over the bed, then leaned forward to watch her. She had kneeled to light the lamp, for the only light was a deep glow from the fire. His steady, thoughtful gaze made her self-conscious, and he saw her hands shake slightly, though her face was calm. Heavy sweeps of her hair kept slipping forward, and she cast them back with her hand, not tossing her head as Runi did. Manui's hair was not raven, but very dark brown, warm in the orange light. Young plainswomen were always slender; but Manui had neither the fragility of Nai nor Runi's lithe firmness. There was a softness about her, a curve at once yielding and supple. The lampflame lit tall and shaking, quivering into black smoke, casting over her rich light and swaying shadow; and suddenly he wanted her, not as before, but fiercely and possessively.

'Manui,' he said, and his mouth curved to see her hands grow suddenly still. He went on one knee beside her, and heard her unsteady breath, and put out a hand to quench the lamp.

'Lamp-fat is running low; leave it,' he said. 'Do we need the light?'

The frost-bitten grass grew withered and tasteless, the herds gaunt and slow-moving, as winter trailed by. The camp was lifeless much of the time, with tent doors closed and fires burning within them. Everyone hungered for fresh food, weary of smoked meat and dried roots; rarely either full-fed or really warm they grew listless and silent. They slept far more than in summer. On the hillsides scarred by the pyres of past winters, new fires burned. The Feast of Ja'nanh passed, with dancing up on the flat hill-tops where they rarely ventured, and a sacrifice of rams to bring them to the mind of the Lord of Heaven again. The days began to lengthen; but this was the worst time, when summer seemed very far behind and the end of winter not in sight. Only the ewes, big-bellied, gave promise of spring.

Neither Nai nor the Golden Ones had been mentioned between Mor'anh and his father for many weeks. There was a quietness in their dealings, which seemed on Mor'anh's part oddly like compassion. The affection between them was stronger than ever, a sad tenderness, deep and regretful; but other bonds had loosened. To those who sensed the change it was disturbing, for it seemed that the Lord and his son were saying farewell—knowing they must part, and bent on parting with kindness. And strangest of all, it was as if Ilna asked pardon, and Mor'anh forgave.

7

pring hid behind each tree and under every stone; but still it delayed.

There had been no frost for many nights; the snow on the hilltops was shrinking, and the streams were loud with water. The earth was softer, and twigs were uneven with knots still too hard and small to be called buds.

Mor'anh, walking from the ewes to where he had left Racho, lifted his head restlessly, turning into the rough wind. The green tingle in the air teased at him, but the breath he drew smelled only of the rain-sodden end of winter, cold and heavy. He felt like a fretting horse held on a firm rein. This time was to spring what dawn was to sunrise, the hargad of the year.

He saw Manui riding her strong brown pony beyond the stream; no one else was near, and he called to her. She raised her hand and urged her pony to a gallop, soaring over the water. He smiled, watching her. He had once drawn Runi's wrath by naming Manui as the best rider among the women or girls, for Runi claimed that for herself. But her Vixen's liveliness was all play; Runi could not have handled the real strength and spirit of Manui's pony so capably. They halted beside him, Manui's laugh making a cloud on the air, while steam rose from Otter, who tossed his head and danced, snorting. Mor'anh leaned down to feel him. 'You have been riding far?'

'Yes, I shall be stiff tomorrow, it is so long.' She sighed with pleasure. 'It is the only thing I envy you men; so much time in the saddle.'

'And you have such a pony, too. I have never seen his equal.' He patted the strong, arched neck admiringly, and laughed at the delight on her face. 'Now I have begun well, I will ask my favour. Will you cook for me tonight, Manui?'

'You are welcome. And your father, also?'

He shook his head. 'He is eating with friends. They would feed me, too, but I like your cooking better. It is true. The food you cook is worth eating even at the end of winter. Better even than Nai makes it.'

She caught her breath. It still amazed her that he could speak of his sister so—as if she belonged to the present and not the past. She looked up at him to see if his eyes belied his voice, but just then the sun broke dazzling through the cloud, striking over his shoulder so that she could not see him clearly. 'Yes, I will cook for you,' she said, blinking and shading her face. 'I must go; Otter is too hot to stand.'

He rode away, and she trotted down to the camp. If Mor'anh came to eat, he would stay till morning. Well, she thought defiantly, so much the better, whatever Ralki said. She groomed Otter and spread his blanket over his back. The sun was brilliant now; out of the wind it might even be warm. She looked for a sheltered spot to picket him, but sun and wind came from the same quarter, and there was no such place.

Manui stirred and woke. The glow from the fire was very dim; the roof quivered a little, as the wind that ended night rose. The covers had slipped down. She was warm enough, but when she felt Mor'anh's shoulders he was cold as stone. Gently she freed her hands and, reaching behind him, drew the blankets up to cover his back. The hairs of the bearskin wavered against her mouth, then danced in her sigh. She slid her arms around him and tightened them, turning her face into his neck.

It almost seemed she had dreamed what frightened her; as if those few freezing heartbeats had never been. And in memory it seemed a little thing, nothing to fear. Only the taste of her terror lingered and would not be denied.

The cold of his absence had wakened her, and thinking him gone she had started up, puzzled and hurt. But he was in the tent. He was poised half crouching, half kneeling, motionless. His rigid stillness, like a figure carved of bone, was frightening. She must have made some sound, or moved, for he turned his head towards her; and it was then that terror shook her. His face was expressionless, but his gleaming black eyes raged, and the look he gave her was like a blow. His hand made a movement, very slight, but so full of anger and violence that she fell down before it, and hid her face. How long he stayed there, and whether she had been awake long, she did not know. He had roused her when he came back to bed, but the roughness of desire could not hurt her. Only the cold, remembered fury of his eyes ached in her mind.

She felt him stir, and loosened her arms hastily. He rolled onto his side and raised himself a little to look down on her. She almost flinched from meeting his eyes, but they were familiar, sleepy and warm, and she had seen that proud and lazy smile before. She relaxed a little, but her smile was tremulous, not as usual a veil across her eyes. He seemed to feel a difference, and stroking her hair back looked at her earnestly, his hand against her cheek. Her wide eyes gazed gravely back, and he sighed.

'Manui,' he murmured. 'Gentle One. Was there ever a woman so well named?'

He laughed at her startled look, and kissed her ardently. For an instant she responded, clinging close, pliant and eager; then the brief passion was gone. She jerked back and pushed him abruptly away, turning her face aside. He released her, staring amazed, then said, 'You are angry with me!'

'I am not!'

'You are. Why is it?'

'I am not angry!' But she knew she was. She resented his good humour, and was angry because he did not know what it was, to be frightened by someone he loved more than daylight. And that was foolish. So she pressed her lips together and kept her face averted, until he firmly turned her head towards him. 'Please tell me,' he said.

She pushed his hand away. 'I please you now, then. It is not always so.'

His amazement was obviously real. 'What do you mean? Manui, when have you ever displeased me?'

'Under your cloak I do, maybe. At no other time.' She was shocked to discover the depth of her own bitterness. 'When you are not in my bed it is different, even if you are in my tent.'

He studied her frowning, then with dawning understanding. 'Did you wake in the night, and I was not there?' She could not answer. 'I think you did. Did I speak harshly to you, Manui?'

'You did not speak at all,' she answered huskily, horrified to hear her voice shake. 'It was the way you looked at me. As if you did not know me, and hated me for being here.' She swallowed, anger crumbling into misery, fighting the wish to cast her arms around him and sob: help me, help me, make me forgive you; if I do not love you I am nothing.

'Eu—!' he aaid, and shook his head. 'I am sorry. I am sorry, Manui. It was not me. It is—' He hesitated. 'It is the God. I cannot choose when he comes to me.' He stroked her hair, pulling some forward over her shoulder, then looked at her again. 'I am sorry.'

As soon as he said 'It is the God' she understood herself. She had thought that Runi had been the cause of the look he gave her. It was a cold wind through her, and his words now were no shelter. For there was Runi; and

She must have made some sound, or moved,
for he turned his head towards her;
and it was then that terror shook her.

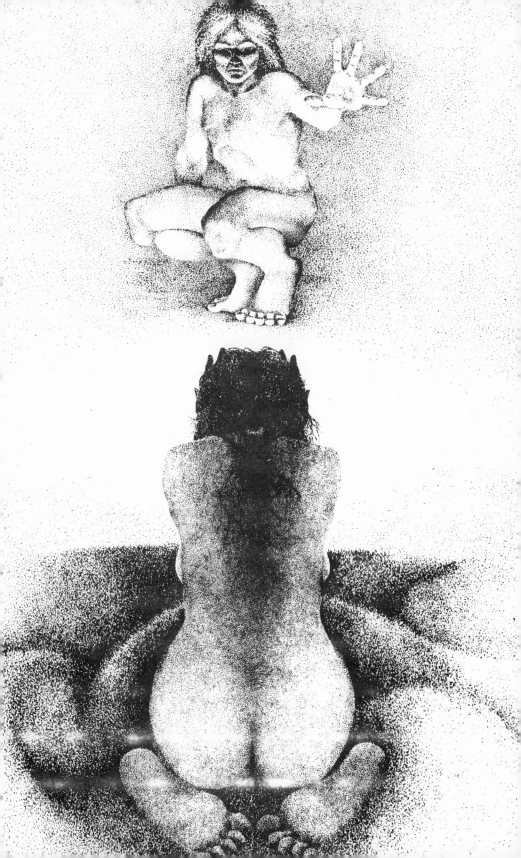

the only words that could really comfort her were words he would not say.

But that was knowledge not to be looked at. So she gave the smile that was a screen before her face and said lightly, 'Do not look so grave. It was the strangeness. I should not have made so much of such a little thing,' and she clasped his neck. He smiled also, and stretched out beside her, smoothing his hand along her side. 'If it troubled you it was not a little thing. I would not do so willingly.' Unexpectedly, he turned his head and kissed her wrist, then said, 'You are good to me, Manui. No, it is true. You are always patient with me, and it cannot be easy. I am lucky to have such a friend.'

Friend. She could not look at him, and did not know how to reply. The word he had used was not one spoken by men to women; their language hardly contained a stronger term. He could not have paid her a higher compliment, nor one that hurt so many ways. 'My lord honours me,' she stammered at last; but just then the Dawn Drum boomed, and Mor'anh cursed, and she could laugh almost easily as he struggled out of bed and pulled on his clothes. 'Dawn comes very soon,' he grumbled.

'It is the spring coming,' she said, hugging the covers round her shoulders. 'Are you not glad of it?' And from the door he looked back with a small crooked grin and said, 'Not always.'

The davlenei were shedding their winter coats. Great clumps of grey hair fell from Racho under his rider's vigorous grooming, and he snorted and shuddered with pleasure at the harsh caress of the reed pad. Mor'anh paused to splutter some hair out of his mouth, and to greet his father, who led his own horse up for grooming.

'Have you seen the Dha'lev today?' asked Ilna.

'Yes. He is restless. I think it will not be long.' His voice lifted at the thought. Ilna looked at him over his horse's back.

'You are very glad.'

'It is spring. Does it not make you glad?'

'Of course.' The Lord paused, loosening a tangle in Hulakhen's mane. 'But it is more than that. You are eager for something.'

Mor'anh's eyes met his warily. 'I am eager to leave the hills. It has been a dreary winter.'

'The cause was in you, not in winter. How will things grow easier?'

'Who knows? A summer is long. Anything is better when we are on the Plain.' He spoke easily, but Ilna was not reassured.

'You choose words to hide your thoughts, not show them! My son—' He swallowed, then shook his head and turned aside. 'Ah, I cannot blame you. You know my mind too well, and I know yours. You will not let your sister go. It has made you mad.'

Mor'anh left his grooming. 'Father!' He caught hold of Ilna's arms. 'Terani! You do not know my mind. You cannot know what is in my heart. I do not know myself. Until Kem'nanh guides me, I cannot. I do not forget what you have said, I think of it. I know you do not think as I do. I do not ask your help. I ask only that you will not make my way harder than it is.' Ilna's eyes were expressionless before his son's urgency, his arms passive in his grip. Mor'anh's voice grew pleading. 'Do not be against me. I am not mad. I can be patient. I am your son. Only, what is coming will come. I ask you only not to stand in the way and make its coming harder.'

'I do not understand you,' said Ilna in a level, stubborn voice, and Mor'anh let go of his arms. 'I do not think you understand yourself.'

'That is true.' Mor'anh began grooming again. 'Often I do not. There are many things I do not understand. But I am wise enough not to stop my ears when Kem'nanh speaks.'

'You are young, and reckless.'

'Maybe. When young, birds learn to fly. That is reckless.'

'They learn by doing as the old ones do.' Ilna mounted, seeming to have forgotten why he had come, and sat fingering the reins. 'No, Mor'anh. You will do as you choose; but I have a Tribe about my neck, and must follow what I know. Let the God decide between us.' He looked down at his son, who continued to groom Racho with hard, even strokes. 'Let there be no anger between us.'

Mor'anh raised his eyes and shook his head. 'There is no anger, my father. Or if there is, it is not mine.'

'No, you do not make me angry.' The chief's worn face creased, and he rubbed his brow. 'Not angry. You make me afraid. . . .'

'I have been talking with Darenu,' said Hran, dismounting where Mor'anh stood talking to the Old Man. 'He says he cannot remember a year when so many of the lambs have died.'

Mor'anh nodded. He had seen the flock-master himself.

'Why should it be a bad lambing?' said the Old One. 'It has not been a hard winter.'

Hran grimaced, and hunched his shoulders. 'Has it not? It has seemed endless.' And for him spring was bringing no end to the bleak time, but a quickening of pain. He leaned against Ranap's shoulder over the sunlit brightness of the new grass, and repeated stubbornly, 'The longest I remember.'

'But your memory is not long,' said the Old One, while Mor'anh turned to look at his spear-brother, stroking his moustache thoughtfully. 'The winter was neither long nor cold. The grass did not fail, and no sickness came to the sheep. Why do the ewes miscarry?'

Mor'anh grunted. 'There is cause enough,' he said. 'I rode over the hill yesterday to the Eregei; their flock increases well, with no abortions.' He looked from one to the other as he spoke. 'But the Good Goddess is not with us. We have lost the Luck of the Tribe.'

Hran's eyes flashed. 'Were we to blame for that, that she should curse us?'

Mor'anh shook his head. 'I did not say she had cursed

us. She may have blessings ready to pour, but we have no bowl to catch them. If my horn is broken and I can draw no water, has the river run dry?' But Hran's brief energy was gone.

'Maybe the calves will die too, then. And the foals. This is a bad beginning to the year.'

'So?' said the Old One. 'A year that begins badly may easily grow better. But if it does not, it is only one year. There will be more. For you, many more.'

'And for you, Uncle,' said Mor'anh; but the Old Man shook his braids with sudden fierceness.

"Not many more! If the Gods are good to me, not many! Do you think I wish for them? If I were given back my strength, then I would never wish to die, but I am old!' He stretched out his hands, and his voice shook with anger. 'Look at them! Once they were strong on spear and bridle, once they drew the bow and held bulls on the rope; now they shake and will not straighten. I am not a woman to ride in a waggon, I am a man, a rider; but my horse is dead, and were he not I could not stay on his back. And my girl is gone, my Velani—she will be weary of waiting for me. She died before you were born. Let me see the Great Plain, where I shall be young again! It is many years since I stood up to dance. And when the drums beat at the Autumn Feast, where were you? I was among the tents, with the children and the sick. I am too old to worship the Goddess. Too old for a woman!' His voice rose with disgust. Hran shook his head, but Mor'anh's wry smile turned to a grimace and a shudder. The old man smiled grimly. 'Ah, that touches you, does it? I have heard about you. Well, if you are ever as old as I am, you will not please the women so much. You will not find them so willing then!'

Mor'anh opened his mouth, then closed it without speaking. Hran laughed aloud at his confusion, while the Old One creaked with amusement. 'Foolishness!' growled the Young Wolf, turning to Racho. 'I have work to do. Hran, what of you?'

The davlenei crouched back at the men's command,

springing up when they were astride. They took leave and cantered away. Hran was still chuckling, but Mor'anh was too pleased to see his mood lighten to mind. A young tribesman greeted them in passing and when he had gone Mor'anh said, 'Is it true that Huldo is courting your sister, Durai?'

Hran nodded. 'He and others. You know she is with child?' He gave Mor'anh an amused sidelong glance, but he only looked astonished and said 'In her first winter! No, I did not. I hear no women's gossip now. Will she take any of them, do you think?'

To the Horse People, fatherhood began only at a child's birth, and was the mother's gift; a man quickened a woman, he did not beget her child. That was the law. A woman who conceived never lacked suitors.

'There is no man she prefers to the others—unless it is Linhai, and it is known he wants Manui.'

'She will not have him,' said Mor'anh positively, even abruptly. Hran said nothing for a while, then mused, 'It is strange that Manui has gone to no man's tent. Linhai chooses well, at least.' He paused, then said thoughtfully, 'The man who wins her will have a woman worth more than many sons.'

Mor'anh drew rein sharply. Hran wheeled and looked at him surprised. Mor'anh said, 'My sister is soon forgotten.'

Hran gazed at him, then looked away. 'Your sister is not forgotten, nor ever will be. But she is with the Golden Ones.' He went on carefully. 'I did not say I would court Manui; I am sure she would not have me. But I could do worse.'

Racho jumped. Mor'anh said angrily, 'Manui deserves better than that!' Hran said nothing, 'And Nai—Hran, you must not despair! Trust me. Trust Kem'nanh—he has not lied to me, I know! Do not forget her; and keep your spears, my brother!'

8

he song of a spiralling, sun-struck bird was the loudest sound in the valley as the Alnei watched the brief ceremony which ended winter and began their new year. They were ready to wander; the tribal banner, loosened from its shaft for the first time in almost five moons, shook and swung in the light breeze.

Though the sun was brilliant, the grass beneath Mor'anh's boots was crisp with frost. He walked towards the King, feeling the weight of their eyes upon him, and the lift in his heart which always came when he stood as he did now; for the people before the God, for the God before the people. The Dha'lev stood outwardly calm; but Mor'anh was not deceived. He stopped before him and bowed, then stepped closer and ran a hand down his nose.

'I greet you, Holy One; and the Lord Ilna greets you, and all of the Alnei greet you. We kneel at the feet of the Horse. Be merciful, Great One, bear us on your back. The moons of winter have passed. Holy One, lead us again into your Plain.' The Dha'lev's ears twitched, turning towards Mor'anh's voice, and he lowered his head, lipping the salt on the proffered palm. The Tribe gazed quietly on the God's chosen ones, the King and the Har'enh, matched in strength and lordly grace as they spoke together, sunlight and birdsong falling about them.

'I am the God's chosen, as you are,' Mor'anh was saying, 'and I have spoken to Kem'nanh, and asked him to guide you where I would have you take us. I tell you this, Great One, only that you may know what is in my heart. I know you will go only as the God guides you, and the Tribe can only follow you, and I am of the Alnei, and must go with them. But I ask Kem'nanh this, as a gift; for a sign.'

The davlani turned one dark, bloomy eye upon him, and made a deep, throaty sound. The young man reached up and pulled free the knot fastening picket rope to headstall, and stepped back.

'Go forth; and the Lord of Herds guide you!' he cried.

The re-davel shook his head and sidled, then, certain of his freedom, arched his neck and blared his exultation, until the hillsides, giving back his bellow, seemed full of thunder-throated stallions. He pawed the air and sprang forward, his herd streaming after. Mor'anh stood in his stirrups to shout, 'The Dha'lev leads! The Alnei follow!'

The column heaved, and began surging forward. Mor'anh whooped, and galloped forward with the other young men who would escort the holy herd. A new year had begun, the Plain was before them; and Winter, the great enemy, though he had made some fall had been thrown down again.

Dusk had fallen before the Dha'lev stopped and gathered his herd to rest; mares and yearlings at the centre, the young horses about them, and the young stallions outside all. It was yet later before the other herds, the ponies and the sheep, the cattle and the goats, were settled to their grazing, and the waggons drawn into the great triple circle of a one-night camp. They lit no Fire of Gathering, but ate, and turned at once to sleep.

The wind of dawn woke most of them before the Drum. The air was raw, the ground damp; those who did not sleep in waggons were glad enough to rise. They set out more quietly that day, the first wildness out of their blood; but their hearts grew ever lighter as their journey went on and the Plain widened about them. The long trail could not weary them while the wind of Kem'nanh blew about them, scented with the freshness of new grass, singing to them of the summer and the plenty to come.

In the deepening blue of the sky the sinking sun glowed deep orange, shadowed smokily on one side so that it looked round and solid, like a great smooth-skinned fruit. Thin streaks of cloud in the sky around it caught its colour, as if the rams which drew Ja'nanh's chariot had left behind wisps from their fiery fleeces. In the darkness of the east, stars shone, and Vani's silver brightened. Hega had not yet risen.

It would have been wiser, thought Manui, to stay with the other young women, crowded close for warmth; it was too cold a night to sleep alone. But she could not stay where Durai was. She felt shamed in the younger woman's presence, touched by a dread she dared not admit; the first stirring of the worst fear that a plainswoman could feel.

She unsaddled Otter, and he began to graze. Her bedding lay at her feet, but instead of preparing it she stood with drooping head, dulled by a great weariness. 'Too cold to sleep alone,' she whispered, and laughed bitterly. What night was not? 'Great Mother,' she spread her hands, 'Great Mother. . . .' But her prayer died unshaped. Raising her eyes she looked at the silver moon, and thought of Runi. Where did she sleep, always defiantly alone? Did she never feel the weight of the night leaning on her, never dread the cold silence of the lonely stars? Did she not feel time flowing pitilessly over her, a river that she knew would drown her some day?

A sound made her turn. The white of Racho's mane gleamed unnaturally vivid in the dying light; he looked unearthly. Mor'anh said, 'I thought I would never find you.'

'Why were you looking?' He laughed, and her breath shortened. Resentment stirred; she sought to crush it and said, 'What do you want?'

He smiled; she saw the gleam in the dusk. His coat was open, baring his deep chest. She seemed to feel already the hard strength of his body. There was a roughness under his voice, like pebbles moving beneath a stream. 'To know if you will share my cloak tonight.'

He came close, reaching out to her; and at once her body was crying its hunger. It was as if even her flesh obeyed his will and not her own. He had no fear of denial. And suddenly many thoughts—of Durai, his confidence, her own lifeless womb, Runi—tumbled confusedly through her mind. Shame and rage shook her; she ducked her head and struck his shoulder. 'No!' she cried. It was a stifled scream. 'No! No!'

She heard herself, horrified. Mor'anh recoiled, astounded by her fury. 'Manui! Manui, what is wrong?'

She took it for surprise that she should refuse him, and her anger swelled to swallow him. 'Nothing is wrong! Need it be? Must I have a reason not to choose to lie with you? Even if it is cold; is that why you came?' He tried to speak but she would not let him. 'Do you expect a welcome always? There is nothing wrong, I just do not choose to share your cloak. Leave me alone; leave me in peace. I do not want you, that is all. Go away!'

She stopped with a gasp, and stood taut and trembling. There was a still moment, then he turned and mounted. 'Whatever I have done to make you angry, I am sorry,' he said stiffly. 'And if my going pleases you more than my staying, I will go.'

'Go, then,' she whispered, standing with face averted until he had left; then she sank to her knees, pressing her fists against her mouth. Her anger spent, she shook with longing and misery. 'He loves Runi; he lies with other women; why must he come to me?' she whispered. She knew she had hurt him, and it doubled her pain. 'Did I say I did not want him?' she asked. 'I said I did not want him. How could I say that?'

For the first time since her childhood she lay and wept that night, for she saw her life clear-eyed, and her heart failed. Even if Mor'anh never won Runi her own happiness was not certain; and what chance could there be that even Runi could refuse him for ever? Then how frail seemed the hope she lived by; yet if that hope failed, what life at all was there for her?

The tents were raised, and the Fire was lit; the Alnei had made their first camp of the year. It was a good place, made more beautiful by the blossoming bushes which grew there—more blessed too, they hoped, for many shrubs were the Goddess's holy *galya*. But though Mor'anh had scouted far beyond the camp, north and west, the horizon of the Plain remained unbroken. Yet, he told himself, there was time between the Moon of New Grass and the Moon of Burning Trees for many things. This year, more time than in others, for spring was early.

Leaning beside his father at the fire that night, he said to the lord, 'I wonder what the Plain is like in winter. I should like to know how it looks.'

Ilna laughed. 'You have seen snow.'

'In the hills, yes.' He shifted, his eyes wide and thoughtful. 'But think of it here; flat and wide and empty. I wonder how deep it lies? Does it keep its whiteness all winter? I am sure more falls here. I should like to see it. One winter I will not go to the hills, I will stay here.'

'And wrestle with the Old Woman? You will not find her so easy to cast down as the tribesmen. What of Racho? And what would you eat?'

'Ve, that is true. But I would like to do it.'

'But you would like to follow the river, too,' said Hran, turning to look at him. 'And more than once I have heard you say that you would like to spend a summer with another tribe. You are as full of wild schemes as a boy.'

'Well, so long as I act always with the judgement of a man, is that a bad thing? You laugh at what I say of the Tribes; do you not want to know more of them? This year, we camped near the Eregei. We know which words they say strangely, we know the name of their lord, they gave my father a beautiful coat.' The Eregei bred fine goats, of

77

whose hair they wove a white, silky cloth. 'Last year, we saw the way the men of that tribe piled up their hair. Four years ago, we were beside the Kar'denei: what do you remember of them, Hran?'

'I remember the men carried falcons, and would hunt with them.' He chuckled to recall it; the Alnei considered that hawking was for women.

'You see, it is so little we know. In a summer, a man could really learn to know a tribe.' They laughed, shaking their heads at him. 'Ah, do you never feel that one life is not enough? There are so many things to do.'

'But all these schemes—Mor'anh, you would have to leave the Tribe!' Hran sat up and faced his friend, who looked crestfallen. 'How far would you be taken? Would you leave the Plain?'

Even to speak the idea was so preposterous that all three men laughed. Khentors knew the world was wide. They did not think that the sun shone only on them and the life they knew. Tribes who had wandered east had told of spending a whole summer within sight of trees as vast as grass, and how the Plain came to an end at last. They had all heard that beyond the mountains lived other yellow-haired men, who were not Kalnat and were yet stranger in their ways. And very far in the south, unimaginably far, there were people whose life was so strange that the Khentor tongue had not words to tell of it. The Alnei knew this was true, because in Mor'anh's childhood a man from this people had come among them; but other plainsmen heard it like the work of a wonderful storyteller. They spoke of this place by the word their guest had most often used of it, 'The Cities', but the name had no meaning for them.

Yet though they knew of the world beyond the Plain and loved to hear tall tales of it, few felt stronger curiosity. Their sense of destiny was strong. They were Kem'nanh's children, to whom the Gods had given the Plain. Other places were not their concern. Besides, though there might be wonders, who could see them but a man who left his Tribe, and who could do that? A man

78

parted from his Tribe would be like water taken out of the river—he would sink into the ground and vanish.

Ilna smiled down at his son. 'You will do none of these things. You will be the Lord of the Alnei after me, and you will have a tribe to picket you.'

Mor'anh bent his head in assent, but said nothing. After a moment he changed the subject. 'We will eat fresh meat tomorrow.'

'You will take a hunt out so soon?'

'There is game. I have not been idle today, I have found it.'

'You must give the wild herds time to grow fat, to increase.'

Mor'anh chuckled. 'Was there ever a father who believed his son was a man? I am the Hunter of the Alnei, father, for the third year now.'

'That is a long time indeed,' said Ilna gravely. Mor'anh made the wrestler's sign of submission, smiling. Hran said, 'Terani, how long have you been our Lord?'

'This will be the eighteenth year. I came to it when Mor'anh was two years old, the year Nai was born.'

It was the first time since her loss Mor'anh had heard his father speak her name needlessly. He turned to look at him, surprised, and for a moment saw Ilna's face clearly, unblinded by familiarity. It was scored with lines. Even his cheeks were wrinkled and no longer firm. There was a pale rim to the brown of his eyes, and his hair was no longer dark hair greying, but grey hair. 'Why, he is old!' he thought, shaken. 'My father is old!'

He looked away, suddenly afraid. Ilna's words, 'You will be Lord of the Alnei after me,' heard so often, pierced him with their meaning. 'I laughed,' he thought, 'because he seemed not to remember that I am a man; yet in my heart I am still a boy, boasting to the others that my father is strongest of all.' Grief and pity wrenched him, and helpless protest. For the first time he wanted to dig in his heels and hold back the turning sky.

He stood up abruptly. 'Hran!' he said, 'Hran, is not this the time to dance the Grass Dance?' Hran rose, agreeing, surprised at his urgency. Ilna laughed: and it seemed terrible to Mor'anh that his father should laugh when his own heart was weeping for him. He shook his head violently, and slung on the drum.

Most drums were played sitting or kneeling, but the White Wolf preferred the long drum, which was slung from his shoulders while he straddled it. He began the beat, and the dancers sprang up. He heard Ralki's cry of laughing rage, and grinned without mirth. Change, he thought, time and change; where is Ralki the Dancer, nimble and graceful, the first girl I wanted, the first woman I courted? Slow-footed and big with child. Is this what a horse feels, when first he knows the weight of a rider? His drum beat more fiercely. The dancers' feet flashed, their bodies whirled past his eyes. Mor'anh bowed his head, pouring his heart into his drumming, and the taut skin roared under his hands. Where did the summer go? My father is old!

The girls danced close together, arms twining shoulders, with quick delicate steps; swaying, rippling, showing the grass how to grow thickly, deep and rustling. The men shouted and leapt, higher each time, urging it to grow tall. Lifegiver, do not fail us, prayed the dance: live, live and feed us, be strong, grow green, stand tall. Life, cried the music, life, life; and Mor'anh's blood cried with it, though not to the grass.

9

herd of the beasts called the Grey Cattle had cropped a wide area of grass close, and now grazed quietly, unaware of the eyes upon them. In the scrub the other hunters crouched, concealed among the longer, coarser grass, and the tough, bitter-tasting stems of yellow flowers. Mor'anh studied the prey. They were big animals, taller and longer-limbed than cattle, heavier than deer, a dusty colour with striped flanks. The skin hung loose about their shoulders, where in autumn they would bear a hump of fat. They had thick, heavy horns, curving down beside their faces and then forward, like pale hair parted at the crown. From time to time one raised its head to look about, or another dropped to the ground to rest. Among the big animals moved small, dark shapes, and Mor'anh grimaced as he saw them. These little deer often sought shelter among a herd of larger beasts, and, being quicker of mind and body than their companions, might give warning of danger. They were antlered, and had long, soft ears drooping by their cheeks; when pricked, they looked absurd on the dainty heads, but few sounds escaped them. However, they were so small they were not lawful prey, so had little fear of men.

The herd was large. Mor'anh calculated, then signalled to his companions to kill two animals apiece. He slid three arrows into his belt, and fitting the fourth to his bow, took careful aim. It was important that the first arrow should kill instantly, without sound; in the brief pause before alarm spread, a skilful archer could bring down another.

He loosed his arrow, and heard on either side the faint whip of bowstrings and light drone of arrows in flight. Along the fringe of the herd young bulls staggered to their knees with at most a faint grunt, almost all shot exactly behind the shoulder. The hunters had their second arrows on the strings instantly, and Diveru, the swiftest of them, had shot his second when his first had barely found a mark.

But one man, Halnu, was unfortunate. The fine bull he had marked dropped down to rest in the instant he released the bowstring. The arrow sped harmlessly over his back, and pierced the throat of a pregnant cow beyond. She fell with a choked lowing, and blood gushed from her mouth. The long-eared deer beside her leapt into the air belling delicately, and the whole herd took fright. The bull Halnu had chosen lurched snorting to his feet, and the man seized another arrow for him. Diveru, Mor'anh, and two others managed to bring down a second victim, but Halnu's arrow, aimed and loosed much too hastily, was no more fortunate than his first. It took the bull in the flank, and the animal swerved, bellowing in furious pain.

Shamed and angry, and horrified at having killed the cow, Halnu leapt to his feet and sprang into the open. Fitting another arrow to his bow he ran forward, but the wounded bull was faster. It turned out of the stampede and charged Halnu. He tried to evade and failed; the horn took him in the side, and as they sprang to their feet the other men heard his scream, and saw him go down under the hooves.

A cold sweat of terror broke from Mor'anh as he seized his spear and ran forward, out-distancing the others. The bull was turning, bellowing, to trample Halnu. Arrows struck it, but it seemed not to care. In a voice like its own Mor'anh roared warning, daring it to harm one of his men. He swung back his spear and prepared to throw, then even as his arm tensed he saw the bull swing round, leaving Halnu, and charge him. There was no time for a spear-cast. He took a grip on the shaft and braced himself. The animal ran itself onto the point where he had directed it, between neck and shoulder bone. The force of its rush struck Mor'anh down; he felt the earth jerked from his feet, the spear bucking under his arm, bruising his side. He trailed from the shaft, his heels kicking for enough foothold to keep him off the ground, clinging grimly to avoid falling under the hooves. There was bawling confusion as the bull tried to reach Mor'anh along the length of the spear; then it pitched to its knees, and a hot rush of blood over his legs told Mor'anh it was dead.

After a moment he got stiffly to his feet and walked to the other men. 'Halnu?' he said, 'Does he live?'

He knelt down by the injured man. Calling to mind all that the Healers had told him, he felt Halnu carefully. He had several broken bones, and a large split bruise on his head, but the worst was the wound in his side. By good chance the horn had had a broken tip, so that it had torn his flesh, not pierced it. But the tear was deep and ugly, and bleeding fast.

Halnu groaned and opened his eyes. They did not wander, but gazed up at Mor'anh wide with pain. He reached across with his unbroken arm to feel his side, but Mor'anh took his wrist and gently put his hand away.

'Leave it. Can you feel your leg?'

Halnu nodded, and tried to smile. 'Too well,' he said hoarsely.

'And the other leg, can you move it?' The man flexed it a little, and Mor'anh nodded. 'It is not as bad as it might have been. Derna, ride swiftly and tell Mnevenh and Lal'hadai what has happened. Hran, bring one of the slings here.'

*There was no time for a spear-cast. He took
a grip on the shaft and braced himself. The
animal ran itself onto the point where he had
directed it, between neck and shoulder bone.*

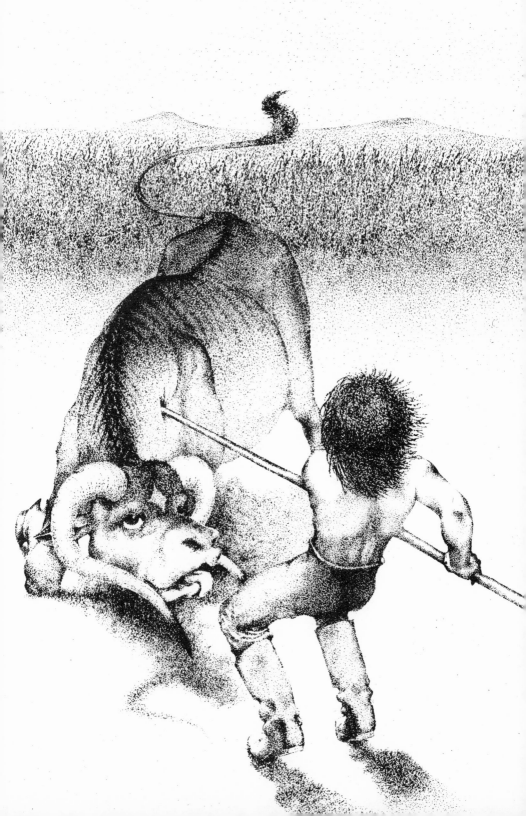

They were as gentle as they could be; but the journey back could only be an ordeal, and he was unconscious at the end of it. Maybe it was as well for him, for Lal'hadai had to clean and stitch his side before the edges of the wound hardened, and there had been no time to prepare one of her drinks. When that was done, Mnevenh the bonesetter was waiting. But Mnevenh was strong and skilful, and there was a quietness about him which drew away fear, as many said his hands had power to do with pain, drawing it out of their limbs. Halnu's wife had come by that time. She did not weep; Khentor men could weep without shame, but not a woman. They lamented for grief, and so Nusani would have done had she found him dead; but he lived, and there was enough to do without wailing. The tears were shed by his children, gathered from their games by the news; so, there being no other help he could give, Mor'anh took them away to comfort them.

When the boy came calling to Halnu's wife, the other women stopped their work and began talking, shocked and agitated. Only in the shadow of an accident that had already happened was it safe to voice their constant fear for their men. Curiosity at seeing them talking so energetically drew Runi aside to join them and hear the news. She was interested but not much moved; and those who were most shaken found relief in turning on her.

'This is what hunting is, you see,' said one. 'It is not a game the men play. Now do you see why the Young Lord will not take you? Is there not danger enough for our men, without you adding to it by your folly and your pride?'

'I am not afraid of the danger!'

Another woman snorted. 'No; why should you be? You know well enough that Mor'anh would never let harm come near you. If you drew peril by your wilfulness, do you think the men would let you face it? No, alas; it would be they who died. No, Runi, I never thought you were risking a goring. Vech! If I thought that would happen, I might add my pleas to yours, that you should go!'

Manui looked round, startled by the malice in the woman's voice. She thought suddenly, 'Why do we hate her so? I have cause, but they cannot have. Why is it?' But Runi seemed not to care, only hunching her shoulders disdainfully, and sitting down.

'Runi!' said Ralki, between scandal and amusement. 'Did you ask Mor'anh to take you on the hunt?'

'Well, what is funny? They take the boys.'

'You did not really expect that he would do it?'

She looked round at them. There was laughter on their faces, and she bridled. 'Oh, I was not surprised at his answer. Vani knows, he does not like the banyei.' But it was an ill-aimed shaft. Women who had watched the Young Wolf flirting with their little sisters laughed mockingly, while Manui said, 'You are not saying he cannot judge who may hunt?'

He was the Hunter of the Alnei, and the chosen of the Lord of Herds. To deny his judgement was too much. Runi shied from it. 'Oh, I would not dare. We all know what a mighty hunter Mor'anh is. No man can bend the bow he bends, nor wield the spear he wields.' She spoke derisively, though at random, and was pleased to see the colour come up into Manui's cheeks, while others glared tight-lipped; and though she did not understand why some smothered shocked giggles, it gratified her. 'Never does his hunting fail. Never do his weapons fail him. The quarry seems hardly to flee him. No, it waits for his spear, it seems, as if it wished to die—does it not, Manui?' She saw the woman press her lips together firmly, but before that she had seen them tremble, and her angry heart rejoiced. 'Even,' she added spitefully, 'the game he does not particularly want!'

All around her women turned with angry cries; and Manui whirled to face her, as pale as she had been flushed, dropping her work at her feet. For a moment she could not speak; but when she did, her voice was steady.

'Why make a riddle-game of what we all know, Runi?'

she said quietly. 'Mor'anh loves you; and that he does is my grief as much as his. But I do not see that it is matter for your mockery.'

For a moment they stared at each other, but though colour rose in Runi's cheeks, her eyes did not waver; and facing her beauty, Manui felt the bitterness of her own inevitable defeat, and turned away. The other women did not watch her go. They looked at Runi, and she met their hostility smiling.

'One day, Runi,' said Ralki angrily, 'you will sting yourself with that poisoned tongue you have, and die of it.' But Runi only laughed.

Vani waned, and was new, grew to the full, and waned again, while Hega more slowly waxed to her pride. On the first day of the moon called the Moon of Yellow Flowers, the Alnei lowered their tents and went north. It was a long wandering; seven days the Dha'lev led them, from first light to sunset, before he found a place to please him.

Hran had not escorted the God's herd; arriving with the waggons he went in search of Mor'anh, surveying the ground as he rode. It was uneven, moulded into hills and hollows; and as he trotted across the likeliest place for the tents, on the long low slope of a hill, where the morning sun would strike, he felt uneasy. Halting Ranap, he looked about him.

The short fresh grass was bright with yellow flowers, but his memory was seeking a different mingling of gold and green. The river cast a wide loop about the hill and the level ground beneath. Hran stared at it, then rode to the brink. It was brimming, the hurrying water glittering, but he saw in its bed a shallower, clearer river, drinking the mist of an autumn morning. Moving along it, he recognised one place then another. But he held off belief as long as possible; until he turned to face west, and looked at the pattern of the mountain peaks. His throat tightened, and his heart swelled; he felt it throb heavily many times, before he urged Ranap on. He knew now where to find his spear-brother.

Mor'anh was standing beside Racho on a hill-crest, and did not look round. Hran had come with words on his tongue, but they died, and he too was silent as he stared away to the dark walls and pale roofs of the Golden People's town. They were working in the fields around it; for a moment Hran looked for a man in a red tunic, but there were many. Then he turned his eyes to his friend. Mor'anh was smiling, a glad terrible curve of a smile, while his cold eyes watched the gate which had framed his last sight of Nai.

his is your doing!'

Ilna's voice shook. His hands opened and clenched over and again. The light flickered as he passed through the column of sunlight leaning down from the opened roof, then turned and strode jerkily back. 'You have done this!' Mor'anh said nothing, only watched him. He was sitting on his bed, leaving the stool to his father, but Ilna did not use it. He stopped by the king-pole and took one of his son's spears from the rack, staring at it unseeing. Mor'anh watched his hands, working on the shaft.

'You are to blame.' The spear rattled back into the rack. 'You meant this to happen. You brought us here!'

Mor'anh spoke at last. 'My father, you speak in anger. You say what you cannot mean. Sit down, my father; be calm and consider.' He waited until Ilna, yielding, sat heavily and faced him. Then he went on less formally, 'Father, how could I bring us here? How could I force the Dha'lev to choose one place or another? Did I mount his back and bridle his head? If I could, I would not dare. I follow the Dha'lev, as we all do; only the God may guide him. Wherever we go, it is the will of Kem'nanh takes us there. It was you who taught me that, when I was a child. How then can you say that I meant us to come to this place?'

'You are the Har'enh of Kem'nanh. You have the ear of the God.'

'No; I have the favour of the God. He speaks to me; but I do not know if he listens to me. I may pray, but is he a feather, to be blown from his own way by my prayers?'

Ilna stared at him, baffled by the undeniable truth of his words, feeling that it was not so simple, shamed by the young man's calm. He tried to keep hold of his anger, but it was slipping away.

'It was your desire drew us here. How, I do not know. But since they took Nai, your heart has been picketed to that town.' Mor'anh said nothing, only looked steadily at his father, his black eyes a door Ilna could not enter. The lord sighed, lifted his hands, and let them fall.

'What will you do?'

Mor'anh thought, 'He knows. He feels what I feel. He is Lord of a Tribe, and Kem'nanh speaks to him too. He sees the shape of things as clear as I do, but it makes me glad, and it makes him afraid.' He felt a remote pity. 'If I were old, I too would be afraid,' he thought, and tried to believe it.

'I will do nothing. What is to happen is in the hands of the Gods; and the Golden Ones.' He smiled, but it could not reach Ilna, who rose to his feet.

'I have watched the men who try to wrestle with you, Mor'anh, and proud of my son I pitied them. Now I feel for them more. I cannot match you. I am Lord of the Alnei, and I cannot command my son. You say to me, "Let what will come, come!" as if it is an easy thing; but the days come down on me now like a stampede of bulls.' He raised his head. 'You think I am old and timid—ah, yes!—but you are not a father. You speak for the God: but I must think of my people, and stand before them.'

'But, they are my people too! Father—'

'Father?' Ilna's quiet voice cut in, and the twist of the word silenced him. 'Father? Yes, I have been a father to you. I have reared you and loved you; taught you and trained you.' Mor'anh listened dumbly, feeling the approach of a grief strange to him, strange to his people. 'I

91

gave you your spears; I showed you to the Dha'lev when you were born. But who it was quickened the spirit that is in you, I do not know.'

They were showing some little boys how to make and throw a noose when the *Kalnat* summons sounded. Hran turned swiftly to Mor'anh; but he seemed unmoved. He went on talking to the children as if he had no other interest, and only when they had trotted away swinging their ropes did he say 'Shall we go out?' He spoke as if he hardly cared, yet there was almost a smile in his eyes. Hran wondered at it. A year before, Mor'anh had met even a mention of the Golden Ones with anger; now, with real cause to hate them, he seemed to welcome them.

When they joined the other men, Ilna was talking to the spokesman. Seven other Golden Men sat in the great painted dray which had brought them; the floor was shoulder height to a plainsman, and carved seats were placed on it. At the back stood the boy with the metal horn. They were drawn by five yoke of red oxen; gay fringed cloths covered their backs, and their short horns were painted in stripes of red and blue. The men wore bordered cloaks and tunics, bracelets gleaming on their arms.

Hran saw Madol at once. He was not wearing the red tunic, but one of yellow bordered with brown, a long blue cloak on his shoulders. Hot, painful hatred rose to choke him; he felt his blood grow rank with it. Madol did not know them. His blue eyes scanned them without interest, as he talked to the only other bearded man present. Nor did the man talking to Ilna seem to recognise them, though Hran knew him for the one who had received their tribute. He looked for the tall man, but he was not there. His eyes returned to Madol. This was Nai's man. She tended his fire, cooked his food, lay with him; maybe the clothes he wore had been made by Nai. Each thought was torment, but he was greedy for the pain, anything to slake his thirst for Nai. He stared at the Golden Man, wondering if a woman would find that square brown face pleasing, if Nai was a willing captive now and sang by his fire. Was he perhaps hating something that was precious to her? But no, that was not possible. That could not be possible.

His demands delivered, Haniol climbed up onto the wain. The driver shouted, and the curly-polled oxen lumbered forward. Mor'anh, watching the cumbersome vehicle turning, smiled. 'They are the same,' he thought: 'So much is changed, I thought they would have too. But they are the same.' He watched their calm arrogance, that regarded oxen and tribesmen in the same spirit. They had not changed.

Hran, his eyes still fixed on Madol, took a stride after the waggon, then stopped. He turned to Mor'anh, who stood watching him with a faint, approving smile. Hran waited, expectant; but Mor'anh only said, glancing scornfully after them, 'Is that a way for a man to travel?'

The tribute-day was grey and cold. The Golden Ones huddled their cloaks about them against the fingering wind, with no sun to brighten their pale hair. Hran looked down on them, then swallowed hard, trying to empty his mouth of the bitterness of fear. He was angry with himself, for there could be no reason to be afraid. He looked at Mor'anh's impassive face, and dread twisted him again. His friend's calm confused him; it was not reassuring. It was like the stillness of a hovering eagle.

He balanced a roll of furs on his shoulder, hiding his face from his companions, and went down the slope. The wind had sharpened, and the Kalnat put up their hoods. Hran could not fail to see that on a windy day there was something ridiculous about men who were wearing tunics, but hooded, they gained menace, and the two impressions jarred.

But they could not hold his mind for long, when he knew who was in this town. He waited a little apart,

93

keeping the furs on his shoulder, and turned warily to look up at the walls. A section was under repair; alternate stakes had been removed, and a pile of new logs lay nearby, but no one was working there. Through the spaces he could see a little of the town. That was good luck undreamed of. The sour juices had gone. His mouth was dry now, and he could not get enough air. He scanned the wall eagerly, knowing his hope almost too frail to stand, but intent nevertheless on the broken view of an open space within the town. He moved away, but the Kalnat, blinkered by their hoods, did not notice. Hran had forgotten caution. He gazed, and then it was as if the weight of his longing had pressed a hollow that must be filled, or the singleness of his passion had borrowed a god's summoning power: for he saw a woman, small and dark, walk into the open.

The furs fell. Gaining the gapped wall, he grasped two stakes and stared between them, unable to find enough voice to call to her. She had changed. She had changed so much, it was hard to say how he knew her. Much of her beauty was gone. She was heavy with child, near her time, and they had cut short her glorious hair. The shapeless, unbleached dress she wore, pressed by the wind close against her body, was ugly and shaming, and without her tight-laced Khentor dress her breasts had sagged. She seemed little more than the embers of herself until, before he could speak, she stopped, looked round and saw him.

'Nai,' he said, his pain dissolved by the wonder and joy in her face. 'Nai.' He stretched his hands through the palisade, and she came towards him with awkward swiftness. Little of her former grace was left to her, but as their hands met again Hran cared for nothing else. The hair that had been cut about her shoulders, too short to braid and falling about her face, gave her the look of a young girl, shocking above her pregnant body; but the face it framed looked older, thinner, with lines it had never worn. Her mouth and shadowed eyes had grown harder, aged by more than one winter. Her bare arms were puckered with cold, and stained with the marks of bruises. Hran thought, 'It was because of her beauty that he took her; why then has he tried to destroy it?'

She closed her eyes and leaned her head against a stake. 'Hran,' she said between laughter and grief, 'Hran, do not look at me. You have not changed, and I have. I am ashamed.'

'Have I not changed? I should have. I have waited long to look at you, Nai. Do not ask me to stop now. Nai,' he could not say her name often enough, the pledge of her presence, 'Nai, you are unhappy?'

'What else could I be? Are you happy?' He shook his head, and she laughed shakily. 'I am a hard-hearted lover, my leopard. Through these moons my worst fear has been that you might be less unhappy than I am, that you might have been comforted. But Hran,' she tightened her grip on his hands, trying to move closer, 'Hran, if you stopped loving me, I could not bear it!'

'Never, never!' He was shaken by her desperation. Seeing the pleading in her eyes he felt for the first time that he was the stronger, and even at such a moment there was sweetness in it.

'What is it like, Nai, in there?'

'It is terrible. I cannot tell you—you cannot dream what it is like. It is a—a *hard* place. I am so lonely, Hran. I only have Marat, his sister . . . There is no comfort in these—houses.' She frowned over the word. 'And the winter; it was terrible. I have never been so cold. I thought I would die. And I miss you, Hran.'

He would ask, though the words stuck. 'Your man—I saw him. Is he good to you?'

She looked at him, then shook her head and leaned her cheek on his hand. 'He might be, if I let him. But he is angry, because he knows I hate him.'

'Is he not pleased that—that you—about the child?'

'Yes! He is so proud, I laugh at him when he is gone! He has no cause!' There was a feline fierceness in her eyes. 'Hran, I am Har'enh of the Mother! Do you think I would let a man quicken me unless I chose? I carried this child when I came here.'

Delight flooded him. Leaning against the stockade he had forgotten the Kalnat, the tribute, forgotten everything but Nai, her hands, her voice, her face. He felt no urgency, only a vast happiness.

'But it troubles me that he will be born here,' she was saying; 'I may lay him in the lap of the Mother, but he will not be shown to the Dha'lev . . . Hran. Hran, why are you smiling?'

'Am I? I do not know. Because you are here. And because you do not love your Golden Man. Nai, it has been a long winter.'

She smiled gently. 'Tell me the news of the Tribe. Greet my father for me. And Mor'anh.' Suddenly her fingers hardened. 'Tell Mor'anh it is true!' she whispered. 'Say I hear it too. And tell him they will not let me be quiet. He will know.'

But at this reminder of their meeting's brevity Hran was shaken with panic, and pressed against the unyielding trunks. 'Nai, the days have been long without you, and there is all my life before me. I want you more than spring and more than morning. How shall I live, if we do not meet again?'

'We will! We will! Hran—!' But then she screamed. Without that warning, the blow could have killed him; even so, he was sent sprawling on the ground, sick and dazed. A blond giant stood over him, shouting. Though Hran's spinning head could not make out the words, he understood the spear levelled at his breast. He tried to roll aside, but his stunned limbs would not obey him. Yet no blow came; and as his head cleared he saw Nai, her arms stretched through the wall, clutching the spear-butt, shouting wildly. Hran began to scramble up as the man, crimson with anger, turned on Nai. 'You scrawny whore—' he said, and drove the butt viciously into her chest. She choked and fell back, winded; but Hran was on his feet, and wild with rage.

96

With a dancer's leap, unerring, he kicked the man's wrist so that the spear fell from limp fingers, and landed poised to spring again. Though no Mor'anh, he could wrestle, and he was past weighing his sacrilege. The big man had no defence against his whip-crack swiftness, and crashed to the ground. Hran fell with him, but twisted clear and sprang up again, heeding neither the other Kalnat watching in disbelief, nor Nai's desperate pleas that he should flee. He waited for his enemy with a wild elation he had never felt before. The furious Golden Man was up again and rushing on him. Hran stepped forward, bent, and threw him over his back, turning swiftly on his heel. Swiftly enough to see how awkwardly the man fell, and to hear his neck break.

For several heartbeats there was complete silence. Then a Golden Woman rushed up to the palisade, stared, and screamed.

Hran was aware of a sudden burst of sound, of Nai almost shaking the stakes as she called to him, but he was numb. He could only stand staring at the great body sprawled at his feet, limbs limp, fingers curled, open eyes blank as pools that mirrored the sky—a blue sky, another sky than the one over Hran. He was dead. It was not possible. He had killed him. Awe and horror engulfed him, and a terrible grief. There had been so much life; and he had destroyed it.

'Hran, run, oh, run!' cried Nai despairingly. But he did not move, and she cried with all her power, 'Mor'anh!'

Hran looked up then, roused by the anguish in her voice. The Kalnat men were coming with raised spears, consuming the slope with their long-legged strides, eager to revenge their fellow and to punish the plainsman's mad impiety. They were before, and the wall behind. Flight was impossible. In despair Hran snatched the dead man's spear, not even thinking how he could use it. Along the wall behind him women's voices called the men on. Hran clutched the spear and prayed for courage.

Then Racho leapt the ditch and came up the long slope

as if the storm wind had taken a body, wounding the ground that had never known hoofprints with his savage speed. He swept past the Kalnat so close that one man fell, and his flashing heels kicked earth back at them. Hran sprang forward as the horse whirled before him, and Mor'anh stretched a hand to swing his friend to the saddle. Hran would have let the spear fall, but Mor'anh seized it. Yet all the while the Young Wolf's eyes were busy elsewhere, searching the wall for his sister. They exchanged one brief intent look, their faces blank of emotion. But as Racho galloped away Mor'anh drew a long shaking breath and let it out in a deep sigh.

The other plainsmen were mounted and riding away; the tribute animals wheeled and cried, then turned to follow. On the ground where the Golden Ones had stood to receive their due, only the hides and furs remained, and a dead man by the wall.

Hran, wrapped in his horror, knew little of the ride back to the camp, hardly knew where he was until they were standing, a mill of steaming horses and shouting men, in the centre of the camp. Ilna was in front of him. 'What happened?' he was saying. 'Quiet! Quiet, all of you! Hran! What happened?'

Hran slid from the saddle and stared at the aging, half-afraid face. 'I have seen Nai,' he said loudly, and they were quiet. 'I killed the Golden One. He hit Nai; and I, I killed him.' He saw Ilna's face collapse, and his own terror overwhelmed him. He fell to his knees and covered his eyes. 'I killed him!' he cried. 'Oh, Kem'nanh! Kem'nanh! I killed him!'

11

n the dusk when the fire was first lit, Hran met the Lord before his tent. The healing woman had given him a drink which had made him sleep most of the day, so that the morning's happenings had retreated from him a little. Having just risen he felt a little unsteady, and the evening seemed colder than usual, 'Terani,' he said. 'Your daughter bade me greet you for her.'

Ilna stood quiet, his face turned a little away. 'Did she?' he murmured. Then, 'And I did not see her, not even from far off. How did she look?'

The ordinary question, springing from feelings he understood, soothed Hran. 'Not well,' he answered sadly. 'She is big with child, but she looks thin, and much older. They have cut her hair.'

Ilna sighed. 'Then I am glad I did not see her. I will remember my daughter as she was. To see your child suffering, and to have no power to help, is the worst pain I know. But I should not call her my child, and she looked for no help from me. When they took her, she called for you, and for her brother, before she called on me. Is it not so?'

'Not quite, Terani. I was not first. It was Mor'anh she called to first, before either of us.'

'Vé, it may well be. From the time they were small, there was no getting a grass-blade between them.'

She called to Mor'anh first, thought Hran, but it was I who killed the Golden Man for her sake. And beneath his pain there wriggled a glowing worm of pride, and he could not quite crush it.

The Young Wolf put back his tent door and came out smiling. Ilna hesitated, then turned away to take his place at the fire. 'Mor'anh,' said Hran. 'Nai gave me a message for you.' The words sounded foolish, and he stumbled over them. 'To tell you it is true; and she hears it too; and they will not let her be quiet. She said you would understand.' He paused, and went on, 'Also, I think I must be purified.'

'It is certain you must; but we will speak of that in the morning, in the Tent. Wait, Hran, I have something of yours.'

Hran stood puzzled until his friend came out of his tent again. 'Here,' he said, arm outstretched. 'This is yours.'

Hran recoiled a step. 'What is it?' he said, though he could see plain enough what it was. The firelight turned its blade to flame.

'It is the Golden One's spear,' said Mor'anh. 'It is yours. Take it.'

Hran shook his head. 'I do not want it. You keep it.'

Mor'anh looked at the spear, but shook his head regretfully. 'No, I have no right. Take it, Hran. Here.'

Half unwilling, Hran put his hand to the shaft, and looked at the weapon. It was taller than he was. The shaft was of pale wood, smooth as bone. The long blade, with a broad point and straight sides widening into shoulders, shone warmly, and the metal that sheathed the butt was figured. It was very beautiful.

'No other man has such a spear among all the Horse People, so I should think,' said Mor'anh.

Hran weighed it. The metal sheathing, though it made the weapon feel light and easy in his hand, did not exactly balance the blade. 'It would not throw well,' he said, trying to find fault where truly he could see none.

100

'It is not made to be thrown. It is not a hunting spear.'

Hran turned it about, watching the light catch it, brighter at the honed edges, shadowed in the groove along the centre. 'How shall I use it, then?'

'Is it not enough to look at it? It is very beautiful. It could only be used as the Kalnat would use it.' Hran met his eyes and saw there a look which appalled him. 'They made it for killing men.'

It was a hunting morning. Mor'anh had risen long before sunrise to pray before Kem'nanh the Hunter, and was with the other men at the river while it was still dark. Vani was sinking behind the mountains. In her light the snowy peaks seemed to float free of the dark mountains, shapes of calm airy beauty: until as she sank they became only a jagged darkness against the fading silver. The men bathed in silence. The Dawn Salute sounded as they were coming up out of the water. The snows kindled, and the green mountainsides were folded with shadow.

Hran stretched his limbs, enjoying the warmth; the water had been achingly cold. The other hunters were keeping a little away from him, but on this morning he did not really mind. He knew why they kept a distance: he had become something strange and terrible, a man-killer, in whose ordinary-seeming hands a dreadful power was hidden. Guilt could be purged in the ordeals of the two Tents, but knowledge could not, and they feared him. It had hurt him at first, but not today. He was content with the sun, the ordinary world. He had just passed through his purification, and the bright morning was all he asked.

Mor'anh said, 'The smell of the Tents clings to you, it seems. It will pass.'

Hran thought, 'It is the smell of death,' and wondered if it would pass, but he said nothing. This was something Mor'anh seemed not to understand. The dread that made men draw back from him Hran could accept, for he felt as they did. What hurt and horrified him was the look he saw on some faces, of envious awe.

101

Kariniol paused, gazing ahead of him. The sun's low rays flooded his face and bared head with gold. He raised his arm in salute.

'Akrol, Soul of Light,' he whispered, 'have mercy on us. Do not deal with us as our folly deserves.'

He walked on as the other men reached him, fitting his helmet to his head again. But Keratol had caught the end of his prayer, and said angrily, 'Folly? What do you mean, Kariniol?'

'Only that if we must do this—'

'*If* we must! Would you let the savage go unpunished? He killed Deram, remember?'

'I know, yes, it cannot go unavenged. I do not wish it should. But I still say that it would have been better to go as we always go, not like this.'

'Unarmed? In peace? And just ask them to give the murderer to us? Are you a fool, Kariniol?'

'When did we ever "just ask" a thing of the Wanderers? We would demand him.'

'And you think they would give him?'

'They might. How can we tell? What do we know of them?'

They laughed scornfully, and he set his mouth. 'What *do* we know?' he thought. 'All we know is what tribute they can provide.' And he felt sure that whatever the power they had over the tribes, it lay in awe, not fear; but his companions disagreed.

'A show of force will impress them far more.'

Kariniol looked around. Fourteen men: two, Keratol and the Master's downy-chinned son, with helmets and breast-plates of metal; the others, like himself, with leather armour. All bearing wooden shields on their backs, spears, and daggers. 'Force,' he thought. 'We are not even carrying our swords.'

'And what force are we?'

'You speak as if we were going to war! This will be enough for them.' He saw Kariniol's ironic look, and his face darkened. 'In Akrol's name! They are the Wanderers! Are you afraid of them?'

102

'No, I am not! No more than I fear the cattle on the mountain; but that does not mean that if I see my bull scraping his feet I will throw stones at him!' Now they all joined the cry of disgusted anger, and his temper rose. 'All right! I will tell you why I do not think we should go like this, and it is not only because I do not think that we shall frighten them. It is because I do not think we should give them lessons, when it seems there are some among them who are willing to learn!'

There was a pause; then their leader laughed derisively. 'Ach, one madman, one. And him we will take and kill, and that will be their lesson, and an end of it.'

Kariniol smiled dourly. He had not expected to be heeded, and maybe after all he was wrong. But he enjoyed one last cut at Keratol.

'So, we will take him. Do you know, Keratol, which one to take? Do not make a mistake, or they might know you are only a man. Who killed Deram? How will you know him?' Keratol looked startled. He had given it no thought. Kariniol laughed mockingly. 'Well, I shall tell you. He is the tallest of them, he rides a red horse, and he has a bunch of red feathers in his hair. Let us hope that is enough. You fools, if we mean to do more than tithe them, it would be wise to look at them more.'

The wind of dawn had fallen; there was scarcely enough breeze now to ruffle the bright feathers in Hran's hair, or to roll to the hunters the heavy smell of the flat-antlered deer.

Hran watched Diveru, who was leading this party; Mor'anh with the other was two bow-shots away. He raised his bow and took aim, loosed, at Diveru's signal, and rejoiced to see his buck fall. A faint breeze moved against his cheek as he fitted another arrow. Then, through the herd, animals flung up their heads with faint snorts and moved forward briskly, but without much fear, until they saw their fallen comrades. Then they cried, and began to run.

Diveru cursed, swinging his bow to try for another

victim, then gave up. He came behind the other men to Hran. 'They scented something,' he whispered, his eyes bright with eagerness. 'A leopard, maybe?'

Hran laughed silently. They all knew how Diveru longed for a leopard skin. But before he could reply, there rose the sound of a ram's horn, beating the air: Mor'anh was telling them the hunt was over. Hran went forward with the other men to retrieve his arrow from his kill. He stood a moment, looking thoughtfully upwind, and wondered what the scent had been. Not a leopard, or they would have been more afraid.

Curious, he walked forward. The grass grew very tall there, in great dark clumps sprouting silver plumes taller than a man on horseback. He trod carefully, but caught no sign or scent of danger that he knew. Then he came round a huge fountain of grass-blades, and met a Golden Man.

He was too astonished to shout; and the young man, whose head and chest were covered by shells of red metal, dropped his spear and clamped his hands over his mouth to stifle his own cry. Then Hran was seized from behind. He gave half a cry before his mouth was stopped, and he began to struggle.

Mor'anh was trotting towards Diveru's party when he heard Hran's cry. He gave a shout, and sent Racho galloping towards the sound. He saw the other men leave their tasks and follow, then he was within the grove of great grass. He shouted, 'Hran!' and snatched a spear from the quiver at his knee. Then Racho burst between two clumps and Mor'anh saw what seemed a horde of Golden Men, all strangely clad. On the far side of the clearing Hran struggled, held by two men; and one of them, seeing Mor'anh, pulled the long dagger from his belt.

There was no time to consider. Giving a fierce cry he galloped straight on, towards the man, levelling his spear. Behind them a man screamed. What followed was too swift to understand. He glimpsed an astounded face, there was a shriek, and his spear jerked out of his hand.

104

Racho stumbled and recovered. Glancing back he saw Hran, his right arm free, seize his hunting knife and turn on the man who still held him. Mor'anh wheeled Racho.

The man he had ridden down lay dead. His hide breastplate could turn many blows, but Mor'anh's spear had had the power of a galloping horse behind it. Another Golden Man was running towards Hran, and Mor'anh kicked Racho into a gallop again. The man checked, seeing them bear down on him, then turned with a shout of fear. It was the sweetest moment of Mor'anh's life, and he rode him to the earth. Then the other hunters came bursting through the grass.

Hran's bewildered young captor wailed and released him, his arm slashed to the bone; Hran darted to join his fellows. One man levelled his spear and ran forward at him, then fell with a scream, Mor'anh's spear piercing his thigh. The Golden Ones fell into a brief confused panic. They ran to form a line, shoulder to shoulder, to fight in a way they understood, facing Mor'anh on his dancing horse and the tribesmen behind him. Then Keratol and another man, fired by fury and pride, gripped their spears and charged. Diveru raised his bow. Keratol choked, faltered, and fell with Diveru's arrow through his throat. The other man gave a hoarse cry, dropped his spear, and clutched his shoulder, staring at the feathered shaft between his fingers.

A taut silence followed. Mor'anh stared at the line of Kalnat, then glanced at the hunters. Their faces showed nothing but watchfulness. He dismounted and ordered Racho away. Hran snatched a spear as the horse passed him, but Mor'anh stood unarmed in front of the tribesmen. The only sound was the muffled groaning of the man with the wounded leg. Mor'anh thought, 'Five of them are down, and not one of us is hurt.'

He spoke. 'Who is chief among you?'

Wordlessly, Kariniol pointed at Keratol. Mor'anh glanced down, then caught a movement and raised his head sharply. 'Do not move,' he said, 'or you will lie as he lies!' He could almost hear them drawing breath, he saw their shocked anger, but the stir died. Other men besides Diveru had fitted arrows to their bows. At his side Hran balanced a spear. He looked back at Kariniol.

'Who will speak for you?' The men shifted, glancing for a moment at the other man wearing metal, but he shook his bent head, clutching his arm, blood spurting between his fingers. 'We all have voices,' Kariniol said at last. The Young Wolf nodded, and took a step forward, Hran at his side. 'Why are you here?' he said.

The tense line of Golden Men slackened a little. One or two of them caught back their arrogant bearing. One man pointed at Hran. 'For him,' he said. 'He killed Deram. We have not forgotten him. He must be punished.'

'He has been punished. We have our own laws. He has suffered for what he did. It is past.'

'It is not past! We have not taken our due!' And another man shouted, 'How has he been punished, when he still lives?'

Mor'anh looked at the man who had spoken, then from face to face. 'To please you, he must die also? You would have taken him from us to kill him? You thought we would let him go?'

He wished he dared look at the Alnei. Kem'nanh, he prayed fiercely, Kem'nanh, keep their reins in my hand. Yet if their faces betrayed anything, the Kalnat had not seen it.

There was one man in whose eyes there was no doubt or unease, only anger at the Wanderer's daring. 'Yes, we would have taken him,' he said. 'We would have taken him and taught you all what price is put on a man of ours. But you would not always have lacked him, herd-boy. We would not have kept him. We would have sent him back to you, bit by bit.'

The air tightened. Hran swallowed painfully. But Mor'anh, staring at the Kalnat in a way no Khentor had ever before dared, answered scornfully.

'And did you think we would have waited patiently

106

while you did this? Did you think we would not come and take him back?'

His voice rose. He felt his people's wild amazement, but fury burned his veins. Kariniol tried to intervene, but from folly or bravado the same man jeered, 'Maybe he would not have wanted you to come. Life would not be so good to him. We would have taken his eyes first—or his manhood—'

There was a stunned silence. Hran gasped, and felt himself turn white. Then Mor'anh gave a deep wild cry, and striding forward aimed a blow at the speaker, his arm swinging straight from his shoulder. His doubled fist struck the side of the Golden Man's head, and with a faint grunt he fell.

An eager shout rose from the plainsmen. The relief helped Mor'anh wrestle down his rage. He looked at the other Kalnat, and saw their levelled spears, and the fear darting in their pale eyes. He gave them a look of scorn, turned his back on them and walked to the tribesmen. His eyes gave them all the command they needed, and others raised their bows. He turned again.

'Lay down your spears.' They hesitated, and his voice grew fiercer. 'Lay them down. Tall man, show them wisdom. We are hunters, we do not miss.' After a moment Kariniol threw his spear to the ground, and then the others followed. 'Derna, gather them up.' The young man ran forward eagerly. Mor'anh stared at the tall man. 'We will not harm you. We will take you to our tents, and tend your wounded. When they are enough healed, you may take them away.' He still spoke directly to Kariniol, and a tremor of anger crept into his voice. 'You will not take Hran. We do not need to be taught what price you put on your friends; we know how we value our own!'

They might have resisted still, if a leader had rallied them, shaken as they were; but authority had passed to Kariniol, and when he told them to yield they did so, and turned to their wounded comrades. The Young Lord stood over the man he had wounded, while they took the spear out of his leg, and kept a stern face, though his stomach clenched. Then he went to retrieve his other spear.

Mor'anh looked at the man he had killed. The helmet had rolled off his head, and he could see his face. He was not young. There were lines about his eyes and mouth, and the hair at his temples was thin. His head was bent back, and his chin stuck up oddly. Mor'anh stared at him in silence, and wondered what sort of life he had ended. It had been such a brief thing, that wrench on his spear, but he could never know all it had done.

The spear stood up from the man's chest. There was a moist stain on his leather corselet. One hand was curled around the spear, the other, fingers splayed around the shaft, pressed against his chest. Mor'anh put out a reluctant hand to grasp his spear, then pulled his hand back. It felt so firm, so—embedded, and the dead man's hand seemed to grapple with him for it. A cold sweat pricked him; he shook with fear and disgust, then grabbed the shaft and pulled fiercely. The body moved horribly, jerking, monstrous. Loathing and panic filled him. Then with ghastly abruptness the spear came free and the man rolled back. Dropping the spear Mor'anh doubled over and was sick.

After a while he felt Hran's hand on his back. His stomach ached with heaving. He straightened and shook his head. 'Did anyone see?' he said hoarsely, wiping his eyes.

'No,' said Hran. Mor'anh's colour was returning. He took up the spear with only a slight flinching, and cleaned it, then turned to Hran with a grimace. Hran said, 'What shall we do with the dead?'

He swallowed. 'They must carry them back to the camp.' The nausea was passing. He walked back to the other men. The Kalnat were gathered, sound men supporting the wounded. Diveru was staring down at the body of Keratol. He too had lost his helmet; thick, curling golden hair was spilt about his head. 'I thought it was a leopard,' remarked Diveru, startling Mor'anh. His dark eyes considered the dead man calmly, without remorse. Then he stooped, and cut off a thick lock of yellow hair. He bound it around the neck of his spear, giving Mor'anh a brief hard smile. And Mor'anh, though his gorge rose again, smiled back at him with a sudden hot delight.

12

t was a strangely quiet gathering about the Fire. So many moods were flowing through the Tribe that Manui felt almost ill with them. Awe at the Golden Ones' presence had cast this stillness on them all, but within the calm they seethed with guilty excitement, and dread, and scared defiance, and a bitter triumph. Manui suffered all these at times, but mostly a dismayed confusion. It seemed wrong that the stars should turn in their accustomed dance above a world so shaken.

Manui raised her head and looked at the Lord. Ilna was like a carving, staring into the fire, his hands clenched on his knees. His face was impassive, but in him was something pity dared not approach, and she looked away. Across the circle from her sat the Old One. He was smiling to himself as he rubbed his beard. Diveru was near him, and Manui shivered to see him. The Kalnat spear lay unobtrusive at his feet, only the very edge of the blade flickering in the firelight, but his hunting spear was stuck upright beside him, and the lock of hair bound there swung and shone.

What must the Golden Ones feel, seeing it? She turned to look at them. They sat near Ilna and his son, surrounded by every comfort the Tribe could offer, fleeces and skins and cushions, a screen to keep the wind from their backs, gay blankets and warm pelts to cover them. The glowing light enhanced what the Tribe still accepted as their beauty. Manui blinked at them, and sought out the wounded she had helped tend. The boy, though his wound had been easiest to dress, looked the worst. He lay with closed eyes, drawn and exhausted. He had lost much blood, but most of his weakness was misery. The man whose thigh had been speared sat with his leg stiffly before him, his face grim with pain. From time to time he gave a faint grunt, and his shoulders jerked. Manui would have pitied them if she dared, but it seemed too great a blasphemy.

Nearest to Mor'anh sat the very tall man, their apparent leader, in the eyes of the Alnei the most splendid of them all. Manui studied him, trying to guess from his face at his nature. But their features were so strange that their expressions were impossible to understand, as impenetrable as their words.

Her eyes slipped past him to Mor'anh, his sombre Khentor face to her blasphemous eyes more beautiful than the whole race of Golden Men. He alone, the heart of the storm, sat calm and relaxed, resting his arm on his bent knee, aloof and assured. Yet the sense of strange incalculable peril hung most thickly about him, so that as she looked at him all other emotions receded, leaving her with fear only, cruel consuming fear.

The stillness of the Alnei did not displease Mor'anh. He had expected it, and was well content that at the end of such a day the Kalnat should find themselves amid this uneasy quiet, the object of all eyes. Only his father's frozen hostility distressed him. He put his hand down to touch the spear lying beside him, and smiled a little, watching Hran as he knelt talking to Yorn, his father. Though possession of a Kalnat spear pleased him, he would leave it in his tent most of the time, and so he guessed would Diveru; but even now Hran was leaning on his, the blade flaming above him. He was called the Long Spear already, much as Mor'anh was called the Young Wolf.

111

Kariniol's eye too was caught by the bronze blade; and whenever he looked away from that he saw instead Keratol's hair swinging gently in the firelight. While he saw them, he could not forget that though they sat here like honoured guests, in an empty tent nearby two of their number lay sewn tightly in leather shrouds.

The quiet oppressed him. He longed for walls about him, logs burning on a hearth, a roof against the night, and only one or two others in the room. So great a gathering of people unnerved him; he would have expected each family to keep to its home. What drew them together? How could they bear so many others around them?

He was cold. The cloth of his tunic did not keep out the wind as leather did, and pride kept him from wrapping one of their blankets around himself. He looked up at the sky, and shivered. He had never seen a sky so vast. By day it was impressive; but at night it was staggering, crushing. He had rarely been outside the town by night, and then only on the mountain, where a man did not stand exposed to the whole sky. Here it was not only above them, it rose up like walls from every side. And here the crowding stars did not stand still, as they seemed to do when seen only in glimpses. They moved as he watched, plunging across the darkness, slowly but perceptibly changing their pattern. It made them seem frighteningly alive, a watching presence.

He felt himself grow dizzy, drowning in the depths of heaven. Pulling his gaze away he stared at the ground, evading the massed faces of the Tribe, and the dazzling activity above and around him. His eyes were daunted; but his ears could not be stopped. In the quiet he heard noises from beyond the camp, the voices of the Plain. Some, near at hand, he recognised as cattle or sheep, but the first time horses called to each other it shook him. But those that came out of a greater distance he did not know, and his mind worked uneasily on them. He refused to ask what they were, but after one especially harsh and savage cry the man beside him stirred uncomfortably and said, 'They can't all be tigers.'

Kariniol answered only by a short laugh; but Mor'anh turned and said, 'You will not hear a tiger; he hunts in the Deep Plain, he would not often come here. That was *dunesh,* that last call; he is a small bear, but he makes a big noise.'

Kariniol nodded, and searched for something to say; but then came a sound he did know, a shivering howl which froze him. Yet to his amazement, the stir through the Tribe seemed one of pleasure. He turned to Mor'anh and said, 'That was a wolf!'

'Yes.' He gave an almost mocking smile. Far off, the wolves howled again, many this time. The fierce clamour stopped the Golden Men's blood, but the tremor that ran through the Alnei was not fear. One of the tribesmen flung back his head and answered them. The mimicry was perfect, and Kariniol's spine turned to ice.

'But—wolves!' To the Kalnat they were the essence of fear, the very symbol of peril. 'And yet your people seem glad!'

The plainsman smiled again. 'They are our brothers. This is the Tribe of the Wolf. It is pleasant when they greet us.'

'And you do not fear them?'

Mor'anh shrugged. 'This is not winter. There is food for them in plenty. The wolf is nothing to fear.'

'Nothing to fear,' thought Kariniol. To him, wolves must be outside a strong wall and locked gate, and then the mere sound of them was terror. Yet these people sat here defenceless, and listened to their howling with pleasure. The sky, the Tribe, both unnerved him; but outside the camp and under the stars was the Plain itself, most terrifying of all. He had looked at it from the mountain, limitless space without boundary or landmark. Yet Mor'anh spoke of the Deep Plain as if this were hardly the Plain at all. And on this they lived, wandering over the emptiness, making no settlement that could keep the desolation out. This where he sat now, this was still the Plain; and when they were gone the grass would grow tall again and drown the memory of their camp. They left no traces behind them, and their frail lives hardly marked the land they lived on.

He was overwhelmed with terror and shame. 'What fools we are,' he thought, 'what fools. They live amid all this: and we thought to scare them with a show of force!'

Kariniol sat alone. His companions wearied him. Save for Sunam, whose broken thigh absorbed all his mind, they were either shattered by fear, or obsessed by indignant rage. Once more he was excluded, but he no longer cared much for that. There were few whose contempt he did not return in full.

Morning made his surroundings more tolerable. By daylight the camp seemed more solid, the Plain less immanent, and the Alnei were less overwhelming going about their work than at the Fire of Gathering. The other Kalnat would return having learned nothing of the Horse People. Indeed, they hardly saw them. But Kariniol watched them with interest. It was for some reason surprising to find that the Dark Ones led lives of their own which went on out of sight of the Kalnat, that they had other faces than the one they showed their masters. Even the sunlight astonished him. In his imagination the plainsmen had always lived in a stormy twilight, enduring cold and hunger. To find the truth so different was disconcerting.

They treated their captives with deference. The adults kept their distance; but during the morning every child in the Tribe came to stare. There were children everywhere. He had never seen so many. Their daintiness charmed him. He had known that plainsmen were small, but never thought what their children must be. And they had none of their parents' reserve. They clustered near him, grinning and giggling, laughing hilariously when he tried to speak to them in their own tongue.

114

As they overcame their awe they sat down around him, trying to talk to him, and pointing out his oddities to each other. His bare legs, to his faint discomfiture, seemed to fascinate and appal them. The children of his own people kept their distance from adults. These played their games around and even through the groups of working women or talking men, confident of indulgence and affection from them all.

'A stranger is a great wonder to them. There has not been a stranger among us since I was nearly as small as they are.'

Kariniol looked up, and saw the young man who had led the hunters; the man who had killed Darinol, and wounded Sunam, and felled Kuniol. The children withdrew at once, bowing. Even the Kalnat recognised him and fell silent, then moved further away. The young man sat down before Kariniol.

'I am Mor'anh, the son of Ilna, Lord of the Alnei,' he said. 'May I know your name?'

There was no need to tell him. Plainsmen called Golden Men 'Lord', though this man had not even greeted him so. They did not exchange names. Yet something impelled him to say 'Kariniol'.

'Kariniol,' repeated Mor'anh. It sounded strange in his accent, and Kariniol shivered, feeling suddenly vulnerable. The plainsman bowed his head gravely, and said,

'I greet you, Kariniol. You are welcome to the tents of the Alnei.'

He spoke with no trace of irony, but even his courtesy, as if to an equal, was insolence. Kariniol, meeting Mor'anh's eyes, was disconcerted to find himself beginning to smile, and quenched it.

'The young one, he with the beard, is he stronger this morning?'

For some reason the question astonished Kariniol, maybe because the youth's collapse moved him to scorn as much as pity. 'He grows stronger, I believe,' he said coolly. Hearing more in the tone than in the words

115

Mor'anh looked at him and laughed. It was a laugh of understanding, in which the other man was invited to share, and reluctantly Kariniol grinned.

'That is a thing which seems strange to us. He is the youngest man among you, and the only one with a beard. Why is that?'

'It is because he is the Master's son—the son of our Lord. He is a noble—that is, he was a lord when he was born.'

'But you do not have a beard, Kariniol.'

'I?' Mor'anh raised his brows at Kariniol's surprise. 'A beard? I have not the right.'

'But you are the leader.'

He stared, then began to laugh painfully. Their leader? So the Dark Ones took his isolation for lordly aloofness! He wished there was someone with whom he could share the bitter joke. Their leader!

Mor'anh was watching him enquiringly. He shook his head. 'No, I am not the leader.'

'You speak for the others.'

Had he done so? Maybe, though even to remember the previous day was dangerous. 'Here, maybe. We are all strangers here.' It sounded weak, but could he say, 'Most of them would not stoop to speak to you?' Certainly not to this strangely imposing young man. 'But they will not hear me when I speak at home. Mine is the least of voices in the Council.'

He was annoyed to find that it cost an effort to disown this borrowed dignity. Mor'anh watched his face with the unnervingly close attention of one trying to follow a strange language. 'Why is that?' he said.

Kariniol hesitated, but evasion was demanding.

'I am new in the Council. I have no land, but my wife—my woman—has, and now I speak there for her. I have no voice of my own. A man who owns no farm—' he saw the frown at the meaningless words, and searched for others, 'a man who—who has no land to care for— who grows nothing—cannot speak in the Council. And a bastard is not allowed to own land.'

116

Mor'anh frowned again. The word on which Kariniol's tongue fell with such angry weight was unknown to him.

'Bastard? What is that?'

'I have no father. He never took my mother for his wife.'

'How then was he your father? How did you know him?'

He looked intrigued, but explanation was utterly beyond Kariniol, who gestured hopelessly and shook his head. After a moment Mor'anh dismissed it and said curiously,

'And this—bastard: it is a bad thing to be?'

'A hard thing. It is to be a child who is mocked, a man who is scorned. It is to be alone; my father was a stranger, and my mother's kin would not know me. And no man would give me his daughter. Sadanat, my wife, was a widow. It is to be poor. I could not farm, nor even choose the work I should do. I am a weaver, a maker of cloth.'

Many of the words escaped Mor'anh, but the bitterness in Kariniol's voice told him enough. 'Then your people lose by their folly. I speak to you as their leader, Kariniol.'

Half the Golden Man's heart was hot with anger at being given the approval of a Wanderer as if it were an honour, but he bent his head and said, 'I am listening.'

Mor'anh said quietly, 'Your people have done wrong. They will suffer for it. You have brought a great evil upon yourselves.'

Kariniol looked confounded. 'What—!' Mor'anh gestured him to silence. He said,

'Because of you, I and my sister lead a divided life.'

For a moment Kariniol doubted his ears. And there was such majestic condemnation in Mor'anh's tone, as if his private grief were a crime against heaven.

'Your sister?' he said stupidly, 'Because of us? How?'

Mor'anh's brows arched in haughty surprise. 'You do not remember?'

And suddenly, frighteningly, Kariniol did remember, and cursed his slowness. Why had he not recognised them? He saw again, vividly, the father's grief, the girl's

117

despair. He remembered Mor'anh's look, which his eyes could not endure.

'The Dark Witch,' he said. 'Madol's slave—Madol's girl. She is your sister?'

Mor'anh watched him carefully, and a bitter smile touched his mouth. Kariniol told himself that 'slave' could not have been understood.

'She was taken at the last tribute. So you had forgotten? I thought you would remember.'

'I had not forgotten. I did not know you again.'

'I remember you. It seemed to me that you told—the other man—to let her go. I do not forget that. I thank you.'

Kariniol shrugged uncomfortably, still shaken by the astonishing accusation 'Because of you, I and my sister live a divided life.'

'And you grieve for her?'

The lift of Mor'anh's head was impatient. 'Hran grieves. My father grieves. They only love her . . . it is not good that we are parted. Our spirits are torn. It brings a curse.'

Maybe the strangeness of the language veiled his true meaning; Kariniol hoped so. If not, this arrogance lay next to madness.

'Because you and your sister are apart?'

Mor'anh considered him thoughtfully. It would be hard to explain. To his own people, he had never needed to try.

'It is not a small thing. Can you understand? We are of the same kind. Nai is Har'enh of the Mother, as I am of the God.'

'Of the God? You—are you a priest, Mor'anh?' It was what he himself had wanted. He had had no other desire, but bastardy disqualified him. And this now must be the final humiliation; to look on a Wanderer and to envy him.

'I am the Priest, yes, and Nai Priestess. But to be Har'enh . . . That is another thing. It is to be one who is taken—whom the God fills—'

He stopped. More he could not say. But Kariniol was

thinking of Madol's complaints of his concubine's moods, and feeling chilled.

'It is not our pain, Kariniol, that brings the curses. It is the anger of those who chose us.'

The Golden Man was silent. Ideas he would have mocked at home seemed possible, reasonable, here. And Mor'anh's assurance commanded belief. Dread stirred in his heart.

He raised his eyes to the Young Lord. 'What is to be done?' he asked quietly.

'Give Nai back to us.'

Kariniol looked at him fixedly. 'Give her back?' he repeated hesitantly. Mor'anh nodded.

'No more is needed. Send her back and all will be well. All will be as it has ever been.' As he spoke he really believed it. 'Speak to the man who took her. Speak to your Council.'

The Kalnat leaned his brow on his hand. It sounded so simple. He could see how easy it must seem to Mor'anh. But he saw with equal clarity a picture of himself proposing to the Council that they should forgo vengeance and that Madol should restore the girl, and he shuddered. Simple: yes, it was simple. But for it to be possible, the world would have needed to be different from the beginning.

'I will try, Mor'anh,' he said at last. 'Akrol help me; I will try.'

13

ariniol gazed with dreamy pleasure as the young girls whirled silently past his eyes. Their faces were calm and rapt. All the dance lay in the intricate graceful movements of their arms and the slight rippling of their outspun skirts. They danced without sensuality. One of them even to foreign eyes was astonishingly lovely, but Kariniol could admire her with unshaken calm. No drums beat to disturb the maidens' passionless serenity. They circled the fire for the twenty-seventh time, then lowered their arms and drifted away into the gathering. The charmed silence dissolved.

Kariniol glanced at the other Kalnat, and caught Sunam's eye. To his surprise the wounded man smiled faintly. He was in deeper disfavour than usual, for talking to the tribesmen; a fact which made him think with deeper hopelessness of the promise which already weighed on him.

'Not much like the last one?' grunted Sunam, and Kariniol nodded. The previous dance, by the men, had been a rhythmic flaunting of agility and strength, and he had felt awed and shamed. They were so hard. Their lithe muscular bodies carried no useless flesh; their waists were as taut and firm as their shoulders. Yet they were supple, too, seeming able to ask anything of their limbs.

The leaps they made in their dancing confounded him. He was sure that the only man in his town who even approached such fitness was the young man who would take the chief part in Akrol's yearly feast; and he was set apart for a year, serving the shrine and training for his run.

Perhaps it is eating so much meat, he thought, wryly. The Kalnat, who lived mostly on corn-meal, were finding so much flesh hard to stomach. They only ate it at feasts. That the tribesmen ate little else, like their dressing in fur and leather, gave an odd air of luxury to their lives.

The dancing, it seemed, was over; but there was still light, and some of the young men began wrestling. It was not possible that the Young Wolf could then long keep his place at Ilna's side. He sat talking to Hran and his father, resisting the wrestlers' calls for a while; but at last he stood up and pulled off his coat. A shout of acclaim greeted him, and his face flashed briefly with laughter. He stripped off all his ornaments but his embroidered wrist-bands, then barefoot and with trousers twisted up and fastened just below his knee, he stepped forward to join the wrestlers.

Manui looked at him poised to meet his first opponent, at the ease and power of his beautiful scarred body, and shivered with desire. She clasped her hands tightly, tensing herself, but her blood sang, and her loins grew molten with longing. She bent her head and laughed to herself, half ashamed and half delighted. He had asked to come to her that night, but still she hardly dared to expect him; it had only happened once before, that he had come to her three nights in succession. It had been so long. Since her rebuff, he had slept away from her every night, until the Kalnat came. She recalled how he had sat before the Tribe as if doubt never came near him; but he had sought her that night for comfort as much as for pleasure—because what he had done appalled him, because, she knew, he could not spend a night alone with the thought of the man he had killed.

Kariniol watched the wrestling with interest. The

121

dances he enjoyed without understanding; but the Kalnat made an art and a mystery of all the skills of fighting,
and this was something to which he could bring his
judgement. It was strange to him; spells of poised stillness and bursts of acrobatic movement almost too swift
for him to follow. The wrestling he knew was a contest of
weight and strength. Even this, the Dark Ones seemed to
make as much like a dance as they could. Glancing aside,
he saw with amusement that most of his companions had
forgotten their pretence of seeing nothing, and were leaning forward with an attention as close and critical as his
own.

Then Mor'anh stood up, and Kariniol forgot to be
critical. There would be no understanding Khentor
wrestling from watching Mor'anh, who made it a whole too
perfect to be broken into parts; but there was the keen
enjoyment of watching supreme skill. Kariniol kept silence until the last bout; but then Mor'anh snatched
victory with a move so deft and unexpected that he could
not restrain a shout of approval. Mor'anh laughed, holding up his arms; then suddenly turned and stepped up to
Kariniol, stretching out a hand in invitation.

The Alnei were instantly quiet. Kariniol sat astounded
and dismayed. He looked from Mor'anh's outstretched
hand to his face, and saw there only laughter, a challenge
made half in jest, a gesture of friendship; so why he
should feel misgiving he could not say. To refuse, to draw
back before the Tribe, was difficult. He looked uncertainly at his fellows, and some of them hissed to him to
stand, to lower Black Cloak's crest and give him a taste of
earth. He stared at Mor'anh again, doubting his open-
ness, distrusting the sparkle of his eyes; but he could not
hold back without shame. Slowly, hiding his reluctance,
he stood up.

Under the shout of delight and fear Ilna groaned, heard
only by Hran. Kariniol listened to the satisfied voices of
the Kalnat with angry disgust. Could they not see that
even in victory he would look a fool? He was head and
shoulders taller than Mor'anh, and half as heavy again.

There was no honour to be gained by defeating him.

Hran rose and went to Mor'anh. 'Are you a fool, my brother?' he whispered, but the Young Wolf's eyes only flashed with excited laughter. He flexed his shoulders and shook his arms, turning to face Kariniol. The watchers grew quiet. The wrestlers eyed each other; Kariniol stepped forward and lunged at Mor'anh; and the Kalnat bayed eagerly.

And then Kariniol knew what he had done. He had opposed himself to the master of a skill of which he knew nothing. Size and strength were not enough. The weight that should have borne Mor'anh down he avoided cat-like, and only a slight jerk brought the big man to his knees. Then as they closed again Kariniol realised with a shock that his advantage of strength was less than he had thought. His body was unaccustomed to such use. He could not command it as Mor'anh could his, could not keep his breath or his balance. He was big, but not hard; weaving was not work to turn flesh to muscle. And he was pitted against muscles of leather, against arms and shoulders that had mastered bulls, and thighs that had learned their strength from stallions.

He understood that now, but he knew that the tribesmen would not see it so. They saw one of the godlike Golden Ones sprawling at Mor'anh's feet. Divinity could not survive such humiliation. He heard their wail of amazement as earth, stars, and firelight reeled about him, and he came crashing; he could almost feel the glory falling from him. He had put the majesty of the Golden People in Mor'anh's hands, for him to fling to the dust.

When his defeat was final and beyond doubt the Alnei gazed in silence as he rose, not even cheering Mor'anh. What blasphemy had long stopped short of imagining, they had all seen enacted. Kariniol knew that the awe in the silence was no longer for him. He carried it as well as he could, smiling unresentfully and turning back to his place. But the other Kalnat too had felt worship withdrawn, and rage and scorn came out to meet him.

*They saw one of the godlike Golden Ones
sprawling at Mor'anh's feet.*

A great weariness was on Kariniol. He was sick of things that were fierce and strange; he longed for his home, for his tall calm wife, for his little step-daughter who never laughed but when he was there. He endured such a morning with his companions that all his bitterness over the wrestling was turned against them, and when Mor'anh came he did not get the cold greeting he had expected. When he asked how the Golden Man was, Kariniol answered with apparent good humour,

'Sore and stiff from that wrestling. Your bones are stone and your flesh is bronze, Mor'anh.'

Mor'anh smiled and disclaimed. 'It was your own strength turned aside, more than mine, which threw you down. It is a skill, Kariniol, that is all. I have been learning it most of my life.'

Kariniol looked at him. He was naked to the waist. 'You are not even bruised, Mor'anh. I am black with them.'

The plainsman laughed. 'We are horsemen, do not forget; the first thing we learn is how to fall easily. But this is not what I came to say. It will please you more to hear than it pleases me to say, Kariniol, that my father means you to go back to your own people tomorrow.'

Kariniol hardly noticed the courtesy. He thought with aching gladness of Sadanat sitting quiet in her chair. 'Back to Maldé?' he cried.

'Maldé? Who is that?'

'No,' he laughed, 'no, not a person. Maldé is the name of our home.'

'Home?'

The Golden Man blinked at the questioning note. 'My house—our town. The place where we live. Maldé!'

Mor'anh's eyes were bright with interest. 'But the way you say it—Maldé—it is as if it were the name of a person. Not as I would say "the camp", "the tent" but as if I said—"Hran", "Yaln".'

'Well—!' he was nonplussed. 'It is our home!'

'It is as if I said, then, "the Alnei", "the Tribe"?'

'Maybe; more like that. But—Maldé is the town, the place, not only the people in it. We are the people, but

Maldé is something else. We could all go, but there would still be Maldé.' He looked at Mor'anh, and saw he still did not understand. 'It is our home!'

Mor'anh laughed, shaking his head. 'Words are strange. Well, it is as I said. Tomorrow you will go—"home" to your own people.'

Kariniol smiled, but a strangely desolate feeling touched him. He thought of Maldé, of the streets where even the weeds were familiar and the dogs had worn themselves places to lie. He thought of his house, with the blessing carved on the lintel, the prayer cut into the roof-tree and the little clay gods guarding the hearth. Home. To the Kalnat, it was the most sacred word they knew; but to the Khentors, it had no meaning at all.

The men easing Sunam onto his litter kept apologising to him, but he only smiled vaguely, light-headed from the drink Lal'hadai had given him with this journey in mind. His leg seemed very far away. Others were making bundles of the dead men's clothing and armour. Keratol and Darinol on their biers lay out of sight. Kariniol stood aside with Mor'anh and Hran. At other times, it would not have been tolerated that he should watch while others worked; but for the present they seemed prepared to allow him the dignity the Khentors gave him, and willing that he should be their spokesman. Unless, he thought, it was just that they thought talking to the Dark Ones the most menial task of all.

Mor'anh said, 'You have not forgotten your promise?'

Kariniol shook his head. He had not forgotten; he wished he could forget. 'Are we ready to go?' he said.

'We?' said Mor'anh, after a pause. 'Do you wish us to come with you, Kariniol?'

He stared, astonished. 'But . . . I thought. We cannot go alone!' Some time before, they had recognised the grim fact that there were barely enough of them to carry home Sunam and the dead.

Mor'anh said, 'Could we show you the way? The mountains are easy to see.'

The other Kalnat were beginning to turn from their

work. Kariniol said, agitated, 'It is not that. But we must cross the Plain. And we are burdened.'

Mor'anh looked at him. Kariniol thought, 'He means we needed no guidance or protection when we came; it is true.' But the Young Lord said only, 'It is not far. You should reach—Maldé—soon after noon. There will be no danger.'

But there was a clamour of protest from the other men, and Kariniol ran a hand through his hair. Turning away from the others he said in a lower, urgent voice, 'What is it? Do you wish to hear me say "we are afraid"? You know it is so. Mor'anh, we know now that we do not know your Plain.'

The Young Wolf looked at him steadily. 'You have spoken as one who means to be heard, and so will I. We have not forgotten why you came. You came to kill Hran; a life for a life. Now you have two more men to avenge. Kariniol, you I would be glad to call my friend, but of the others of your people, what shall I say? We are not fools, to walk into the tiger's jaws.'

He smiled, but Kariniol only gave him a harassed look and hurried over to the other Kalnat. They talked hotly together, while Mor'anh and Hran watched. Angry voices were raised, but in a moment Kariniol came back. He said abruptly, 'How if we give our word that no hand will be raised against you?'

Mor'anh looked narrowly at his tense face. 'What oath will you swear?'

'I will swear by Akrol the Soul of Light.'

'You only?'

'We will all swear.'

Mor'anh looked at the other men, then back to Kariniol. 'We swear oaths on a spear,' he said at last. 'Where is yours? I must trust you for the oath, Kariniol, that it will bind them. Let them swear now; then you, on my spear and on yours.'

When the others had spoken Kariniol grasped the two shafts and took his oath. Mor'anh did not understand all the words, but he watched the man's face and was satisfied. When Kariniol had ended he put his own hand to the spears. 'Mor'Inkhlen!' he cried, 'Spear of Truth, Avenger! Hear and remember!'

It was hardly past noon when they came in sight of Maldé. A blue haze hung over the town, and the pale thatch sparkled. Mor'anh drew rein and leaned forward, looking at it as he had done from the same place when they came to this camp; as Nai had done from there, the day they took her.

Kariniol stood gazing. Mor'anh said, 'Will they see us? Or shall I blow my horn?'

'Blow,' said Kariniol, and began walking down the slope. Mor'anh sounded his horn a few times, then looked back thoughtfully at the tribesmen. They had been much amused that the Kalnat were afraid to cross so small a stretch of Plain, and by day at that. But though they had enjoyed the joke, the Golden Ones had not.

'Derna!' he called as he dismounted. The young man pushed forward eagerly. He had been the wittiest of them all on the journey. No likeness to his sister showed in his face, nor in his admiration of Mor'anh; but it did in his tongue.

'We will go to the boundary, but you, Derna, will stay here with the horses,' he smiled a little at the young man's crestfallen face, 'and maybe while you wait, think of the worth of courtesy.'

He took the halter of one of the litter horses and led the way downhill. Four Kalnat took the biers, the others plunged past Mor'anh. There were women, now, running out of the gate and down the hill. Mor'anh kept his mind on getting Sunam smoothly down to the ditch.

Four men came at once to carry him away. There was a great clamour of voices, glad and angry. Kariniol was greeting a woman and the child she carried. Mor'anh waited, watching him, but he showed no sign of looking round. Then almost in chorus, three women began weeping; a thin woman who crouched sobbing by one shroud, an old one who wailed, and a young girl who cried desperately, over and over, 'Keratol! Keratol! Keratol!'

Mor'anh flinched. He nodded to his companions, and led away the horse he held. The commotion behind him grew, while the girl called on and on, wild and monotonous as a bird. At the top of the slope he glanced back. Kariniol's wife had gone, and he stood at the ditch waving. Mor'anh raised his hand, and turned to Racho.

Then Derna, feeling he had been treated like a boy and shamed, put heels to his horse and plunged shouting down the hill. Mor'anh whirled and yelled after him, but he did not heed. He would salve his pride and defy the Golden Ones; he would break the first law, as the Young Wolf had done, and ride his horse within their boundary.

The horse leapt the ditch near the Kalnat. The Khentors watched frozen. Derna made a wide sweep over the grass, whooping mockery and defiance, then rode back for the boundary. He had almost reached it when a man shouted with rage, and hurled his javelin.

The air was driven from Derna's lungs in a deep cry. He fell from his horse, which neighed with fear and fled up the hill. The tribesmen groaned and surged forward, but Mor'anh shouted, 'Stay here!' threw Racho's reins to the nearest man, and ran down the slope.

Derna lay on the grass, trying to rise, the javelin by him. Mor'anh knelt and put a supporting arm under his shoulders. The young man's eyes, amazed and afraid, stared up at him. 'What is wrong?' he whispered, and groped for Mor'anh's arm. Mor'anh shook his head. He did not know what to say. 'Lie still,' he said gruffly, returning the feeble grasp of Derna's hand strongly. His face was stern and calm. The earth under his knees was soft with blood. 'I fell,' said Derna, astonished. Then his face contracted with pain, and he gasped suddenly. 'Young Wolf!—You did not tell us—You did not say—!' His eyes strained wider; he cried out through his teeth and struggled briefly; then he shook, and gave a moan, and the life went out of him.

130

Mor'anh felt the sudden weight on his arm. After a moment he laid Derna gently on the grass. He could hear voices of the Kalnat again, but they meant nothing. Even grief held back. He knew only that Runi's brother lay dead before him, and how was he to face her?

Kariniol was in agony. The oath was broken. All hope of friendship must be at an end, if such hope had ever been. He was a fool to have thought of it. There could be no friendship now, no trust, no honour; all that could be defended now was the ancient mastery of their people. And there knelt the threat to their rule, there alone on the grass. Only the memory of words spoken defended him. More words, and Maldé was free of the threat, and Kariniol of the promise that weighed so heavy on him. The oath was broken already. And what did any pledge matter, set against the danger from Mor'anh? Could he consider his own honour at such a time? Could Maldé be left in peril, for the sake of his pride, and a dishonoured oath?

'Kahuniol!' he shouted, 'Catch him; hold him; don't let him escape!' But he did not move himself. The men nearest Mor'anh, more than willingly, rushed forward. The Young Wolf sprang to his feet, but made no attempt to flee. The men grabbed and pinioned him roughly, but he did not struggle, only stared at Kariniol in disbelief. Kariniol looked aside from his face. 'The killer of Deram does not matter. This one is the head and the heart of the trouble,' he said. Mor'anh's eyes blazed with scorn, and he could not bear it. 'Kill him,' he groaned, 'kill him, and all is well . . . '

He reached for a spear. He would have struck, if only to close those black eyes and stop that look of furious contempt. But a man snatched the weapon laughing and said 'Later!'

Then Mor'anh spoke. 'Now I see what the word of a Golden Man, and the name of Akrol, is worth. It is a thing worth learning, even too late . . . Give my people our dead. We did as much for you.'

One of the men picked up Derna's body and carried it

over the boundary. The tribesmen were coming slowly down, and Mor'anh called out to them. 'Go back!' he shouted. 'Go back! Do not come too close!' Kariniol groaned, and clenched his hands. 'What could I do?' he cried, and met Mor'anh's unendurable eyes imploringly. On the crest Racho whinnied, rearing against the restraint of the man who held him. The cloak left flung across his saddle slid to the ground. Seeing it, Mor'anh laughed bitterly. He was glad he was not wearing that. At least none of them would have his bear-skin cloak.

They marched him roughly up the hill towards Maldé. He would not fight. It was hard to bear himself with pride, but his rage helped him. There was a crowd gathered already, and he would not lower his head before them.

The stink of the town, the crowd, smote him at the gate, making his nose flare. He stared back at his mockers, and at every jeer grew haughtier. His fierce eyes never wavered nor changed; not even when they met eyes not blue but black, in a white appalled face. He looked at his sister, as she at him, with no sign of recognition.

On the hilltop the Alnei set down Derna's body and watched silently. The Young Wolf did not look back. They stared until he was through the gate and out of their sight, then turned hopelessly away. But Racho, when they tried to lead him away, snorted and dragged back, and neighed in shrill anger. Even within Maldé Mor'anh heard him, time after time, pealing his wild dismay.

14

or'anh opened his eyes and heard the bronze chains rattle as he moved. He had not been sleeping. He doubted if he would ever sleep again. He did not much regret it. Sleep was nothing. The pleasure lay in waking refreshed, and it was the waking he was likely to lack.

It had grown dark again. The small barred window showed no light outside; no snatches of sound came in. It was night once more, then. His second night as a prisoner; and the next day would be the day they buried the men he and Diveru had killed. On that day, said the man Kuniol, they would begin to make him die.

He tried to swallow, and sat up slowly, leaning against the rough wall. The weals on his back burned as they touched the logs; they had whipped him before they chained him. He moved his arms as gently as he could, for the heavy bands galled his torn and swollen wrists. Every part of his body hurt him. They had delayed the pleasure of killing him, but not of beating him. On the day they took him, and all through the day just past, they had come at intervals to do so. It was as bad as the time the bear had hit him, only the bear had been fighting for his own life, not hurting him for sport. One eye he could hardly open, three of his ribs he knew were broken, and his cuts and bruises were without number. Kariniol would not be envious now. Then he shook his head weakly, because he feared that if he thought of Kariniol he would weep.

His mouth was dry and stiff; he had had neither food nor water since they took him. The room stank, and he shook with cold; he hoped it was cold. In the faint light he stared all round him again, then closed his eyes that he might not see the smallness of his prison, and thus might prevent the horror that shook him. Never before had he been inside any place for so long. He felt foul. He had always been vain of his body, fastidious as all plainsmen were, but now he was sticky with sweat and blood and ordure.

He sat perfectly still, sinking back through the darkness in his head, trying to slip free of his body. But he had never found in stillness the ecstasy that released him from his flesh, and now it was less possible, with pain clutching at him. Memories, clear but brief, skimmed his mind like darting birds: a tent taking shape, his father laughing, fledging arrows, Hran and Ralki dancing, a horse's arched neck in the sun; all things he had lost for ever. I am going to die, he thought; I shall die here. But life beat obstinate in his body, and he could not accept it.

How long would it be until dawn? And how would they kill him? He had heard one man say that they should bury him living in the grave of the man he had killed, but no one else had taken up the idea. Only Kuniol had hinted; they would 'begin' to 'make him die'. He shivered uncontrollably, remembering what the same man had said about Hran. 'We would have taken his eyes from him first—or his manhood—.'

His eyes, or his manhood. Was this their intent? They were right, lacking either he would have no desire to live. He felt sick with dread. His manhood, his eyes. He clenched his teeth, trying not to shake. He was ashamed. Did courage depend so much on daylight and a sound body? His eyes. And he could not even defend himself, he could only stand helpless and wait. His manhood. 'Manui!' he croaked, startling himself, suddenly craving in despair her pliant warmth.

At times throughout the first afternoon he had heard Racho calling from the hillside, and once in the morning. He had not seen Nai again, nor heard her voice. He felt alone as he had never felt in his life, not even in the time of his manhood ordeal.

'Kem'nanh!' he cried hoarsely, and flinched as his voice came back from the walls. 'My god, my Lord, where are you? Have you forgotten me?' But he knew where Kem'nanh was. He was out in the Plain, his own realm, far from this place of walls where his chosen lay chained, even his prayers imprisoned.

A beam of moonlight edged through the window, falling near his head. For a moment he thought it was moonrise, and still early in the night; then he realised that here it might only mean that Vani had begun to move past a roof. He lay so that the beam fell cool on his battered face, and saw a bright curve swelling from behind a gable. Strangely, gazing at the silver goddess he did not think of Runi; he thought only, with desperate longing, of the Plain all silvered, shimmering as the grasses tossed.

Voices outside the door roused him. He strained his ears, but the walls were of split logs and he could understand nothing. They went on for some time; then there was silence. A little later the door shook, and someone bumped against it.

He grew tense. 'No!' he thought. 'Not now! Great God, not now—not in the dark!' There was a scraping noise, of someone inexpert taking the bars from the door; then it opened a crack. A dark figure slipped in, closing the door and standing still beside it. His heart drummed violently.

'For Nai . . . I came for Nai . . .'

Mor'anh stirred, astonished. A girl's voice, and she spoke in his language. He sat up slowly, gazing where she was, listening to her quick breath. No light fell on her, and she seemed only a deeper blackness; but for her trembling voice, a demon of Hargad. Why had she come? For Nai . . . what did that mean? The women who had come to see a captive barbarian had come in groups, giggling, and by day. Why did she not move?

'Who are you?' he murmured softly. His eyes ached too much, and he closed them, drooping his head. He heard a few hesitant steps, and some rattling, then a short silence. He felt rather than heard her kneel by him. Then there was only swift uncertain breathing.

He looked up suddenly, and she started. There was a radiance about her head, the moon making a silver halo of her hair. He could see no more, save that for a Golden Woman she did not seem very big. On the floor by her were two pitchers. Several times she put out her hand, then drew it back. 'She is afraid of me,' he thought, 'bound as I am.' He almost laughed, but pain tore him, and the sound became before he could stop it a soft moan. He caught his lip. 'Who are you?' he said again.

'My name is Marat,' she whispered. 'I am Madol's sister. Nai asked me to come . . .'

She moved, and the moonlight caught the metal that she held: and he grew rigid, staring at it. 'It is a knife,' he thought. 'She has brought it so that I can die before they torment me.' It would be easy; to pierce his throat, or his heart, or to open his veins. It would cheat them. He shuddered with horror. I will not do it! No, nor shall she! Not even to save the pain. Nai cannot have sent her—Nai would not think I would—Nai would know better!

He looked at her. 'Have you come to kill me?' he asked with forced calmness. 'Because if you have, even if it is in mercy, I will not let you. I will suffer any torment they have for me, but I will not let go of my life one heart-beat before I must.'

'*Kill* you?' she cried softly. 'No! Ah, no! Nai sent me—I have food and drink. Quickly.' She picked up one of the jugs. He took it, wincing as it touched his split and swollen lips; it was water. He drank it gratefully, his stiff cracked mouth softening. When he had finished, she

136

gave him the broth. He paused, and said, 'Where is the man who was watching?'

'Still there. I gave him a drink Nai had made. I said it was from Madol . . . he had the watch before. Nai said I must tell you she would have come, but Madol knows she is your sister, and will not let her out . . . Have you finished? This is a file . . . it is for cutting your chains . . .'

He drew in his breath sharply and twisted to his knees, forgetting the pain. He gazed at her in wonder. 'You can set me free?' he breathed.

'Yes . . . It is Nai's doing. I only said . . . since Madol would not let her leave him . . . She is my friend. I never had one before. I know you are all sorry she is here, but oh! I am so glad!' Her soft voice fluttered on, barely audible, as she bent over the chain, rasping at a link. The pain of the shackle moving, grating on his raw wrist, was excruciating. He wished he could see her more clearly. When the light fell on her face it made only a meaningless jumble of light and shade, leaving him only her hair, netting the moonlight.

'Will it take long?'

'Not too long. Kahuniol's watch lasts until dawn, and we never go out of doors at night.' She paused. 'I had nearly forgotten. Nai said I must give you these.' She gave him his brow-band with the wolf-tail, and his bear-necklace. 'They gave those to Kariniol, and he gave them to Nai. He did not wish to keep them.'

'Shall I work at that?'

'You do not know how.'

'How do you speak our language?'

'My mother was a Horse Woman. She was—like Nai—'

'Ah. Tribute.'

'Yes . . . but my father loved her. She was not unhappy; and he loved me, because I was her child, better than Madol, his wife's son. I suppose that is why Madol dislikes me. Mor'anh, this will take too long!'

Her voice shook. He murmured, 'How much have you done?'

'One ring—almost. I thought it would be quicker—the smith takes no time. I am not strong enough to make it bite deep.'

'Let me see.'

She drew back. He could not see, but he could feel how thin the metal was worn. He needed the chains before him. He drew a breath, then stretched out on his back, rolled over, and twisted to his knees again. His battered body stabbed with protest, but he could just reach the weak link.

'Give me the—that thing.' He pushed it through the chain and twisted it, shivering with pain and effort. The bronze snapped suddenly: so suddenly that his straining arm shot out to the farthest limit of the chain.

His body leapt with the shock of agony. He would have screamed, had he not stifled his mouth in time. Tears flooded his eyes. Every muscle tingled with anguish, and new blood gushed over his hand. But one arm was free.

Marat gasped with relief. 'But the other? We have no time for the file!'

He stood up unsteadily and leaned on the wall, feeling sick with pain. He would not yield now. Two women had freed him of hunger, thirst, bars, a guard; and one chain. If he could not do the rest, he did not deserve to be a man.

'I am Mor'anh of the Alnei,' he muttered fiercely. 'The Spear of Heaven, the White Wolf, the bear-slayer. I am the Har'enh of Kem'nanh. I will not be bound. I am the son of the storm . . .' He felt along the chain. The links were of bronze thick as his little finger, fixed by a staple even thicker. But the staple was driven into wood.

He grasped the chain in both hands and braced himself. 'I am named for the lightning,' he told the darkness. 'I sleep under tiger-skin, I ride upon the wolf-skin, I fought a leopard and won before I was a man. Do not think you can hold me!'

Marat drew back, scared and baffled. Mor'anh drew deep ragged breaths, summoning all the power he had, his eyes blindly intense. He could feel his strength gathering, rising till it shook him. He bunched his muscles, and pulled until fresh blood broke from all his wounds. A wild rage rose through him 'Kem'nanh!' he muttered, gathering himself; then cried aloud, with imperious trust, *'Kem'nanh!'* And it was as if he called in an open place; there was no echo.

Then he felt a cold wind roar through the walls and fill him, and put forth his utmost strength. The air around him shook with power; and the oak cracked, and yielded the staple.

He staggered backwards, laughing breathlessly. The chain swung from his wrist, the staple at the end holding a chunk of pale wood. There were splinters at the foot of the torn wall. Mor'anh laughed again, 'Kem'nanh! Kem'nanh!' he crowed softly. 'My father, you came!'

He stooped, and picked up the ornaments Nai had sent, and the file. 'Marat.' She stood staring dazed at the wall. 'Marat!' She looked at him. 'May I take this?'

She nodded, pulling herself together, and picked up the jugs. They slipped through the door; the guard sprawled motionless beside it. Mor'anh paused to replace the bars, and gave Marat the cup the man had drunk from. 'Maybe they will think it was all magic.' He laughed, but Marat looked at him fearfully and said nothing. She led him quickly through the dark twisting streets, and at last to the gapped palisade. Sudden doubt shook her. 'Can you get through?'

'Marat, the Plain is outside; I will get through if I must eat wood like a beaver.' For the first time he could see her. She was nearly as tall as he was, and her face was not so pretty as her voice. But in the moonlight she looked smooth and pale, a girl carved of ivory. He paused, looking at her. 'Marat, what if they discover you? Do you want to come with me?'

She stared and shook her head without thought. 'I? No, no. Go quickly now.'

By turning sideways he could with much twisting and pain struggle through the widest gap. Once outside he turned. 'Marat, I cannot thank you enough.' Her face looking through the stakes was shadowed, but light

*He could feel his strength gathering,
rising till it shook him. He bunched his
muscles, and pulled until fresh blood
broke from all his wounds.*

shimmered in the hollows of her big troubled eyes. 'The Good Goddess bless you. Farewell.'

He loped down the grassy slope. The ditch he had hardly noticed before was now a painful obstacle, but he crossed it. He paused and saluted her again, then went on up the long low hillside. The God-given strength and ease was passing, and once more he ached and shivered and throbbed. At the crest he looked back again. She was still standing, a dark shape between the stakes, gazing after him. She stood so, even after he had vanished over the hill.

15

hen dawn broke, Mor'anh was lying in a hollow sunk in exhausted sleep. Even the light did not wake him; but when the sun fell on him, warming his cold flesh, he stirred. His body was wet with dew. His bruised eye was so swollen, he could not raise the lid. After a few moments he began to rise.

The drained feeling that always followed the God's possession had this time persisted even after sleep. He was thirsty again, and though he felt no hunger he was weak with lack of food. As he stood up he staggered, and his legs trembled. He had never been ill, and this present feebleness was worse to him than pain.

A flight of birds skimmed by him. They were the birds of summer, the first he had seen that year. He made the gesture of salute to Ir'nanh, Lord of Life; but at that moment he did not feel that the Dancing Boy could help him. He moved forward, walking unsteadily up the slope.

Even in his perfect strength walking would have seemed very slow to him, who had never walked far; now he felt he hardly moved at all. 'Kem'nanh! Kem'nanh!' he cried silently, but the God did not reply; as if he said, 'I broke your bonds and gave you strength to flee; you must help yourself now.'

He did not know how long he had been walking, when he stopped and looked about. Surely the camp was not so far? The sun was nearly three handspans up the sky. In an unlucky moment he tried to decide on his direction. While he did not question, only followed his instinct, all had been well; but as soon as he began to reason, his confidence crumbled. He stared around, but all ways were the same, and he had no recollection of the way he had gone when he first left Maldé.

He was a horseman. Dismounted, distance and even direction confused him. It was the mastery of horses that had made his people free of the Plain. Not lightly were they called the Horse People. The Davlenei made their lives possible, and lacking them they lacked all. Mor'anh felt he had never known before how great was Kem'nanh's gift, or understood so well why the sign of manhood was to ride a davlani.

'Racho!' he cried out despairingly. 'Racho, Racho!' Then he shook his head, and plunged on.

But Racho, who had refused to follow the other men back to the Tribe, who had refused to go even with Hran and Ranap when they sought him, who had lingered for nearly a day outside Maldé, had not yet given up hope. Sometimes nervousness and loneliness drove him from his vigil, and he would gallop back towards the camp, until he came within sight and smell of the herds; then he would pause, and graze a little, and stand fidgeting a while, disturbed and doubtful; until he turned to race back to the place where he had parted from his rider, to stand watchful and eager above the town again. He was drinking at a stream not far from Maldé, when the wind drifted a fragment of sound to him, and a faint scent. He flung up his head, and after a moment began to trot upwind.

Mor'anh knew he had reached the end of his strength. He had crawled up the last slope; now he rolled on to his lacerated back, not caring for the pain, if only he could rest. At least he would not die in the place of walls; the

144

God's mercy had released him to the Plain. He closed his open eye, and sighed.

He did not notice the soft hoof-falls until they were almost at his ear. Then Racho lowered his head and blew his warm sweet breath over his friend's face. Mor'anh opened his good eye and stared, then sat up with a weak cry of gladness. 'Racho! Racho, my heart, my brother!' The davlani whinnied joyously, and the Young Wolf struggled to his feet. 'Son of Kem'nanh, re-davel, true friend! O Racho!' He embraced the horse, weeping with relief. Racho nudged him, and crouched back; Mor'anh got himself on to the saddle. Cautiously, the horse moved forward.

Racho had not allowed Hran's attempts to unsaddle him; the Long Spear had only taken the reins from his bridle, lest he fall because of them. So Mor'anh had the stirrups, and the decorated throat-strap to cling to. But it was hard to keep his seat. He lay on Racho's neck, not attempting to guide him, rolling with the motion. Racho went as smoothly as he could; but at last Mor'anh drifted away into darkness and soon after slithered down Racho's shoulder to the ground. He made no attempt to rise. Racho pushed at his shoulder, but he only groaned, and lay still.

Racho raised his head. He could smell the camp, he could see the horse-herd, but his rider lay unmoving at his feet. In despair the re-davel stretched his neck and screamed in anguish, then screamed again. To a Khentor there was no sound so appalling; it brought Mor'anh to his senses. 'Racho! Racho!' The great horse stooped his head again; Mor'anh crawled to his knees, but could not stand. Moving painfully he took his brow-band and slowly fastened it around Racho's horn. 'Go to Hran,' he whispered. 'Hran. Go to Hran.' The horse moved forward hesitantly, then tossed his head and cantered away.

After a while Mor'anh felt a horse's gusty breath again, and saw white-feathered hooves. He turned his head, and saw dimly a fall of white mane. 'Heu, my brother; I will try again.' He could hardly open even his good eye. He got to his feet at last and clutched handfuls of mane, but could not make a spring. 'Down, my friend. Down,' he croaked, pressing on the horse's back. After a moment's hesitation the davlani moved, not crouching his quarters as Mor'anh expected, but sinking right to the ground. It was certainly easier to mount so, and the Young Wolf straddled the warm back. He leaned forward to grasp the throat-strap, but his hands found nothing, and he clasped the horse's neck instead; then he realised that there was no saddle, either. He shook his clouded head, and opened his eye. The leg he saw was grey, but not Racho's storm-colour; it was silver, like the starlit clouds.

Carefully the Dha'lev rose to his feet, shivering a little at the unfamiliar weight on his back. He smelled blood, and chains dangled against his legs. But some power curbed his wildness, and he walked slowly forward, so smoothly that Mor'anh was not even shaken.

In the camp, the token had been understood. Hran was running for his horse, and Ilna was leaping like a young man to Hulakhen's back: while the horse no man had ever ridden came bearing his rider with gentle skill.

Hran saw them first and called out in wonder and disbelief, leaping to the ground. Ilna followed. The King Horse stopped before them, and Mor'anh slid from the back that only the God might mount, to lie at his father's feet.

The day after the return he woke to see Runi kneeling in the middle of the tent. She looked at him, but did not move or speak.

'Runi,' he said softly, astonished, then looked away from her to gaze at the roof. After a while he said, 'Derna is dead.'

Her mouth quivered. 'I know,' she said. There was nothing else, and after a moment he turned to look at her again. Her face was flooded with tears, her body shuddered with silent sobs. Her grief, that he could do nothing to lessen or soothe, crushed his heart. 'Forgive me,' he whispered; but she only hurried from the tent.

But it was not Runi's grief that weighed on him as his strength returned, though it was a suffering not his, the burden of which he must share. Three days after his return it began, and for four days it invaded his dreams and underlay his waking thoughts, threading his blood with anguish and casting on him the shadow of a desolation whose cause he did not know. He thought he understood. It was Nai's grief he felt; some anguish too great for her to contain alone was crossing from her heart to his. And what it was, he dreaded to discover.

The healers set six days as the time he must rest, and Ilna enforced this. As well as time to recover his strength those days gave him time to think; to think above all of the favour Kem'nanh had shown him, bringing him out of Maldé and back to the Tribe, commanding the Dha'lev to bear him on his consecrated back. Within his grateful pride, he was afraid; the God was coming closer and closer to him. Since the attaining of his manhood, when alone in the Plain he had first known the God's possession, and understood that he was the Har'enh, the signs had come ever more often; and in the months since the loss of Nai, Kem'nanh had claimed him more clearly than ever.

Once he had thought this was a favour the God showed him, a gift, a sign of special love, and he had been awed, proud, and grateful. Now the awe had overwhelmed the pride, and gratitude seemed presumption. As he felt Kem'nanh's nearer approach, he remembered uneasily the patient days in his new manhood spent working Racho on the long rein, teaching him to understand and obey. What had the God put on him? A garland, or a halter? He was ready as he had always been, to give whatever was asked of him, his love, his loyalty, his trust and utter obedience; but not till now had it occurred to him that maybe the God wanted more. What if the chief

147

*Carefully the Dha'lev rose to
his feet, shivering a little at the
unfamiliar weight on his back.
He smelled blood, and chains dangled
against his legs. But some power
curbed his wildness . . .*

part of his life were not enough, but Kem'nanh demanded it all, so that there was none left for living to
please himself? Maybe Kem'nanh wanted not simply his
worship and obedience, but all his will, all his self:
wanted him.

16

or'anh stood before his tent in the dawn, watching the young boys and girls gathering. Most of his hurts were healed, though his ribs were still bound. But the marks on his wrists would not fade quickly, while the perfect beauty of his face was marred forever by a scar which puckered one eyelid and brow. His left wrist was still weighted with a shackle, for the file had broken before its work was done. Fortunately they had been able to move it enough to dress his wrist, and the metal was bound with fleece so that it no longer galled him; but they were troubled that he wore it still, and might do so all his life. Mor'anh accepted it with calm. No matter, he said: it would help him to remember.

It was the first day of the Moon of the Dancer, also called the Moon of the Young Lord, and the day to honour Ir'nanh. Summer had come. The young people Mor'anh watched were wreathed and garlanded, carrying other garlands and rods decorated with flowers and feathers. This was the one feast where they, the young and un-proved, took the chief part, honouring the God with his own gift, their brief and careless youth.

The place where they went to worship was doubly sacred to Ir'nanh, for not only did a tree grow there—indeed three trees—but a stream ran among them. Lead-

151

ing the way, dancing in double file, went the banyei who would go to the Goddess at the next feast, and the boys who in this very month would be sent out to seek their manhood. After them walked Ilna, Mor'anh in his Priest's robe, and Hran with the other young dancers; and behind them Vanh led the singing children.

This was a well-loved feast. There was no terror in it, and it marked the beginning of the year's best days. Vanh strolled by the singers, waving his hand to keep them in time, nodding or frowning as notes pleased or offended him. Hran, moving aside, clapped his hands to give the dancers the beat, occasionally gesturing to guide them. They came to the Tree itself, the one which grew alone with space to dance around it. The others were beyond the stream, their trunks tangled with bushes. The young dancers wreathed around the tree, the singers too encircled it, and behind the Lord and the Priest the flower-crowned worshippers whispered and laughed.

But the Dancing Boy was not only god of youth and flowers; he was also the Doomed One, the Lord of Destiny, the Destroyer. Standing before him, Mor'anh felt no less awe than in Kem'nanh's presence; and more fear, for he did not understand Ir'nanh so well. Gaiety and terror were so strangely mingled in him, who remembered and foresaw all things, yet still was Lord of Laughter. When he went through the circles into the shadow of the tree and raised his eyes, he felt how apt an emblem of Ir'nanh was a tree. The leaves and blossoms tossed merrily in the sun; but behind them was shadow, and their bright beauty was borne up by strong many-branching limbs, the unbending firmness of the trunk, and the earth-fast roots.

When he spoke, there was a movement among the bushes beyond the stream: but Mor'anh did not notice, and the young worshippers behind him did not waver. But others had seen. When all was over and the offering made, when the lower branches of the Tree were gay with garlands and the rods all stood about the trunk, then some of the men leapt the stream and moved carefully up

152

to the bushes. Puzzled, Mor'anh stood by Hran at the edge of the stream. 'What are they doing?' he asked, and at that moment there was a hoarse wild scream from the thicket.

Mor'anh and Hran sprung to the far bank. The men were calling to each other, and from the undergrowth the tearing screams went on. Three of the men were stooping among the bushes, and Hran and Mor'anh plunged through to them.

In the small clearing a girl crouched, waving her scratched bruised arms and rigidly spread hands before her, turning her head aside oddly as she screamed. She was dirty, and sick, and ragged; but her ripped dress was of wool dyed blue, a Kalnat dress. Her tangled brown hair half covered her face, and her eyes were fixed on nothing.

'Quiet!' commanded Mor'anh, and the men fell silent. The girl's screams gave way to weaker cries of fear, and she moved her head confusedly, not turning to look at the newcomers. Mor'anh said more quietly, 'Now, what is this?'

The girl moved. She sat up and turned her face up, but her eyes strained sightlessly. Her hands groped; feeling the air, or trying to push back the darkness. She stopped crying out. 'Mor'anh?' she said huskily. 'Is that you? Is—is Mor'anh there?'

He knew her then, though his eyes would never have recognised her. He stared appalled. 'Marat!'

All the way back to the camp she chattered like an excited child, talking without object or pause, hysterical with relief. When Mor'anh set her down and sent for Lal'hadai and Manui, she laughed gaily. 'I know about Manui, she is Nai's friend. I know Lal'hadai too, she is the healing-woman. Am I not right? Mor'anh, why do you call Lal'hadai? Mor'anh! Are you there?'

'Yes, I am here. You have cuts that need tending. No bad ones,' he said, as she felt anxiously along her arms. This was true, there were only scratches and grazes on her limbs, though many were red and puffy. 'But some of them look sore, and Lal'hadai's ointments are soothing.' He did not mention the swellings on her head and arms, nor the great broken bruise on her temple. She said nothing for a moment, then sighed.

Marat had never had much beauty; now she had been robbed of the little she did possess, leaving her gaunt and sallow. Her hard-featured face, high-cheeked and bony, needed good health and high spirits to make it attractive, and now it had neither. Her hair was darker than he had imagined it, brown, and at the moment listless; and it was a surprise to see that her eyes were tawny-brown. They at least had always been pretty, large and wide-set; but now they were painful to look at. His heart ached with pity; and with shame, for surely he was the cause of this.

'You are quite healed now?' she asked in a calmer voice.

'Well, bones are slower to mend than flesh, so my ribs are still sore; but I am strong again. You see, Lal'hadai is wise and skilful. It will not take her long to make you well.'

'I hope so . . . there is not much, only bruises, and I ache so.' She tried to smile, then whispered, 'But my eyes—my eyes!'

In her voice he heard the echo of himself, and shivered. 'They are not injured, Marat. There is nothing that I can see. Maybe they will heal of themselves.' The door darkened, and he looked up with relief. 'Marat, here is Manui.'

'Manui?' The sick girl put out her hand, and Manui took it. 'Nai has told me of you; she said you were her dearest friend.' She paused, then added irrelevantly, 'You have lovely eyes, she says.'

Manui looked startled, and Mor'anh laughed. 'So she has; very lovely. Marat, there is much to talk about, but I will return later. Manui will take care of you.'

When he came back, Lal'hadai was leaving the tent. She looked at him and shook her head. Away from the door she said softly, 'I have done all I can. But she will die.'

He was shocked. 'Why? She has no great hurt. Why?'

'I am a healer, Young Wolf, not a seer. I know only what I can heal, and what I cannot . . . I know when life has begun to go. I cannot say why. But I think she has never been strong. That wound on her head—my mother told me she knew a man who went blind when a horse kicked him there.' She looked at him bleakly. 'I am sorry. I will fight for her as for my own child; but there is death in her.' She moved a little away, then said, 'Look at the scratch inside her right arm, and the one on her neck—there are others like them—'

Marat was washed, and Manui was combing her hair. He could see no cause for her to die. Surely Lal'hadai was wrong. But when he spoke and she put out her hand, he saw the scratch Lal'hadai had meant. It looked angry and swollen under its poultice, and thin red streaks threaded away from it.

'Where have you been?' she asked.

'To see a man named Yaln. His wife has given him a daughter, born this morning; when else could Ralki the Dancer bear her child? And because this is a feast day of the Lord of Summer, they wish me to go with them to take the child to the Dancer's Tree. That is where we found you.'

'What were you doing? I heard the children sing.'

'Offering to Ir'nanh . . . Marat, Manui will tell you all you wish to know, but now tell us: how did you come to be at the Tree?'

She began slowly, 'In the morning, when they found you gone, most people said Nai had done it, but Madol said that was not possible. Then Kahuniol—the man outside, you remember—said it was witchcraft, and many people thought it was true; and some said it was the little gods who guard Maldé, who did not want you there. Then someone accused Kariniol, and he did not deny it. So they put him where you were, and Kahuniol too. But the funeral for Darinol and Keratol began then, so they left their punishment. Oh, and on the second day of the funeral, Nai's baby was born—' Her voice faltered. Mor'anh thought, 'It is that, then,' and said aloud, 'That should be told when Hran is here. Go on.'

'Well, Kariniol would say nothing at all, and of course no one believed Sadanat when she said he had been sleeping. But by the time the funeral was over, no one thought it was his fault. So they said the greatest fault had been Kahuniol's and at last he said it was not witchcraft, but he had taken the drink Madol had sent, and Madol said he sent none. So on the next day—it had been my turn in the hut—they decided what to do to me. It was Kariniol who persuaded them not to kill me, but to throw me out of the town to find you if I could. And he tried to tell me which way your camp lay.'

'What will they do to Nai?' interrupted Manui fearfully.

'Nothing. She belongs to Madol. Only he can punish her. So they drove me out. But Madol came and some others—it was the women, mostly—and they got stones and threw at me; and some of the boys followed me over the boundary and stoned me. Then one of the big stones hit me on the head. When I woke again, they were all gone, and I could not see.'

Her voice shook. After a moment she went on.

'So I could not even go as Kariniol told me. I wandered a long time, I don't know how long—I think there were three nights. I could not find anything to eat, but just before the second night I came to the stream. I was terribly thirsty. Then I dared not leave it, so I went along beside it until I came to those bushes, and I hid among them. I stayed there till you found me.'

She stopped. Mor'anh bent his head. 'Vé, Marat, I am ashamed that you should suffer this for helping me. You should have come back with me as I said.' He looked up as his spear-brother came in. 'Here is the Long Spear. Let us hear it all. Tell us of Nai.' Hran stepped forward eagerly; Mor'anh looked away from his face.

156

'She had her baby the second day after Mor'anh went.'
She heard Hran's delighted exclamation and turned her
face uncertainly towards him. 'A little girl. Is that Hran?'

'Yes, I am Hran. Tell me how she is.'

'Nai is well. The child is dead.'

The brightness was shocked from Hran's face. Manui
gave a cry. Mor'anh, who thought himself prepared,
found he was not. Grief and anger overwhelmed him.

'Nai is Har'enh of the Mother!' he cried. 'She could not
bear a dead child, nor one that died of its birth! The
Goddess would not allow it!'

Marat said, 'It is true. The child was born strong. She
was small, but well made and lively. Nai was very proud
of her.'

'But how came she to die?' cried Hran. 'If she was so
strong, how could she die?'

Marat swallowed, reluctant. 'Tell us,' said Mor'anh.

'Nai was pleased with her but—but Madol was not. He
said a boy would have been some use, but who wanted a
girl? And—and she did not look like him. She had much
black hair. If she had been fair he might have softened
. . . but he said he would not rear a child who was not his.
So when the funeral was over he took her away from Nai
and left her on the mountain.'

They were stunned into silence. After some while
Mor'anh spoke. 'He did what?' His face felt stiff with
shock and rage. 'He killed her? He killed the child?'

'He did not kill her—he left her to die—'

'He killed her! To kill a child!' The blasphemous horror
of it choked him. 'Did he know what he did?'

'Of course. He had—had the right—' She trembled,
confused, imprisoned in her blindness, unable to see
their faces. 'It often happens, especially with girls. There
are too many born . . .'

'The Golden Ones kill their *children*?' Marat put a hand
to her head. She understood the grief, but not the disbelief, in Manui's voice. She could only repeat, 'It happens
sometimes. He had the right.'

157

'He had no right!' cried Hran. 'The child was not his, she was Nai's. And no one has a right to kill—and a child!'

Then Mor'anh rose to his feet burning with wrath, and his deep outraged voice silenced them. 'No, he had no right. Who could talk of such a thing? Any man not wholly accursed would spend his last strength to defend a child. But he did not know all he did. This child was the daughter, the first-born, of the Har'enh of Mother Nadiv! He will be cursed! May the Great Goddess strike him, may she rot his bones and wither his loins! He will be cursed!'

17

ven in one day, Marat had grown more haggard. Looking at her, Mor'anh began to believe Lal'hadai. The Golden Girl shook continually, and the swellings at her joints gathered; she said she ached, that her arms and legs hurt her. 'I must have grown too cold, those nights, and now I have a little fever,' she said. 'I feel better, though. I do feel better. Lal'hadai says the best thing is to rest, and keep warm and eat well. And everyone is kind. I do not think they ever leave me by myself by day. Manui is always here. I wish I could see Manui. Is she pretty?'

He was startled to realise that he did not know. There was no face or body he knew better, but whether she was pretty, he could not say.

'Your father—the lord—has been here too. He talked to me for a long time; about Nai, and the time when you were children.' She laughed. 'I never heard a man talk about his children before.' He could believe it. He could believe anything of a people who put babies out on a mountain to die. Coming of a race to whom the Tribe was everything, and children, the life of the Tribe, the best gift of the Gods, he could not imagine that people living different lives might see them differently.

'Are all tribes like the Alnei?'

'We have our own customs in some things, our own

dances; but in most things we are the same. In the big things; the laws, and the worship of the Gods. Why?'

'I wonder if my mother's tribe was like this. She was a woman of the Shenerei. She was not taken like Nai, she was tribute asked for. If my people—if the Golden Ones asked for a woman, how would you choose her?'

'I have never seen it done. But the custom is to choose only from women without children; and we would keep aside the Priestess, and any whom the Gods had marked. We would ask Kem'nanh to make the choice . . . But you must rest, Marat, and I have work to do.'

She heard him move, and put out a hand to detain him. All her gestures and movements were those of a small woman, though she was almost as tall as Mor'anh; it gave her a clumsy pathos.

'May I ask one more thing? It is easy to answer.'

He laughed. 'Ask, then.'

'Your father said, and Nai said, that you killed a leopard while only a boy. Is that true?'

'Yes: but you must not think I was a little boy. It was not long before I became a man. But it is remembered, because a leopard is one of the skins of honour.'

'I know that. Nai told me; and the others are the tiger, Lin'hai the White Wolf, and Kha'voi the black bear: and a man may only wear their skins if he has killed them with his spear.'

'Vé! You are a plainswoman!'

She laughed. 'I have seen your bear-skin; you wore it when Hran killed Deram, and you came to save him. They call you Black Cloak in Maldé, did you know? What happened to your leopard-skin?'

'You mean Nai has not told you?' She smiled, flushing. 'Ah, that was the beginning of my quarrel with the Golden Ones. It was my glory, and I wore it for a cloak. A leopard-skin is the most beautiful of furs; long and soft, pale gold, and the black spots have white around them. We went to give tribute—not at Maldé—and I wore it, though I was told not to . . . The Golden Men too thought my cloak splendid; they took it. They said it would cover

160

their Lord's footstool.' He smiled at her expression. 'No, do not grieve. It was long ago, and my wilfulness deserved it. I have lost things I loved more to them since then.'

They tied back two sections of the tent wall, so the sweet summer air came to her, and the noises of the Tribe. She ate, and rested, and claimed every day that she felt stronger; but very soon it was plain that Lal'hadai's eye had not deceived her. Only Marat did not know. It was true she had begun to despair of her eyes, but saved so unexpectedly from the terrors of the Plain, even blindness was a grief she could bear. Safe and cared for now, she knew no reason why she should die. The aching of her sweating flesh, the pain in all her stiff limbs, these were only the signs of a slight fever caught when she grew chilled, which left her strong enough to eat and talk; it would soon pass. She never dreamed that death could reach out to her from the past, nor that it lay coiled in her like a sleeping serpent. So while her poisoned blood throbbed through her body, she looked forward happily to the time when she would be strong again, a woman of the Alnei; and all those who came near her took care not to shake that precarious happiness. There would never be need for her to know that she was far more her father's daughter than her mother's, that she would be a Golden Woman always. While she lived, she was the spoiled pet of all the Tribe. All save Runi.

The worst of Runi's grief for her brother was over, but she was filled with bitterness. She felt his death had been little cared for, hardly noticed beside the fact that the Golden Ones had taken Mor'anh when they killed Derna. Even her tender-hearted father, though he wept for his eldest son, had seemed to think the loss of the Young Wolf the greater evil. But Mor'anh had come back. The God had taken care to rescue and restore him, while for Derna there was no return. The wind had taken her brother's ashes, and in the rejoicing over Mor'anh's return it seemed that the same wind had blown away all memory of him.

She would have vented her misery on Mor'anh, when he was healed; but then the Golden Woman came. Runi did not share in the gratitude with which the Alnei welcomed her. To her Marat was a Golden Woman, a woman of the people who had killed her brother for nothing, for a harmless boyish jest. Yet Ilna sat for hours talking to her, the women devised endless ways to make her food palatable to her. Vanh sang and played to her, the children brought her their toys, everything that could give pleasure to her blindness, anything good to feel, or hear, or smell, was brought to her tent; even the kittens of the Goddess's cat. Hran and Mor'anh gave all their time to the sick ugly stranger, the Kalnat woman. Only she herself held aloof; and when no one seemed to notice or care that she did so, her fury grew.

It was early on the sixth day of the Moon of the Young Lord. The milking was not yet finished, and Mor'anh was still among the herds when a small boy on a pony galloped up crying shrilly 'Young Wolf! Young Wolf! Mother says go quickly—it is the Golden Girl!'

He feared to find her dead; but the woman at the tent door said 'We cannot make her speak. We found her so this morning. Come and speak to her. Maybe you can comfort her.'

Dismayed, he went in. Marat lay with her face hidden, shuddering with spasms of sobbing, not heeding the women trying to soothe her. She would not turn her head; her fingers were clenched on her hair, pulling it across her face, and they could not loosen her grasp. Her weeping racked her; she snatched her breath in low moans. Mor'anh looked at Manui, who shook her head.

'This is not good for her. She is exhausted, she cries because she cannot stop. It is woman's frenzy.'

He touched her shoulder. 'Marat!'

As soon as he spoke, she broke into frantic screams, muffled by the fleeces of her bed. She beat away his hand. He recoiled and looked around at the women. 'What has happened!'

162

Most of them shook their heads; but one said fiercely, 'This is Runi's work!'

The others gave a faint shudder, looking at Mor'anh; but he only stared at the speaker, bewildered. 'What?'

'I saw that little viper come away from here. The Gods only know what she has said, but there is no mercy in her, and she has poison enough in her tongue to do this without putting forth her strength!' She stopped on a gasp, facing Mor'anh half in fear: but he only said uncertainly, 'Little viper?'

The woman who had first spoken swallowed and was silent. He looked to Manui, but she shook her head anguished, 'Do not ask me!' Then another said, 'She is all spite and jealousy. May the Good Goddess cause her to cut herself with the edge she has to her tongue, and may she bleed to death of the wound!'

He did not reply. He looked down at Marat, and his heart shook. He felt crowded and stifled. 'Leave me with her; I will see what I can do,' he said hoarsely. 'Manui, you stay; no one else.'

They went. He grasped Marat's shoulders and raised her. Her face, desperate with misery and terror, shocked him. She wailed and thrashed, flinging her head about, her fingers still knotted in her hair, blind eyes clenched shut. Her breath jerked and crowed. Panic gripped him; he did not know what to do.

Manui pushed him aside. 'Hold her up,' she said, and he obeyed. Manui grasped Marat's hair, holding her head still; she hit the Golden Girl's cheek four times, so hard Mor'anh protested. Marat's cries stopped abruptly: she gave several odd indrawn whoops, then snorted and was quiet. Her head fell back and her arms fell loose.

He laid her down and looked at Manui, reproaching her roughness. She did not heed him, only began pressing fleece soaked with cold water to the girl's face, wiping her brow, her eyes and cheeks, talking gently to her all the while. Mor'anh gazed. A terrible grief was waiting to be faced; he clung to the moment, and watched Manui.

After a while Marat stirred; she whimpered and tried to sit up. At Manui's nod the Young Wolf raised her and drew her to lean against him. 'Mor'anh?' She whispered, 'Manui?'

'Yes, we are here. There is no one else. Marat, what happened to distress you so?'

She did not reply at once. At last she said, her pretty voice choked and roughened, 'The girl called Runi: is she as beautiful as she says she is?'

His heart died. He could not speak; but Manui answered steadily, 'She is very beautiful.'

'And—she says you love her, Mor'anh. Is it true?' He could not answer. Her wavering voice grew insistent. 'Is it? Is it true? Manui!'

He met Manui's eyes, seeing in them only the reflection of his own pain. She nodded mutely to Marat, then remembered. 'Yes,' she whispered, 'yes. Yes, it is true.' All at once she began weeping helplessly, without a sound, turning her face away for shame. Marat said,

'It is no wonder, if she is as beautiful as she says. But, Mor'anh, it is not true that I ever thought you—loved me. How could I be so foolish? I did not think it. I know you are kind because you are sorry—because I helped —so it is not fair to call me a fool for thinking—a thing I never thought.' She stopped on a gasp. Mor'anh began to speak but she said 'Wait', and steadied her breath.

'I know I was never beautiful. But there was no need—why should she taunt me with being ugly? Why must I know? If she is so lovely, what can it matter to her? Does my being ugly make her more beautiful? What have I done to make her so angry? I never spoke to her before. I never wished her harm.' She hardly raised her voice, but the dead misery of it was hard to bear. 'Mor'anh, I am sorry, but I think she is cruel. And she said—such things. I know you say things Kalnat would not; often Nai shocked me. But Runi . . . she made me afraid. It was night when she came—at least, I did not know, I—she would not tell me if it was night or day. She laughed at me. She never let me know where she was—sometimes

164

she spoke right in my ear—I could not see. She was trying to frighten me, Mor'anh; that was worst. She wanted me to be afraid.' He felt her trembling. 'I was afraid. She mocked me for being blind. Is it my fault? Is it? Mor'anh, she hates me, she does, she does. Why should she? What have I done?'

He looked in agony at Manui, but she was striving to master her tears. He said, 'I do not know. Marat, this is all untrue. You are ill and you are scarred, but that will pass. You are not ugly. Do not believe anything she said. She is—she is jealous. Because all the Tribe honours you. Because she has always boasted of her courage, and you really are brave, she envies you.' He felt she did not hear, that she was only waiting for him to stop. When he paused she said quietly,

'Why did you not tell me I am dying?'

Her voice trembled. Manui raised stunned eyes. Feeling Marat begin to shake again he said roughly, 'Life and death are with the Gods. I am not a god, we are not gods, to have knowledge to say "You will die".'

'Runi told me I am dying. She said everyone knew it—everyone, everyone—that they all speak of it. She did not believe that I did not know. She said'—tears of terror spilled over her cheeks—'she said that you would not be sorry. That you are waiting—She said that you think while I live you cannot ask her to come to your tent, but when I die—you can take her—'

He shook with rage. 'She lied worse than she knew. Marat, hear me. I call on Kem'nanh to witness, and the Goddess, and by all my spears I swear, may I die if ever she puts foot into my tent! Mor'Inkhalen, hear me!'

Manui stared at him, but Marat was not to be comforted. She had begun to sob again, from fear alone. 'It is true, then, it is true. I am dying. Why, why? What is the matter? I am getting better! Please. No, please. Don't let me!' She clung to him desperately, and he held her, powerless even to comfort her. 'Akrol! Akrol!' she cried out in her own tongue, 'Give me the light!' She wept hopelessly, 'But I am getting well, I am, I am.' That she

165

repeated over and over. He knelt beside her, holding her, for a long time, while she whispered insistently; until her voice faded and grew quiet, and she seemed to sleep. Then he laid her gently down, and went to the back of the tent. Manui attended Marat in silence, but when she looked where he sat, his head bowed against his arms, she was riven with grief. She would have given him back his image of Runi, if she could.

Mor'anh watched the dying girl, and thought 'This is my doing.' And he thought of Derna, and the dead Golden Men. The world was suddenly full of death, violent and inexplicable, death at the hands of men. And it came from him: the lightning-bolt, the destroyer. He grew chill with horror. How had he become a cause of death to so many? His heart was heavy with guilt, and when he thought of Runi, grief and shame overwhelmed him. For hours he sat there, until Manui called his name quietly.

Fever raged in Marat. Her body burned and shook, her eyes glittered. When he touched her arm she cried out faintly, and her skin scorched his hand. They spoke to her, but she did not hear, or found the effort of replying too great. She was too weak even to move her head. He crouched by her, watching how swiftly, at the last, her fire burned away.

Towards sunset she spoke. 'Is Mor'anh here?' Her voice hardly stirred the air. He had to stoop low to hear her speak. The words rustled faintly in her throat.

'Bury me,' she whispered. 'In the sun. Do not burn me; not like a plainswoman. Bury me in the earth . . .'

18

he was talking and laughing with a group of banyei when he found her. He watched a moment in silence, as he had paused before laying Derna's body on the ground, though he knew he was dead. Then he said 'Runi'.

She looked round, her green eyes sparkling. 'I greet you, Young Wolf. What do you want?'

'To speak to you, Runi. Come away.'

She failed to notice the strangeness in his voice. She shrugged her shoulders and tossed her lovely head. 'You are speaking to me. Why should I leave my friends?' She laughed provokingly, and the girls giggled.

'Runi!' he roared. Lunging forward he seized her wrist and dragged her to her feet, and she screamed. The girls squealed and scattered. He shook her furiously, then turned and dragged her away. Sick with fear, she stumbled behind him, in terror of his anger; not even for what he might do in it, but just of the force of his anger itself.

It was to Nai's tent he took her; and once in he flung her hard away from him, so that she staggered to her knees. She scrambled up and crouched in terror, appalled. He stood beyond the king-pole, unmoving; in the dim light he loomed large, and Runi trembled.

Mor'anh said, 'At last I understand. Now I see you as you are: little viper. I long believed that you did have a

167

pride that was more than another woman's. I thought it made you more worth winning. Now I know better.'

There was more than fury in his voice; there was contempt. She gasped shudderingly, and put her hand to her mouth. His voice rose, rich with anger.

'It was never more than pride—was it, Runi? Conceit, a lust to see yourself above other women. You are beautiful, so you wished to flaunt it. I loved you; and because the Tribe honours me you gloried in my love—for no other reason. You wished to triumph, so you wore my love like a trophy, as I wear this bear-skin—See who I have cast down! But to be my woman would not be honour enough. They might understand that, those other women you despised. Besides, others can claim to have lain with the White Wolf, and you wish to lead, not follow. So you chose to reject me. You would mock me and scorn me, and they would stare and wonder, and you would be covered in glory. And so you fled me; but never too fast or too far, lest I abandoned the chase. And as for my pride, or my pain, they were balls for you to toss.

'And you are cruel. I could have seen that long ago, but I would not admit it; more shame to me. I know how you have taunted Manui. How has she deserved your scorn? To love and ask nothing, to give with both hands—does that make her fit for your mockery? Are all who love fools, then, Runi? Is that what you thought of me?' For an instant his voice cracked, then steadied. 'Great Mother! You, to scorn Manui!'

His words beat on her head like hailstones, and she hid her face behind her arms; while her brain beat with terror, he does not love me, he does not love me.

'But Manui is too strong for you. She has a patience and a dignity you cannot touch. So that victim was not enough. Then came Marat.'

There was a moment's silence. Runi trembled.

'Why, Runi? Why did you do it? Were you truly jealous? Did she get too much honour? Or was it only that she was weak, and you strong; she helpless and you pitiless; you willing and she easy to hurt? Ah, you scorpion! Outcast, friendless, blinded, dying; what was there to make you hate her? How had she wounded you? Why did you envy her? She had so little, so little: why did you destroy what she had?'

He came towards her, and she wailed with terror, beating her hands on the ground. 'I will beg her pardon! I will go to her now and beg her pardon!'

He looked down on her. 'Will you?' he said softly. 'Marat is dead.'

She crouched silent, her long hair trailing on the floor by her hands. She thought of the Golden Man he had killed, and her teeth chattered.

'Get up,' he said.

She began to fumble to her feet. He thought, 'Where is her pride now, and the courage I never doubted?' Her fear made him angrier, and he put out a hand to jerk her to her feet. She swayed and clutched his arm, looking at him in terror and appeal.

There was sweetness in humbling her. Anger had not killed his body's longing; her beauty shook him as never before. Her fear was a goad, stinging him with thoughts of holding and hurting her, of punishing her with his desire. He longed furiously to force her, enjoy her submission, possess her at last. This hating lust, that sought pleasure in pain, was new and dreadful to him, but it rose as fast as his anger. He clenched his hands and remembered they were in his sister's tent. Runi stood shivering, abject with dread. She put out a beseeching hand to touch him. 'Mor'anh . . .'

The back of his arm struck her and flung her to the matting again. He clenched both hands around the king-pole and stared at her. She lay crumpled, her face hidden, shrieking faintly, 'Forgive me—forgive me—'

His throat worked. 'Get out,' he whispered. He was a man, he would master himself and stop short of his desire. 'Get out.' He stood rigid until her scrambling feet had gone, before loosening his grip. Then he slid to the floor, leaning against the king-pole. He sat slumped there a long while, and at last the tears came. He had not wept

169

for longer than he could remember. Outside the sunset burned away, the Fire was lit, and the Tribe gathered; but he stayed where he was, alone where the darkness thickened.

The Alnei buried Marat as she had asked, in her blue Kalnat dress, on the top of a hill where no shadows would fall, her face turned to the mountains. It made them uneasy. It was hard to cover her with earth, hard not to feel when they passed her grave that she lay there listening to their footfalls. Maybe even the spirits of the Kalnat had their own customs. But the Khentors burned the flesh to free the soul and it was difficult not to believe that since her flesh was unconsumed her spirit lingered. Runi above all feared her ghost, and crawled every night into the tent where her young brothers and sisters slept, lest she be alone in Hargad, when ghosts are strong.

Four days after Marat's death, an embassy came from Malde.

They sent in a herald first, a young boy with a blue staff bearing two bird wings. Ilna did not know the sign, but he understood the meaning, and sent some Alnei boys back with the Kalnat child to bring in the messengers.

There were five of them, all older men. Mor'anh saw only one familiar face. Ilna received them in his tent. They greeted him very courteously, and began civil unhurried conversation as they made themselves comfortable on the rugs spread for them. Ilna sat in his chair, and Mor'anh like a dutiful son on the floor beside his father. The Golden Men tried not to see Mor'anh.

When all the greetings were over the spokesman, whom Mor'anh recognised as the man who had taken their tribute, said, 'We have been sent by the Council of Malde, to seek an end to the trouble that has come between us.'

Ilna looked astonished, but said only, 'I would welcome such an end.'

'There has always,' said Haniol, 'been peace between

your people and ours.' He ignored Mor'anh's ironic look. 'We did not wish this peace ever to be broken. We of Maldé have never been harsh masters. When a tribe has pitched its tents near us, we have not asked too great a tribute, and we have not, as some towns have, added to the laws which our forefathers made and yours obeyed.'

Ilna inclined his head, assenting. He did not hear their speech with the same ear as did his son: for him, the spell the Kalnat had laid on his people for generations still held. And Mor'anh kept silence, with lowered eyes.

'And over this last month,' went on Haniol, relieved that young Black Cloak had not spoken, 'all this has changed. How has this happened? We look back and ask ourselves, and it is hard to say how it began.' ('Ai, ai,' sighed Ilna.) 'Let us say it is some of our young men, and some of your young men. We know what young men are; their blood is hot, their hands are swifter than their minds. They find it easy to quarrel, but we who have to mend what they have broken, find it hard.

'Our young men have fought. Where lay the first wrong, who can say? Surely there has been folly on both sides. But this is the end of it, that three men of Malde are dead, and one man of your people. The young men have done enough. It is time to take the matter away from them.'

He paused, looking earnestly at Ilna. The old Lord's face was grave and attentive. 'Do I speak truly, Lord Ilna?'

'You speak truly. Go on, I will listen.'

Haniol gave a quick glance at the young man, but he sat quiet, fingering a band of fleece on his wrist. He went on, 'Three men of ours are dead, and only one of yours. We might wish to go no further, and let silence cover it; but we have a town to rule, and our people are not pleased. They ask for revenge.' He saw Ilna's eyelids droop and his jaw harden, and the lord's son raise his eyes with a brief flash. He chose his way carefully.

'But what is revenge? Can it bring back the dead? We want this ended, we do not want more blood shed. Yet we must give our people some sign. We Kalnat have a custom to end these troubles, which we call the blood-price.'

He waited, but before Ilna spoke Mor'anh said, 'Forgive me, my father, Lords. Lord, you say that you are sent by the Council of Maldé, and that the Council did not wish the fighting that has been between our people, but it was all the young men?'

'That is right,' said Haniol, encouraged by his tone of deference; then Mor'anh raised his head.

'Then the party that the man Keratol led, who came with your Lord's son among them—they were not sent by the Council of Maldé? And the man Darinol, who died on my spear—how old was he?'

Their smiles stiffened, and their blue eyes grew blank. Mor'anh curled his mouth, but his father said, 'Young Wolf, this is over and forgotten. Lord, what is this custom you speak of?'

Haniol cleared his throat, his balance shaken. 'The— the blood-price? It is better than asking blood for blood. When a man is killed or wounded, there is a price paid to his kin. We come asking for this.'

To a Khentor it seemed a strange custom; but Ilna said, 'What is this price?'

'The penalty set by our laws is this; ten head of cattle, and ten sheep, for every dead man.' Mor'anh looked at him sharply. 'And for the man who was lamed, five head of cattle, and five sheep; he cannot work, his family will be hungry. When this blood-price is paid, we shall have peace again.'

'What of our dead man?' said Mor'anh.

They froze again. After a time Haniol said carefully, 'Maybe some of the blood-price should be remitted. What do you say?'

'I? I spoke idly. All this is for my father. I ask no "blood-price". I could not put a value on Derna's life and say, that is his worth.' He smiled at them savagely, and they sat rigid. Ilna said as if he had not heard, 'This seems

172

good to me. I agree to this, to end the trouble, so no more blood is shed.'

'That is good to hear!' cried Haniol. 'The Lord of the Alnei is wise! And I have words from the Master of Maldé. He says, if you are willing to make this bargain, then on the fourth day after the full moon bring the cattle to Maldé, and come with them yourself.' Mor'anh kept his head bent, but all his face tensed and narrowed. 'Come, and bring with you as many of your people as you wish; and the Master will make a feast for you. And he will give you gifts, things that you lack, of wood, and of bronze, to make the peace firm.' He rose smiling to his feet.

Ilna and his son rose also. Mor'anh said to his father very swiftly in their own tongue, a smile on his face, 'Do you believe anything they have said?' Ilna stared and answered, 'Why should they lie?'

He did not reply, but turned again to the Golden Men, still smiling. 'Where is my friend Kariniol? Why did you not bring him, who is so wise and knows us so well?' Then he answered himself, 'Ah, but there are no oaths to be sworn.'

When Ilna had taken leave of them he returned into his tent. His son still stood there.

'You mean to do as they ask?'

'It seems best to me. These sheep and cattle are little to give, to have this trouble ended.'

'Little! It is much when we should not be asked it. When did we seek their lives or their harm? Why should we give it?'

'Maybe you are right. Does it matter? They have come seeking to end the quarrel now.'

'There is an easy way to end a quarrel—never to begin it again. They need never have come to us, if they wished to end it—they could let silence and time cover all that has passed. They do not wish to end this quarrel. They want to win it, in any way they can.'

'And what do you want?'

173

'I want it ended. I want peace, but not as they say it. We have always lived in peace, they say; so might the falcon say to the hare, which he eats at will. It is sure they did not wish the peace broken. We give them much, and take nothing, and have never been a trouble to them. They despise us, my father; always they despise us. They think we are fools, that they can cheat at their will. Do you truly think they give each other what they have asked of us, for blood? Why, they have not enough cattle!'

'Maybe they do not. Does it matter?'

'It matters that they mock us. It matters that they lie to us, and think we do not know. They keep us like herds—all of us. Not the Alnei only, all, all the Horse People. They keep us like cattle to milk at will, and they think we have not even horns.'

'What would you have us do? They are the Golden People!'

'And we are the Horse People! So they are bigger men than us, but what of that? We have seen them die like other men. What if they are taller than us? Face them on Hulakhen, my father, and you will not find them stand so high! Who made them our masters?'

'The Gods!'

'So you say, and I know you believe it. So have we all said, for how long who knows? Who first said it, I wonder? Was it a Golden Man? I think it was their spears, and not the Gods. But we did not know Kem'nanh then. We have a mighty God, now, the father of a great people. Father: Terani: Lord: you ask me what do I want—what do *you* want?'

'I want my tribe safe, my people safe,' whispered Ilna. 'I want the world as I have always known it.'

Mor'anh was silent. In a moment he said, 'Well, we will give what they ask. You have given your word, and even when we do not swear by our Gods, we are not Kalnat to break our promises. And this feast he spoke of—what of that?'

'We will go. What else? Why?'

'Father, I do not trust them. I fear their treachery. They

have broken such a pledge once; and that man Haniol, who seemed so honest, he lied without pause all the time he talked.' Ilna did not speak. 'Will you still go?'

'I will.'

'With many men, in friendship?'

'Yes. Mor'anh, in courtesy I can do no less.'

'In prudence you could. They will try to trick us—they think us worthy of nothing else. You should not—'

'Mor'anh!'

He fell silent. The old Lord looked at him with burning eyes, then sat down heavily.

'Mor'anh,' he said. 'Who is Lord of the Alnei?'

But he did not say it as a man might say, Is this my hand?; he asked it as a question for which he sought an answer. His son looked at him with love and pride.

'You are, my father,' he said gently. 'Kem'nanh grant you long remain so; for we will never have so good a lord again.'

19

T he Moon of the Dancer grew to the full, and began to wane; and on the fourth day of its waning the Alnei gathered the beasts of the blood-price, to take to Maldé.

Mor'anh had persuaded Hran, and Yaln, and Diveru, and all the other men he could sway, to go as if for a great hunt, with spears at their knee, and their bows ready. He had decked Hulakhen as befitted a lord's horse, and now stood by Hran in the place of gathering before his father's tent, combing Racho's mane.

Hran, leaning against Ranap, said, 'You fear treachery from them?'

'Why should I not?'

'The Lord does not distrust them.'

'My father is a man so honourable, he can see no dishonour in other men. I am less noble. Where I have been betrayed once, I will not trust twice.'

Ilna came out then, and the young men straightened, Hran bowing a greeting. The Lord looked at his horse's festive trappings, at Racho, fringed and tasselled, and at the collared spears. He smiled slowly, loosing Hulakhen. With a gesture taking in the horses and the weapons, he said, 'What is this for?'

'To honour them, father,' said Mor'anh blandly.

He grunted sceptically, then catching his son's eye smiled again, as if he were not displeased. He said, 'We know we are old, when our sons begin to protect us.'

Mor'anh grinned a little. 'Are we ready?'

'You are,' said his father, grimly amused, 'but it has been for nothing. I do not mean you to come.' He stopped Mor'anh's protest. 'Neither you nor Hran; they know you both. If I took you, it would look like insult. Do not look like that, Mor'anh. I do not distrust them as you do, but I will not go waving your black cloak in their faces. My son! Am I too old and foolish to go alone?'

'It is not that. You know it is not. But I think there is danger, and I would be with you.'

Ilna did not answer at once. He looked up at the sun, so that every crease and furrow of his face was drawn by a clear line of shadow, and then round at the camp. His eyes were full of love and regret. He drew his reins through his fingers and said.

'You may be right. There may be danger. But I do not know where it might fall, and that is another reason for you to stay here. You fear a trap at this meeting, but I keep thinking of us riding away and leaving the tents, with the women, and little ones . . . if they wished to punish us, there is the quickest way. We cannot both leave the tents. You must stay here.'

For a moment Mor'anh thought of asking which was the real reason; but in his heart he knew his father thought them both true, and together irresistible. So he only said 'What of Diveru? Shall he stay or go?'

'He shall come, if it makes your mind easier.' He turned to the Young Wolf. 'I am too old to become another man, Mor'anh. I must choose my way as I have always chosen it.'

Mor'anh bent his head. Ilna turned to mount; then with his hands on the saddle he paused. He looked at Hulakhen, then mounted slowly. Mor'anh stood at his stirrup. There was comfort in looking up into his father's face. It restored the world, even though that face was no longer strong and handsome between black braids.

177

The Lord looked down on him, the same look of yearning in his eyes as when he had looked over the camp. He said to Mor'anh, 'Do not try to live so many lives. I am Lord of the Alnei, and sometimes Kem'nanh speaks to me also.' He leaned down and put a hand on his son's shoulder. 'Guard our people well, White Wolf.'

Then he gathered his horse, and moved away, and the other men followed him. They rode out, driving the herd of animals across the Plain to Malde. And at the town, the Golden Ones were preparing already to receive their guests, with the gifts of wood and sharp bronze they had promised Ilna; for they had decided it was no longer disgraceful to use their swords against the Khentorei.

Mor'anh set sentries, but himself remained at the centre of the Tribe, working before the door of his tent. He had not stripped Racho; he stood weaponed and caparisoned, held only by the lightest of picket-knots. If they did raid the camp, he would be ready, but he did not fear it. He sat all morning outwardly absorbed in smoothing a spear-shaft; but his mind was following his father, riding proudly to the Kalnat feast, and dread hollowed his belly.

When the horns blew, he knew he had been right. They would never have come back so soon if he had not. He pulled Racho loose, and swung to his back.

He kept to a trot until he was clear of the tents, then launched Racho into a gallop. He had not far to go. If any doubt remained, it vanished at sight of them. They were not returning in eager haste; this was flight. As soon as he saw them his eyes went searching for a dark brown horse, straining across the distance. When he could see Hulakhen galloping before them, and his father upright in the saddle, he gave a great shout of joy.

But then they met, and he saw Ilna's terrible pallor, and the vivid blood that splashed and glistened on the saddle and horse-cloth. He seemed unhurt, from the front; the wound was in his back, spilling blood over Hulakhen's quarters. He was hardly conscious, though his hands gripped the reins and his body rode his horse with the instinct of more than forty years. Mor'anh knew at once, with utter despair, that Lal'hadai would be helpless.

His eyes were closed when they laid him on his bed and left Mor'anh beside him. The sword had thrust upward, piercing his lungs; he lay drowning in his own blood. Wild with grief Mor'anh grasped his shoulders, crying 'Father! Father!'; not 'Teras' like a man, but 'Teri! Teri!' as if he were a small boy.

Ilna's eyelids quivered. He looked at his son, then his head rolled to the side.

'Well, Mor'anh,' he said with difficulty, 'it was as you warned me . . . they were treacherous. I remember, before the spring, you said to me, Only let what is coming, come; and now it is here.'

Mor'anh could not speak. He shook his head in agony and sank to his knees by his father, taking the square brown hand which had been so strong and leaning his brow against it, groaning softly.

'You would not have wished this? I hope not . . . but my son, if you had known, it could have made no difference, if the God guides you.' He kept pausing, to muster breath to continue. If he tried to breathe deeply, an odd sound came from the wound itself. 'I am one of the first. There will be many, many others . . . Ve', my poor son; do not break your heart when all this comes; it is Kem'nanh's doing, not yours . . .' He stopped, and struggled again.

'It was too hard for me, Mor'anh. I could not will what He willed. I was too afraid. But Kem'nanh loves you, my son. You will be—strong enough—'

He gasped, and stretched his head about. Mor'anh wept, making no attempt to stop.

'A horn—I hear a horn. Is it one of the boys?'

'No one, father. No one is blowing a horn.'

Ilna moved, and sighed, then closed his eyes. 'You are a good son,' he muttered; his voice gurgled a little. 'Proud, and wilful; but such a son as no other man ever had.' He stirred a little. 'Nai . . .' His head moved fretfully. 'There is a horn; I hear it clearly.' Mor'anh shivered

179

with grief and awe. Ah!—It is his; the Horn-blower. Come away, come . . . the hunt is over.' Suddenly he opened his eyes and looked at his son, and said clearly, 'Mor'anh, I always thought the Feast and the Gathering were for us. Now—I wonder. Who does he call from the hunt, and what was the quarry?'

He clenched his mouth shut against the blood. For a moment his eyes looked into Mor'anh's clear and compelling; then their grip loosened. And though the eyes looked still, Ilna had gone from them.

When he stepped out, he emerged into a silence so deep, it seemed even the birds were hushed. A crowd had gathered, and he straightened to meet the anxious appeal of all their eyes. He said nothing, but his face told them the truth, and a low wail broke from them. Some of the women sank to their knees, beating their fists on the ground, raising the mourning cry 'Rahai! Rahai!' Hulakhen tossed up his head with a soft worried snort. Mor'anh looked at his father's horse, and grief took him by the throat. He bent for a picket rope and knotted it to Hulakhen's headstall. 'I will groom you soon,' he said, as if offering comfort; but the davlani pulled his head up, ears moving uneasily, and gazed past him to the tent entrance.

Mor'anh turned and saw his friend. 'Hran,' he said, walking towards him, 'Hran.' He grasped his shoulders. 'My brother, take care of yourself. I am losing everyone I love.'

'Diveru is waiting,' said Hran. 'Do you want to talk to him?'

Diveru's face rarely softened into emotion; now it showed some regret, but much more grim anger. 'Shall I tell you how it happened, Lord?' he said.

The title shocked Mor'anh like a frosty morning. In truth Diveru was using it too early, before the Tribe chose him; but there was no doubt they would do so. 'Come into my tent, then. You too, Hran.'

He went to his bed, to stretch out on his tiger-skin, then sat instead in his chair. Diveru sat before him.

'There were many of them waiting for us,' he said. 'Two or three for every one of us. And we were deceived at first, because few of them were carrying spears. Lord Ilna thought he had been proved right, they meant no harm. Some of them came down to us. Lord Ilna knew one of them. This man smiled, and counted the animals, and they drove them away. But the other men did not come to meet us; they stood on the hill, and your father stared at them. We had not got off our horses . . . Then the man who did the talking said, now we should go to the feast. Some were ready to dismount, but Lord Ilna did not move. He was looking across the ditch, at the way the men were standing; in neat groups, all looking one way. He said to the Golden Man, "Where is your Lord, who called us here?" I saw his face as he spoke, and I think he knew then that something was wrong. The man said he was waiting in the town for us; that we were to go up there to the feast.' He looked briefly disgusted. 'He talked much, and smiled all the time. The other men were beginning to come down to us. Your father said, "We have come here as you told us, and brought what you asked; and you said there would be an end to the trouble." The man said, "So there will be." But then another man came up to your father and said without greeting him, very loudly, "Where is your son?" He was trying to smile but he could not, and his eyes were hot. He said to the other man, "Black Cloak is not here." Then I think your father had no more doubt. He said to the first man, "Thank your lord for us, but we will not go to his feast. We cannot go into the place of walls." He was backing Hulakhen while the Golden One was still talking. I could see he was angry, and I think he was afraid. Then the second man shouted, and—' Diveru paused, shamefaced. 'We had not feared them much, because they had no spears. But they wore a kind of quiver at their belt; and at the shout each man put a hand to it and pulled out a long knife.' He

181

swallowed. 'There was a lot of noise—shouting, and the horses, and someone screamed;—and I heard the smiling man shouting angrily, "Not yet! Not Yet!" Your father called to us to ride; they had already wounded Yorenu, and someone else. Hulakhen had run forward, but Lord Ilna would not go until we were all away: and while he held back, the second man ran up and stabbed him. Then Hulakhen bolted.'

After a time Mor'anh said, 'Would you know the man again?'

'Yes. So would you, White Wolf. It was the man you knocked down, when he said how Hran would have died.'

Mor'anh flinched. Kuniol had begun to hate him then; and his rage, denied revenge, had festered, until unable to reach Mor'anh he had struck where he could. Had his own arm in some way driven the blow that had killed his father?

After Hran and Diveru had left him, when he emerged from his tent, he found an old woman waiting. She said timidly, 'The women are ready. May we go into him, Young Wol— Young L—' She stopped, confused.

'Yes. Go in,' he said. Women were there to receive you at the end, as they had been at the beginning. In between a man ruled his body as he chose, but they had it first and last.

The drums had begun already. Thin smoke still rose before the Goddess's tent, but every other fire in the camp was smothered now. He could hear the wailing 'Rahai! Rahai!' The mourning had begun.

His father was dead.

His loss hurt him physically, a hard clenching pain in his chest that made him gasp. The hand that had checked and guided him was gone, the mould that had formed him broken. He had forgotten the parting of their minds, forgotten Ilna's reproaches and his own impatience, their battles of wills, only remembering the love that had never changed.

He thought of the old woman stumbling over his

182

name. How could he be called Young Lord, when there was no longer an Old Lord? He was not the Young Lord now, nor the Young Wolf, nor even one of the young men. He was no man's son.

The banner of the Alnei had passed to him. They were his people now: he was Terani, the father of many. An era in the life of the Tribe was over; as always at the death of a Lord. But Mor'anh knew that more had died with Ilna than with any Lord before him; and no man had ever picked up the burden he shouldered now. An age had passed, not only for the Tribe of the Wolf, but for all the Horse People.

PART TWO
The
Son of Kem'nanh

20

or three days the Alnei mourned their fallen lord. There was no hunting, nor any work beyond the necessary tending of the herds. All day the slow drums beat, and the women wailed. A blanket dyed blue covered the door of the dead lord's tent; by every tent door stood a blue-shafted spear. No food was cooked, for no fires were re-kindled. For three nights the Fire of Gathering went unlit, and in the place where it should have burned they raised Ilna's funeral pyre.

Wood was rare on the Plain, and precious. It was never burned except for this sacred purpose, and it had happened that bodies of those who had died in summer had been carried for several moons, even back to the winter hills, before their souls could be freed. But for the funeral of the father of a Tribe, enough fuel would always be found.

There was a tree whose wood they gathered wherever they found it; the dancing tree, irvelhin, sacred to Ir'nanh the Destroyer. Green or dry, it burned with raging fierceness, and gave great heat. For the death fires of most men, a little of this must suffice; but for Ilna, half the pyre was built of it.

Through the days of mourning, the women kept Ilna's body in the circle of tents behind the Tent of the Goddess;

187

but on the third night they re-opened the back of his tent and carried him in. For the last time the Lord of the Alnei lay on his bed, awaiting the dawn and his pyre. At dawn Mor'anh came, with Ilna's only living brother, a sister's son, and Hran.

Ilna lay clothed as for a feast, with all his ornaments, his cheeks freshly shaved. A strange tangy smell hung about him, from the women's anointing. Gazing on his father's face, Mor'anh felt desolate. The features were familiar, but the face was empty. Ilna's body was an abandoned tent; his spirit had parted from his flesh, and waited only for the flames to free him for his journey. Mor'anh stooped lower; but the smell of oil and herbs and treegum did not belong to the man he knew, and seemed to forbid a nearer approach, or any intrusion into that utter privacy.

The bier was formed of blue spears laid across tent-poles and covered with the dead man's saddle-blanket. On this they laid him, pillowing his head and shoulders with a grey wolf-skin, and spreading under his feet his saddle, its fresh-washed fleece still showing faintly the stain of his blood. Amid the wailing and the drums they bore the Lord of the Alnei through his people and up to his pyre. They laid him on the matting which covered the platform and drew the spears from under him, standing them at the corners of the pyre. They hung a grey wolf-mask from each spear and stood the banner of the Alnei at his head. By his side lay the three spears given him by his father at his manhood feast, by his spear-brother, and by his wife's father.

Then Mor'anh fetched Hulakhen, and led him to the pyre. A trace of some familiar scent, the horse-cloth maybe, excited the old horse; he snorted eagerly and pulled forward. But the couch bore only a corpse, not the rider he sought, and his pleasure vanished. He stood patiently while Mor'anh cropped his mane; and when the young man turned away to lay the springy pile of hair under Ilna's right hand Hulakhen stretched forward and nosed the saddle and horse-cloth again, sad and puzzled, then hung his head and gave a low whinny. Mor'anh took his head-stall again and caressed him. 'It will not be long,' he whispered. The Khentorei did not send a horse to follow his rider—davlenei were sacrificed to the God, not to men; but the token Ilna took into the Great Plain would soon draw his old companion after him. Meanwhile Hulakhen lingered, the very symbol of loss, a horse left riderless.

Later that day Mor'anh came alone to the pyre, coming with a son's grief to lay offerings on the bier of his father. He brought a small leather casket from Ilna's tent, containing the old Lord's treasures. It held a great swathe of his wife's hair, kept for this day so that she, who had died in the sickness when there had been too many dead to give anyone more than token burning on a common fire, might share in the dignity of his funeral. There were relics of his children's childhood; a brow-band the small Nai had made for him; and a leather pouch holding a few things, ordinary or even broken, that he had valued as a child. Looking at them the White Wolf felt again how little a man knows even of those he loves best, and how much of his father's life he had had no share in. There was a knife-handle in the bag, broken and discoloured, child-sized, of bone carved into the shape of a fat little wolf with nose on paws; it was strange to think of his father the Grey Wolf as having been once Linalnu, the Wolf Cub.

He closed the bag and put it back in the casket. There was nothing but a pair of ear-rings, valued not for any memory but for their beauty and strangeness; these Mor'anh did not mean to burn. They were delicately worked, of metal once yellow but now rather brown and discoloured, and two lovely white stones, smooth and softly sheened, like the moon through thin cloud. They had been a gift to Ilna from the stranger from far away, the man neither plainsman nor Kalnat. Mor'anh had not thought of the man for a long time, but as he looked at the jewels, an idea quickened.

The casket he placed under Ilna's left hand, by his

favourite spear and his horn. On his father's breast he laid his own best-loved ornament, a pendant of sweet-smelling resin, and with it his brow-band with the white wolf-tail. He put at Ilna's side the spear he had taken from Hran, but there was no other memento of his sister he could send. It hurt him bitterly, that Nai was not there to honour her father's pyre.

There was a flower growing plentifully near the camp which bore its blossoms in long orange tassels. By sunset, so many children had pushed bunches of this flower between the logs that it looked as if the fire were kindled already. Among them was a paler gleam; Keratol's hair, bound there by Diveru. When they gathered for the burning, the sun was balancing on the mountain peaks. The flower-decked pyre glowed in the sunset, and the blue spears began to look black. Mor'anh stood apart from the other men, waiting to set the torch.

The drums stopped. Silence fell on the ears like a blow. Into the quiet the Old Man's voice rose, speaking for the Alnei.

'Ilna, why have you lain down so early? Get up, young man, that is my bed you lie on; rise and give me my place. Ai, Ilna, why did Horn-blower call you and not me? You were a strong river refreshing many, and I am a dry stream-bed. You died in your strength, Lord; you were not sick, you were not feeble, it was a man's hand ended your life. Ai, we lack you, Grey Wolf! You were a wise leader, a strong lord, a kind father to us. Why did you leave us? We had need of you! The tent is empty, the saddle is empty; Terani, why have you left us? You were honourable, Ilna; you kept your promise, and trusting your slayers you rode to your death. You put out the hand of friendship, and the long knife pierced you. Ai, a curse on the men that slew you! Ai, ai, a curse on their roofs and walls! Terani, it is bitter to lose you!'

The lamentation rose. Women sank to their knees, beating their breasts and the ground, shaking their loosened hair as they wailed 'Rahai! Rahai! Rahai!' Men took away the banner from the pyre, and the blue spears.

The woman who kept the Goddess's Tent in Nai's place came forward carrying a pot of fire. She offered it to Mor'anh, and he set his torch to it.

The torch was of irvelhin, and burst with fire. The flames were deep blue, streaked a little with orange. Holding it high Mor'anh stepped up to the pyre, and called on Ilna's lingering spirit.

'Goodbye, my father! Great grief takes leave of you, but great joy waits to greet you, and we weep for ourselves and our loss, not for you. You have forgotten grief, and Kem'nanh's Great Plain is before you. A swift journey, my father! Goodbye!'

He thrust the torch into a layer of brushwood, which caught crackling; the wood around began to burn, then with a roar the irvelhin took fire, and in an instant the pyre was raging with flame.

The heat drove the circle wider. Thick curls of flame leapt up the walls of the pyre, dark blue and orange coiling together. The men raised their horns and began to wind them, in a long salute. Mor'anh took his, but had to let it fall. His grief suddenly overwhelmed him, and he wept without restraint. At first he covered his face, but that hid the fire from him, and lowering his arm he gazed into the flames, letting his tears fall unashamed. The small things burnt first, with little golden puffs of fire; then the hair and fleeces began to wither, and the spears to smoulder. There was scarcely any smoke, but the dusky air shuddered with heat. The fire danced high, almost hiding the lord; and amid all Ilna lay calm on his couch of flame, as a man must who seeks immortality.

Most people hid their faces when the body took fire, but Mor'anh stared on, though his vision was blurred with tears and the heat-warped air. Ilna's flesh, loaded with oil and spice and resin, burnt with its own flame. For an instant he saw his father, still looking like himself, sheathed altogether in blue fire; and then the centre of the pyre, built mainly of brush for this purpose, fell in. The old lord's body dropped from sight, and the blazing walls toppled in on him. With an ecstatic roar the holy blue fire

*The fire danced high, almost hiding the lord;
and amid all Ilna lay calm on his couch of
flame, as a man must who seeks immortality.*

of the Lord of Life coiled skyward, only flecked now with orange, tossing sparks up into the blue darkness; and the White Wolf hid his face in his arm as he wept.

Gathered about the re-kindled fire, the Alnei could see how the gap at their heart grew wider. Beside the Priest's stool where Mor'anh sat there was a great space, with the Lord's empty chair, and the Priestess's stool. The Old One, speaking for the Council, stood before them. The people were very quiet, lest the old unsteady voice be lost.

'The Alnei are a lordless people. Ilna has gone to the Great Plain, and his place is empty. We must choose a man to fill it. A man to guide us, and keep our laws unbroken, and to speak for us. A man who is wise and strong, who sees far off and whom danger does not find sleeping; a man who will not bow his back nor cover his head before winter, or drought, or sickness, or fire. A man we may love as a father and follow gladly; who knows the ways of beasts and the secrets of the Plain. Do I speak the truth?'

They answered 'Yes', but without clamour. They knew the end, and were waiting.

'The Council has talked long together. Now we come to you. There are many worthy men in the Alnei, cunning hunters and wise counsellors, but we have one among us who surpasses us all.' He paused to gather breath; Mor'anh gripped his stool, his blood leaping unevenly.

'Alnei! We offer you Mor'anh the son of Ilna to be your Lord and Father. Will you have him?'

The eagerness of their assent brought colour rushing to Mor'anh's face. The Old One raised his arm.

'Does any speak against him?'

There was an almost imperceptible pause; then they cried 'No! No! Mor'anh! White Wolf!'

The Council leaned towards each other laughing. The Old Man turned to beckon Mor'anh, tears in his faded smiling eyes. Mor'anh rose, pale and very earnest, and moved forward to face the Tribe. Beside the bent frail figure his youthful manhood blazed gloriously. Har'enh of Kem'nanh, strong and beautiful and proud, he was theirs. Their joyous acclaim changed and sank, became almost adoring, while he stood shaken and moved.

The Old Man spoke again, turning to him. 'Mor'anh, Spear of Heaven, you have long been our Priest and our Hunter; now we ask you to be our Lord. Will you lead the Alnei?'

Into the sudden quiet Mor'anh said slowly, 'If it is your wish to do me such honour, I will be your lord.' They answered eagerly; but he held up his hand. Now, when they were pliant as river-clay, was the time to speak. 'If I am the Lord you want, I ask no better thing of life,' he said. 'But are you certain you wish for me? I am not the man my father was, and I will not be the Lord he was. Do you wish to follow where I may lead you?

'If I am your Lord, I will live my life for you. Beside you I will care for neither horse nor friend, woman nor child. I will plead for you with the God, I will rule you as justly and as well as I can. But I am the Har'enh of the God, and must obey him. If he lays a command on me, I will lay it on you. If you put yourself in my hand, I must put you in his, for that is where I am. Are you willing that I should do so?'

He listened calmly to their reply, having expected no less. Then he raised his voice again.

'But there is one way he leads me, where you may not wish to follow; my father would not do so. Do you wish to stay in the shadow of the Golden People, or to leave it?'

A sigh rippled through them. The words had been spoken at last. But none spoke, only gazed at him expectantly.

'If you will be ruled by me and by Kem'nanh, then you cannot be ruled by them. If their harness is pleasant to you, choose any lord but me, for I cannot bear it. We have never raised a hand against them, nor desired anything of theirs, nor sought their harm at all; and when I think of the hurt they have done us only in this last year, my heart is sick. We are not men to them, we are beasts they keep to use at will—no, we are not even beasts, for we care for our herds and defend them, and we would scorn to kill the beasts we hunt by a trick, as they killed my father. They care only for what they can take from us, and they do not hesitate to reach into our heart. They took from us our Lady, the Luck of the Alnei, the chosen of Nadiv, as if she were a fine heifer, and when we cried out against it, they laughed! They mock us, and lie to us, and trick us, and they think we deserve no better!' They watched him spellbound; he flamed with the passion of his anger. 'We! We are the Children of Kem'nanh, the Sons of the Wind, the Horse People! Shall we bear it longer? Who are they, to use us so? Who made them our masters?'

They shuddered at his daring, but there was not one who had not asked it of himself in his heart. One of the young men scrambled to his feet: 'They are only men, that is all! We all saw; the greatest of them could not stand when Mor'anh wrestled with him. He ate dirt at the Young Wolf's feet like one of us!'

The tribesmen laughed, and another man cried, 'And they die like men, too! We have seen them; go to the women who shrouded their bodies, and ask if they are made of flesh like us!'

Already the idea long hidden in their hearts was taking colour from the light. Mor'anh felt the excitement flowing through them. His heart rose; he knew he spoke for them, and not to them, when he cried,

'I am not likely to forget what their rule means; they have set the mark of it on me!' He raised his left arm, and the unbound bronze shackle flashed. 'I have been wounded by tiger and bear, by leopard and wolf, beside lesser animals; and those scars I bear with pride, for they fought me and knew what I was. But the scars the Kalnat set on me, this, and this, and the stripes on my back— there is no pride in them, for they bound me when they beat me, and they whipped me like a law-breaker put to shame, and it was sport and laughter to them! Each scar burns my soul. Feeling this, shall I bow my head to them? Kem'nanh humbled Kariniol before me, and he brought me out of the place of walls; were not these clear signs? Shall I ignore them?'

They shouted eagerly, but an older man rose and said, 'White Wolf, we feel the bitterness you feel, and our hearts too are sore. But if we say we will serve them no longer, what shall we do? Shall we never come near them?'

'If we never came near them, that would be well, but that is not for us to choose. What shall we do? We shall refuse them tribute, we shall refuse them obedience; they cannot rule us if we will not be ruled. It is hard to ride an unwilling horse; and they are not Horse People!'

They laughed, but someone said, 'And if they come to force us? What then?'

'Twice they have tried to do so. Who among us would ever trust their words again? And when we faced them openly, it was not we who died.'

'What is this?' said Diveru loudly. 'Is death a stranger to us? We meet him on every hunt. Is a Golden Man fiercer than the white wolf? Is he stronger than the bear, that we should fear him? They have a thirst for blood, but is it greater than the leopard's thirst?'

All round the fire men were on their feet. Mor'anh cried, 'Diveru speaks truly. We have no need to fear them, we who are used to facing enemies much fiercer. When they hear the wolf-pack call, they shake and grow pale. What should we fear? Can a man die unless Horn-blower calls his name?'

The Alnei were chattering and shifting like a flock of birds preparing for their long journey, both eager and hesitant. Never had there been such commotion at a Fire of Gathering. Even the women had forgotten to keep their voices low and were talking and arguing energetically. Manui's eyes darted about as she tried to judge how their resolve was tilting. She shook with excitement, agonised at being unable even to speak to help him. She could only cry out for quiet, when the Old Man lifted a hand and shuffled forward.

'It is time for me to speak,' he said, when there was

silence. 'Listen to me, Alnei. It must be for something that I have lived to be so old. When I was young, I heard what Mor'anh hears; but no god was with me. I could not make other men hear it, and I have lived all my life with their harness on me, knowing how it galled. No man knows the bitterness as I do. So hear me now. To let a time like this pass is a sin against all gods. If a tree refused to blossom in the spring, it would live a barren wasted life. So shall we. This time of choosing may not come again. Let it go by, and it may well be that the Horse People will pass their days in grief and dishonour. The God has sent us signs, he has sent us his Har'enh; dare we turn our back on Kem'nanh? If we do, may he not cast us from his hand? I thank the gods that they have spared me to see this day; maybe I shall see their shadow pass before I die!'

Then the Alnei felt their hearts beat as one heart, and their choice was made, and voicing their thoughts a man stood up and said,

'We will have Mor'anh for our Lord. Terani, lead us. We will be guided by you, and we shall obey the Golden Ones no more!'

21

he tent of the Lord was spacious, suited to the dignity of its occupant. It oppressed Mor'anh; when he woke in the night, he found his high mood gone. He was unused to lying alone in a tent, and this was far larger than the Priest's tent, four times as large as Manui's. His bed was twice as broad as any he was used to sleeping in; neither his tiger-skin nor his cloak covered it.

'It is not so wide as the Plain, and that has been my bed; and the stars are a higher roof than this,' he told himself. But still he felt lonely. There was an empty tent either side of him, and beyond them the tents of the God and the Goddess. He wondered if anyone slept within hearing. He was too tense to sleep again, and lay staring into the darkness, waiting uneasily for the drum of dawn.

When it came, it brought no relief. It was a cool clear morning, yet he breathed as if stifled. His heart beat heavily, and his body cramped with tension.

He sat most of the morning in the porch of his tent, trying to master his body. The muscles of his neck were taut, his scalp pressed on his head; his hair had risen. The sickness swelled in him, and the dizzy shaking. He knew now what this was, but it had never before grown so slowly or so strongly. His careful breath hissed through his teeth. The tribespeople passed him on tiptoe. They set food near him, but he did not notice it.

At noon thunder crashed, though there were no clouds. Mor'anh stood up. Voices called, amazed and fearful, as it boomed again. The young Lord gasped. The air shook again, and he turned and marched swiftly into the Tent of the God. Jerking the curtains together he stood in the secret place. 'Come, then,' he whispered. 'I am here. Why do you not come?'

His blood seared his bursting veins, his bones ached as hard as his flesh. There was no one there. He was sick, and blind, and alone. He fell to his knees, then on his face, his hands clutching the earth. The world turned about him. With all his will and terror he clung to his mind. The strain grew worse; he would have screamed, but his throat was locked; and still no word came out of the darkness.

The walls of the tent shook. His body stabbed with sudden agony, and he leapt to his feet with a hoarse cry. The darkness beat at him, driving him out; he bent his head and ran staggering from it. His head was roaring, and his feet could not feel the earth. He flung the door-curtain back, and met the wind.

It lashed his hair about his head, and battered his body. He thought he yelled, but could not hear. Spreading his arms he leaned on the air, opening his mouth; he swallowed it thirstily, filling his lungs. The men and women crowding at a little distance watched him fearfully.

As suddenly as it had risen, the wind ceased. Mor'anh stumbled forward, crying out in loss and reproach. Pain and sickness had gone, but he had lost the world with them. The raging darkness still possessed him, and he could not see; and the vanished wind drew him after it, an intolerable yearning.

He cried out in fear, stretching out his hands, calling on his friends; then he snatched them away from the hands that came quick to grasp and comfort him. They stood in

200

one world, and he on the threshold of another; if they touched him they might hold him with them. He must be free. The longing that possessed him was terror too, a despair and surrender that he could only feel as death. But if this was death, then death was what he most desired. He spun on his heel, stamping his foot fiercely, crying out again, enraged. They were everywhere about him, pressing up and calling in words he did not understand. He felt their fear and it maddened him. They were tangling him in a net of their own feelings. They maddened him. They smothered him. He must be alone. He must have air to fill his bursting enormous lungs, space to contain the stretch of his colossal limbs. They must let him go. They crowded and contained him. He must break out. He must flee their terror and his, or frenzy would turn to madness, and power to destruction. His spirit, vast as the sky, battered at its cage of bones. If his tingling heels drummed the ground, the earth would crack. Out! Out! They must let him go! Only the Plain was vast enough and silent enough, an emptiness to be filled; and out of that breadth the summons came, which his longing answered. There in the loneliness he was awaited.

He arched his throat and called out again, with the voice of a stallion, a monarch's bellow: and Racho answered him. Mor'anh moved forward, stiff, heavy with power. The Alnei fell back from him. He called again, and Racho replied, coming with tail flying and standing mane, surging to a standstill before his rider. With a twisting leap Mor'anh bestrode the re-davel's back, and his frenzy possessed Racho also. Head reared back, haunches crouching under him at every bound the stallion fled with his rider at a bolting gallop. Mor'anh rode him as not even a plainsman had ever ridden before, leaning back as though trailing in the wind of their speed, his hands barely touching Racho's hide, but his thighs clove to the horse's side as though they were one flesh.

201

The same terror drove them both, a true panic, the madness of the God, though they were not fleeing before that gale of power but rushing headlong into it. Mor'anh felt the grasses lash at him, the still air wail past his ears with their speed; and with every stride the power grew. But he had yielded to it now so utterly that it surged through him without resistance and found no more to batter down. Having nothing left to lose, he had no more to fear.

Racho reared back, neighing, and went on more slowly. Heat rolled from his body, but though his chest heaved deeply he showed no sign of weariness. Mor'anh felt the great muscles surging under him, springing and eager. Blinking his clearing eyes he saw the stallion's head held high, crest standing; he was no longer driven by Mor'anh's longing, but drawn himself. The air throbbed. Ahead of them it grew not bright but intensely clear. They stepped into it, and the first breath seared their mortal bodies; but after that it was delight to breathe. There was a salty tang to it, and its clarity made every blade of grass distinct and vivid.

And there before them stood He who had called.

Racho stopped. With a snort and shudder he stopped, he bent his knees, he knelt; he bowed his head and touched his horn to the ground.

Mor'anh slid from his back. He was on his feet by the horse. He stepped forward. Awe and dread were breaking his heart, but he had no strength to resist, and went forward as he was bidden. Then his body too had no more strength, and he fell to his knees, stretching out his hands imploringly; and they were caught, and held.

He knelt surrendered, leaning on that great strength. Here at the source of the storm was safety, was refuge and stillness. And the grip of the hands that held him was firm and warm.

After a while he spoke, huskily, his head bowed against his arms.

'Why did you hurt me so?'

'Why did you fight me?'

202

Mor'anh trembled. He could not say he heard the voice; it entered him through every sense, filling him. The depth, the richness, the splendour of it overwhelmed him. And the warmth, like the grip of the hands that sustained him. The One whom he had always felt most near in the cold roar of the wind, the bleak storm: there was warmth in him.

Again the voice, deep and wild, beautiful with creation's mightiest music. 'You struggled so hard, how could I not hurt you? Like a timid girl at her first Feast!—Mor'anh; my son. Look up.'

He raised his head. Before him was One who wore the form of a plainsman, a lordly black-haired man, neither young nor old, in the pride and summer of his strength. But he was on a mightier scale than mortal men, and the magnificence of his beauty was hard to bear. The splendour of his shoulders, the powerful grace of his limbs, the majesty of his head. His face Mor'anh could hardly bear to look on, nor to meet the brilliance of his green dark eyes. He was vibrant with masculine potency over which Time had no power. His presence overwhelmed the man. And Mor'anh was confounded over again by the simplicity of his glory. In him pride was mere humility, for it was no more than perfect knowledge of himself. He had no need to prove himself, or show himself as other than he was.

He spoke again, a smile in his voice. 'Answer me, my son. Why did you fight me?'

Mor'anh whispered, 'I was afraid. You wanted so much. I wanted to keep something of myself.' He shivered with shame at the memory. How could a man say the God asked too much? If he found a man worthy of his use, it was honour past imagining or deserving.

'You have been like a bird afraid to use its wings lest it lose the bush it perched in; like a foal afraid to take its mother's teat. You are mine. How could you be yourself apart from me? Stand up, my son, and face me.'

He rose unsteadily, and faced the God.

'Do you know me now?'

Then his body too had no more strength, and he fell to his knees, stretching out his hands imploringly.

'You are Kem'nanh, my only Lord.'

'I am Kem'nanh, and your Lord; and I am your father, who quickened the life in you. In the same form you see me wear now, I got you on your mother Ranuvai.'

Mor'anh gazed and could not speak. He thought of Ilna. He thought of his priestess-mother, keeper of so many secrets. Had they known? He shook his head, dazed. Surely Kem'nanh meant to speak to him in symbols.

'How can that be?' he stammered. 'Your spirit has touched me, but I am a man. How can I be the son of—of—' He could not say it: of a God.

'When I take the form of a man I am a man, a true body with living seed, and thus I fathered you. Your mother was a woman of great wisdom and power, favoured of Nadiv before I honoured her. Ilna was chosen to be your father under the law given to your people. Most of your spirit comes from Ranuvai; your body is mortal, as all born of flesh must be, and could not bear too much divinity. Yet you are truly my son. You are six parts man; but the seventh part is divine.

'Listen well, Mor'anh, and know the reason for your birth. For you were not born of desire but will, and by design, and the design was not mine.

'This you all know; the world Kuvorei made has been spoiled. To our grief, the spoiler was one of us; for even the Gods can sin. Only Kuvorei is perfect. What He Whose Name Is Taken Away sought to do was not done, for against the Maker his will may not prevail. The balance is marred. But though some stumble, the Dance goes on. Ai, alas, my brother! He was cast down; but harm he did do, and the worst he did to man.

'Man has gone awry and given his will to wrong. The world was made to be whole: we, Gods whose natures can be known, to link you to Kuvorei; you, with thinking souls in mortal bodies, to be a bond between us and the animals. But man has forgotten this, and that which should have joined now divides. Man, made Lord of the mortal earth, has abused his trust and tried to make himself its master. Such was the sin of the Nameless.

'Yet man himself is not what the Nameless would have him be. You have fallen, Mor'anh, but you have not submitted. After all the time that has passed, despite man's ignorance, his pride, his fear, still his heart turns towards the Gods. Still he remembers what he was, and his longing is towards what he has lost. And be assured, He who made you will not let you go.

'Each man feels in his heart the break in creation, and tries many ways to close it. Not all is forgotten. Some men remember their duty to the earth they tread. You remember that man was given care of the beasts. And He who made is not ashamed to mend.

'How that may be done only Kuvorei knows. But man has a part in the long labour, and may help restore what he helped to mar. Yet he has forgotten the knowledge he had, and forsaken the power given him, and they cannot be regained. So we put some of our power in your hands. We give you the Magics. First and to all, the Earth Magic; but the others to their chosen holders in the right season. Such a season is now.

'This is why I begot you: because the Alnei and the Khentorei need a lord at this time who is more than just a man. The Khentorei are my people and have long known it; but out of the Khentorei I have chosen the Alnei. You first Mor'anh, and after you all the children of your body, shall wield the power I give you, and bear it, and keep it from doing harm. It is the Wild Magic I put into your hands: power over winds, and over beasts, and the spirits of men, and much besides. It is a terrible strength; yours to use, but yours to guard, and you shall answer for the use you make of it. You alone, if you do your part, will not be safe from it. The Wild Magicians will need strong spirits. Peace will never be theirs. That is why I put my blood into the Alnei, whom I have chosen to bear this burden. You will be first among the Tribes, Lords of the Plain; and every man of the Alnei, so long as the Tribe endures, shall call himself the Son of Mor'anh.

'So I lay commands on you. The first you know. You

207

may serve the Golden People no longer. But remember, when you have thrown them off, treat them with friendship as far as you may, and never use them as they have used you.

'When you are a great people to whom lords of lands you do not know send gifts, remember this. You shall have no bond-slaves, and you shall not take tribute by force.

'The Lord-ship of the Alnei shall henceforth pass from father to son, and your line shall never be broken. I will favour your children, and theirs, and all the Alnei down the years, with beauty and strength and understanding beyond other men's. Let it never be forgotten, that I am your father.

'I would have you obey this; let no woman of the Alnei be given to a man of another tribe, so that she leaves the tents of her people. If a man wishes to leave his own tribe that is well, receive him among you. But see that all your children remain Alnei.

'I charge you never to change the laws and customs you have now. Other tribes will do so, but let the old ways be remembered among you.

'Never forget that I am Lord of the Wind and that you are a wandering people. Follow my Dha'lev, and cling to nothing that pickets your hearts. If you build yourself walls I shall not follow you within them. When you put your faith in them, your trust in me is gone.'

Mor'anh stood enraptured, gazing at Kem'nanh, hardly conscious of hearing his words, though not one did he lose or forget. He wished to fix the aspect and presence of the God in his memory, but it was impossible. He could no more have held the river in a drinking-horn than Kem'nanh in his mind. Adoration swamped him. He sank in it. He had never guessed that it was possible to feel such happiness. All the things he had accounted pleasures, the company of friends, riding his horse, the hunt, victory at wrestling, the love of women, all these were nothing, were childish toys, beside the joy that now possessed him, the ecstasy that is Kem'nanh's gift.

'I have taken a visible body to appear to you, Mor'anh, my son, that you might find it easier to hear me. Henceforth I will come to you as I have always come, but you will find it easier to bear. Go now, Spear of Heaven, Mor'anh of the Alnei. Rule my people well. Keep a strong heart. Trust in me always. Always remember that I will never leave you.'

The great voice sank into silence. Mor'anh went down on his knees. He felt what might have been a hand, briefly touching his head. A wind sighed coldly about him, and for an instant the world rocked: he bowed lower. Then Racho neighed wild and desolate; and when he raised his eyes he knelt alone on the ordinary Plain, and the Wild Rider had gone.

22

heir fourth camp lay deep in the Plain. The grass grew long, thick with blue and crimson flowers, and the heavy heat clung between the stems. It was the Moon of Storms, the beginning of the rut, and the air was fierce with the cries of stallions and bulls and rams. Two moons, Sheep Shearing and Long Days, had passed since the Alnei had made Mor'anh their Lord. Some were beginning to dare to speak to him again as if he were the Mor'anh they had always known, the Young Wolf, not the Son of Kem'nanh. What he told them of the destiny of the Alnei was less daunting than the knowledge that Mor'anh had stood before the face of Kem'nanh, had spoken to him, put his hands in the hands of the God; the fact that their God had chosen them less awesome than the fact that he claimed their Lord as his son.

It had been a hunting morning. Hran and Mor'anh lay beside the river after bathing, watching their horses enjoy the water. 'I do not know why you made Diveru the Hunter,' Hran was saying.

'To be Lord and Priest both is enough.' Mor'anh answered lazily. 'While I was Hunter too I felt I was talking to myself all the time. Vé, it is hot. If there is no wind soon there will be another storm.'

'It is too hot to sleep these nights. I spend most of the time walking about trying to find a breeze.'

'Can you find no better way to tire yourself?' Mor'anh chuckled, but Hran was silent. The Lord opened his eyes, then sat up and said more gently, 'Hran, are there no women in the Tribe to please you? Since my sister was taken you have tied your breech-lace with a double knot. It is not good. I would not have you forget Nai; but you need not love a woman to find pleasure with her.'

Hran frowned, and continued to skim reed-heads at the water. After a while he said, 'No. I know you think so. But perhaps there is need not to love another woman.' He turned to his friend. 'What are you saying? That I must learn to want other women? That Nai is with the Golden Man for ever?'

'No! She must return to us. Kem'nanh will give her back to us. You will have Nai in your tent, do not doubt it. Did you think I would forget the Golden Ones?'

'Who could think it? You have kept us learning our weapons afresh all summer . . . no, I did not think you had forgotten.'

Mor'anh said nothing, but the laziness had gone from him. Then he said, 'Hran, look here'. He slipped a pouch from his neck and out of it tipped two jewels. 'Do you know what they are?'

The Long Spear exclaimed over them. Much rubbing had restored some of their gleam. The gold was worked with marvellous delicacy into a mesh of plant-tendrils, two or three of which wound about the pearl so that it was safely held, but hardly concealed. Hran traced the liquid curve of one golden strand. 'They are beautiful! Well, I see they are ear-rings. Where did you find them?'

'In my father's tent. They brought to my mind the man who gave them to him. Do you remember—oh, many years ago, before the Sickness—a stranger came, one winter. Do you remember?'

Hran turned his mind back. 'Faintly,' he said at last. 'He was tall and pale; he said he would die of the cold.'

211

'This was his gift to my father. Ilna never wore them—they are not ornaments for a man. They are from that stranger's land, from The Cities.'

Hran looked confused. 'Yes?' he said questioningly. Mor'anh leaned forward.

'What do we need, before we meet the Kalnat again? Think, Hran! If they choose to fight us, we have our spears, but after that, hunting knives. While they have their long spears, their knives, the long knives I have not seen, which killed Ilna—all of metal. I will not let the Alnei follow me to their deaths. We need weapons, Hran.' He saw that his spear-brother still did not follow his thoughts, and laughed. 'Look, my brother, look at this ear-ring. They were skilled men with metal who made that.' He looked at his friend's appalled face, and grinned.

'What do you mean?'

'I shall go to The Cities.'

Hran was struck dumb. He stood up, and sat again. He pulled his hair loose and ran his hands through it, and cried out.

'The Cities! Mor'anh, you are mad! No one knows where that is! You would never find it! Mor'anh, forget this. Do not go. You would never return, the Tribe would never see you again. You would be lost to us!'

'I must go. Weapons we must have; shall we get them from the Golden People? Shall I go to them and say, "Make us long knives that we may kill you"? Or would you have us face them with what we have?'

Hran could only shake his head. 'But The Cities! It is so far. O Mor'anh, we will never see you more!'

The anguish in his voice moved Mor'anh. 'Hran, my brother, do you forget Kem'nanh? He is with me, and nothing shall keep me from returning, I promise you.'

'But how will you find the way?'

'The stranger told me. I have remembered much, Hran. That is another thing that makes me sure the God means me to go. I remember that I used to follow the pale man, and ask him questions all day. And I asked him how he

would find The Cities again, and he showed me,' he
hesitated, 'I forget what he called it, it does not matter, I
did not understand it. He said it was a picture of the land,
but it did not look like it to me. But he traced his way on
it, and told me how to follow it. Mostly I shall be following rivers. That night I told my mother about it.' He
paused. 'She told me I must never forget it. She looked so
seriously at me, and spoke so solemnly—it was about two
moons before the Great Sickness. I suppose her death so
soon following made it even more important to me to
obey her. I told myself the whole way every day until it
sank into my mind. I never did forget. I had not thought
of it for a long time, until I saw those ear-rings. But I still
know it.'

Hran groaned. 'How can you be sure?'

'Hran! That man, the stranger, who was so pale and
could not bear the cold and wore ornaments fit for a
woman—*he* found *us*! He had heard of a people living on
the Plain, and came to find if it was true. He had no one to
tell him the way. I, I have been told the way, and I *know*
The Cities can be found. Shall I, the Son of Kem'nanh, be
so much less bold than him?'

'Let me come with you!'

'I do not think so. It will be hard without you, my
brother, but I would wish you to be here. You know my
heart better than any other.'

'When will you tell the Tribe!'

'Not yet. I shall not go until after the Feasts.'

Hran stood up. He knew Mor'anh's decision was
made, and argument was useless; and the Tribe would
not oppose it, as they would not oppose anything their
Lord willed. Beyond doubt Mor'anh would do this terrible thing—go alone out of the Tribe. And dear as he was
to Kem'nanh, could Kem'nanh still protect him, so far
from the Plain?

The summer ended. It was in the Moon of Flocking Birds,
when they passed in great masses following the sun
south, that Mor'anh told the Alnei of his intention to go

the way the birds went. They wailed with fear and grief, and implored him not to do so, but as Hran had foreseen, they yielded before his confidence. In time, the idea grew acceptable to them—even to the Long Spear. Only Manui watched the time draw on with unabated dread.

They turned south, and the Deep Plain was behind them. Mor'anh remembered his wish to stay all winter on the Plain, and see how the snow lay when the Old Woman pitched her tent among the grasses. It was less than a year past, but he remembered it like another life, when he had been another man, young and unburdened, Ilna's son. And he smiled, like a man ten years older remembering the schemes of boyhood, not knowing how youthful still was even this amusement.

The Moon of Burning Trees passed; and in the fourth day of the Moon of Great Feasts they pitched their tents in the valley where they would pass the winter. The Dha'lev led them to a good valley, deep and well-watered, sheltered with thick woods. It was the last camp he would choose for them. He had been their King for seven years, and his prime was passing. Before a younger horse could put him to shame they would send him to the Great Plain, where he would live in eternal honour.

That feast, the Feast of Kem'nanh, was the first at which Mor'anh took his place as Lord as well as Priest. The welcoming of the new men came first, and when their plaits were gone and their men's spears in their hands, he led each round before the Alnei, crying his name and his horse's name, bidding the Tribe know them. Then they sent the women and girls away, and the true Feast of Kem'nanh began. All the men went bare-chested and barefoot, their heads plumed with horse-hair, and the dancers wore horse-tails too. But Mor'anh, leading the dance, wore trousers made of the hide of a stallion, with feathering at his wrists and ankles, and a mask of horse-hide over his head. The mane danced above him, and the black hide of the horse's neck covered his shoulders; the horn rose from his brow. In this dance he always lost himself. He became a stallion, prancing and stamping, swinging his horn, smelling the wind; all his movements and attitudes those of a horse. He was the Great Horse, the herd leader, King of a Tribe, honoured by plainsmen above all living things. He tore the ground and arched his neck, bellowing his challenge to rivals. When no answer came he shook his shoulders and neighed with scorn. Above the drums the deep horns sounded the rich music which pleases Kem'nanh more than any other, and behind their Lord flaunting in his pride the three lines of horsemen stamped the ground and pawed the air, tossing their plumes together.

The dance over, Mor'anh went into the Tent, while the men outside sang to the God. When Mor'anh came out, he was carrying the great cleaver of flaked stone.

He had only been a man five years, so this was the first horse-sacrifice he had made. When they led the Dha'lev up to him he looked at the animal's majesty, his superb unconquered pride. He remembered how tenderly that great back had borne him. He thought, 'He fought for the right to stand where he stands now; it was his choice.' But not since his first hunt had he prayed so earnestly for a steady hand and a strong arm.

The Dha'lev died, and the tribesmen wailed with grief as he spilled his silver mane on the bloody earth. Mor'anh marked each tribesman, from the Old Man to those made men that day, with the horse-sign on their breast in the Dha'lev's blood. Then they raised the King to his waiting pyre, and sent him to the God.

Other feasts passed, and last came the oldest of them all, the Feast of the Mother. Dawn on the first day of it broke over tribes without women: even those too sick to walk had been carried away. None of the men knew where the women went, or what they did; few dared to guess.

The sun set. The children were put to bed; the older boys rode off the keep the Watches in place of the men. Vani drifted in and out of cloud, not the cold crescent of the banyei, but full and golden.

A drum boomed. Its heavy single beat rolled down the

215

hill, and Mor'anh and Hran grinned briefly at each other, as always more than half afraid. They walked with the others out of the camp and up the blazed path into the trees: for the only time in the year, the men obeying the women. Ahead of them the summons quickened, an urgent double beat.

The path ended in a broad clearing. The fitful moonlight was brightened by a circle of huge fire-bowls tended by old women, who fed them with twigs and leaves from which rolled sweet smoke. Further up the hill, the drum beat on. The men spread in a circle around the clearing, not speaking, or even looking at each other now. They began to stamp, in time with the drums. Then the faint sound of singing drifted down to them.

The singing wound nearer, a chant so ancient that it was sounds rather than words; and the women came dancing slowly down the hill. They came in a long twining file among the trees, swaying as they sang, sounding their own instruments; rattles with tongues of bone shivering together, or little longhandled drums. They wore robes of soft deer-skin, belted at their waists but unsewn, which glowed yellow in the soft light. Their faces were masked, only their mouths uncovered, and the masks painted. It would be hard for a man to know his own sister or wife among them.

They passed through the circle of men and closed their own circle within it. The dance quickened. The drumbeats crowded closer until the heavy air shuddered with them. The women stepped around the fire; the moving robes bared pale sides, and legs naked from hip to ankle. Their eyes, hazed with the galya they had eaten, glowed through the masks. They wove their line in and out, now dancing close to the men, swaying their bodies towards them until they reached out, now skimming away. Mor'anh watched the twining arms, the swinging hips and rippling shoulders; he heard himself call out to the women, who laughed and cried out wildly. Their blood was running hot with the galya and the drums. They drummed the earth with their heels; the smoke rolled between them to the men, who gasped in its dizzying sweetness. The song still rose and fell, but the words with no meaning but mystery began to melt in other sounds. The music quickened, and the Goddess's drug flamed through their bodies; the night, the fire, the moon swung dizzily around them; they beat their bare tingling feet on the earth and cried out longingly. The night was thick with unfocused desire, men and women delirious with the Goddess. In front of Mor'anh a tall slender woman swung her body in a rippling curve that dragged a groan from him. Then one woman gave a shrill frenzied cry; they all joined it, flinging up their arms, and the circle broke. The slim woman straightened like a cracked whip and sprang forward, darting past Mor'anh. He heard the gasp of her laugh, saw a flash of green eyes, and whirled after her.

She sprang nimbly through the trees. He let her keep a bound ahead until they had gone beyond the other worshippers, then caught up with her and seized her waist. She turned at once, her arms clasping him as fiercely as he held her. They fell to the leafy ground and coupled without a word. Her wild laughter shivered on until he stifled it with kissing; after that only the rustling leaves broke the silence.

After a while they moved to a deeper hollow under one of the bushes, and sank deep in the worship of the Goddess. She was a fierce and eager lover, as full of laughter as desire; when she laughed he almost knew her. He thought at first that the night would never be long enough for them; but they slept at last, Nadiv's frenzy spent.

He woke when the night grew colder. The woman slumbered exhausted, nestled deep into the leaves. The moonlight fell mottled through the bush, gleaming on the pale abandon of her limbs. Her black hair lay tossed all about.

He moved closer. At the Feast the holy herb had raged in her veins; now they were only themselves, and he wished to know what wildness he could wake in her. Her

217

She sprang nimbly through the trees.

lips parted, shaping her sigh of pleasure; she woke and began to draw back, fending him away with smothered laughter; but when he grew insistent she yielded with the faintest of protesting sighs.

When he woke again she was gone. He walked down into the still womanless camp and found Hran. It was unlucky for a man to speak of the Feast, as unlucky as for him to name even to himself the woman who had lain with him; so only Hran's grin mocked his friend for his late return, and when the Long Spear's vivid green eyes gleamed with laughter, the Lord refused to trace the resemblance or put a name to his memory, and only grinned back.

The Feasts were over. Winter had begun. And before Vani could wane far, Mor'anh meant to ride to The Cities.

23

he drum had not sounded when Manui looked out of her tent. She shivered. 'It is thick frost.'

'That is good. Winters are easier when the frosts begin early.' Mor'anh reached for his boots. 'Come back from the door then. You will take cold.'

That was true. But she stood unmoving, gripping the door-flap, gazing at a world ghostly and dim under the starlight. The pale silence offered her bleak fellowship. There were times when the only refuge lay in stillness. She was colder than the frost already.

Mor'anh stood up, stamping his feet into his boots, and glanced across to her. She had begun to shake with cold. He shook his head ruefully, and went to her. 'Manui . . . !' he said, gently chiding; he drew her away from the door. She turned without speaking and leaned against him, and he held her firmly, feeling her trembling. Cold soaked from her flesh. She looked pinched, pale and haggard; and he could no longer pretend not to understand.

Her body ached with her violent shivering. She felt weak and ashamed. She had striven for so long not to burden him with knowledge of her love; but now all pretence was ended, and her strength spent beyond pride. Often she had resolved to take his love-making more lightly, and always at his first touch her passion had betrayed her, but never before so utterly.

He felt her shiver again, and rubbed her arms briskly. 'Now see what becomes of disobedience. I told you to come back.'

She managed to smile. He must not carry away such a cold farewell. But despair was crushing her. She could have borne it as easily had he said he was riding to seek the Great Plain—more easily, for the Great Plain belonged at least to their own world.

'I am rebuked, Terani.' They looked at each other, searching for words, but Khentors take leave of one another so rarely they did not know what to say, and had to fall back on kisses.

Mor'anh never found as much pleasure with any other woman as with Manui; that night had banished even the memory of the Feast. While it lasted, he had known nothing beyond themselves and the moment that drowned them. Now the cold morning was come, and a long solitude lay before him. His desire was touched with fear, and loneliness breathed on his neck. He could have begun the night again; but the first blow of the Dawn Drum parted them at last. He would be looked for at his own tent, and must go.

The sun was well up when he took formal leave of the Tribe, and the whole world was sparkling. On tent roofs and other places where the frost was thin it had melted already, leaving drops of water lit with rainbows. Where it was thicker it shone; every leaf and grass-blade glittered, and the world was a glory of light.

Again they sought some way of leave-taking. There was no form of words to use. No man left his tribe unless cast out for a great crime, and no leave was taken of an outcast. The only parting they knew how to make was from the dead. It would be ill-omened, to say to Mor'anh, 'A swift journey'.

The Old One moved to Racho's head. 'Mor'anh, Lord of the Alnei,' he said, 'once before you rode away from the tents, though then you did not go alone. Then we said, "Go forth a boy and return a man", and you came back to us riding Racho. Now, you set out with your re-davel; you go forth a man, and who knows what you will have become, when you return? But we pray as we prayed then: Kem'nanh have you in his keeping, and bring you back to us safely.'

The swarm of attendant children soon fell away, then after a while the boys who had appointed themselves outriders. Only the ten pack-ponies trotted behind him, and Hran beside him. His spear-brother kept him company for many miles; but at last they drew rein. The day was more than half gone, and Hran must be back in camp by dark. Their parting could be delayed no longer.

Hran turned Ranap, and they faced each other. After a moment Mor'anh said, 'You know my horn-call. I do not think I can be gone for less than three moons, and it may be longer. But after the third moon, begin to listen for my horn.'

'We have ridden stirrup to stirrup for many years,' said Hran. 'Even for one season only, my side will feel strange without you, my brother.'

'And mine without you. Watch over my people, Long Spear. May the winter not be hard. Do not let the Old One die while I am gone. Guard yourself well, my brother; better than any.' He looked north. 'Say my name every day to the Plain lest it forget me.' Then his tone changed. 'And do not let anyone neglect his weapon practice. Be as strict as with your dancers.'

Hran smiled and said, 'I know I do not need to say it, Son of Kem'nanh, but: the God go with you. When winter leans towards spring, we shall look for you.'

They rode their horses close and embraced; and then, for the first time either could remember, they gathered their reins and rode away in opposite directions.

After two days, Mor'anh came to a forest. It was the first land-mark he had to find, but he was almost astonished to see it there where the City-man had seen it, as if eleven years could have undone the work of hundreds. He gazed at it with some awe. From the hillcrest whence he first saw it, he could see how far it stretched; east and north-east to the horizon, and south away round the curve of the mountains, as close as a lamb's fleece. This was the end of the Plain. The hills of winter, and the Kalnat mountains, he had always known; but this was strange, a new kind of country entirely.

For three days he rode around the forest's edge, almost in its shadow at times, watching the trees curiously. He could have moved more swiftly, but he was held to the pace of the ponies. They were strong and enduring, and swift for their size; but they could not have matched Racho's earth-devouring stride.

On the fifth day, near sunset, he came to the river he had been waiting to find. It was broad, but not too broad to swim, and he made camp on its farther bank. He lay awake long after dark, staring at the embers, listening to Racho and the ponies tearing at the grass. A strange stillness was invading his heart. No plainsman would call himself alone while his horse was with him: but he had only once before been so long without human company, at the time of his manhood test. Then he had known what he was doing, and why, and that all his fore-fathers and fellow-tribesmen had done the same before him. Even so, it was always a time of dreams and strange visions, from which all boys emerged changed; Kem'nanh had first claimed him then. But now he was doing something no plainsman had willingly done before, and so putting himself altogether in Kem'nanh's hand. It was in solitude that the God's madness fell on men; his terror waited in lonely places. But he could spare those who trusted him enough; and who should trust him, Mor'anh thought, if not I?

The next day he rode no longer east but south, follow-ing the river downstream through the forest.

Once under the trees, he saw that they did not grow very close together, though at the river's edge they crowded more, leaning out over the water like sleepy thirsty cattle. There were often wide stretches of grass, and low bushes; the ground was splashed with sun. But he was nearly overcome with awe. Any place where a tree grew was holy, to him; here where they grew in numbers past counting, it was almost too holy to bear. By day he saw few animals, none he knew, only one or two leaping in the trees, but the forest was full of birds. It was Ir'nanh's country past doubt. Even now when the trees were spreading their leaves beneath them the birds were active, calling and singing constantly. But their bright sounds and the rare animal noises were but the embroidered border; the garment was silence.

Often he felt that he was not alone, that he was watched and even followed, but he laughed at himself. Once on the first night under the trees he woke with a shock and sprang up sure that for an instant he had seen a girl's face; but there was nothing, and he lay down again. Maybe some animal, bolder and more curious than the rest, had come to stare, and if his fancy made dark-eyed girls of shadows and leaves, that was no wonder.

The next day brought no sun, but lashing rain. The river blended with its banks, and the dull dripping trees on the far shore were half hidden in mist. Mor'anh's cloak grew heavy with water; he huddled into it and laughed wryly. 'Lord of Summer, if this is your place, where are you?' he called. But there was no one to understand and answer.

Next day they they came to a place where the river divided about a large island, and against the island on either bank was a wide gap in the trees. When he rode out into the gap and looked east he saw that it continued, a broad path through the forest.

'Like a river in the earth,' he said. He talked aloud often; the longing to hear another voice grew daily. Twice he had thought he had heard someone: a clear young voice saying, 'Who are you?', another time a lower voice, 'Where are you going?' Each time, after the first shock, he knew that the silence had not been broken, that the voices had sounded only in his head. Racho had heard nothing. So he gathered his mind firmly, and prayed to Kem'nanh to preserve him from the solitude that can take away a man's knowledge of himself. He still sometimes felt the eyes of the forest on him, but no longer tried to catch a glimpse of the watchers, sure there was not even a beast, that it was only the oppression of the stillness. And now he had grown more accustomed to that, they did not seem so close.

For while he stayed on the road they could not approach him, not daring to leave their trees. They watched him from among the branches, too quick and quiet for even a Khentor to glimpse. Quite soon the trees thinned, and the true forest gave way to broad empty spaces with scattered clumps of trees. They could not follow him there, and would not if they could; only to smell the air of it brought back their thousand-year-old grief as fresh as dew, the fallen trees and the lost comrades.

For six days Mor'anh followed the road. It had been falling into decay; the stones that had once surfaced it were broken and buried, the ditches beside it choked, but its course was still clear. Often they passed areas of broken ground, with lumps of stone visible through the grass and weeds. Once he saw a field of stones. When he rode round them they seemed to have been flung down at random, except that they were all much the same size and shape; but when he climbed onto the large stone at the centre and looked over the field he saw that they made a pattern of lines all following the same curve and flowing from the centre stone: or to it. The sweep of the curve made him think of the golden tendrils on the ear-rings; but why men had made the stone pattern he could not think, and he did not like the way the lines all came swirling in to his feet.

That was the fourth day along the road. Vani was dark that night while Hega was full: the patterned stones came weaving into his dreams, all coiling towards the malignant moon, until it seemed that the stars had learned a new and sinister dance, and he woke sweating with horror not daring to sleep again lest the dream was waiting for him. Certainly, he thought, he had been alone too long.

After six days they crossed another river; the road ran through it, so that the ponies did not need to swim, and Racho did not wet his belly. At the edges, by the deep water, many of the stones were loosened, but there was still a smooth firm path along the centre. On the third day after that they passed some great fingers of stone, like tree-trunks of rock, round slabs piled high. They stood either side of the road, in pairs, with other chunks of rock about them. One of the hugest lay across their path, half embedded in the smashed road. He puzzled over them, staring back after them long after he had passed. The vanished people of this country had it seemed treated stones like toys. What sort of men had they been, to pile them up or make patterns with them like children at play, for no apparent purpose? Had they been giants, to use them so carelessly?

He pondered on it until he slept, but next morning it was soon put out of his mind. For at the very beginning of that day's journey, soon after sunrise, they came to the Great River.

havoi, his people came to call it in after years, the One Who Divides; the great river which flows almost the width of Lelarik, richest realm of Vandarei, drawing its waters from mountains far in the north and from wild southern hills, as well as from the tall peaks where it rises. Vandarei was a name as yet unknown, her history just beginning as this plainsman stood on the bank of the river; many generations would pass before Lelarik's rise and fall, but Shavoi was there already, bearing her great burden across the unborn land.

Mor'anh gazed astounded. On such a breadth, had it been land, a whole tribe could have pitched its tents and loosed its cattle. He could hardly see the trees on the far bank. Small waves lapped gently on the shores, but all that might of water moved with hardly a sound, with less noise than the rivers of the Plain. The low sunbeams glinted and sparkled on its surface, and but for the changing pattern of their glitter, he would scarcely have known that it moved.

'Racho,' he said, 'I hope our journey does not end here. Only a bird could cross this.' But at that moment he would hardly have been disappointed if he could go no farther; he had seen a marvel.

The road ended in a broad flat place at the river's brink,

with narrow upright stones spaced along its edge. Mor'anh's way turned northward. He was to ride upstream until he found a way to cross the river. They travelled beside it for two days, and Mor'anh never tired of it. It was there that he first noticed how mild the weather had become, like a warm spring although winter was well advanced. There were even flowers in bloom.

Several times he saw craft out on the river. The first time it startled him; but then he thought he should have guessed that people who knew this great water well would have found some way of riding on it. Once, one of them was close enough for him to see a man moving on it. The plainsman waved his arms and shouted; the riverman looked across and raised his arm before going on with his work. The small encounter excited Mor'anh greatly. His journey had not been for nothing. He had found a land where men lived, men who were neither Horse People nor Golden People: The Cities was surely a reality, and could be found. His relief equalled his exhilaration. The world grew firm again. It was a place where men lived, not where he wandered alone among relics of dead giants.

On the evening of the second day after leaving the road he saw where another river, flowing from the south, joined the great one. His heart leapt; that must be his last guide, the river he must follow to its beginning. He camped over against it that night, and went on in the morning with nervous eagerness. His next objective was surely near; and about noon he found it.

It was another wonder. Men had stretched a path across the water. Shells of wood were linked by ropes as thick as his leg, and across them was laid a path of huge planks of wood. There were gaps in the line of shells through which low craft could pass. When they stood at the beginning of the path, he saw it rising and falling in gentle waves; and when they moved on to it, it boomed strangely under the hooves.

Crossing that river was the most terrifying thing he had ever done. Neither he, nor Racho, nor the ponies,

229

had ever known anything but the steady earth beneath them. The ponies neighed with fear, scared by the noise their feet made, and the more they milled the greater grew the noise and their fright. Mor'anh had to dismount to calm them; and then he felt for himself the slow heave under his feet.

He gripped Racho's saddle for an instant; sweat broke cold on his skin, and he felt dizzy. But his voice was steady as he soothed the frightened animals, and Racho did not fail him. When Mor'anh remounted the re-davel moved forward unhesitating, and the ponies followed close.

Over land, the distance would have been a short canter. Here it seemed endless, as they went slowly along the path that swelled and boomed. Mor'anh looked down at the water beneath them, and the wrinkling skin of the river, and his heart beat in his throat. When the ponies smelled the shore ahead, they jostled eagerly, but speed might make them slip, and he made them keep to a steady walk until they trod firm earth again. A little way from the bank he stopped and made much of them, finding his own legs shaking with strain.

But they were over the Great River, and elation filled him. That night he lit his fire in the land between two rivers, and next day, turned his face to the south.

He rode beside this last river for nineteen days.

In this land, the very colour and texture of the earth was strange. It was hard to the touch, and crumbled drily between his fingers, unlike the soft coolness of the black soil of the Plain. This was almost red, and often yellow rock thrust through it; the land showed its bones here. Yet it was beautiful. The season being late, the memory he carried away was of a golden land; the short grass was dusty gold, and where that could not grow the tawny rocks glowed in the sun. The trees were at first the kind of tree he knew, with bare dun branches and their pale leaves drifted between them, though they were much smaller than the forest trees; but the further south he rode the commoner became trees which had kept their leaves. Some were tall and straight, with rough russet trunks and deep green leaves so thin and small he could hardly call them leaves. They lay deep under the trees, looking soft until he felt them, though they made a springy scented bed. Others were low, slim trees with narrow glossy leaves. Nowhere did they grow close, and they became more scattered daily.

The land was not flat, but a series of ridges and valleys. The river swiftened often, and clamoured over rocks in its bed. It had grown shallow, and was so clear it seemed shallower, and it was cold enough to take his breath. The little rivers and brooks that fed it were yet clearer; when Mor'anh and the horses crossed one, their shadows fell not on the water but on its bed, and the small stones under the streams sparkled in the sun. There was no lack of water for the animals, though now the grazing was poor, except along the river bank.

Each day it grew hotter. Mor'anh was amazed and perplexed, for midwinter was only a moon away, yet it was hotter than any summer he had known. They travelled now into the night, resting in the hottest time after noon, Racho and the ponies browsing, or drowsing in any shade they could find, while Mor'anh stripped and lay on the short pricking grass, soaking in the sun. The earth was warm under him, and the rocks often too hot to touch.

Vani reached her full and waned. She too had changed: he saw the shadows on her face more clearly, and though she shone brighter she seemed more frail. In this bright air the red moon too seemed fairer. He only knew Hega dull and lowering; here, though still unfriendly to his eyes, she glowed.

He felt his loneliness worsen; the wish for human companionship had become a hunger. He had wearied of the sound of his own voice, to which no other voice replied. He missed the Tribe bitterly, and the knowledge of the distance that parted them was a pain which grew heavier daily. He conjured their faces at night, Hran, the

*Men had stretched a path across
the water. Shells of wood were linked
by ropes as thick as his leg.*

Old One, Manui, Diveru, and Runi: and Nai and his father. For loneliness had one trick left to play on him. One separation seemed like another, and he often forgot that they were no longer in their tents.

He rode stripped to the waist, yet though it grew ever hotter, there was no heaviness in the air. Its clarity was as pure as the water in the brooks. The river had branched again, and was truly narrow now. It sounded constantly, rushing with gayer speed over a steepening bed. Often it lay below them in a little gorge, or they rode beside it between walls of golden rock. Trees were rare now, but there were many shrubs with slender whippy branches and slim tough leaves. The air was hot and tangy with strange scents.

One evening he saw the lights of a village, far away across a hillside. His desire to be with men urged him to go to it, but he felt a strange reluctance, an awkwardness and shame, and after hesitating a while he rode on his way. By his solitary fire he told himself it would have been only pointless delay. Mor'anh had never felt shy before.

Vani waned, and as she drew towards the dark the land grew strange ahead of him. In the distance it rose up; but not into a mountain, for there were no peaks. Not even a mass of hills; as they drew closer the upper height still seemed flat, a smooth hard line, and the slope was a single cliff the length of the horizon. The river wound towards it, and each day it rose higher.

When the silver moon had two nights to live, he made camp at the foot of the slope. The height above cut the sky in half. When he lay down to sleep the darkness was full of the river roaring along its narrow bed. He watched it curving white over the rocks which hindered it, and remembered how it looked where it met the Great River, and they made a smooth plain of water. 'Other things I have seen young, and growing old; but I have watched this river from age to youth. Yet its age is still there; and when I looked at it then, at the same time it was young, leaping over these stones.' He thought: 'This is how the

234

Gods must see Time, and the lives of men; not as something which passes and is gone, but which is all there, always. While we, moving with the water, see the trees on the bank pass and think they are gone for ever.'

The ascent was hard and slow. Racho and the ponies were Plain animals, unskilled in choosing their footing; the strange terrain made them nervous. Mor'anh led Racho, looking for soft ground, fearing to lame one of them on the stones. They rested often; at least the grazing was better than it had been for many days. Mor'anh dared not lose the river, but when they had to make a long cast away from it, the sound would guide them back. Here it was yet louder and swifter, often leaping from shelves of rock as much as Mor'anh's height, with a gleeful roar. Once the White Wolf slipped into it, and the force of it made him stagger, though it scarcely reached his knees.

When they came to a level place broad enough to rest on, with a slope below it not so steep as to endanger the animals in the dark, he was glad to stop, though there was still plenty of daylight left. He had time to look at something he had never seen before, the land spread out below him. This northern slope soon fell into shadow, and twilight came early, though sun still shone into the land below. It had not darkened beyond evening when he lay down, but he slept at once, exhausted.

They had hardly begun their journey next day when their way was barred by a sheer cliff more than four times Mor'anh's height. Yet Mor'anh, gazing dazzled and delighted, did not regret the delay, for over the cliff the river poured in a glory of flashing whiteness. The water battered into the pool at its feet, foaming and creaming; the haze of spray chilled his face and danced in a rainbow above him. He left the horses and clambered up to a little ledge of rock beside the cascade, holding to a dripping bush, drenched by the glittering spray. There he stood as in a trance, overcome by the beauty and tumultuous joy of the waterfall. On the Plain, in the domain of a wilder, fiercer, power, Ir'nanh the Boy, wielder of the darting lightning, Lord of the transient summer, was a God of life's fleeting brightnesses; like a singing bird swooping over the grasses. Here he showed in his splendour, in the power of his gladness, like a great swan who sits back on the river and beats his wings, exulting. The cataract soared over the cliff and plunged shouting in the pool below, the drops that struck him bruised like stones; but before him the torrent seemed still, so unchanging was its ribbed wall. Mor'anh felt a solemn gladness, and a stirring, as if he were on the brink of a mystery.

Late that afternoon they reached the crest. Ahead and to either side the new land stretched out, a vast platform of earth and rock. The air was cooler, and yet more limpidly clear than in the sparkling land below. When he looked back, their climb seemed impossible; the ground fell away, folded and tumbled, reaching the gentler earth in a distance seeming little more than its own height.

They could have travelled some way before nightfall, but as soon as they were well away from the brink Mor'anh turned his tired beasts loose to rest and graze. He examined them well, but found no signs of lameness, then he made his fire, and ate. Stars began to flitter in the green of the western sky: when full dark came, with the swiftness to which he was growing accustomed, he saw stars in the south that he had never seen before. He sat up watching them, feeling at last that his journey was almost done.

25

t was a land of bright pale colours, light green, pale yellow, blue, as if the sun had bleached it. Even the earth was a softer colour than in the land he had just left, a pale fawn. It was Ir'nanh's country no longer; a calmer god ruled here.

The river wandered over the level land, but the trees and bushes growing beside it marked its course, and he could ride across its wider curves without fear of losing his only guide. It was time to begin looking for the place that would be his journey's end; and he felt at a loss. The stranger had told him that 'The Cities' meant a great place, or many places; and that one such place was called 'a city', and that it was where his people lived, a place fixed and walled. There had been other names he used, but Mor'anh had forgotten them, as he had forgotten the descriptions which had linked to no reality he knew. Now he searched the land ahead for something he could call 'a city' but could see nothing yet.

At one place the river had cut itself a little valley with sides higher than he could look over from Racho's back. He was riding along this, enjoying the shade and the breeze, when from ahead of him he heard thin piping, and caught the smell of goat. He felt that strange reluctance again, a wary desire to see before he was seen, and went forward quietly. He turned the point of a corner, and gaped.

Not four spear-lengths away a girl sat on a shadowed rock, piping, with goats grazing round her. Her curling brown hair, rather tangled, fell behind her shoulders; she was very young, to judge by her sun-dappled breasts, and as she sat with her side turned to him she seemed to be completely naked. He did not know which shocked him more, her nakedness, or that a girl should be given charge of a herd: both sights made him blush with shame. Then the goats began bleating and staring, which made her turn her head; he averted his eyes and began to greet her, but she leapt to her feet with a shriek and bounded away. He saw then that she was clothed, though only in two strips of red cloth tied about her waist.

He stared at her terror-stricken flight, her red garment flapping, the goats galloping behind her; then rode on, astonished and rather hurt. No other woman had ever shown such horror at sight of him. He felt his face carefully, and laughed; his hair and moustache were unkempt, and his beard had grown, covering his face almost to the cheek-bones. Maybe a man astride a strange horned animal, naked above the waist and strangely clad below, wild with black hair and uttering strange noises, might be alarming. He bathed and groomed himself with care that night, shaving his cheeks with much grimacing, though he could not take off all his beard, combing and trimming his hair and moustache. He thought long about the girl, wondering most that she tended a herd; that one fact seemed to imply so much about her people.

Almost as soon as he set out next day, the river met with a road—one in good repair, this time. Far ahead, at the end of the road, he could see a solitary mountain, low and truncated, like a smaller version of the land itself. It was soon after dawn, and the shape was dark against the sunrise. When the sun rose higher he could see it more clearly, and scanned its slopes for a sight of the dwellings of men, hoping they would not have another steep climb.

The morning wore on. Before him the flat-topped mountain grew steadily larger; indeed, it seemed to approach very swiftly. There was something strange about it; it looked too distant, or not distant enough; he could not get the scale of what he saw. As the sun swung southwards, shadows moved across its slopes; the great outcrops of rock from its face seemed very regular. He studied it doubtfully, feeling a quailing in his belly. Then suddenly his eyes adjusted, and he knew what it was he saw; and it was not a mountain far off, but a city close at hand.

The shock stopped his breath. He had imagined it like the Golden Men's stockaded towns. He could have dreamed of nothing like this. He felt drenched in shame, appalled at his ignorance. His impulse was to turn and flee. He actually turned Racho's head. Then he came to his senses, and summoned his pride, and went on.

Soon he could see men moving on the walls, and on the flatsided towers, broadening from top to base, that strengthened every angle of their many sides. Then the huge sloping walls of tawny stone loomed above him, and the massive gate-towers. Mor'anh dared not let himself pause, or he knew he would retreat. Racho's head was high and attentive; he was curious, and doubtful, but not alarmed so long as his rider did not hesitate. The gates were guarded by armed men. Over short orange tunics they wore others of polished metal scales; their arms and sandalled legs were bare. Their tall rounded helmets were crested with orange. Each held a pike, and had a large curved shield, straight-sided, standing by him. The gateway was a great square arch; as he rode its shadowed length he saw the massive doors laid back against the walls. Then he came out into the sunlight within the city.

The stench of the street was the first thing to hit them, so that the animals snorted and tossed their heads; it was as bad as the smell of the Kalnat town. Then the people in the street noticed him. Some boys shouted, and all at once he was the centre of a crowd. The men at the gate

239

had not moved or glanced aside as he passed, so that he had thought strangers were commonplace to them; but these people called and stared and pressed around him jostling one another, women as bold as men. He had grown so unused to people that he found he had to struggle with something very like fear. They were not unfriendly, and they did not seek to hinder him, but he found he had stopped anyway, confused by the clamour of words he could not understand. Then from behind sounded a noise, like a horn but higher and harder, and more precise than the Kalnat horns. The crowd began to melt away, and those who lingered were pushed back by men with the metal-scale tunics, until Mor'anh found himself between two lines of these scaled men. One who seemed their leader came through the file, raised his flat hand to Mor'anh briefly, and led the way forward.

The plainsman followed bemused. They went swiftly along broad paved streets until another high wall faced them with closed gates of metal that was bent and twisted into patterns, before which another man waited as if expecting them. He and the leader of the men with Mor'anh exchanged salutes; one spoke and the other replied. Their voices were so quick and unemphatic that they must have been repeating mere formulas. The first man turned away from the gate and saluted, again so brisk and blank-faced that he could not feel it to be a greeting, then spoke sharply to the men, who turned swiftly and followed him. They turned as if he had pulled them; and it was then that Mor'anh noticed how strangely they moved, all their legs moving together, twelve feet striking the earth as one. He turned to stare, but now the metal gates had been opened, and another double file of men waited to lead him in.

He could hardly keep from gaping at the building which faced him. It was like a hill of stone. Slopes made of piled narrow ledges rose to broad platforms with walls along their edges, lines of slim stone trees shadowed paths by tall blank walls, roofs rose one level on another; and everywhere was the sound of water, and clumps of

240

green. As they drew closer, he had to tilt his head back to see the roof-line.

The men led him to a broad slope of the narrow ledges. There was a blaze of sound from the strange horns, and a group of people came across the flat place above. Men whose scale-tunics were of yellow metal sprang down to line the slope, and as the foremost of the men reached the topmost ledge, they and the men about Mor'anh shouted and fell to one knee.

Eight men bore up a canopy under which walked three people; behind came a group of more plainly dressed men. The three under the canopy were all splendidly clothed, but Mor'anh looked at the man in front, on whom maybe the fate of the Alnei hung, and no further. He was tall and slender, with smooth brown hair about a fine pale face, not young, but not yet old. His steady eyes and mouth held command. He moved a hand; the musicians fell silent, and the kneeling men rose smartly. The men holding the canopy poles became immobile. Mor'anh gazed up, and the lord met his eyes and spoke. He greeted Mor'anh in a light cool voice, with words he could not understand; but their tone, and the look of his grey-green eyes, was re-assuring.

Mor'anh swallowed. He had not spoken to a man for a moon and a half, and for a moment feared that no words would come.

'I greet you, Lord,' he began, then realised that he was using his own tongue, not the speech of the Golden Ones as he had decided. He went on in the language he thought more likely to be understood, 'I cannot speak your tongue, Lord. Is there any man here who knows the speech of the Kalnat?'

It was then that a miracle happened. The group of men further back shifted, and one came down. He bowed and spoke briefly to the lord, who gestured assent. Then turning to Mor'anh he said,

'If you are, as I think you must be, one of the men who call themselves the khentorei, from the plain in the far north, then I know a few words of your language.'

*Eight men bore up a canopy under which
walked three people; behind came a group of
more plainly dressed men. The three under the
canopy were all splendidly clothed, but
Mor'anh looked at the man in front, on whom
maybe the fate of the Alnei hung, and no further.*

He spoke slowly, with hesitation. His voice was even and lacking emphasis, so that the sound of some words was strange, but the language was that of the Tribes. Mor'anh's face lost its careful impassivity. The astonished delight that leapt in it needed no translation, and the Lord smiled.

From his heart Mor'anh offered gratitude to the Gods, to Kem'nanh, and to Ir'nanh, loosener of tongues, who had gone ahead to prepare his way. 'I am of that people. I am Mor'anh, the son of Ilna, Lord of the Alnei. I come bringing your Lord gifts from the Men of the Wide Lands, and am come to ask his help for us.'

The interpreter turned to translate. Buoyant with relief, Mor'anh looked about him, and at the other people before him. Towards the back of the canopy was a young man clad even more richly than the Lord. Then the person he had not yet seen clearly, who had been hidden by the Lord, moved, and he saw, with surprise, a woman. He looked at her briefly, then looked again. But the interpreter was speaking.

'You stand before the Lord Yu-Thurek, Lord of our City, Jemaluth. He bids me greet you, and says, Lord of the Alnei, Mor'anh, you are welcome to the land of Bariphen and to Jemaluth, the City of the Wise.'

Mor'anh dismounted and went forward. He laid fist to shoulder and bowed before the Lord Yu-Thurek; but the Lord of the City stepped forward to the very edge of the canopy and gave Mor'anh his hand. Mor'anh had never felt a hand so smooth-skinned and soft-fleshed. There was no strength in the Lord's grasp; the strength was in his eyes. Grey-green and calm, they smiled on the plainsman; the eyes of a man who lived more in thought than in the passing moment, over whom passion had little power. Mor'anh felt abashed under their gaze.

The other man had ordered his words, and when the two Lords stepped apart, he went on,

'The Lord Yu-Thurek asks you to be his guest, and bids you make his—his tent—', Mor'anh grinned, '—his *roof* your own for as long as you wish.' He hesitated. 'He bids me call men to lead away your horses. Will they go with them?'

'The ponies will: but it will be best if I take Racho—my horse—where he must go. And they will not go within walls.'

When this was translated the splendid young man laughed, then checked at a glance from the woman. The Lord spoke, and another man came down the slope. The speaker said, 'I am to come with you, and see to your comfort. The Lord says, when you have shaken off the dust of your journey, he will offer you—', he looked harassed again, 'the horn of greeting.'

Mor'anh bowed; the Lord bowed; the scaled men turned, and they all moved up to the flat place, the lesser standing back until the canopy had passed. Mor'anh looked up at the woman again, but she did not turn her head. He was left with the interpreter and the second man, who was eyeing him curiously. He said smiling,

'How do you know our language? Have you seen the Plain? Is it possible? Are you the man who came to our tents?'

The other bowed. 'I am that man. My name is Ya-Buren, and eleven years ago I was a guest of the tribe Alnei. I learned your speech then, but I fear I have forgotten much.'

'I should have foreseen that your words would lead me to your own place! It is good to speak with men again, Ya-Buren. Will you lead us, then? Would someone shave my beard, before I meet your Lord again? This is my horse, whom you have not met before; his name is Racho.'

His spirits were rising to jesting. Had he known, Ya-Buren would have smiled. But he was an earnest man, and he remembered that plainsmen thought highly of their horses; so he bowed and greeted Racho gravely, before leading them away.

The royal rooms were on the north side of the Palace. The room where Yu-Thurek greeted Mor'anh again and gave

245

him the cup of welcome was cool, as was the cup itself and the pleasingly sharp drink it held. Mor'anh gave thanks in the phrase he had learned from Ya-Buren; the Lord's brows rose, and he spoke. 'The Lord says, your quickness rebukes us,' said Ya-Buren. He had a bundle of thick white sticks beside him, from several of which he had peeled a long strip of thin hard skin, and he seemed surer of his words. 'And also, his daughter and son wish to greet you.'

Mor'anh had been wondering if the woman was wife or daughter, and trying not to look at her, ever since he came into the room. Now he turned to the young man, but it was she who stepped forward first, and as he spoke her name Ya-Buren bowed deeply. 'The Princess Jatherol.'

She was tall and slender, made unlike a plainswoman, with deeper breasts and fuller hips, so that her waist looked yet smaller. City-women wore light flowing dresses; the soft cloth of hers clung over her breasts and her hips. She met his eyes, which were level with her own, as easily as another man might, holding out her hand; but looking at her he felt how long it had been since he had lain with a woman. The hand she gave him was smooth and cool, and softer than a child's; he drew a breath, and held his eyes to her face. He could not judge her beauty. She had silky curling hair of soft brown, long light-green eyes, a soft skin; it was a cool face, at odds with her body.

The Prince, Yo-Pheril, was easier to greet, though he talked so fast that Ya-Buren could not keep pace, and much of what he said could not be put into the Khentor tongue. He seemed to Mor'anh to lack the bearing of a Lord's son, to have no consciousness of being the Young Lord, his father's right arm. His assurance was no less than his sister's, but of another kind. Still, his open friendliness was irresistible.

Mor'anh turned to signal to the men who carried his bundles. The Alnei had chosen their gifts by those things the Kalnat seemed to value most highly; but as the men began to untie them, Mor'anh was shaken with doubt. Could people who lived as these did, find worth in anything the Plain could offer?

But there was no doubting their amazement and pleasure as the furs and the pliant dyed hides were spread before them. Yo-Pheril knelt to examine more closely a decorated drum, Jatherol caressed a carving, but the musk was presented on bent knee direct to the Lord.

Ya-Buren translated their praise of the gifts, and added, 'These are things we rarely see, Lord Mor'anh. Ivory—furs—why, only half of this would be a lordly gift!' Mor'anh bowed, then sat down, taking the cup a servant offered him. His tension was lessening. He looked at Jatherol, and dared at last to let his eyes and mind dwell on her. Then Yo-Pheril picked up a horn and began to blow it, and Yu-Thurek, laughing, stopped him.

'Lord Mor'anh, I think you can see how your gifts please us. But when we met you said that you had come to ask our help. What help may we of The Cities give you of the Plain?'

Mor'anh drew a breath and took the ear-rings from his pouch. 'These are Ya-Buren's gift to my father. Looking at them I thought that here where they were made there would be men skilled in the use of metal; and as I look about I see it is so. We have no such skill; indeed, we have no metal. But we have great need of weapons. There are men we must fight soon, and they have red spears, and long knives like the one Prince Yo-Pheril wears at his side.'

'A sword; swords,' said Ya-Buren.

'Swords. We have spears which are nearly as good as theirs, though of stone; but only knives we use for hunting, of stone or bone. We must fight this people soon, it must be; and my people will die if I do not get them weapons of metal. Will you make them for us? That is what I come to ask.'

His eyes spoke as persuasively as his deep urgent voice; they looked at him silently as Ya-Buren translated, impressed by his unstudied intensity. After a while Yu-Thurek's words came back to him.

'There is nothing hard in this request. I see no reason why Jemaluth cannot give you what you ask. But the day grows hot. It is our custom, Lord Mor'anh, to rest through the heat of the afternoon. My people will take you to the room they have prepared for you. This evening we shall feast you, and tomorrow we shall speak of this again.'

26

hey had given him a room on the north-west corner, with great windows and a wide arch leading onto a broad terrace, from which steps led down into a walled garden where Racho was lodged with the ponies.

Even his bed was of stone, a low platform each side three paces long, spread with mattresses and cushions and a heavy embroidered coverlet. He had both men and girls to wait on him; the girls seemed chosen for their prettiness. Some were smooth City-dwellers, but there were others, darker and smaller, yet quite unlike plains-women, for they had smooth brown skin and their hair curled. They had bare arms, and skirts unsewn at one side. He watched them thoughtfully, but he feared his ignorance of their customs, and the girls' shy manners discouraged him.

As the sun set he was walking on the terrace, watching Racho feed from a tripod in the garden below. He had bathed luxuriously—there was a bath sunk in the corner of his room—and been shaved. The attendants had taken away his dusty clothes and boots to brush, and he wore a long loose robe, with little heel-less slippers that were hard to keep on his feet. He felt light and elated. The long strain of his journey was over, and no longer preoccupied with doubts he was free to enjoy without reserve the strangeness and luxury about him.

From his terrace he could look out over the walls of the Palace and see the buildings of the City beyond. He could see how far it was to the huge outer walls, and guess at the number of people those walls held. It was never quiet. There were noises not only of men, but of things he could put no name to. His curiosity was sharpened; he was greedy to see and learn it all. He had seen wonders: the forest, the Great River, a path laid upon water, Ir'nanh's mighty waterfall; but Jemaluth eclipsed them all, a living marvel. He thought of the towns of the Golden Men, with wooden walls and straw roofs, their paths paved with hardened dirt and edged with weeds, and he laughed with scorn. Yet they despised and mocked his people, while the Lord of this great City had received him courteously, and called him Lord Mor'anh. He felt a new kind of anger with the Kalnat, as if they had sought to deceive him.

From her terrace above Princess Jatherol could see one part of his, and glimpse him as he strolled in the sunset. She had been taught by Ya-Buren how the nomad plainsmen lived, but this stranger walked the stones of their palace with the assurance of a Prince of Bariphen. She watched him for a while, but her women were waiting.

When she was dressed and adorned, she went to her father. Yu-Thurek was seated at his toilet table choosing his jewels. She leaned against his chair, and he glanced up smiling. 'Advise me.'

She turned over the jewels, holding them near the brown watered silk of his robe, then chose a set of clear yellow stones. She drew out a chain, and let it flow from hand to hand. 'Shall we give him the swords, then?'

Her father arched his brows. 'Well, we have not said so yet. You know better than that, Jatherol. We must move through the right forms.'

She shook her head. 'I do not think our guest would

understand them. I think this time we must do business like common men—break a stick and call it a deal.'

'Where do you learn these phrases? From Yo-Pheril, no doubt. Well, maybe, though I think you underestimate him. I shall ask you to call a Chairing, for one thing, and I am sure he will understand that. Berethol is recovered enough to attend, is she not? Well, do you object?'

'To giving him the swords? Not at all. Only—' She paused, aware that her studied indifference was leading her into feigning.

'Well?'

She examined the lid of a pot of paint. 'This is a new thing surely; that a City of Bariphen should concern itself with barbarian chiefs and their wars.'

'Jatherol, you astonish me. You know better than to speak so. What, the Princess of Jemaluth speaking with the vulgarity of a lord from Inthukar? While I govern, Jemaluth will find nothing beneath her concern. When we think ourselves too great to deal with any we do not think our equals, our end is written. I thought that was the first thing you learned.' She looked at him earnestly in the obsidian mirror. 'That reason is enough. But there are others. You have listened to Ya-Buren, you know as much as I do of the plainsmen. Barbarian chiefs and their wars? If he came from the south, maybe; but you have heard Ya-Buren say that the plainsmen do not make war. The tribe he visited did not know what he meant. For the worst crimes their punishment is not death, but expulsion. Think of those crimes, too.' (Jatherol smiled, 'Eating horse-flesh,' she murmured.) 'Murder is not one of them. It was not remembered, Ya-Buren's chief said, that it had ever happened.'

Jatherol was conscious of regret, and tried to cover it with lightness. 'Things are changing on the Plain, then.'

'Indeed; alas, maybe. But I should be most surprised if this is a war between tribes. Recall that Mor'anh said that their enemies are already armed with metal. I would think they are the Kalnat. Come, think like a politician.

251

The Kalnat are becoming stronger all round the coasts in the north, and even through the swamps and into our coastlands. Our ships can no longer put in for water or repairs in safety. If this young man's people attack them, it may stem the growth of their power before it becomes too great a danger to us. Also, let us not forget that Bariphen lives by trade. It is a melancholy fact that swords are easier taken up than laid down. They will need more weapons, and where will they bring their northern treasures but to Jemaluth, if we have treated them well?' He paused, adjusting an ear-ring. 'My last reason is less solid, but I am not sure it is not the most important. There is, it seems, a nascent power in the north, and from the knowledge we have one of potentially enormous power. Do you not agree we ought to secure the friendship of this people for Jemaluth?' He smiled at her reflection. 'And there is the reason that needs no explaining. He came to ask our help; and this is, after all, Jemaluth.'

She piled the jewels back in their casket. 'This is Jemaluth. It is well for him that he came to us and not to Inthukar.'

'Your reasoning is a little astray tonight, my dear. It was not chance; he came to us because Ya-Buren had gone to them. He would not have gone out from Inthukar seeking knowledge.' He gave her an ironic smile. Her dress was the colour of electrum, her rustling robe darker, like clear honey. Her hair, paint, jewels, scent, were all exquisite. 'But you astonish me, Jatherol. Do you really consider our guest no more than a "barbarian chief"? You look very lovely. I like that dress; I do not think I have seen it before. Is it the one you thought too good to wear for the Prince of Ko-Phitel?'

Ya-Buren came to guide Mor'anh down to the feast; it seemed they had a room especially for eating in. They walked through wide cool corridors, where the perfectly smooth floors and straight walls amazed Mor'anh. One wall of the corridor did not shine like others, and it was decorated with lines and patches of colour. Mor'anh looked at it doubtfully, wondering why the City-men found it pleasing. Then he stopped, his hands clenching, angry and dismayed.

Before him stood two Golden Men, each as tall as Kariniol, their yellow hair and long spears gleaming. They flanked the door. At first he took one of them for Kariniol, but their faces were strange. 'What are you doing here?' he demanded fiercely in Kalnat. Then, his senses returning a little, 'Are you from Maldé?'

The big man looked at him, his blue eyes bewildered, and saluted with his spear. Though the familiar shape, it had not the red gleam Mor'anh knew. The Golden Man spoke to Ya-Buren in the language of The Cities, and the scholar said 'Do you wish to speak to the guard, Lord Moran? He does not understand you.' Then he guessed the mistake, and laughed. 'No, no, Lord; these men were born in the City. They are part of the Golden Guard.' Mor'anh cooled, looking at them with less hostility, and he smiled grimly as they saluted him.

He entered to a crash of music. The men and women rose to greet him, and bowed as he passed between them. The first woman astonished him so that he almost checked, for her eyelids were blue as a lizard's throat. Then he saw that every woman there had eyes as vividly coloured, and that the men too were painted. The servants led him to the top of the room, to a table on a raised platform. The table was of stone. He half expected to find his chair the same, but it was of polished and padded wood.

There was another blaze of sound, and Yu-Thurek entered with his children. Mor'anh rose with the others, and watched their approach. Yo-Pheril glittered in the lamplight. The Princess's dress rippled and shone like water; he had never seen silk before. It was so fine, it moulded even her thighs as she moved. When she took her place at the table, the deep folds of her robe fell straight and hid her body, and he was almost glad. Once again he was surprised to see her take the place of honour, while Yo-Pheril sat on his father's left. Indeed, the Lord himself took the less magnificent of the two central chairs; it was Jatherol who sat under the golden canopy.

He asked Ya-Buren why the daughter was placed above the son, even, it seemed, above her father, and the other man laughed. 'Yes, she sits above them both; I thought it would surprise you. It is because she is her mother's daughter. Yu-Thurek is Lord for his life, but he became so by marrying the last Princess. The man chosen to be Jatherol's husband will be the next Lord. Yo-Pheril is a Prince because of his high blood, but he will not follow his father. Power goes through women here.'

He turned to look at her, amazed, and met her eyes. She smiled. Her eyelids were green, but being nearer he could see that they were painted, as was her mouth. She laughed at his scrutiny and spoke, leaning forward that Ya-Buren might hear. Her dress was cut low, baring part of her breasts. Ya-Buren said 'The Princess fears by the way you look at her face that you do not admire it.'

'Tell her, it is only that I have never seen a woman's skin painted like that. Say no, I admire the Princess entirely.' Ya-Buren translated without emphasis, but the Princess had watched Mor'anh's eyes and heard the cadence in his voice; she drooped her lashes and turned away smiling.

The feast was long, with scores of dishes, and long pauses through which musicians played. The variety of food bewildered Mor'anh. Nearly all of it was vegetable, though strangely disguised; there was little meat beyond fowl-flesh. Some of the rich spiced sauces pleased him, though he hardly knew what he ate. It was not food that could be eaten with fingers, and they had a variety of delicate tools, spoons, and tongs, and skewers; he watched Ya-Buren to learn their uses.

He soon became aware that all the richly dressed men and women were watching him with an interest as absorbed as his in them, nodding and smiling whenever they caught his eye. He had not suspected how strange and fascinating he seemed, with his black hair and eyes, his graceful energy, his deep resonant voice. Ya-Buren told him how he had been announced: Lord Mor'anh, Prince of the Plains. He shouted with laughter, and there was a ripple and a sighing; even the Princess Jatherol stirred in her seat.

When the eating was done, servants cleared the tables, then set them with wine and fruit. Musicians played, entertainers came, tumblers and jugglers, and last of all girls who danced. Their dancing was strange to him, but they were pretty and moved gracefully. Darkness went from blue to black beyond the curtained arches, and through the high windows he saw stars; he was amazed at how far into the night they sat.

Over the next days he roamed Jemaluth with Yo-Pheril for companion, until he began to know the City a little.

He was learning their language with a swiftness that astounded them, from Ya-Buren and from Yo-Pheril; within days he could talk easily about ordinary things. His quick ear and accurate memory amazed a people whose own powers of listening and remembering had been dulled by centuries of literacy. Yu-Thurek mocked his daughter gently for her surprise (which she acknowledged to be unreasonable) at the plainsman's intelligence, but it had astonished more than her. And Jatherol was even more amazed at the ease with which he had taken to their life, the assurance with which he walked amid his unfamiliar surroundings.

Mor'anh now treated the Prince like a younger brother. Yo-Pheril was something he had never met before, a young man free to play like a child. Now he knew him, he no longer thought him lacking in sense, yet there was still a lightness about him, and there were times when he seemed more girlish than his sister. Mor'anh could not conceive of manhood without responsibility. Yo-Pheril was a good-looking young man in the style admired in The Cities; slender and graceful, taller than Mor'anh, with a face tapering from his high cheekbones to his chin, a narrow delicate nose, mobile mouth, and long eyes with drooping painted lids. His voice was light, but they were none of them deep-voiced; Mor'anh's vibrant tones still woke a fluttering of silk sleeves among the women. Being a young man, the Prince wore long loose trousers under his tunic, not a long skirt as his father did. Mor'anh still found the sight of men clad like women amusing, though he liked the long open robe they put on when formally dressed.

He had seen the temple of Jemaluth's guardian god, where the law-courts were, and the temple of the god of the springs, where the outer courtyard was the city's public fountain. There the river he had followed rose in two springs within the sanctuary, whence it was led in conduits from basin to tiled basin before flowing out of the temple and finally through its own gate in the city wall. There were two other springs within the city, each enshrined within a smaller temple. They had a deep reverence for this pure water; drinking it was their only daily religious rite. Few crimes were punished more severely than that of fouling a spring; and water was a thing in which they took great pleasure. No noble's house was without at least one fountain, and even smaller houses had their pools.

He saw the score of colonnaded courts and shadowed terraces where the scholars and philosophers from whom Jemaluth took her title met: men, Yo-Pheril told him, from every city in Bariphen. Ya-Buren himself was not a native of Jemaluth. They looked at Mor'anh hungrily, but his knowledge of their language was not subtle enough for him to talk with them, and they had regretfully to let him go. These men were housed and fed by the city; they had no other concern in life but the search for knowledge and understanding. Mor'anh was surprised to find that though they served no god, they were esteemed far more than priests. Indeed, the City-people gave their gods respect rather than worship. The Goddess, who was regarded as only the guardian of the family hearth and pregnant women, received affection, but not fear or adoration; the sun was not Lord of Heaven to them, but a faintly malevolent power. They had a tower where offerings were made to him four times a year, twice when he had gone farthest away, twice when he stood overhead; but for the rest of the time the priests who served there were concerned only with keeping the calendar and marking the hours of the day.

They had found a way of reckoning these without the sun, for often Mor'anh would hear the first hour blown on their trumpets while the sky was still dark. All his life it had been dawn which woke him, by its light or by the Drum; now he would lie in the great bed, watching the darkness above the City thinning, and never know exactly when the sun rose. It was in that time of cool quiet, when the breeze rippled the curtains of his room, that the strangeness of finding himself where he did returned. Then the room in which he lay, the Palace and the City would grow remote and marvellous again. The times of solitude with leisure for thinking of the new things he had learned were grown rare; he valued this morning time, and the long afternoons of their strange fractured days, which they ordered to avoid the sun. He lay alone, after the first few days. Among his early discoveries was that he was waited on by bond-servants and slaves. He was shocked to find what that meant, and never felt at ease with his attendants again. The memory of the maids' smiling compliance filled him with shame; he did not want to take a girl to bed when he knew she could not refuse.

It was a reaction that Yo-Pheril and his friends could not understand; they could not imagine why he found it humiliating. For the first time he had learned a custom of theirs in which he found nothing to admire, and it distressed him that he could not make them share his disgust. He began to notice things anew that he had hardly regarded at first. He saw that the men and women who sat around the gates and in the squares were not idling away time they were too old and sick to spend usefully, but were begging for their livelihood. He realised that the gangs of children who roamed the City were not making

257

vicious mischief for play, but were struggling for their lives. Once he had been puzzled by the women loitering along the streets at night; now he understood, he found the knowledge appalling. Coming of a people with few possessions, it took him some time to recognise poverty, and to see that here, to own little was a disease that people died of. He knew now why they were escorted after dark. He had thought it was to honour them. It would be strange, he thought, to be unsafe walking alone among the tents, but he understood now, that a City was not a Tribe.

hey were a people of stone, as the Kalnat
of metal; they loved it. Even the cup in
Mor'anh's hand was of stone, ground
thin and polished. He said this to Yu-
Thurek, and the Lord laughed, agreeing.
'Stone . . . it is the bones of the earth.
Our mother has beautiful bones.' He turned his own cup,
holding it to the light, and his face softened with pleasure. Mor'anh leaned back in his chair, watching Jatherol
walking on the terrace in the moonlight. Yu-Thurek said,
'What are you, then? If they are metal and we are stone,
what are you?'

'Oh, of the beasts, our sharers of the earth. We love and
know them.'

'Yet you hunt them,' said Yo-Pheril.

'How else would we live? But we understand them, we
live among them and suffer their fears. We know them as
they are, and love them for that, not for the use we can
make of them. That is why it is a thing we punish, to
harm them without need. The Gods have put them in our
keeping.'

There was silence a moment, then Yu-Thurek said, 'Do
you mean that men were created for that reason—to take
care of the animals?'

Jatherol had entered, and stood listening. Mor'anh
looked at the Lord, but his face was perfectly earnest. 'We

have always believed it was why the Khentors were made,' he said carefully. 'To protect them, and guide them. We share the earth; but only we were given wisdom.'

Jatherol looked at him with grave wonder. The Lord was silent a while, then laughed softly.

'Could it be as simple as that, after all? Could everything be simpler than we think? You must let the philosophers discuss that with you, Moran. Listening to them I have often wondered if the Gods meant to set us such riddles as they wrestle with.' After a moment he said, 'There are some who have begun to speak with envy of your life; did you know, Moran?' They had none of them quite mastered the check in his name, nor the breath at the end. 'They talk of nobility and simplicity and dignity, and living close to the earth.'

It was strange; the complexity of their life dazzled and excited him, while they were stirred by the lack of it in his. Doubtless each was envying what he did not understand. He set down his cup and said,

'To me too our life seems very good: but it is not easy. The summer is one thing; but I think if these people knew what winter can mean they would envy us less. To be close to the earth—it is like being close to a tiger: it may not be pleasant. Yo-Pheril, there are two of your friends who say this, Ya-Thoron and Yu-Bareth. To them I would not say this, because it seems to insult them; but had they been born on the Plain, they would not have lived to be men. I have heard my strength praised, and my health. Well, all my tribesmen are healthy and strong; those who were not are dead. My mother never lost a child, but she bore only two, and was a favoured woman; I know another who has borne eleven, and never reared one to the age of learning. The women comfort her saying that the children they lose here are theirs for ever in the Great Plain, where my mother will be childless; and doubtless it is true, but here, year by year she weeps.' He shook his head. 'It is not all cruel. There is summer; the tiger is beautiful; it is a good life. And we have the Tribe. That is best of all.' He looked at them earnestly. 'It is not only the fellowship. There are words I have heard here which seemed strange to me at first: "have pity on the widow and the fatherless". I have heard it said of good men to show they were good "he pitied the fatherless and the widow". But it did not mean he wept for their grief, as I thought; it meant he sheltered them and fed them, when no one else would. Among us, a widow is only a woman whose man is dead, and those without fathers do not go hungry. Nor do the old, or the sick, or the crippled. No one struggles for life alone. No one sits in the dust and stretches out a hand to me as I pass, or dies un-noticed in a corner.'

'Lord Moran, say no more! And Jemaluth takes pride in being a city governed by the laws of virtue! We are shamed.'

He shook his head. 'I do not speak to shame you. Your city has made the world wider for me. The Tribe too can be merciless. There is a girl in my tribe—a woman cannot be cast out—but she is almost an outcast in our midst, because she is afraid to live the life of a woman. There is no place for her. Yet is it her fault? It is true she takes, and gives nothing to the Tribe. But if she were crippled or foolish we would pity her; because she is strong and clever and beautiful we do not. May it not be that her heart is crippled? Or her spirit lame? She is cruel and angry, but how has her nature been twisted, when here it might have grown free?'

In the gloom before sunrise he waited before the great gate to take Racho out for exercise. Whatever the sun-priests said, the Captains of the Gate knew that day began with light. Not until the sun had risen were the ox-teams led from their stalls in the base of the great towers and harnessed to the massive chains that opened the gates. Mor'anh had not seen them opened before, though he had watched the closing more than once. In

261

the evening a crowd always gathered, but now he waited with one man dozing in an ox-cart, and a youth with a traveller's pack and staff who eyed him with interest and envy. The ox-drivers shouted and cracked their whips, and the teams leaned into their harness. The soldiers talked and laughed, adjusting the last buckles of their armour as they waited to pass through and mount guard; the drivers yelled at their animals; the oxen groaned and laboured; but the huge gates made no sound as they swung apart. They rose as they opened; if there was ever need to close them with great speed their own weight would do it, but usually the ox-teams were used to brake their closing. Now men were waiting to chain and wedge them back. Between them light grew, and the watchers saw day unfolded to them.

Mor'anh rode until the freshness of the morning was past, and returned by the horse-fields where the chariot ponies of the army grazed. He slowed to look at them, then dismounted and examined some closely. He had a low opinion of the City-dwellers as horsemen, and few of them could ride; but still he had been surprised at how little use their chariots were to them. He had not before seen the herds; now he wondered no more. They were small gentle ponies; they looked well on a parade ground, or trotting a light chariot around the streets. They were pretty and graceful, but vigour had been bred out of them long ago.

When he had bathed and changed, he went seeking Yu-Thurek. Jatherol watched him come leaping up the staircase that led to the royal terrace, and smiled. The Palace tailors had copied his leather clothes, which were too warm for Bariphen, in cloth; he was wearing a suit of crimson linen, preferring strong colours to the pastels they wore. He looked well in it; it was no wonder that Yo-Pheril and others were beginning to imitate his fashion. Though, she thought, if they too meant to let their coats swing open, they would do well to wait until they could bare chests as firmly muscled as his. Though probably they would not dare; in Jemaluth it would be thought most immodest. She wondered if anyone had told the Prince of the Plains so, and hoped they would not.

'Yo-Pheril is not here,' she called. He looked up and laughed, shaking his head. She went back to the cushioned bench where her book lay. He reached the terrace and came to perch on the balustrade before her. 'I was not looking for him, but for your father. Is he here?'

'He was walking here with two friends until a moment ago. He will return soon.' The scroll had lost her attention, and she laid it down beside her. He bent forward and looked at it.

'The marks look like broken twigs. What do they say?'

'This is poetry. In this poet's time, they tried to use as few words as they could; sometimes it is good, but when a poet writes only "Pool-flower-stone-lovely", I think I am working harder than he has, and stop reading.' She smiled as he shouted with laughter.

'Oh, what else could one of your poets say! "Pool-flower-stone-lovely." Oh, I shall remember that. That is Jemaluth. Only a City-man could have said that.' He laughed down at her; and she realised with a slight shock that he was laughing not at the poem, but at Bariphen. She had never imagined that he might find some things about them amusing. He picked up the scroll.

'And with these broken twigs, you can hear what was said far away and long ago. It is a powerful thing. Maybe I must learn it.'

'Moran, how much do you mean to do! Have you time for that too?'

'Not this winter. But maybe when I return.' She looked up sharply. 'Oh, I mean to return, Jatherol. And Yo-Pheril is to come—ah, here is your father.' He rose to greet him, and she had time to calm her face.

'Ah, Moran, now I do not need to send to find you. My chief armourer has come. He has decided how best to make your swords, and has one to show you.'

263

'That is good news. And I have decided something. I know what the Alnei may give you.'

'You have already given us much!'

'That was a gift of another kind. No, I speak of something else, which may help Jemaluth, if you will accept it. I went to your horse-herds this morning. I understand now what you have told me, that you can use them little. I cannot say what I want to say in your tongue; but you must know, or your horse-keepers will tell you, that you will breed in weaknesses unless your stock is strengthened. I think you have no wild herds in this land, am I right? Well, we will bring you ponies, not to use in your chariots, but to strengthen your ponies' blood. Do you want this?'

'Moran, no gift could be more welcome! I am no horseman, but I have heard that my grooms go like pilgrims to gaze on your pack-ponies. Would that you could give us some of your skill, too.'

'Well, why should we not? There is a road between us.' He paused as two other men came onto the terrace, and Yu-Thurek turned. They bowed to Jatherol, then to him. 'Ah, Ya-Rophel! Lord Moran, this is our chief armourer, who has brought his work to show you.'

The man stepped forward. 'It was a nice problem, Lord, but I am pleased with our answer. A very interesting problem, but I think we have solved it. We discussed it with the captains too, of course. Well, this is what we have made.' He beckoned to his companion, and took a bundle from him. 'Yes, here it is.' He unfolded the cloth, and held out the weapon. 'Would you like to take it, my Lord Prince?'

Mor'anh lifted it carefully. The metal blade was cold, and he flinched a little from its touch. It was not the hot sunset colour of the Golden Men's weapons, but paler, more like grass at summer's end. Hilt to tip it was a little longer than his arm. The blade ran straight for most of its length, but where it began to narrow it began to curve also. The point was very fine. When he grasped the hilt

264

he was surprised to find how light the weapon felt. He exclaimed, and the armourer smiled.

'That is the balancing, Lord Prince. That is where the skill is. It is not sharpened yet, of course. The outer curve will be sharp, and both sides of the point. Will you tell me, is that grip comfortable to your hand?'

'It seems strange, to ask if it is comfortable.'

'Oh, but very important! Think, if you could not grip it firmly. Or if it galled your hand. It is meant to hurt your enemies, not you!' He laughed cheerfully.

Mor'anh shuddered. The sword did sit easily in his hand, almost too snugly. He took the blade in his other hand, and looked at it again, imagining the edge ground bright and sharp. It was made to kill men; it could have no other use. It was a terrible thing.

When the armourer had gone, Mor'anh stood leaning on the parapet, his face grim. After a while Yu-Thurek said, 'Ya-Rophel has done his work well. What are you thinking? Is it learning the use of the sword? I am sure you need not worry. You will not find it too hard.'

He laughed faintly. 'No, Lord, I think I fear to find it too easy. Ya-Rophel has done his work too well; my hand closes so readily on the long knife. I have a new prayer: I pray that the sword in my hand will always gall me . . .' He turned and looked over the balustrade. 'Sometimes when I see where I am leading my people, I grow afraid. After I had killed the Golden Man, I felt such horror . . . I had never guessed how easily it can be done; and now I cannot forget. Whenever I am angry with a man, the knowledge will be there: I could kill him. Will the terror of it always hold my arm? The Golden Ones do not feel it, and I think your people do not. I see how easily your son's friends will call upon a man who insults them to fight, and Yo-Pheril says men have been killed like that.' His hands clenched on the stone coping. 'Maybe this sounds foolish to you. But there is a name my people have for themselves; ker'ivh meni, the gentle people. I do not want to take that name away from them.'

'And yet you plan to fight the Kalnat.'

'Not plan; not unless we must. Not if they will let us go without it. But they will not. They are a people who have no fear of killing. I have seen death many times —mostly of beasts, but of men too. And killing is death, only showing a different face. Each time I have killed, I have smelled the bitterness I must drink one day. And so I say, Lord, I fear the spear in my own hand as much as the spear in my enemy's hand.'

'And yet you will face this,' said Jatherol, 'so that you may free your sister?'

He smiled. 'No, not that only. Or even chiefly. I thought so once—but the loss of Nai was only the torch set to the fire. The fuel had been gathering all my life. Now I do this because Kem'nanh commands me, and for no other reason.' He turned back to face them. 'We have never had a word for what we seek now, but you have one you use often, "liberty". I did not know that name before. Well, I know my "liberty" is worth fighting for, only I do not know if it is worth killing for.' He paused, pulling the embroidered border of his coat between his hands. After some while he said softly,

'And I listen to myself saying, I know this, but I do not know that, as if I am waiting to choose. And yet: very often we say, I will think about it more, but while I think I will do this, and this, and this. Then when we have done our thinking and come to make our choice we find it is made, there is no choice left. All those things we did only while we thought have made it, and when we look back we cannot see when we chose our way.'

'Now you talk like a philosopher. Will and fate; fate and will; which is stronger? Yet you say your god leads you, Moran. Surely, then, you are not troubled?'

'I know I follow Kem'nanh; but still I fear. The Har'enh follows, and Terani fears. I do not think the Gods are always thinking of our peace and happiness when they guide us. I think they have their own reasons. It is their right. But what obedience brings us may not please us at

266

all. Jatherol, I once said to you that I must obey Kem'nanh because only then do I have quiet. I was answering lightly. A man should not obey his God because this will bring him strength, or happiness, or peace. He should obey because it is his God, and for no other reason.'

28

he fountains rang softly into their pools, and the tame water-birds shook their feathers. The shadows of the drooping leaves swayed over Mor'anh's face. While he kept his eyes closed and lay quite still, he could almost think himself into being cool. But not quite. The winter solstice was eight days past, and the sun was on its way back.

The garden he lay in was famous. There was even a soft lawn coaxed into greenness. Mor'anh stroked his fingers gently over the grass-blades. A breeze moved the leaves and shook the fountains' drops into a different music. The Princess sighed. 'Qethadol, your fountains always make me think of Ladrekor.'

Mor'anh sat up, blinking in the sun. He had been thinking of the Tribe, and their faces were still in his mind as he opened his eyes on the young nobles. For an instant they seemed strangers again; it seemed impossible that this garden and the Plain were in the same world, and that one man could know them both. He wondered how he would ever find words to tell the Alnei of this place. 'What is Ladrekor?'

Jatherol sighed again. 'The most beautiful city in Bariphen, they say. Its river has seventeen springs; and the main fountain has many bowls so made that as they catch the water they sound different notes. So the city is called Ladrekor of the Singing Fountains.'

'It is the name, that is all,' said the other girl. 'Probably it is nothing wonderful. But it does sound more interesting than City of the Wise.'

'And Yo-Pheril is to go there on a visit,' said Jatherol to Mor'anh, 'which annoys me, because I cannot, ever.'

'Cannot? Why?'

Yo-Pheril smiled. 'The penalty of power, my sister. A Princess cannot leave her city, Moran. A superstition, our philosophers say; but it has the force of law. The people would expect the walls to crumble if Jatherol left them.'

'Never go out of the City?' Mor'anh looked appalled, and Jatherol laughed.

'Oh, through the gates into Jemaluth's land, but I may not travel to another city or its lands. But why should I wish to? It is only Ladrekor that I would like to see.' She broke a small cake and threw it to the birds, who flapped and gabbled. Their host, Yu-Bareth, said, 'Are those new bracelets, Prince Moran? I have not seen them before.'

'You should not call him Prince,' reproved Yo-Pheril. 'He has rule, so he is a Lord. And you do not keep memory of your forefathers, do you, Moran? You cannot name your grandfather's grandfather?'

Mor'anh shook his head smiling, then was stunned to realise how true that was. Other men had long ancestries whether they could decorate them with names or not, but he was the first generation of his line. Who had begotten his father?

'And besides, Lord is the higher title, and he should be given it. Now you may ask your question.'

'Thank you. Lord Moran, are those bracelets new?'

Mor'anh looked at the polished, engraved bronze band on either arm. 'Only as bracelets. I wore them when I came here, as a shackle the Kalnat had put on me. One of your men took it off for me. Then he made these of the metal. I shall wear them always, and my sons after me.'

'Have you any sons?' Jatherol asked. How strange, not

even to have wondered if he had a wife. But surely he would have spoken of her?

'Not yet, but I shall have.' He grinned as they derided his certainty, and lay back on the grass. Jatherol looked at him, ivory skin and hair like jet on the bright grass. 'It is an unsubtle contrast,' she told herself, but it almost stopped her breath.

When they had been silent a while, the Prince said, 'Moran, I have remembered something. That road you followed to come here—I have heard of it before. It is the relic of an old realm, called Barithor, peopled by men from Bariphen. They cleared the forests, and built cities and roads—five cities, I believe—and traded along the rivers. The realm stretched between the rivers as far as the sea. But in the end the estuaries silted, and the land became swampy and too unhealthy to live in, and the realm came to an end. Long ago. Nine Jubilees; four or five hundred years, since the last city was deserted.'

'But that is—that is ten lives of men, or more! And yet you remember!'

'Well . . . the records are incomplete, but they remain.'

After a while Mor'anh said, 'And the rivers drove them away. They belong to the Boy too. It was Ir'nanh's punishment, because they destroyed the trees.'

Yu-Bareth looked interested. Jatherol said, 'Maybe that is so; it is said to be a haunted forest. Yes, I know; but Ya-Buren is not a fanciful man, and he believes it. He says he heard voices in it.'

Mor'anh sat up. 'What? Speaking to him? That is strange; so did I.'

'Did they curse you? He says they railed at him, and he had evil dreams.'

'Each of you understood them, did you?' said Qethadol. 'What well-taught ghosts, to know your language and ours.' She laughed, then stood up. 'Here comes my stepmother,' she muttered.

Mor'anh grimaced. He liked Yu-Bareth, Qethadol, and their elder brother, and their father: but not their father's young wife, who never lost a chance of languishing her

270

long eyes at him. Had what she offered been less tempting, he might have laughed and disliked her less; but he could not laugh at Pheruthal.

This was the one puzzle he had been unable to solve. Their manners of greeting, of eating, the hundred small ceremonies they wove into their lives, he had mastered like one playing a game he does not understand, yet enjoying his own skill. And in most things of more moment, his natural courtesy was enough. But in this one thing it was not enough, and there were no formalities to learn, and it was hard to ask advice.

In the Tribe, he would never have sought to make love to another man's woman. Here, the young unmarried women whose favour he would have courted among his own people might talk to men as equals, might display their bodies alluringly, but he soon learned that they must be treated like girls not come to womanhood. Slaves whose bodies were not their own to withhold brought shame into the bed with them. Prostitution repelled him. Convention said there was no other kind of woman. Even had convention matched truth he would have found it easier than he did when reputed honest wives smiled invitation, and lovely wantons like Pheruthal blatantly offered themselves. Yo-Pheril and his friends talked lightly of affairs, of lovers and mistresses; there must be some safe and honourable path through that field of serpents, but he could not see it, and feared to take a step.

Yet the pleasure of love-making had long been as necessary to him as food, and far more easily won; the lack of it was sorely felt. And there was Jatherol, his daily companion. Between the women he wanted and could not have, could have but did not want, and wanted and could have, but with dishonour, his confusion and exasperation grew, until withdrawing to his room that afternoon he took refuge in memory, and lay thinking of Manui with heartshaking longing.

Mor'anh dropped the thin curtain and walked across the moonlit terrace. The talk and music faded as he went slowly down the steps; on the level place halfway he paused, savouring the beauty of the night. The flowers planted for the darkness were opening; in the pool below, the silver moon was reflected half full. Her light shimmered on the silk robes of the woman standing there, and stretched her shadow up the steps to his feet. She turned smiling to greet him.

He came to stand by her, leaning his arms on the wall of the pool. Along the beams of moonlight, fish gleamed briefly. The silver embroidery on his coat flickered in and out of shadow as he moved. She stood looking at him, feeling the moment grow timeless, filled with a still delight.

His figure was reflected indistinctly in the water. She smiled, remembering his first encounter with a mirror. She had had to explain the use of it, and at first, as with the paintings, his unaccustomed eye simply could not see the image. But she still remembered with pleasure how he had looked when he understood that the face he saw was his own, how wonder had been replaced by the slow exultant grin he could not curb.

'You have left the feast early.'

'Yes; they have begun talking of things I do not understand. There is a word—I have forgotten it already. What is it, when a man ends his own life?'

'Suicide?'

'Yes. They have begun talking of that, and praising it. It seems they think it a noble end. This I do not understand.' The thought shocked him deeply. 'Do you truly think this? This great gift the Gods give, you will cast it back at them?'

'It is done far less than it is talked of, Moran. But yes, we do praise it. You must know by now that we are people who like to order our lives. I think many of us would rather arrange our meeting with death, than be taken by surprise.' She laughed as she spoke, and he listened incredulous.

'Let me be taken by surprise! Death is the great enemy, and who would go willingly to him, holding out his

272

hand? No, let Horn-blower choose my time.' He shook his head in wonder. 'Who but you of The Cities could do it!—to talk so coolly of this thing, and to laugh as you do so! To make rules and manners for dying!' He turned to her. 'This in your people is strangest of all to me, Jatherol. They take everything apart and look at it with their minds. Even beauty they make rules for. Do they not praise you part by part? I think they say to you that you carry your head well, or have well-shaped ears, or graceful hands—', she began to laugh, 'or your bones will age well. But which of them has looked at you whole, as I have; and which of them has said as I do, Jatherol, you are beautiful, and I desire you?'

Her laugh choked into a gasp, and she blushed in confusion. It was his turn to be amused.

'There is no answer you can make, I know. That is why I never said it before. I should not have said it now. Forgive me.'

She was angry to find herself trembling. Was her sophistication so easily overthrown? 'There is nothing to forgive. In Jemaluth, all may speak as they please; but there is nowhere all may do as they please.' She glanced at him, but he was looking at the water, not at her. 'Now let us speak of something else. How does your sword-training go?'

'Well, I think. The Captain is a good teacher. And Yo-Pheril helps me; he practises with me. He is very good at it, it seems to me. Is it so?'

'Yes. He has a name as a swordsman.'

A fish leapt out of the water through the moon's image, shivering the silver. He watched it tremble into wholeness again. 'I must learn well and fast . . . I have been here more than a moon, Jatherol. When this moon is waning, I must go.'

'So soon?'

'It is not long to be here, I know. But I have been long away from the Alnei, and I have still the journey back to them. I must be with them before spring.'

'But you will come back, you say.'

'Oh, yes. Not next winter, but the one after that I shall come, bringing the ponies I have promised. And when I go back to the Plain then, Yo-Pheril will come with me. You will come to know the Alnei well, Jatherol. This is only the beginning of our friendship. There are many years to come.'

'Only the beginning,' she repeated, and turned to meet his eyes. They looked at her gravely; there were no secret meanings hidden in them. He spoke as a Plainsman, not a City-dweller who knew how to double-edge his words, but she was the very soul of the City of the Wise, and her words would serve her as she chose. She spoke firmly, as one who makes a pledge. 'Yes, there are many years ahead. We will be better friends yet, Prince of the Plains.'

Inside the Palace, the wide corridors and dim staircases breathed coolness; outside, the brazen sun kneaded his flesh, and the bright stone beat in his eyes. Yet his friends still strolled unperturbed, and talked of things they would do before the hot weather came. He wondered how even custom could make it bearable.

The day of his going was fixed: the fifth day of the white moon's waning, a full month after the winter sun-feast. It was more than three moons since he had left the Tribe. They would soon begin looking for him; and the Dha'lev would be growing restless long before his journey was over, smelling the wind for spring.

His yearning for his people and for the Plain grew daily, an ache for the feel of the wind, the scent of the grass. There were times when he was wearied by the unyielding stone beneath his feet, his eyes and flesh bruised by the solidity of all around him. He longed to sink his eyes in the cool green of the Plain once more. He hungered to feel his mouth shaping the words of his own language, and to hear it spoken again by low Khentor voices. There was still pleasure in the company of City-dwellers, and fascination in their City; but he yearned for people to whom his ways and thoughts were not strange.

He wanted the ease of Hran's company, and Manui's love. He had not thought to miss Manui so bitterly.

And yet, the last evening came too soon. The stone lamps shed their soft light on Yu-Thurek's dining room, and the moon on the curtains made them a shimmering, rippling fall of silver. Mor'anh looked around at the luxury of the room; even the air was made sumptuous for them, very delicately scented. He said, 'When I have been gone a while, I shall begin to doubt my memory.'

'Then we are the more certain of your coming back to refresh it,' said Yu-Thurek. Servants were removing the traces of their meal, and setting tables with wine and fruit. Mor'anh took a yellow fruit, and turned it between his hands. 'This is something I shall miss.'

'Is there no fruit on the Plain?'

'Oh, yes, when we find it. But none like this.' He ate it slowly, relishing it. Yo-Pheril laughed.

'It is not your last; we can take some with us.' He was to travel with Mor'anh as far as the Great River. Mor'anh only smiled in answer, and settled back in his chair. It might be the last he would ever eat so, sitting by a lamp of golden stone, with the feel of silk against his oil-smoothed skin, hearing harp-music fall through the perfumed air. Jatherol gazed entranced at his sybaritic composure.

Pages had entered, and Lord Yu-Thurek motioned them forward. 'So, Prince of the Plains, your first visit to us comes to an end. We must make it as hard as we can for you to forget us. Jemaluth has given her gifts to the Alnei; these our gifts to you, our friend.'

One by one they laid them before the White Wolf. A robe of heavy green silk, its black border embroidered with silver, and a belt plated with silver. From the Lord a necklace, and a sword of a rare new metal, grey and gleaming, a metal harder than bronze, keeping an edge better, and, it was said, holding hidden fire; a sword such as only Lords and great Princes bore. Yo-Pheril gave him a jewelled baldric and a scabbard; and Jatherol, two women's robes of silk, one golden and one crimson; one for his sister, she said, and one for his wife, if he had one, or when he chose one. Also she gave him a lamp of thin stone carved like one of the flowers that floated on their pools; remembering the poem he laughed, and again at her last gift, of a mirror.

When Mor'anh had thanked them, and the servants had gone, Yo-Pheril said, 'I have this for you too; it is not a gift like those, only a curious thing.' He gave it to Mor'anh: hollow like a horn, lighter and frailer than stone, but quite unlike the flimsy shells Mor'anh had seen before. The outside was dull blue-green; the inside grey, and faintly iridescent. One end was bluntly pointed, the other swirled open. Yo-Pheril said, 'Do you remember asking me where rivers went? And I told you the sea, but could not tell you what it was like. I got that shell from a man who has seen it; and he says that if you put it to your ear, the noise you hear is the voice of the sea.'

There was only a swirling, at first: but then he heard it; the hiss, the soft roar, the echo of a distant boom, the sound curling over and down, again and again, muffled remote thunder. His eyes grew spellbound. It went on, endless and unresting, tireless, relentless, wave after wave. New distances opened in his mind. He knew at once that it claimed kinship with him. Long years before Khentor feet would tread a sea-shore, when the hunger for wide wandering had touched none of them, he sat in the palace of a city of an inland realm, and listened to the calling of Kem'nanh's other Plain.

He took it from his ear at last, and handed it on to Jatherol. 'So that is where rivers go. No wonder that it draws them.' He shook his head, and laughed suddenly. 'I have come to the City of the Wise; and I have forgotten to ask my own question! Lord Yu-Thurek, I did not ask the hunters of truth. Maybe you can answer me. Tell me, does the river flow in the bed laid down for it, or does it choose its own way?'

Yu-Thurek smiled. 'Be glad you did not ask them; you would be there still. It is a question we have all asked them, in many ways. They cannot say, and nor can I. But this I can tell you, Mor'anh; that a stream near its source is easily turned aside, but once the river is old and its bed deep, it must flow in it for ever.'

29

he great court was in shadow. So soon after dawn, the stones had not lost the chill of night. Yet early as it was, the people of Jemaluth were massed along the road leading from the Palace to the gate. Mor'anh could hear, beyond the walls, their swelling murmur.

Racho pushed his nose into his rider's shoulder, and Mor'anh fondled him. Yo-Pheril leaned on the side of his chariot, yawning a little, shivering at the morning's coolness. At the foot of the stairs stood two great palanquins, canopied and gold-crusted. Eight fair-haired bearers stood by each. Even for Kalnat they were big, the biggest men Mor'anh had ever seen.

Trumpets blew on the terrace above. The gold-armoured guards shouted and fell to their knees. The Lord and his daughter beneath their swaying canopy descended. Mor'anh stepped forward, then stopped, awed.

Yu-Thurek was dressed as usual with sober magnificence; but Mor'anh had never seen Jatherol so splendid. Her dress was not of pale rippling cloth, but heavy orange silk, the hems two handspans deep with gold. Her outer robe, which all but hid the dress, was stiff with gold, and its high collar stood up rigidly behind her head. She wore a round flat-crowned head-dress beneath which all her hair was hidden; chains of gold hung against her cheeks. She was weighted with jewels unlike any he had seen her wear before, heavy and ornate. Mor'anh had never seen her pre-eminence so clearly demonstrated, and was a little shaken.

'I should have taken leave of you last night, Princess; while I still dared to call you by your name.' She smiled, and her eyes beneath their painted brows and gilded lids were unchanged. 'We will not say farewell, Moran. Only "until we meet again". May you prosper. Night and morning Jemaluth will watch the roads for your return.'

She put out her hand, but when he took it the rings were hard against his fingers, and instead of speaking he bowed, fist to shoulder. The bearers knelt, and Jatherol moved forward. Under the sumptuous weight of her ceremonial garments and archaic jewels she moved without her liquid grace, but with great stateliness. The Lord stepped easily into his palanquin, but the Princess had to be handed to hers by attendants. Mor'anh mounted; Yo-Pheril gathered his reins; the Golden Men rose, lifting their splendid burdens. The trumpets blew, and the escort formed.

They passed through the wrought gates, Jatherol's orange palanquin first, the Lord's behind; after them came Mor'anh and Yo-Pheril, side by side. They went with slow majesty towards the City's gate. The road was almost choked not only with crowds, but by canopied chariots, priests in poled carrying-chairs, nobles' litters. At the Gate there was a space of calm, under the arch where none but the guards might ever stand; but outside the City, the crowds began again.

Jatherol and her father came down from their thrones at the gate, and mounted the walls to watch the travellers out of sight. Gazing after them, Jatherol said suddenly, 'Do you think we have done wisely?'

'In sending swords to the Plain? I think so. Or if not wisely, justly.'

She moved her head a little to look at him; her collar made it difficult. 'When you talked of a new power in the north, there was something you did not mention. Do you know what I am thinking?'

'That they will overthrow the Kalnat, and learn their strength; and that some day, our turn will come.'

'Well?'

'It may be. But the Bariphen to which that happens, if it ever does, will not be the realm we know. The world must change.' He raised his arm to Yo-Pheril, who had looked back. 'And I daresay we may deserve it, by then.'

Jatherol was silent, following Mor'anh with her eyes. Turning Racho to look back for the last time he saw her standing on the wall facing the sun, a tiny glittering figure, like the image of a goddess.

Mor'anh and Yo-Pheril, with their train, travelled along the road; this time he would follow a swifter way to the Great River. On the third day they descended from the plateau by a ramped road which wound back and forth across the slope. It took half a day; Mor'anh remembered his two-day scramble ruefully. Below, the road ran on.

'It isn't bad, remembering its age,' said Yo-Pheril, driving his chariot by Racho. 'It could be re-paved, though.'

'Is this too part of the old realm, then?'

'In a way: it was a main route to it. It doesn't get much use now—though maybe its second blooming is coming. To think, after all these years, the old realm's road will be used to travel to a place and a people that the men who built it never knew existed! I won't think it, it makes me shiver. I wonder who is coming after us?'

Yo-Pheril had never travelled for so long. He had expected never to leave Bariphen, and his high spirits made this journey far less heart-wearying to Mor'anh than the other. He had wondered how the Prince would endure the lack of comforts on the journey, but Yo-Pheril was undisturbed. It seemed to enhance his pleasure; he was hardier than he seemed. The servants raised a tent for him every night, but he preferred to lie out, as Mor'anh did. He talked and questioned constantly. Since Yu-

Thurek had consented to his own future journey to the Plain, his curiosity about the life there had redoubled.

Mor'anh found it hard to make clear to him what a Tribe was. Even when they agreed that it was not like a city, nor a family as Yo-Pheril understood it, nor an army, it was not easy to say what it was. The Prince persisted in thinking of it as Mor'anh's to command, as if his fellow-tribesmen were subservient to him. At last as they bathed in a small river one evening, Mor'anh suddenly said, 'Listen, Yo-Pheril; you have heard me talk of the Great River? I have said what a mighty water it is? Well, that great river—it is this little river too, and the river I followed to find Jemaluth, and every small river, every stream, that has flowed into those rivers. Even this trickle among the ferns, that I can stop with my finger, that too is the Great River. Yet all these little waters, like single lives, they make something that has a soul and a life of its own, always changing, and always the same. That is what a Tribe is like.'

Morning and evening he practised swordcraft against the Prince. He would never have Yo-Pheril's long-learned skill that made supreme effort seem polished ease, nor did he have his dash; but his eye was good, and his reactions quicker than his friend's.

When they came in sight of the Great River Yo-Pheril, gazing from the hill-crest which gave the first view of it, was deeply impressed. 'No wonder my father thought it necessary to send a message to the ferry-men. Are these the haunted forests I see beyond?'

'No. Those trees do not grow close. That is where the fallen stones lie, though.'

He had been wondering how he was to make the crossing, but the ferry summoned by the Lord of Jemaluth was waiting where the road ended; a fenced raft, towed by two boats. It was large enough to take Racho, the ten ponies, and himself. There he parted from Yo-Pheril, with affection and regret. The Prince wished him well with the City-dwellers' traditional blessing: 'The Gods send you health, happiness, and a handsome wife!' Mor'anh laughed and said, 'It is likelier to be granted than my wish for you; but I say as I said to your father and sister, I wish you a good horse beneath you, your people about you, and the wind in your face always.'

The ponies, though becoming hardened to strange things, liked the raft as little as the bridge. He had to give them all his attention as the big dour rivermen leaned on their oars and the bank fell away behind them. Not until they stood on the landing-stage on the northern shore could he look again for his friend. The sun was in his eyes, but far away across the river he could see the group of men, small as seeds; and before them, like a chip of jewel, one figure in light bright green. The distance was too great for movement to be seen; but still, when he had mounted he sat and waved his arms before riding away.

Returning, the way seemed shorter, or his eagerness moved him more swiftly. He rode aside after strange sights less than on his outward journey. It was strange, when he rode through the fallen stones and broken ground, to think that here had been a city like Jemaluth. It was not easy for him to think that he looked at something which had been, and was not; that the past was about him. To find himself in two times at once was as hard for him as to stand in two places at once, and as disturbing. Plainsman that he was, the City-dwellers could not teach him soon to think of Time. For his people, years and centuries withered like grass and were gone; the past was as mysterious as the future, and stories of it vague as prophecies. To be able to number the dead years, to name their men and know their deeds, to look across them as from the cliff-top he had looked across the land below, seemed almost as marvellous as to see into the years ahead. As marvellous, and as powerful, for how it increased life!

When the true forest began, he remembered his voices, and Ya-Buren's. He rode looking about warily. But maybe for that reason, he neither saw nor heard anything, nor felt any watchful eyes. Yet now he knew their history, even the trees seemed to whisper grief to him. At last he stopped the ponies, and rode Racho across the ditch and among the trees a little way. 'Be easy!' he called into the silence. 'The Dancing Boy avenged you. He made the rivers poison them, and long ago their cities fell.'

The road reached the last river; but he did not turn north. He rode on to the water's edge, and found his hope answered. It would have been hard for the ponies, laden as they were with swords and gifts, to have swum this first and last river; but here too the road ran on under the water, to the island, and surely beyond.

The crossing was slow. He tested the footing carefully, for the current thrust hard, and it would go ill with a pony which fell. The river was full, and seemed bitterly cold; in the north, the snow was melting. It was growing dark when they reached the far bank, and night had fallen before he had attended to all the animals. But there was wood in plenty, and he built a fire that warmed them all well into the night.

He woke next morning to the realisation that no more rivers divided him from the Tribe, and that the sun-graced mountains in the west held, somewhere among their northern foothills, the winter camp of the Alnei. Elation flooded him. He felt that a spring to the saddle and a swift gallop would bring him among them at last, that if he now shouted 'Hran!' with all his power, his spear-brother would hear him. He knew in truth he still had a long journey, but his heart was bursting with triumphant joy as he set out that day.

He had succeeded. He had braved the loneliness of the lands where no men lived; he had crossed the long emptiness, and seen the marvels. He had found The Cities, whose existence they had all doubted, and been received there with honour. At the end of the terrifying journey he had found unlooked-for friendship, and people who gave the help he asked generously. The world was greater and stranger than he had dreamed, and the Golden

People much less. His faith in Kem'nanh had been fully answered, more than fully; and after it all, he was returning safe. His heart almost cracked with happiness, and he sang as he rode.

The last part of the journey took five days. For four of them he threaded a way round and over the lower slopes of the mountains. On the fourth day, about noon, they came over a crest and saw spreading out northwards, seeming at their very feet, sudden space and smoothness: the Plain at last. He shouted with joy, and Racho neighed. Even the tired ponies pulled on eagerly, sniffing the wind, sweet with the smell of springing grass.

His heart thudded like a lover's as he watched the level land draw closer; the ground flew away beneath them. When the last hillside was a bow-shot behind them, when the grass stretched level all about and they stood once more on the black earth of the land the Gods had given them, Mor'anh dismounted and flung himself to the ground. He spread his arms as if he could embrace the Plain and pressed his face to the grass, weeping with joy. After a while he rose, and prayed to Kem'nanh; then he went on until it was time to make the last of his solitary camps. He slept content that night. When he rose in the morning he opened his gifts, and groomed himself for his return to the Alnei.

Hran had made a watch-place on the hill east of the valley's mouth. From there he could see far over the Plain, north and east, and every possible hour he spent there. He had resolved not to begin looking for Mor'anh too soon. 'After the third moon', he had said, 'begin listening for my horn. It cannot be less than three moons, and it may be more.' And he had replied, 'When winter leans towards spring.' So he had let three complete moons pass, and after the third full moon had let it wane before beginning to watch. Only with the fourth new moon had he begun his vigil. Now he had spent the greater part of thirteen days in his rocky nest, standing leaning on his spear, or crouched out of the wind with his back against the rock. Tonight would be the fourth full moon; spring had begun, and the fourth month nearly ended.

Some of the Alnei had despaired of Mor'anh's return as soon as his confident presence was no longer among them. Others had felt their faith sapped through the winter. Now, as the new grass began to grow, and the young King Horse who had never met the Lord became restless, there were many whose hearts began to fail, and who looked at Hran fearfully, as if some knowledge must come to him. Manui was withering in pale silence. Only the Old Man never doubted, and Hran; Hran would not even speak of hope, declaring it was certainty, and asking which they doubted, Mor'anh's faith or Kem'nanh's power. Yet even he sometimes felt he watched with neither certainty nor hope, only stubbornness.

So he was feeling on this, the fourteenth day of the year's first month. He could see nothing of the smoke-hazed camp from where he stood; only trees and a steep rocky path to his left, with Ranap at the bottom of the slope, to his right an even more precarious path, and before him the Plain and the sky. It was a sunny day; the green of the young grass shone and rippled. But he had watched since daybreak in this windy perch. He was cold to the bone, and near despair. Now the shadows were lengthening again, and turning eastwards.

And then he saw a moving spot out in the green, that separated into eleven specks. Too often he had been deceived by wandering animals; but these seemed to move with purpose. He caught his breath, and even as he shaded his eyes to look again there came faintly the sound of a horn, blowing a call he knew.

Then he gave a great yell of joy. He hurled up his long spear and caught it, and flung it up again whirling in the sun, a wheel of fire; and he saw something flash in answer above the little caravan. The horn sounded again, and raising his own he replied, blowing on and on in wild delight. In the camp they heard, and everyone dropped their work. Then men ran for their horses and boys for their ponies, while others only ran. But Manui

*Then he took the sword that was the Lord's gift
to him, and the mirror that was the Princess's
and whirled them above his head as he rode.*

pressed a hand to her side, grown faint with sudden hope.

Hran came leaping and sliding down the steep path, and the women and children gathered around Ranap needed no answer but his joyous laughter: 'He comes! He comes!' While Mor'anh too laughed for gladness. Then he took the sword that was the Lord's gift to him, and the mirror that was the Princess's and whirled them above his head as he rode.

Thus he came back to the tribe, Mor'anh Lin'harn on a lord of horses riding over the sunlit plain. His robe was edged with glancing silver, as if a light ran round it, and light flashed above his head, glittering and blazing from his hands. For it seemed that he wielded white flame in his left hand and cold fire in his right. He whose name was Spear of Heaven, he seemed armed with the weapons of a god, like Ir'nanh's burning spear itself. Awe silenced them briefly; then a voice cheered, and they shouted,

'Mor'anh! Mor'anh! Ai, the Spear of Heaven! Hai-ai-ai; Mor'anh Mer'inhen, Mor'anh of the Lightnings!'

30

he fire roared exuberantly, an endless skein of red stars streaming from its peak. Sometimes a gust of wind blew one side hollow while smoke and flame belched from the other, making the dancers yelp with laughter and skip out of reach; but that night even a scorching was a joke. They had scoured the woods for this huge Fire of Gathering, and the valley was sweet with woodsmoke.

Mor'anh sat on the Lord's chair, his happiness blazing like the fire. He still wore the silk robe, the silver embroidery looking like trickles of flame. Tomorrow night would be for telling his story, not this riot of gladness. The noise was surely carrying to the next valley. The dancers leapt endlessly about the fire, sometimes a proper chain, more often small groups or solitary men dancing out their exultation. Hran was not among them; the Long Spear did not leave his spear-brother's side. He shone with happiness and relief, even the lack of Nai overwhelmed for one evening.

Mor'anh felt that he was talking ceaselessly, greeting and joking and answering, tumbling out whichever of his recollections lay nearest his tongue, basking in their love. His brilliant eyes were wide, gazing about, renewing his memory of every face. He had not yet spoken to Manui; he had glimpsed her in the crowd when he rode in, but she had not been close enough to reach in the confusion. She had come late to the Fire, and seeing her moving to a place among the women, he had sprung to his feet and called, 'Manui!' She had stood confounded, blushing so that even the firelight could not conceal it, while any reply she might have made had been lost in the Tribe's laughter, as Mor'anh sat hastily, embarrassed himself at so far having forgotten custom. Hran said, laughing, 'Is that City manners?' and he answered lightly, to cover his confusion, 'No. For in the City, unless you are a woman's kinsman, you may not greet her until she has greeted you.' They whooped, and begged to be told more, and his breach of custom was forgotten.

His new title had grown to him already; Mor'anh Mer'inhen, Mor'anh of the Lightnings. When he had left, the Old Man had said that once, going forth a boy, he had returned a man; going forth a man, who could tell how he would return? He had come back in their eyes a demigod at least. Their shadowy history had held no heroes until now, so they could not name what they saw in him. But he was leading them out of the shadows, into the times when men would be named and remembered, and they had given him already the name by which the ages would know him.

Manui loosened her plaits with shaking fingers, and began to comb out her hair. Fresh washed, it sprang out of the braids and slipped away from her combing. She gathered a handful and smelt it, seeking the fragrance of Ralki's herbs; then let it fall, shaking the dark torrent about her shoulders and back.

She should feel happier. He had broken custom to greet her, and when she left the Fire he had caught her eye with a smiling signal he took no pains to hide. She could not understand why she felt nearer tears than laughter. For four months she had lived only for this day, for weeks had dreaded to find the fulfilment of her long hope turned to bitterness after all; and now when fear and doubt were overthrown, she could not rejoice. It had been Ralki who had scolded and bullied her into preparing herself fitly, Ralki who had been sure he would come to her. Manui had felt too much, and it was all turned to pain.

She could hear the happy uproar at the Fire still; he would not leave it yet. She must shake off her daze to greet him as she had dreamed of doing. But even as she formed the thought, the doorflap moved, and he spoke her name.

A small cold breeze blew in with him, stirring the edge of the robe he wore, so that the faint light went flickering along the silver; his left hand rested upon his sword-hilt. The unfamiliar outline made him look a stranger. She rose swiftly, gripping her fingers together, the blood rushing from her face. She tried to speak, but her throat choked the words.

There was a charged silence. 'Manui?' he said again, at last, but there was already a hint of doubt in his voice. She tried again. 'Mor'anh,' she said with an effort; then desperation loosed all the wrong words. 'You have been long away. Was the journey very hard? I had begun to wonder if you would return at all.'

'To wonder?' She saw surprise stiffen his face, and hated herself. He answered, 'Not hard. Only long and lonely; but worth making.' He paused for her to speak, but if she could not find the right words at least she would not say the wrong ones. After a moment he said coolly, 'Has the winter been hard?'

'Hard? Yes, hard,' she almost croaked, knotting her hands in agony. 'Very hard, yes, very hard.'

Had she answered lightly again he would have gone. But he hesitated, and said almost humbly, 'Everyone else welcomes me, Manui. Will you not? I thought you would be glad to see me.'

'Glad?' she cried. 'Glad?' She fled across the floor and cast herself against him, clinging tight. 'Mor'anh, oh, Mor'anh! I thought you would never come back!'

He closed his arms around her, laughing shakily with

relief. 'I did not know—I wondered what had happened—who—Manui; look up—' But she pressed her face into his shoulder, crying incoherently, 'So long—all winter—I could not bear it. So long—and The Cities; and I thought it was for ever; and the cold. I was afraid to wake every morning. All that time, and never knowing—and then to expect words, just like that. And to laugh—after four moons—to laugh!' She shuddered. 'I will laugh, but not yet. I know I am happy, Mor'anh, but I cannot feel it yet.'

He held her closer, shaken with a tenderness that astonished him, and bent his face to her hair. 'Oh, I have missed you, Manui. I have missed you so much. How good your hair smells; I had forgotten. There is so much to say. Look, I have brought you a gift. No, don't look; you can see that later. Look at me: Manui.'

The lamp burned on. Later, when she got up to pick his robe up off the floor and he trimmed the wick, he said, 'They make these of stone . . . they gave me one. You shall see it.' She put her arms into the robe and stirred the folds, and he grinned. 'Oh, yes, you look well in it. Be careful, Manui; the long knife has the sharpest edge I ever felt. Oh, if I talked for a week I could not tell it all . . . How would you like to sleep in a stone bed?'

'It would depend on who else slept there. Mor'anh, that is no way to treat this coat!—'

She stirred cautiously in his arms, turning her head to see his closed eyes and peaceful mouth. But he said, 'Don't move, I'm not asleep,' and she settled again. He sighed. 'Talk to me. Say something.'

'What is the gift you have brought me?'

'You can't see yet, I don't want to move. Say something else.' She pinched him, but he only laughed.

'Were the women in The Cities beautiful?'

'Some of them. Much like other women.' He opened his eyes and grinned at her. 'The Princess, Jatherol: she is very beautiful.' She pinched him again, smiling, until he caught her wrists and wrestled with her gently, then

292

buried his face in her neck. 'But however beautiful they were, they were no comfort to me. Did you miss me, Manui?'

'Have I not told you? Do not make me remember. Every moment I lived was like eating meat without salt . . . Why do you make me say these things?'

'I am sorry. Look, the lamp is flickering. Sit up; let me show you your gift while there is light.'

When he put the mirror into her hands it puzzled her as it had him. 'No, this is how you use it. Hold it there; and it shows you your face. Do you see?'

She did. She looked at her reflection in silence for some time, and she thought of Runi, of the beautiful City-woman, of many others. He knelt there, his eyes expectant, so sure his gift would give her pleasure. Indeed it did, as did the thought that he had not noticed, or did not care. She saw he had not praised her eyes falsely, and her hair was thick and glossy; but for the rest, it was only an ordinary, pleasant face. She turned it over and looked at the decoration before she said, 'It is lovely.' And she did not know whether her painful laughter was blessing him for not knowing, or reproaching him for making her know.

He did not wake until long after the Dawn Drum, not until she had risen and opened a flap of the roof, letting in the sun. As she sat combing her hair, watching him dress, she was struck by the sheen of health on him, so unlike everyone else's winter-weary look. 'They will have been crowding your tent door since sunrise,' she said. But he only laughed and replied, 'Then they should have had more sense.'

She smiled, then looked down to tease a tangle out of her hair. She said softly, 'Will you come here tonight?'

He did not answer. She stood up, furious at her folly, and picked up his robe, shaking and folding it. She offered it to him, but he did not move, only stood looking at her. At last he spoke.

'Manui,' he said. 'Did you know I love you?'

The shock was too great for gladness. It rushed over her, leaving her breath only for a stifled 'No'.

'No. It surprised me too.' He took her face in his hands, gazing at her gravely. She stood as though movement would lose her everything.

'This tent has been a place I sought. But you are right. I should be found in the Lord's tent. I am not the Young Wolf any more. Would it grieve you never to sleep here again?' He looked round regretfully, then back to her. 'Come to my tent, Manui. My tiger-skin is lonely. The Princess sent a silk robe for my woman, and I would choose to see you wearing it. Will you come?'

'Yes,' she said.

Belief came, and joy too great to bear. She felt she saw the world made new, and all the Gods turn smiling faces to her. Her spirit was singing, and out-dancing Ir'nanh; but she only said 'Yes' and stood holding his robe out to him. She gave a sudden amazed laugh, and he smiled.

'Who should have my spear? Your sister's man? Tell him to bring a spear to the Fire tonight. No. I must speak tonight—tomorrow. Come, smile, my pigeon . . .' He stooped and kissed her lightly, then took his robe, picked up his sword, and was gone.

After a moment she sat down weakly. At first she felt regret that the present hour must pass; and then the realisation came, that there would be no more need to prolong such hours. She understood at last that this was only the beginning of happiness; and she feared only that she would not know how to endure such joy.

Runi felt that she could not bear another year like the last. She had endured the winter in an obscure hope that when Mor'anh returned he would have forgotten her offences, and she would be restored to the place she had once held. She would see the hunger back in his eyes, and know that power was hers again. Maybe she would go to the Goddess in the autumn. In the desperation of her loneliness, with only her father and younger brothers and sisters still tolerant of her, she felt she could even find the courage to be a woman.

She could not have spoken to Mor'anh at the Fire; but next day she watched for him. She saw when he went to the horse-herd to greet the new Dha'lev, and saw the path among the trees he took; she loitered there to wait for his return. Walking back deep in thought, he heard a quick surprised sound of pleasure, and looked up.

Runi stood before him, smiling uncertainly. 'Terani!' she said gaily. 'It is good to see you back!'

He inclined his head astonished. 'It is good to be back.' He looked at her coaxing smile, her hopeful eyes, and was strangely reminded of Pheruthal, waiting along garden walks to ambush him with her beauty. Only Pheruthal had never made him feel as Runi did.

He knew that he had never known her. He knew the girl he had loved for more than two years had never existed, that he had created her himself out of his own dreams and Runi's beauty. But the dreams were not yet forgotten, and the beauty was real. He had forgotten how real.

'It—it has been strange—not to see you for so long.' She had never had to find words before, only to accept his homage, or reject it.

'To be strange is not always to be bad. That I have learned again this winter.' He watched unbelieving as she stepped nearer. There was pathos in her attempt at—what? What was she offering? Did she know? What would she do, if he took hold of her? His mind pitied her; but his body did not.

'Oh, it was bad this time, Terani.' But it was not Terani who had courted her. Abandoning the search for words she looked up at him, green eyes glinting. It was a look he had seen a hundred times; and amid the rush of emotions it woke, he thought astounded, 'She means to bend my neck again!'

He drew a breath. 'Well, it is good to see you, Runi. But

I am waited for.' He stepped firmly past her without looking aside; and he had walked some way before he realised he was still holding his breath.

The Khentorei say there are three ways of loving. There is the love of tigers, which is fierce but not deathless; for passion spent, tigers part, and a pair hunted will each escape as it can. There is the love of lions, calmer and nobler than the tiger love, deep and warm; for the lion will fight as his family escapes, and die for them at need. So Mor'anh loved Manui. And last there is the love of leopards, who will fight side by side, or flee together, or perish together, but who will not be parted. For if a leopard is killed, its mate will stay by the body and die sooner than escape alone.

Runi had been Mor'anh's leopardess. Such love can only be given once, and his had been wasted. Runi had proved unworthy of the Lord of the Alnei; but what he had given he could not take back, and she was his leopardess still.

Never had a bride been claimed so. No suitor was ever secret, but Mor'anh threw his spear to Manui at the Fire of Gathering. He rode his caparisoned horse into the circle of firelight and called 'Duranoi!' He had prepared himself with care, and even Hran was moved at sight of him. 'Duranoi! Come forth with your sister Manui!'

The murmur of pleased approval brought a glow to Manui's face as her sister's husband led her out into the space before the fire. She too was in her best, but she had no splendour to match his. The Alnei saw nothing amiss in that; it was fit that a bridegroom should outshine the woman he sought. Mor'anh raised one of his collared spears, and it stabbed the earth between Manui's feet. 'Duranoi, I would be your brother!'

'I have your spear, Terani.'

Mor'anh took up the spear Duranoi threw to him, but he did not then ride away. He circled Manui and her brother, leaned from the saddle, and scooped his bride up before him. With a triumphant yell he sped away into the darkness. The Alnei cheered, and Duranoi, followed by others whose mounts were picketed near, ran for his own horse to pursue them. Mor'anh led them beyond the waggons and three times about the camp and herds, while Manui clung to him laughing in delighted terror, before he rode back to the centre of the camp and lifted her down at his tent door. Hran was there, to tie the curtain after them and keep the door from the bride's kin; but Duranoi and his friends did not contest with him long. Soon the dancing began, and when he had rubbed and picketed Racho, Hran went to lead them in rejoicing.

Mor'anh was resolved to ride to other tribes before the Spring Wandering began, and tell their lords how things had changed among the Alnei. It was possible that the men of Maldé, or other Golden Men, might visit their anger at one tribe on another, and he wished to warn those he could reach. Before the sun was high, he and Hran were riding across the river. Some women were gathered nearby. One called boldly, 'You are out early for a bridegroom, Terani; we thought better of you!' Only Ralki would have dared. He joined their laughter; and another woman answered, but so that he should hear, 'Not early for a father, Ralki; he's going to fetch her the mare's milk.'

'Not yet; you think too well of me, sisters!' he said cheerfully. Then catching the looks they gave each other he drew rein, startled. 'What do you mean?' he said.

Manui was making the Lord's tent her own, so busy she hardly noticed Mor'anh enter, until he spoke. 'Oh! I thought you had gone!' she said, turning; then, 'What is that?'

'Mare's milk.'

She looked up at him. She was trying to look stern, but could not stop the smile. 'Ah, who told you?'

'Some of the women—they thought I knew already.' He was glad they knew he had not. Now no one could think he had taken her to his tent for that reason. 'Why had you not told me?'

'Everything came at once. I wanted to save this last

297

thing, just a day or so.' She took the leather beaker. 'They tell me this is very nasty. Are you angry with me?'

'Angry! At such news! How could I be angry!' He cast himself laughing into his chair. 'Are you pleased, Manui?'

'I have waited so long. I had begun to fear it would never happen. Now I have everything. I am more than pleased.' She raised the beaker, and drunk the strong-tasting milk quickly. 'Vech, it is nastier than they said.'

'When will he be born?'

'He! You are very sure. The Good Goddess may send you a daughter.'

'I hope she will; and when she comes she will be most welcome. But this will be my son. When will he be born?'

'Six moons from now. In the Moon of Storms, about the full moon.'

'The Moon of Storms! When else could my son be born? The son of the lightning-bolt, and born in the Moon of Storms!' He caught her up in his arms. 'My father must have willed it. How does it feel, Manui, to be the mother of Kem'nanh's grandson?'

She leaned her head against his. 'I try not to think of it. But I have waited years to be the mother of your child. That is enough for me; and a greater thing than—than the other, that I do not like to say. What will you call him?'

'I shall call him Ravalsh. Ravalsh, the son of Mor'anh—'

'Ravalsh?' She looked startled. 'Dawn Thunder? But that is a horse's name!'

'It is a man's name from now on. Ravalsh. How will you bear us, my Manui? The Gentle One, to be the woman of the lightning, and the mother of thunder!' He set her down. 'I must go. Hran is waiting, and I must go to the other lords. Ravalsh. Ravalsh. I like it better each time. Say it, Manui: Ravalsh, the son of Mor'anh, the son of Kem'nanh!'

31

here were times when Madol wished he had never taken his Wanderer concubine.

As a houseslave, she had never been very useful; nor had she brought much pleasure to his bed. He had never brought her to willingness, only at best to sullen exhausted submission. And from the beginning she had unsettled his house. The other slaves were afraid of her, while as for Marat—a bastard half-sister was small loss, true, but it had been galling that a foreign slave held such sway over her. He had never been able to humble the girl. She met favours with disdain, and was uncowed by neglect or brutality. There were times when she made even him afraid, and it had been worse since he had exposed her baby. He blamed all his ill-luck on her; the barren cows, the sick bull, the failing crops. He never saw a smile on her face save when news of some misfortune came to him. And it made him furious that she did not conceive. When he had taken the other child from her, he had sworn to get one on her himself, but she had said coldly, 'I shall not let you'. Not could he. All his other bond-women bore children to him, but not the Dark Witch.

He even wondered, now, what beauty he had ever seen in her. Now that he was soon marrying, she would be more trouble than ever. The suggestion that he might sell her back to her tribe he met with derision, though he had thought of killing her. But Kariniol got to hear of that, and sought him out to say that if harm came to the dark girl, then he, Kariniol, would kill Madol and not care for the punishment. Kaniniol had been growing odd, since the business of Black Cloak's capture and escape; so Madol had let the girl live.

But worst were her weird moods. They came often, but were most disturbing at the first full moon each autumn. Then she seemed crazed. The second time he had locked her in an outhouse, but she had got out, and roused his neighbours with her singing, while her dancing was still a by-word for indecency with those who had seen it. He had dragged her to his bed, and that had been the only time he had got any great pleasure with her. But when he spoke of it she had stared stonily and said, 'Not me. It was the Goddess.'

Now this winter past had been worst of all. She had sunk for hours at a time into a delirium of terror, wailing softly in her own tongue saying, a half-caste slave said, that she was lonely, that he was gone, so far; lost, lost, lost; until even he began to recognise some words. He half hoped she would die, but feared the ghost she would make. It unnerved him. Such grief and horror could not be in a house and not bring ill-luck upon it.

Her strength had returned with spring, but she was not less disturbing. A month had brought her from despair to a fierce elation, as frightening as the worst of her frenzies. He would hear her singing to herself at times, a soft happy sound that froze his heart. There was a jauntiness about her that he felt bode him ill. Worst of all, she spoke prophecies now in their language. Once he saw her gazing raptly at the rafters, and she said, 'This roof will let snow when winter comes again.' She walked more lightly, and looked at those who treated her ill more mockingly; she stopped among the sowers one day and said merrily, 'Why sow that the horses will eat?'; and once when in a rage he whipped her and chained her in the logshed she only laughed and said, 'Yes, you can shut me up now, but wait for the lightning. When all the walls are down, what will keep me in?' Mostly she simply watched them, with closed mouth and secret eyes, the air of one who means, 'It would be better for you if you knew what I know,' but will not tell. A servant asked her why she spoke her warnings since no one believed them; she answered gaily, 'But I like them not to believe me.' When Madol heard that, it scared him.

But she prophesied no more, after a certain day. Standing at the well with other women she stiffened, her eyes fixing; she cried out as if astonished with gladness, and called aloud,

'Listen: listen: do you feel the air? A wind is coming. Can you not hear it? A great wind, a great wind! A wind is coming: and those with roofs must make ready to see them torn off!'

When the second moon of the year was new, in the fifth day of New Grass, the Alnei followed their King into the Plain. Mor'anh rode Racho at the head of the column now, not cantering with the young men about the King Horse. This Dha'lev was still almost a stranger to him, a young horse, broadbacked, all black, save for his forelock and the feathering of one hoof. There had been times when Mor'anh had wondered what would happen if the Dha'lev led them to pitch their tents near Golden Men who were strangers. But when Hran asked him the same question he laughed. 'The God leads the Dha'lev. He knows what he means us to do. If it happened, we should refuse tribute, I suppose. But it will not happen.'

'Can you be sure?'

'As sure as if I rode the Dha'lev myself and knew where to guide him. Why would Kem'nanh lie to me? The Alnei, and the men of Maldé; we are like cats and serpents, enemies fated for each other.'

The gifts from the City were laid away now, or as familiar as Mor'anh's necklace of silver chains and rough emeralds, or his flower lamp. All the Alnei could describe

301

by now everything their lord had seen there, though Mor'anh often wondered if he had been able to give anyone a true picture of Jemaluth. The only thing he had shown only to Hran and Manui was the shell which held the sea-sound.

But the swords were in constant use. Day after day the tribesmen laboured to make themselves swordsmen, and Mor'anh strove to pass on what he had learned. Most became moderately skilled, some would never learn the use of it, and some, like Hran, seemed to know without learning, as if they only needed to remember artistry laid aside for a time. Hran especially had a judgement, a grace, and a deadly deftness, that would in time make him a swordsman the equal of Yo-Pheril. Mor'anh, watching his spear-brother admiring and appalled, soon left the teaching to him. When they had learned the use of the weapon they had to learn to fight with it on horseback, and there they could only teach each other; the City-men had had no advice to give. They had to teach their horses not to fear the clashing metal and the blades flashing about their heads; but the skill must be learned first, or an injured horse would learn the wrong lesson, and far worse, and would have his faith in his friend and rider shaken. Seeing the work to be done, Mor'anh prayed to Kem'nanh not to bring them to their enemies too soon.

Spring warmed into summer. The Moon of the Young Lord passed, and Mor'anh had been Lord of the Alnei for a year. The boys were sent out into the Plain, and Mor'anh, blessing them as they left, promised they should return to a better tribe in the autumn. For a little while their mothers stifled anxious weeping, then looking at the swords blinking on the practice-ground, feared for their men instead.

The first time that the God had possessed him after revealing himself, Mor'anh had been astonished with delight, for Kem'nanh had come as gently as a father touches his sleeping child. Now he never struggled against him, but watched for the God's sign eagerly, the possession did not rack him in coming. He felt the Lord of Herds always near, a presence at his right hand as Hran was at his left. The feeling was so strong that when a man rode to his right side it made his hair rise. Even in their bed, Manui must sleep at his left.

The Moon of Sheep Shearing came. For days, everyone laboured among the flocks. Mor'anh, working with Hran, set the struggling sheep he held back on its feet and released it, while Hran scooped up the stinking fleece and added it to the pile for the children to carry to the women at the river. Rubbing his brow on his arm, Mor'anh watched the sheep, who had ceased staggering away and grown calm, and was now beginning to realise that it was free of its wool.

'The fleeces are heavy this year,' said Hran. 'They are all saying that everything prospers now you are Lord.'

'In summer that is easily thought. Let them say it next year, and I shall be glad.' The sheep, lightened and cool, gave a hesitant skip, and he grinned. 'Look; she thought she had forgotten that trick . . . no more today. Let us go to the river.'

At sheep-shearing, there were so many eager to bathe away the wool-oil at the end of the day that it became like another Gathering, all sport and laughter. But they could not linger; sword-practice must go on. Hran, indeed, had no wish to delay it. As they walked he drew his sword and began sporting with it, making it whoop through the air, carving hot brightness. Mor'anh drew back and watched with perplexed wonder. He wondered if Hran had thought at all of the purpose of his new art, or if, as with dancing, he was simply delighted by the harmony of movement. Mor'anh, though better than most, would never excel, simply because he did not like swords. He could see the beauty of his, could admire the craft that made it, catch his breath at the brave show of its flashing blade, but the more beautiful it seemed, the more it appalled him. He had strength, control, judgement; he lacked nothing of mastery except delight in his work. He had always loved supremacy, and sought to excel in all he did, but in this, he resisted his skill.

Manui bloomed. Pregnancy, or happiness, suited her. Her face smoothed, and her lovely eyes glowed: she had never been nearer to beauty. She remembered how Ralki had been irked by her lessening agility, and laughed at her; she herself seemed to grow more graceful, not less, and walked now with confident gaiety. She never doubted she would bear Mor'anh the son he wished for. Once he grew half repentant, and asked if she wished for a girl, but she laughed at him.

'Whatever you or I wish for, it means nothing. The Goddess gives as she chooses. Son or daughter, I do not mind. But no doubt the Mother will listen to Kem'nanh, if he wishes you to have a son.

'It is not that I would not welcome a daughter. I shall. I want a little girl, but—'

'—but all men want to see their sons. I know.' She was making a sling to carry the child in, and paused as she pulled some stitches tight. 'Yet you will have to wait for your desire. When you say "my son" you see him grown and taking his spears from you, while I see a small boy; and when you speak of a daughter, you mean as you said, a little girl, while I think of my daughter as a young woman.' He grinned, admitting the truth of it. 'You lose your girls, and we our boys, when they grow.'

The Moon of Long Days waxed, and Manui's time drew near. The Dha'lev cried to them to follow him again, and they broke camp. They had been deep in the Plain; now he led them west. Mor'anh rode before the Tribe with a thudding heart, tense and silent. Wherever they pitched camp now, Ravalsh would be born there.

The King Horse hesitated twice, investigating sites, but each time he went on as if lashed, always west. They crossed two rivers, and once had to rope and picket the Dha'lev while the long column closed to a length the men could protect. At last they could see the horizon broken by the mountains. When they drew near, the great stallion slowed, smelling the air, hesitating for guidance, until he turned and trotted north-west. Even he was tiring, and glad when the God left his back, and let him rest.

They had not come to the same campsite. They had approached from the south this time; the low contours were not the same, and they were the other side of the river. But they all knew the shape of the mountains now. They pitched camp first, and only at sunset rode out; and then they saw it. Maldé, with the smoke hanging above it, and the sun's last light burning orange on the pale thatch of its roofs.

32

f there had been anyone who still doubted that Kem'nanh willed this end, he did so no longer. It was certain they they were doomed to finish the struggle where it had begun; with Maldé. Now the hunting cat was couched, and waiting for the serpent.

For this Mor'anh called no Council, but gave commands. They were not to ride too near the Golden People's border, or offer any discourtesy; but they were to let themselves be seen, and not hide which way the camp lay. If the Kalnat came, they would be civilly received. 'What the Gods will shall be done,' he said, 'but let them walk open-eyed to their fate. We shall not lead them there, nor tempt them, nor trick them.'

Hran was surprised and a little disturbed. He thought of the saffron silk robe lying waiting: what of Nai? But Mor'anh was unshaken. 'It is in the Gods' hands. But it must be their doing, not ours.'

Two tribes had camped near Maldé that year, and each yielded tribute. The Kalnat thought the world restored to its proper order, and did not hesitate to send to the third tribe.

When the embassy came, Mor'anh had not long returned from the hunt, and was working over the kill. He did not go out; the herdmasters received the demands, and the embassy departed. The Alnei watched Mor'anh expectantly, but he gave no orders. He was told that tribute was asked, and laughed, and did nothing.

Vani was frail; the nights belonged to baleful Hega. Four days after the tribute should have been rendered, Maldé sent again. A small embassy: one young man attended by two servants. He was haughty and curt, demanding to see the Lord. Mor'anh received him before his tent, making no effort for splendour; but it was plain the young man did not recognise him. He delivered his rebuke, and demanded swift obedience, with heavier tribute for a penalty. He had dressed to impress. Mor'anh gazed while he spoke at the finery which once would have awed him, and smiled in his heart. When the Golden Man had finished, Mor'anh replied mildly, 'We heard your demands, and understood them. But we do not give tribute.'

The Golden Man stared at him unbelievingly. 'What did you say?'

'We do not give tribute.'

His face grew crimson, and the servants boggled. He began to remonstrate, but not delivering his considered speech and so amazed, he could not find words of authority. Mor'anh listened calmly until he had done, then said, 'You have brought your message and we have heard it. Now you have an answer to take back. We give no tribute.'

The Golden Man departed clutching at his dignity, but Mor'anh's eye kept them from laughter till he had gone. Then he said, 'Put a watch on the way from Maldé. We will receive the next more fittingly.'

Shocked and furious, Maldé made the embassy to this insolent tribe the day's first business. The morning was only half gone when the scout came to say that the ox-cart was on its way; and all work ceased.

When the Kalnat came to the waggon circle and blew their imperious summons, no crowd gathered. Only two men appeared to greet them with great courtesy and asked them to enter the camp. They refused, and demanded that the Lord come out to them; but the tribesmen, though very polite, were immovable. At last, already ruffled, they climbed down from their wain and followed them.

The tents were very quiet. They soon saw the reason when they came to the open place at the centre. All the Tribe must have been massed there. The two men led them forward, then left them.

Mor'anh faced them, mounted on Racho. The banner of the Alnei was planted at his right; to his left stood Hran and Diveru. The Kalnat knew then what tribe it was, when they saw the spears on which those two leaned; and they knew Mor'anh too, even without his black cloak. Their leader began to speak at once.

'What is this folly? Why have you ignored our demands and slighted our messenger? Beware. You have roused our anger against you. Where is the tribute due to us? No Wanderers have ever escaped tribute, and no other tribe refuses it now. Have the Gods made this tribe mad? If you are the Lord, explain! Obey us now, and there still may be mercy for you. The tribute is doubled, for your disobedience; but maybe nothing worse will befall you, if you obey now, and beg our pardon.'

'Nothing half so bad shall befall us,' said Mor'anh quietly. 'I greet you, Haniol. It is long since we spoke together. But it seems your last messenger did not speak as I told him to. We told him plainly, that we would give no tribute.'

'As you *told* him to—!' The Kalnat stared, almost too amazed for anger. They had none of them ever talked to a Khentor who was facing them on his high horse; they had to look up to his face, and their composure was shaken. The Tribe was silent, and the two men by the Lord gazed at them calmly.

'Without doubt Akrol wishes you to be destroyed!' Haniol gathered his wits. 'You will give no tribute? Have you forgotten who we are? What are you, to deny us our due? No, it is plain now; Akrol remembers your past crimes, and has driven you mad, so that you will be destroyed!'

'We will not be destroyed. Certainly a God has done this, but we are not mad. We see clearly now. You ask who we are? I shall tell you. We are the Horse People, the children of Kem'nanh, and he has opened our eyes. We will give no more tribute, because he has forbidden it.' Suddenly he smiled, but without softening his eyes. 'Let us say we have forgotten who you are. We will begin again. We will live in peace; we do not want what you have.' The Golden Ones listened dumbfounded. 'We might even live in friendship. But always,' he said, 'always, now, as equals.'

They sucked in their breath, and let it out in shouts. 'Equals!' cried Haniol, 'Equals! No other tribe speaks so!'

'They too will grow wise.'

'No other lord has ever so insulted us. Your old lord would not have done so!'

'True! He would not. But you killed my father!'

His eyes blazed at them; the spokesman fell back a little and as he did so Madol pushed out to the front. He drew his head down into his shoulders, hissing.

'Cattle-driving savage! Dung-eating barbarian! Equals? You should be grateful we come to show you what men are who live in houses! How dare you speak to us so!'

Mor'anh moved. Madol's face flinched, and he stepped back. But the Lord only raised a hand. No one stirred. Mor'anh's burning eyes did not waver from Madol's face, and the Kalnat stared mesmerised. The Khentor reached behind him, and shrugged a robe to his shoulders, clasping a belt of silver about his waist. Still his eyes did not flicker. Madol was white. At last Mor'anh spoke.

'I am Mor'anh of the Lightnings, Lord of the Alnei, Kem'nanh's chosen Tribe. Who is this talks of barbarians?' The Kalnat men stared appalled at his robe, his baldric, the rings, the necklace of emerald and silver. His wrath seemed to make him rise taller.

309

'Listen to me, Yellow Dogs! I have seen a city like a mountain. I have met a people who cut stone like cheese and make water dance for their pleasure. I have talked with lords and ladies who never carry any weight greater than the weight of the ornaments they wear, whose skin is fine as new petals even on their fingertips. They wear cloth that is like water, and the air is made sweet for them to breathe. I have walked under the shade of stone trees with those who stalk truth in the City of the Wise, and feasted with Princes who wear jewels as the morning grass wears dew. I saw Golden Men in this city; but they were servants who stood at the doors, or carried their masters where they wished to go. I have been the guest of a lord whose house would cover all Maldé, whose gardens grew the length of twenty spears above the earth. And this great Lord calls me his friend and equal, and names me as Prince of the Plains. I have learned the ways of men who live in houses; shall I tell you of them? Shall I now be awed at your wooden huts? When you have learned to pave your streets, when you have learned to make water come where you bid it, then come again to call me savage!'

He had scattered foreign words among his speech, but its meaning was clear enough. The Alnei stirred excitedly; the Kalnat drew together, pale with shock and anger. After a silence Mor'anh said, his voice calm again, 'Do you understand yet? You have taken your last woman from the Alnei; your last cow, your last sheep, your last hide. Must I tell you again? We will give no more tribute!'

Then at last they understood that they were ten men in the camp of their enemies. They turned to go, but Haniol said, 'We will return, Black Cloak. We will come with anger and strength, and what you will not give we shall take, tenfold and more!'

But Mor'anh answered only, 'You may come; but what you take is with the Gods.'

The Moon of Storms was three days old when the last envoys came. Mor'anh laughed, thinking he should have guessed that they would meet then, and began to take thought for what lay ahead.

He counted the roofs of Maldé, and even reckoning two fighting men for every house, it did not seem many; he changed two to three, and still the number was fewer than the men of the Alnei. Then on the fifth day of the moon the men he had set to watch the town began to tell of men going out north and south, and west into the mountains, who did not return by sunset.

After two more days, men began coming to the town carrying weapons. Most came in small groups or singly, but two larger forces, each between twenty and thirty, came from north and south.

Soon they saw men out every day on the level ground before the town, exercising. They saw them practising with swords and shields and spears, but no one used arrows, or ever threw a spear. It seemed the Golden Men's way of fighting was for two lines of men to run at each other with spears held shoulder-high, then to fight hand to hand with spears or swords. However, it seemed they realised this would not serve against Khentorei. After the first day they began manoeuvring in a new way, forming a close line of shields and slanting their grounded spears to make a line of bronze for the horses to run against.

The Alnei had made the last of their preparations. Every man made a pectoral of thick hide to guard his horse's breast. Some also made shields for their throats, but these irked the davlenei, and few would endure them. The men covered the horses' pectorals with adornments, but no one bothered to make armour for himself. Horn-blower knew every man's hour. No one could live beyond it, or die if it had not come.

Mor'anh watched the exercising Kalnat every day, and it still did not seem to him that the Golden Men took tribesmen seriously as enemies. The only sign that they had given real thought to the task before them was the spear-wall. His first sight of that had made him grimace, though he believed he found a way to weaken it. Yet the

311

Golden Men practised that less than anything, as if they hardly expected to use it. Mor'anh wondered if they believed that it would come to a meeting of spears.

Two days after the full moon the scouts of the first watch sent a boy to bring the Lord out. He came, and the man who gave place to him at the top of the slope said as he crawled down, 'It seems plain what it means; but we thought you should see.'

The army of Maldé was drawn up before the town. Mor'anh had to admit that it was an impressive sight. The long front rank of men with polished breastplates and helmets hid the less well equipped men behind; when the flashing spears were raised above their heads, they were like a meadow of bronze. Some of their old splendour had returned to them. Fighting was to them the finest art, the highest pitch of life. The Kalnat had ever thought war a nobler state than peace. They looked in that hour as men look who are doing the thing in which they take most pride. When a man in a long blue robe walked through their lines, and they lifted the helmets from their golden hair, even Mor'anh was moved once more by the beauty of the sight.

The blue-robed man walked to a small platform of stone, and began to perform some ceremony. He killed two birds, and smoke rose from the stones. He began a prayer; but before he ended it, Mor'anh felt the air grow cool, and the brightness was blotted from the armour as a cloud hid the sun. Far off, thunder growled faintly, and the long lines stirred. The priest turned and spoke for a while, seeming to try to diminish the omen; the White Wolf grinned. Then the men began to come forward, each pausing before the priest. Mor'anh slithered back down the slope.

'They are ready, then. We too must prepare.'

33

or'anh would have kept watch all night, not once as the other men, except that he would not have it thought that unease kept him from sleep. Now in the third watch he walked from sentry to sentry, greeting them softly and looking into the darkness. The night was like an unlit tent. Heavy cloud covered the stars and moons, and there was no wind. The air was still, save for the drums. They never fell silent for long. The darkness throbbed with them. The tribesmen slept, untroubled by the music that had lulled their infancy, but Mor'anh hoped that the men of Maldé found less ease. There must be many who lay wakeful, thinking of the bad omen and hoping for better luck with a new sun. Surely the pounding in the night must shake their rest and sap their courage.

He had led the men away from the te⌐.ʊ, towards the Golden People's border. They would ɯeet them as they came from Maldé, not where the battle could endanger the herds and the tents. He had not truly known what this meeting of spears risked, until he had parted from Manui; then fear of what could happen if the Golden Ones overcame them gripped him. She had given him a smiling farewell. 'And you may find a slenderer woman when you return,' she said, 'I think he has chosen his day with care.' Now he longed to know how things were with

her. Maybe she had gone already into the circle of women's tents. The camp was near, but many men would
have liked to speak again to their women, and he could
not be the only one to go.

The stars were hidden, but behind the clouds the night
turned on, and Mor'anh lay down to sleep. The drums
throbbed. Among the tents they could be heard; the boy
who had come to mount the Dawn Watch kept looking
west to the sound of them. In the heart of the camp, the
Lord's tent stood empty. By the waggons Runi saddled
Vixen. Ralki rose from her bed again, but her daughter
slept contentedly, and she knelt down idle. In Maldé, in
her hiding-place, Nai lay wakeful, listening to the drums.
'Hran,' she said softly. She pressed her hand against the
wooden wall, and laughed gently.

The men keeping watch heard the Dawn Salute sounding from the camp as they went to wake their comrades.
Mor'anh stood up smiling. He rubbed his face with dew
to freshen it, then pointing to the east laughed aloud.
'See!' he cried. 'Their sun does not shine on them this
morning, either!'

They ate and drank. Though sunrise showed dimly,
the cloud hung still and the day was slow to lighten. The
air was warm and heavy.

The men gathered, checking their weapons, caressing
their horses. They had all come proudly decked in all
their ornaments. Mor'anh walked among them, making
sure that every man was certain of his task, cheering
them with his gay confidence. He had put the best fight-
ers in the front rank, and behind them, in case they were
to face the line of spears, the swiftest and most accurate
archers. Soon a scout came to say that the gate of Maldé
had opened, and they mounted. They walked forward,
over one crest and a second, and then saw the Golden
Men.

There were no more hills between them, only a long
slope. The Kalnat stood on a level place within their
border, but many bow-shots from their town. They had
not thought to meet their enemies so soon, nor to see

them so formidably prepared; they were intending a punitive raid, not a battle. Un-nerved, they grounded their spears and made their line almost where they stood.

But the Khentors did not charge. They drew rein and sat gazing at Mor'anh, and he looked round, impassive and considering, as if interested chiefly in the sky. Then he rode Racho out from the line, and turned to face into the Plain.

'Kem'nanh!' The heavy air dulled but could not stifle the invocation. 'Lord of the Wind! You told me that you would put the wind into my hand! Give it to me now! Father! Give me the wind!'

For a moment there was utter stillness. Then it seemed the earth sighed; a cool air breathed upwards. The grass shivered, and the manes of the davlenei flickered. It breathed again, more strongly. Mor'anh stretched out his hands before him, then drew them slowly in; and the wind came with them.

The heavy cloud stirred, and began to roll. The strengthening air pushed at their backs and rushed down at the Golden Ones. The Kalnat reproached Akrol bitterly, remembering how their own plea for an omen had been answered. Mor'anh gave a shout of triumph, and wheeled back into his place. 'Alnei! The Wild Rider goes with us! Now!'

They surged down the slope, gathering speed. Mor'anh blew his horn, and they began to canter; they were within three bow-shots of the Golden Men. The wind bore them on. The space lessened; the Kalnat gripped their spears. At Mor'anh's shout the front rank of horsemen opened, letting the archers through. They had arrows ready aimed; they loosed, and the arrows sang among the Golden Men. A man stood up shouting and fell down; the second flight came while the men hit by the first were still gaping, and the third fell as swiftly. Already the spear-line was gapped. The archers fell back and the spearmen, their line already looping to drive hardest at the gaps, gripped their shafts hard against their sides. Mor'anh cried 'Harai! Harai Alnei! Hai-ai-

ai-ai-!' He urged Racho to a gallop, and the charge became an ecstasy of speed, with fear out-distanced and
scattered by the wind. There was a whipping of air, all
but lost in the clamour, as the archers sent another flight
high over their heads; and then the two lines met.

Mor'anh and Hran found that Kalnat breastplates were
not proof against Kalnat spears with the weight of a
charging horse behind them. The men they struck fell,
any cry they gave lost in the rising noise. Mor'anh
stopped for the spear planted by the man he had killed,
and others took the idea, snatching up the spears of fallen
men. The palisade had broken, but the charge went on,
surging over lines of Golden Men, slowing as it did so,
until the forces were mingled and grappling.

The men of Maldé had not fought many pitched battles, and never against an enemy they could not meet foot
to foot. They knew how to fight men who fought as they
did, but not how to resist such weight. They had to learn
anew as they fought. But they were brave men, and
stubborn, and they could not believe in failure. They
clamped their shields to their breasts, drew their swords,
and fought grimly.

Mor'anh almost forgot to draw his sword. He was wild
with exultation. He hardly knew he was in a battle and
men were dying, only that his people were about him
shouting his name, and that his God was filling him. His
spears gone, he rode unarmed long enough to have died a
dozen times; but he seemed to the men behind him
invulnerable, clothed in a glory that turned back bronze.
'Harai!' he shouted, and drew his sword; and they
pressed after him crying 'Harai! Mor'anh Mer'inhen!'

During the forward thrust someone yelled at him 'The
banyei!' and snatching a glance back he saw black hair
tossing; but there was nothing he could do. They pressed
on until they had passed right through the Kalnat army.
They turned, and paused for a moment; then they thrust
back into the battle.

Mor'anh, wielding his sword ruthlessly, was aware of
a horrible happiness. He smelled blood, and heard men

screaming with pain, and knew that Racho was trampling them as he pressed forward; he saw things that at any other time would have appalled him, and he laughed. Hran was fighting like a man enraptured, who sees one thing and presses towards it no matter what stands between. The Golden Ones held rank no longer. They were spreading far over the grass, fighting in tight out-facing groups. Hran saw where Madol stood in one such group, and rode towards them with a glad cry. Mor'anh followed, but a lone Kalnat came rushing at him, so he was too occupied to see how his spear-brother fared. He only heard Hran's shout as he wheeled away; and before he knew more, the noise of the battle changed its tone, and the Golden Ones were in flight.

The Khentors shouted exultantly, and plunged into pursuit, but Mor'anh sounded his horn, calling them back. Though some turned reluctantly they came, following him a little aside from the ground they had fought over, where lay a third of Maldé's army. It seemed marvellous to Mor'anh that so many should have come unscathed through such red chaos; more marvellous that so few Alnei lay among the fallen. Surely, now, he thought, they would know they could no longer treat the Horse People as herds; now they would call for an end to the fighting. Then Hran shouted 'Look!' and seized his arm, and he turned to look across the fields to Maldé, and grew still with astonishment.

The Master and other elders had watched the fight from the gate-house. It had taken them some time to believe what they saw, but when they understood they lost no time. All Kalnat knew what befell a town which lost a battle. None of them remembered that the Alnei did not know, and would have had no thought of a sack. The townsfolk were beginning to flee to the refuge of the mountains before the men broke. When Mor'anh looked, the gate and the road beyond were crowded with women and children, old people, and cattle. Out of sight, many more streamed from smaller gates, to take rougher but shorter paths.

Mor'anh, wielding his sword ruthlessly,
was aware of a horrible happiness.

The soldiers saw too, and realised that indeed there could have been no hope of out-distancing horsemen to the town and barring the gate. Their people had no more reliance on their protection, and the storm-wind battered as them in reminder that Akrol had given them out of his hand. Yet as they looked at the straggling helpless column of those who fled, pride filled some and battle-rage others, while many were driven by love alone; and they turned and re-formed their ranks. They dared not wait to face another charge. Those who still had spears balanced them at their shoulders, and raising the war-shout they ran forward, at the moment when Mor'anh, staring at the townsfolk, suddenly shouted 'Nai!'

At his side Hran took it up like a battle-cry. The dreadful exhilaration rose in Mor'anh once more. He did not know why the people fled, he did not know why the Kalnat chose to die when they might have lived, but he knew that under the strokes of his sword were falling his long-hated enemies, and that within sight the town lay open that had held his sister captive. He would have taken her peacefully, if they had so consented, but there was more gladness in winning her back so. He would have spared the Golden Men, if they had asked mercy; but if they preferred to die, he would give them their wish. In the sun that pierced the storm-gapped cloud, the lightning of his grey sword flashed and fell.

When they broke a second time, he did not call the tribesmen back. Thrusting unheeding through the rout, he and Hran rode stirrup to stirrup to Maldé. The last of the fugitives screamed as they rode up, some turning back, others struggling forward. The plainsmen reined in instinctively; but while Mor'anh stopped, Hran leapt to the ground and ran into the town.

Mor'anh stood still. The frenzy was fading, his mind growing clear again. He looked at the pitiful cavalcade, the sobbing children and haggard women. 'Where are you going? Why?' he cried. 'We will not hurt you!' But they did not heed him, or stared in baffled, appalled terror. Glancing down he saw that he still held his sword;

he moved to sheathe it, but it was so bloodied he did not like to do so. He turned Racho, and looked back. The Alnei had shattered the last semblance of a line, and all resistance. They were hunting the Golden Men, harrying them as they fled. All Mor'anh's fury was gone, and energy was draining out of him. He watched the fleeing men still trying to draw the Khentors away from their families. Pity overcame him, and desolation. He let his sword fall to the ground, and raising his horn blew the call for the end of the hunt. Come away; let them be; enough.

They turned from their quarry, not sorry to do so. He watched them as they dismounted and began moving among the fallen, seeking their own; soon he saw them begin to carry aside the wounded, while others caught and led away the riderless horses. 'And the Golden Ones. Look to them too,' he whispered. He felt terribly weary. Soon he must go down to join their labour.

His mind shaped faces he feared he had seen lying there, whom he dreaded to see again with certain knowledge. Yet it must be borne. Some Kalnat women who could no longer be restrained by their fear had broken from the column and were running down to the battlefield. Someone should go to bring Lal'hadai and the women. Mor'anh moved; but as he did so the air about him thickened, making Ranap and Racho toss their heads snorting; and above, Kalnat pausing on a mountain shoulder to look back at their home, raised a keening cry.

In after days the Kalnat said, and many believed, that the Khentors had burned the town; but it was not true. They, who fear fire running free above all perils, would never have done so. Some spilled lamp or abandoned kitchen fire had begun it, and now the wind, channelled by the narrow streets, was fanning it strongly. As Mor'anh turned, a fresh twist of the wind brought a wave of smoke rolling over the wall above him, and billowing in the gate. He heard the crisp sound of burning. 'Nai!' he shouted with alarm, 'Hran!' Springing to the ground, he ran through the smoke into Maldé.

Once through the smother by the gate it was not so bad, but flames were running along eaves and leaping between thatched roofs. Every moment there was less smoke and more flame. For a heart-beat Mor'anh paused; the Khentor's fear of fire is deep, a fear of the blood, not the mind. Then he ran forward again, calling for his sister and his friend.

Abandoned chickens and stray dogs squawked and yelped in the main street, and rats and mice scampered about his feet. The heat was growing, and wind-caught sparks stung him. He could see neither Hran nor Nai along the wide street, and the thought of entering the narrow side streets filled him with horror. Then he heard Hran's voice, and glimpsed him along an alley, casting about and calling Nai! Nai! Mor'anh was about to go to him, when behind him he heard another voice. Hran turned with a shout, plunging through the flames. Further along the main street a smaller figure appeared, darting through the smoke, springing over piles of burning straw. Mor'anh started eagerly; then stood still, to let them meet. A house blossomed suddenly with fire; and against its light he saw his sister run laughing to her lover's arms.

34

y noon the wind had slackened, and the only clouds were streaming like white banners in the bright sky. The mountain paths were almost empty. The smoke from burning Maldé was thin, and the flames among the blackened walls pale in the sun.

Mor'anh stood within the door of his tent. Outside were the sounds of rejoicing, but his grazed heart was grateful for the dim quiet. He had left to Hran the triumph of bearing Nai back to the Alnei, a living emblem of victory. The first celebration had seemed to belong more fitly to them, with their unshadowed gladness. The tumult of his heart was too great for him to rejoice so soon, nor could he ride away from the hurt and the dying. But now they were all back in the camp.

He thought at first that Manui was not there, since she did not greet him. Then he became aware of her soft breathing, and saw her sleeping in their bed. She lay straight and slim, and by the bed stood a cradle.

He lit the flower lamp and looked down on her; and a gulf of sorrow opened in his heart. She was his woman, the one he had chosen, the wife he loved. Why did it still matter what she was not? It was a betrayal, to look on her sleep and feel such grief. He knelt and touched her hand, shamed by his treachery. Where could he have found a better woman? Free to choose, he had chosen her, who had no equal; his comfort and strength, the lover he delighted in, the friend he trusted. There was nothing to regret. Nothing: save that his will had no power over his longing.

He turned to the cradle half reluctant, afraid that after all he would not be able to feel the gladness so long prepared; then he saw the child in its nest of fleeces, and his heart grew still. It moved its dark head against the creamy wool, small limbs thrusting against the softness, and gave a grunting cry of effort; and joy broke through him.

Gently, he gathered the top fleece around him and lifted him out of his cradle, sitting back on the edge of the bed. 'Ravalsh!' he said softly. His son. He gazed at the baby, dizzy with rapture. He had thought so much about this moment that it was strange to find himself so unprepared. But the child he had imagined had never been more than the echo of this reality, never half so alive. He brimmed with delight, gazing absorbed and fascinated. He had expected the creased face, the strangely wizened body, but not that these should proclaim such lusty health. Nor had he been prepared for the energy of his jerky uncertain movements, the fierceness of his small cries, the force of will in the tiny body he held on his hands. This was a person, a stranger. He was meeting his son.

He touched a finger against the baby's cheek, and laughed to see how quickly he turned his head to snatch with greedy working mouth. He wished he would open his eyes. He smoothed his hand over the dark hair, entranced and terrified at the softness of the head beneath, feeling the downy delicacy against his palm. The child's arms moved as though he were fighting, his hands clenched into fists; his feet rubbed past each other, heels kicking into his father's thigh. Mor'anh was amazed again at the vitality in the tiny frame; that something so frail could be so fierce! The strong grip of his

324

fingers, though proverbial, was still astonishing. Then the child gave a gasp and a shiver, and woke. The flailing of his limbs ceased, and he opened his eyes.

For the first time Mor'anh met the eyes of his son. 'Ravalsh' he greeted him; the baby blinked. He gazed up at his father with a look of calm wonder. Mor'anh was enchanted, and then suddenly overwhelmed with fear. He cradled Ravalsh in the crook of his arm, and looking down into those hazy eyes he knew for the first time all that fear could be. He had been afraid before, but the danger past the fear had been forgotten. Now he must feel it always, the dread that is the penalty of love, the aching to protect what cannot always be protected. He had put the life of his heart into another's keeping, and he was invulnerable no more.

He became aware of a change in Manui's breathing, and looked up at her, smiling. She said, 'You have found him.' He looked down again. The baby was twisting his head, his lips pursed. 'He is sneering at me,' said Mor'anh, and she laughed faintly. The charmed stillness was broken, and the world came crowding back. He thought of all that had changed since he parted from Manui; but he said only, 'We have brought Nai back.'

She sighed with gladness. 'And the Golden People?'

'They have run away . . . most of them.'

His throat tightened. Walking on the battlefield he had heard his name spoken. It was Kariniol. He was dying; there was nothing to be done. Mor'anh had knelt and spoken to him; the Golden Man had looked at him, then his eyes had wandered away. 'Mor'anh,' he said again. He had nothing to say, nothing to ask. He had only wanted someone to recognise him, and to hear his name spoken once more before he died. Mor'anh shook his head, and said, 'Their place is burning.'

'What did Nai say?'

'She laughed more than she talked. She will be here. When she knows you are awake, she will come.' What his re-union with his sister meant to him he could share with

325

no one, not Hran, not Manui. 'All things go well for our son. He will be laid in the lap of the Mother by her Har'enh. When was he born?'

'Not at dawn. I hoped he would be, and thought it for a while. Kani told me I shouted with anger when the salute came, and he did not. But soon after, when the storm began, then he was born.'

'That was when we rode at them . . . Kem'nanh gave it to me. I called on the wind, and it came; and we knew then that the Golden Ones were already thrown down.' He lifted his child up before his face. 'When you were born, it was dawn for us indeed, Dawn Thunder. I hear the sound of the hooves in your name. My son, you are the first of our people to be born out of their shadow!'

After a while he said, 'When the fighting was over none of us knew what to do. I felt I wanted to ride after the Golden Ones and say, "What happens now?" ' He had never thought that they would run away. Nor had any of the plainsmen. Already Mor'anh was aware of a new feeling among them; astonishment and bitterness, as if they had been betrayed. They had dared to defy the might of the Golden People and to strike at their sanctity, to assail the shrine before which their feet had halted for so long, and they had found the shrine was empty, had always been empty. Where they had dreaded, they now scorned. They might have forgiven their former masters much, but never the swiftness of their surrender.

Manui said softly, hesitant, '—But what of our people?'

He lowered Ravalsh, mastering his face so that he looked stern. 'Not many died,' he said carefully, 'though many are hurt.' He busied himself with the fleeces, striving with himself. He could feel her troubled eyes. 'Not many; but they were all.' He drew a sharp breath. 'Yaln,' he said, to explain his tears. 'Yaln is dead. I am ashamed to face Ralki.'

She put out her hand to him. 'Their deaths are not of your causing. You only obeyed the God. Horn-blower called them, or how could they die?'

He nodded. 'I know.' But the shame of having

widowed Ralki was not the grief that made his heart writhe. He stood up, hiding his face from her. Manui was silent. The child in his arms gave a tiny sharp sigh, and he looked down. When he could control his voice he said, 'Today I am learning what fatherhood means. I am Terani: shall I not weep for my children?'

The sharp agony had passed. No doubt it would ambush him again; but meanwhile, had he not causes enough for gladness? He was young, and a Lord. He was Mor'anh of the Lightnings, God-begotten, and Kem'nanh had kept faith with him. He had seen his enemies flee before him. He had avenged his father. He had taken his sister in his arms, and known the world made whole again. He was holding his son, who would never know the shadow of subjection.

He gave a sigh. 'There is much to be done, I must go. Nai will be here soon to see you; to see you both.' He looked at her and smiled. 'But this I cannot delay. I am taking my son to show to the Dha'lev.'

The silver grass swirled silently about Racho's legs. The boundary trench brimmed with shadows at his feet; he snorted a little as he was urged on, but jumped it easily in the darkness. There was none to forbid their crossing. They moved at a slow trot, the davlani prick-eared and curious, perplexed by his rider's behaviour.

It was not usual to ride out of the camp at night. Behind them the Fire of Gathering burned on, far past the usual time. The rejoicing Alnei danced tirelessly. But Mor'anh had risen and left them, and sought Racho. Hran and Nai were gone; Manui and Ravalsh sleeping. The mountain drew him, and he had a grief to face which he could not yield to among the Tribe.

As they crossed the place where they had fought, Mor'anh let Racho slow to a walk, then stop. Their shadow lay before them. The very ground seemed to breathe pain. Mor'anh swung Racho to face Vani, and his cheeks were glittering. 'She will not dance for you again, Lady,' he said. 'I saw her fall.'

She was dead. Haughty Runi had been brought low, her black hair spilled in the dust. Runi was dead, a bronze blade in her proud heart. When he and those with him had turned after the first charge that took them through the Kalnat ranks, they had seen her, they had watched her go down. And Mor'anh had not flinched, though every eye had turned to him. But after, when all was done, he had come to find her. He had gazed on her lovely face, the black lashes of her sealed eyes, her cold mouth, her pale tear-stained cheeks. Then he had taken her in his arms and laid her head on his shoulder and stroked her streaming hair and wept, for all that was gone, and all that had never been.

Now he bowed his shoulders and wept again, deep shaking sobs that released his knotted grief, stretching and easing his soul. After a while he wept not only for Runi, but for Yaln; for Ralki, beating her own grief under her feet as she led the dance to welcome Nai; for Kariniol. He wept for the end of striving, for relief, for gratitude. He wept to empty his heart of turmoil. He wept for guilt, and pity, and weariness.

He raised his head at last, feeling drained and clear, like the storm-scoured sky. Vani shone impassively; he looked at her uneven curve and sighed, rubbing his hands over his drenched face.

Mor'anh rode Racho far from the boundary, up onto the higher ground, until he came to a flat shoulder from which he could see the town. If he looked east, he could see the glow of the Fire, and the breeze brought the faint sound of drums. Exuberant with triumph, they danced on. But the mountains were silent behind him, and he looked down into the ruin of Maldé.

It was little more than a charred shell. The roofs shone pale in the moonlight no more; the walls could hold no more captives. The smell of burning still hung about it, and a few piles of ashes still glowed dully, but the flames were dead. Even though he looked on it, he could scarcely believe in its destruction. He was Mor'anh, the lightning-bolt. Where his anger struck, nothing remained; only the embers smoked. So the Alnei sang already.

He found it hard to comprehend how complete was their victory. His first experience of the irrevocable suddenness of war was terrible to him. Only a day ago the town had lived, had sent out a host of men. Now the Golden People had vanished among the mountains. The Alnei had offered them help, food, healing herbs, almost pleading with them; but they would not stay where the Khentors were, preferring to drive their carts away up the steepening roads. Where they had found to shelter from the sweet summer night they feared so much, Mor'anh could not guess.

When the fighting was over, he had prayed that he might never again know such a meeting of spears. Now he understood that Maldé was only one town, that other Golden Men might try to force them back to obedience, that other Horse People would follow the Alnei. What had begun could not be soon ended. He sighed. His eye travelled over the trampled cornfields, pale under the moon, and out to the Plain, the realm of the great hunters whose innocent fellowship the Alnei had forsaken.

'They need not have died,' he said to the silence. 'I thought they would talk. They need not have fled us.'

Racho whinnied softly, and Mor'anh laid a hand on his neck. 'Well, they have gone, Racho. We need fear them no longer. No, but we have a worse thing to fear. Ourselves; each other.'

After a while he stirred and looked about. 'Tomorrow we will come and gather the stray cattle,' he said. And Nai could maybe tell them if the strange grass growing in the fields was good for anything. Maybe Maldé would still provide wood enough for the pyres, and the hills were open to foraging now. He yawned. He was too tired to be happy, but he began to be aware of something like satisfaction. Happiness would come.

Night wheeled about the Picket Star. The fire-glow was

Then he had taken her in his arms and laid her head on his shoulder and stroked her streaming hair and wept, for all that was gone, and all that had never been.

dimming; the drums were silent. The Alnei were going to rest at last. And the Lord of the Alnei thought of his tent, where his wife and son lay sleeping.

They did not take the same path down, but one which led them past the gate of Maldé. Mor'anh lingered before it, gazing through the gaping gateway into the desolation. There was nothing left in his heart but pity. 'It is our home!' The place that remains when all the people have gone.

'This was never what I sought,' he said aloud. He stretched out his right hand. 'Kem'nanh, Father, if there is guilt, let it fall only on me.'

The silence was unbroken, but the answer spoke in his mind.—'My son, you are too proud. Such burdens are not for you to claim.'

He smiled faintly, and turned away from the ruin, moving towards the boundary. 'I claim nothing. I ask nothing. Only stay with me.'

—'Always.'

They cleared the ditch. Racho's tail rippled silver as he quickened his pace. Mor'anh's back was to the Kalnat lands. He was cantering back to his people, and the soft night wind blew in his face, sweet and wild with the scents of the Plain.

ABOUT THE AUTHOR

I was born in London right at the end of World War II of mixed Irish, Cornish, Somerset, West Highland stock, with the Sun and Moon in Capricorn and Aquarius rising—thus giving Saturn three places on my birth-sign, which is not fair. So I started off with a promising identity crisis and this was improved when, at two, we moved to rural Essex. Perhaps this accounts for the verbal and intellectual precocity which made me, very unwillingly, a rather lonely child.

I have been asked why I write fantasy. First, I am sure I would have written, anyway. And I did not intend to write for public consumption. In early days I thought it purely private and that if I wrote for publication it would be "realistic" novels. . . . I learned to read very early, at two-and-a-half. At five I had an almost adult reading ability, but adult books were more than the child could cope with. So I found the great store of literature that age and popularity have reduced to emotional simplicity—not that "reduced" is the word, but the emotions are clear, basic, strong, while the stories can be told in rich, exciting language—folktale, myth, and legend. These, with the later addition of history, were my diet. Oddly I read very few children's classics: Ransome, a little Nesbit, Treece, Saville. But my knowledge of children's books was professionally gained later when I became a librarian. Nor did I encounter adult fantasy until I was twenty.

So my head was stuffed with heros, quests, castles, oaths, causes, Kings, Gods: and not surprisingly when I began to write that is what came out.

As for the specific form, Vandarei, it began as a playworld, the sort that a lot of children have, and I was of course the Queen, the character about whom I created the adventures. But I had the disposition of a pedant. I didn't really want to pretend: I wanted to know, to be sure, to get it right. So even in its childish form this playworld had a tendency to become concise, factual. As I grew older, horses became a passion and the playworld developed into "Equitania"— the horse motif strengthening. During this time the history of the country itself assumed an importance and I began to actually write. At fifteen, however, the last links with "Equitania" wavered and the name "Vanderei" appeared. The Queen was abandoned and ceased to be an avatar of myself, becoming a character whom I manipulated, but with whom I no longer especially identified.

The major facts about Vandarei, the outlines, were fixed by the time I left school at sixteen, but there was a lot of refining, modification, to come. One of the most important of these was the separate development of the Harani (*Red Moon and Black Mountain*) and the Khentors. Originally, all were Vandarins alike: the Harani simply being the royal house and the aristocracy. But they crystallized into very different, I hope complementary, peoples. So did other peoples of Vandarei, partly because I recognized that so vast a land could not be ethically, culturally, or linguistically homogenous: but the Harani and the Khentorei grew in stature and mystic significance as they did in individuality. And in the end, the Khentors took most of my heart—I am only sorry that having reached a satisfying mode of life, they have no impetus to do much. They remain the same. It is the more restless, troubled, burdened Harani who produce the stories: and who, being an "I" people produce the individuals, while the low-ego nomads, the "We" people, do not so often, unless touched by the Gods. If I try to define the different fascination of each of them for me, the interest of the Harani lies in their burden of responsibility, their separation from others by the power entrusted to them, the difficulty of reconciling destiny with happiness. The Khentor appeal is more atavistic, based on simplicity, harmony with nature, and so on: briefly, for me, they achieve the delight of closeness to the life of nature combined with the richness of human community.

Obviously my world is very real to me, but since cutting loose from the Queen myself, I have never been dominated by it. Of course, the older, the more complex a creation gets, the less it is amenable to manipulation, and the nearer it gets to an almost organic life which imposes its own logic; so that invention can often seem like discovery.

Of course, I originally embarked on Vandarei because it is an expression of the material, acquired or internal, that I have to use, but my pleasure in fantasy can be partially defined. I get a kick out of postulating ways of life, societies, then examining how their members work and live, also, in introducing one exotic, incalculable element, like magic, into a human situation. What I wish to say really is that I do not consider fantasy a light form, one which evades the vicissitudes of reality. It uses strangeness and glamour, but if that is a lack of seriousness I share it with Homer, Malory, Milton, Blake—although obviously no comparison is intended. I deny that reality is defined by drabness. Indeed, fantasy is "unrealistic" only in externals: it is within ourselves; and it is in our relationships with others that we live. These are reality. I may bring different tensions to bear on my characters, but I hope that only serves to underline their basic reality, and the humanity which is the perpetual concern of the writer.

—Joy Chant